Dating Little Miss Perfect

Cassandra O'Leary

Cover design by Kylie Sek at **https://kyliesek.com.au/**

Edited by Liz Dempsey at **https://theerroreliminator.wordpress.com/**

Interior book design by Cassandra O'Leary using Atticus

Cassandra O'Leary, Author

Melbourne, Australia

cassandraolearyauthor.com

To my sweetheart of a husband, who asked for a completed manuscript for his birthday. Here it is!

Better late than never . . .

Contents

Chapter One

HotAussie007: Hi stranger. Talk dirty to me!

Eden heard her smartphone ding and knew who it was before she looked. She grabbed her phone. Yes, it was her anonymous *almost* boyfriend. Hardly anyone messaged her. And that tingly anticipation in her lower belly, no one else had that effect.

She shouldn't be doing this at work. It seemed naughty. A little dirty. But she was addicted to messaging him. As with any addiction, she couldn't help herself. Taking a deep breath, she straightened her pristine white lab coat and smoothed back a lock of hair escaping her high ponytail. Silly, considering they couldn't see each other, but she wanted to look her best.

Eden tapped out her response... No. *Delete!* She wouldn't go all the way totally sexy. Not at work.

LittleMissPerfect: Hey big boy, what's up?

HotAussie007: That's it? Nice dirty talk. You're a real bad girl LOL

LittleMissPerfect: I'm at work. Covert messaging in progress *side eyes*

She scanned the lab. Her fellow science geeks were absorbed in their work, some plugged into earbuds as they conducted experiments or typed up reports. Felicity, her research assistant, was focused on analyzing the drug assay.

All clear.

HotAussie007: I'm working too. Coffee break. What are you wearing?

LittleMissPerfect: Not telling. You have to guess. Some men fantasize about my prim and proper outfit. And what's underneath...

HotAussie007: Gah! Librarian? School teacher? Am I close? Stern, bossy, smart as a whip. I like this train of thought *daydreams*

LittleMissPerfect: I'm picturing you in underwear over tights. I've got this whole Clark Kent/Superman fantasy going on...

HotAussie007: *choke* Standard office gear today. Sorry to disappoint. But you can be my Lois Lane any day.

LittleMissPerfect: You're making me shy *blushes*

HotAussie007: Don't be shy. I like you.

Her belly flipped. *Likey like.*

HotAussie007: Will you meet me IRL?

Meet him? In real life? Her skin tingled, heat rising up her throat and across her cheeks. *Oh God.*

It could go spectacularly wrong, but she wanted to meet him. She wanted. Bad. All this online flirting had her mind intrigued and her body set to explode at the merest hint of a sexual fantasy. It was weeks since they'd ditched the dating site for one-on-one chats. But they'd kept things casual. And anonymous.

She'd chickened out of meeting him once already. Maybe she'd been smart. What if he took one look at her and bolted out the door? What if he didn't go for geek girls? What if she couldn't be sexy and funny in real life?

Eden loved the banter they shared online. But it was way easier to sex it up virtually with a faceless man than to flirt with a real, live, hot and sweaty human. Oh, but she wanted hot and sweaty.

Time to bite the bullet, to see if he was as funny and sexy as he seemed in their chats. She was dying to know what he looked like. Perhaps she'd indulge his librarian fantasy.

> **LittleMissPerfect:** You're on. Sweep me off my feet, big shot. Get back to me with a time and place. I'll wear something strict.

> **HotAussie007:** *dies* Will message later

Eden stared into space, indulging in her superhero fantasy. But Superman was too boring. This situation called for Thor. Lois Lane morphed into the spunky scientist Jane. With her long dark hair and subtle curves hidden under a lab coat, she did look a little like Eden. She'd help Thor save the world and hold on to his hammer... She'd happily oblige her hero. Strong, powerful, built like a pro wrestler but with a caring side. He'd do anything to protect her and save humanity.

As she was stroking her bare thigh near the edge of her summer skirt, a looming presence materialized behind her, sparking warning tingles across her nape, making the tiny hairs stand on end. Eden knew who it was. The man had timing. Bad timing. And he'd snuck up behind her bench in the open-plan lab. Was he trying to make her uncomfortable?

A few words rose to the front of her mind and they weren't polite. Eden tried to keep it cordial with the bane of her professional existence. "Donohue. To what do I owe the pleasure?"

She swiveled on her stool to face her work rival, and not for the first time, she wished Finn Donohue's looks matched his unpleasant personality. Instead, he had stunning sea-green eyes, tousled caramel hair, and over six feet of hunky height. All the muscles. None of it made him more appealing. It just didn't. Okay, his Aussie accent made him a tad more attractive. But only a little.

Odd how she was surrounded by Australians, online and at work. A little alarm went off in her brain but she ignored it. This particular Aussie was definitely annoying.

Finn heaved a long-suffering sigh. "You know why I'm here, at least you should. The final clinical trial report. It's three days overdue, Eden."

He leaned over her, drumming his fingertips on the bench, invading her personal space. She crossed her arms under her breasts, and his gaze tracked down to her V-neck for a second. Eden stared at him without speaking until he slowly blinked and met her eyes.

Her lips stretched in a mock-friendly smile. "It's *Doctor Robinson*. And as I said in my email, I'm still waiting on the blood test results from the LA lab. I can't magically make them appear on my desk here in San Diego."

Finn straightened. "Well, keep me updated. We need to get this drug to market ASAP, and I won't be held accountable if you don't deliver your end of the project."

Eden waved him away. "I get it. Now, shoo!" She must have scared him because he took a step backward. Smoothing down her skirt, she sighed. "Go back to your marketing cubicle. Relax in a beanbag chair and sip your hipster coffee. Send some tweets or whatever it is you do, and let the smart people do their jobs."

He narrowed his eyes. "Right. Wouldn't want to interrupt all that important texting, *Doctor* Eden." Finn shot her a glimmer-of-death glare, then turned and strode from the lab.

She did not admire his retreating form in his sharp suit. Broad shoulders, slim waist... firm butt. Nope, she scarcely noticed him.

He'd caught her slacking. She had to be careful. Her future at Magna Smart was precarious. From now on, she'd be the consummate professional to ensure her team received the special projects funding. Patients depended on her, on the heart medication that could save their lives. Years of research had gone into Magna Smart's new drug.

She'd built up a team of good people who deserved a chance to prove themselves. They wanted to see the project through to completion and have their achievements recognized. She deserved recognition too. Plus, she needed the job. A big-ass mortgage didn't pay itself. If she lost the project, she'd be downsized faster than you could say, 'you're fired.' And finding another job at her level would take months, not weeks.

The funding would *not* be wasted on Finn Donohue's marketing team. Again. The amount of funding his team received last year versus the paltry amount for her scientific research team was appalling. Eden's gaze snagged on the memo from a few months ago, stuck to the partition behind her workspace. She reread it, her fists clenched in her lap.

Memo

To: All Staff, Heads of Department
From: Dr. McTavish, CEO Magna Smart, USA

> *All departments now have the opportunity to compete for the current round of Future Smart Special Projects Funding recently announced by our parent company, Magna Smart Pharma (Europe). As part of this outstanding initiative, I am pleased to announce I have been appointed the arbiter of project suitability and likelihood of success, i.e.*

, commercialization potential, revenue generation, and talent recognition for the United States arm of the company. A total of US$10 million in new funding is available for approved projects.

Department heads are to compile detailed proposals on their special projects for my initial input and approval by 1 March. As this opportunity was conceived as a 'Best of Breed' initiative for ideas that will impact the consumer business, proposals are sought from consumer-facing units, including Marketing and Business Development, Research and Innovation Commercialization, Information Technology, and Medical Science Partnerships.

If relevant teams choose not to take up this excellent opportunity to submit Future Smart Project proposals, management will, of course, carefully consider resource reallocation in future endeavors. The US Operation will aim to put its best foot, or feet, forward as the case may be.

Signed,
Dr. McTavish

Eden shook her head, dismissing the urge to throw tacks at the stupid memo with its implied threats.

She pushed Finn Donohue to the back of her mind too. She needed to concentrate on this potential thing with HotAussie007. Soon she'd meet him. In. The. Flesh. That was fantasy and a half — enough to stop her heart *dead*.

Finn had finally escaped his painful conversation with that woman. *Thank you, Jesus, or Odin. Whoever's listening.* He stomped down the corridor, his feet beating a rhythm like a call to war.

Doctor Eden could suck it, in his humble opinion.

If only that thought didn't make his blood run as hot and thick as the chocolate sauce on his favorite banana split. Eden's lips, that petulant pout and the tempting curve of her mouth when telling him off, nearly had him saying, or doing, something stupid.

The way she talked down to him, as if he wasn't worthy of breathing the same air as her and the other snooty scientists in her lab, as if he was something she'd scrape off her surprisingly purple Doc Martens and shove in a doggy-do baggie. But it wasn't worth spending any more time thinking about. Not how she spoke, not the words, and especially not her hot little mouth.

No, he needed to focus on his work. He stormed along the polished concrete and glass corridor toward the Marketing and Business Development Department, at the opposite end of the building to Eden's research lab. His jaw clenched as he recalled her final dig: *Let the smart people do their jobs.*

He'd show her smart. He had plans, damn it. Big plans. He had so much on his plate it was hurting his brain, but he didn't deserve her scorn. He'd try to be her ally if he could.

Swerving off route, Finn pushed open the heavy fire door to the spacious courtyard between the two main buildings and sucked in the salty sea air, breathing deep and filling his lungs with oxygen. It was a little humid out there but much better. Not so stifling. Outside, still standing on the concrete paving of the company's campus but overlooking the Pacific Ocean, he could breathe.

The courtyard boasted an architectural centerpiece — a man-made stream bordered by blocks of granite ran down the sloped ground before dropping off a step into a small water feature. Finn plonked himself on the edge of the polished rock by the clear, running water and rolled his shoulders, shrugging off the tension. He came here whenever he needed to find his calm. Chant some 'oms.' Whatever.

He wasn't the only one catching some rays. Quite a few of the worker bees had escaped the hive to eat lunch or work on their laptops outside. Surveying the scattered geeks and admin staff, he spotted one of his guys: Nate, their new website analytics guru.

Nate caught his eye and nodded once, his long black hair flopping over his eyes. The younger man picked himself up and ambled over, touchscreen laptop in hand. He needed a haircut, big time. No one would take him seriously when he looked like an overgrown student who'd escaped from a frat house.

"Hey, man, you okay? You look stressed out."

Nate needed a makeover in how he spoke too. Finn was his manager, and as such, he deserved respect. Before he moved to the States, he'd thought Aussies were laid back. But some of these Californian dudes were so laid back that they were almost comatose.

"I'm fine, thanks. Just taking a breather." Finn held up a hand to shield his eyes from the blinding summer sun. Beautiful day, as always. He'd rather be surfing, for sure. Maybe at Bells Beach back home.

Nate nodded, his head bouncing like one of those bobble-head dashboard ornaments Finn bought for his Chevy. "I want to show you something. Can you spare a few minutes?"

Finn dipped his chin in Nate's direction. "Sure. What have you got?"

"Weirdness with the website. A whole lot of traffic from eastern Europe, and considering Magna Smart doesn't trade there, it stood out. Could just be a blip, but it could be something more."

Nate pulled up a graph on his screen and showed Finn the data. He talked him through the usual site traffic, mainly from the US and Canada, with some hits from Asia on particular products. The eastern European thing did seem odd. The pattern was out of whack compared to previous months, and Finn had read a lot of records lately. There were also large file transfers happening that Nate hadn't seen before. The younger man shrugged, as if to emphasize his uncertainty. "There could be a new partner or a reseller we haven't heard about, sending traffic our way. Or, not to be too doom and gloom, it could be bad news. A hacker or someone else targeting our site. Do you think we should check with IT?"

"Absolutely. Get your information over to Data Security and see what they reckon." Finn dragged his hand back through his hair and gazed out across the vast expanse of blue sea and sky. "Great day for surfing."

"Surfing's not my thing, but I'd like to try that one day." Nate pointed to the clifftop to the right of the company's complex, where a couple was preparing to jump. It wasn't an emergency. They were strapped into a tandem hang glider.

Finn and Nate watched in silence as the couple launched off the cliff, hovered, and then lifted in an updraft of air. It looked impossible, or at least implausible, but they flew. Amazing. They swooped and glided on invisible trails of wind, rising higher still before tilting downward and skimming across the ocean. After a couple of minutes, they disappeared from view.

Finn sighed, brushed off his weird mood, and stood. "Yeah, I should try hang gliding." *Before I head back home to Australia.* The depressing thought popped into Finn's head, uninvited. He turned to Nate and shrugged. "Guess we should be getting back. Let me know what you find out about that blip."

"Sure thing, boss man."

"Don't call me that. Finn will be fine. Mr. Donohue, if you're feeling formal or we're in a meeting with the Establishment."

"Can do, Finn." Nate saluted.

With a shake of his head, Finn headed across the courtyard to the opposite building, back toward the concrete bunker housing his team. But before he went inside, he succumbed to the urge to get his own back on Eden. Speaking to his smartphone's dictation app, he drafted a quick email:

"Doctor Eden,

I greatly appreciated your attitude in our earlier chat. Your reminder of our formal work relationship and the importance of letting 'smart people do their jobs' was timely. Please find attached a file you may find of interest.

Your humble servant,
Finn Donohue
Manager, Marketing and Business Development
Magna Smart Pharmaceuticals
Attach file: Civilization"

"Send."

It was juvenile, and she'd most likely hate him even more, but he couldn't resist. When the cartoon titled 'Civilization' came up on his Twitter feed earlier, he'd immediately thought of her.

The cartoon depicted the slaves of ancient Egypt hauling rocks and lugging cartloads of tools to build a pyramid. A lone female figure stood at the top of the pyramid, raised on a lofty platform, shaking a finger at the workers below. Her long robe, black hair, cat-eye makeup, and jewels made it obvious she was the famous Queen Cleopatra. The caption nailed it.

Work smarter, not harder, that's my motto. Civilization will thank me later.

He'd probably put his foot right in it. Still, it was better to be the shit-stirrer or even the one stepping in it than to be the excrement. *There* was a life philosophy.

Now that he thought about it, Eden kind of looked like Cleopatra, the classic Elizabeth Taylor version. Beautiful. Imperial. Scary. But irresistible, nonetheless. The way her lush breasts rose as she crossed her arms underneath was hypnotic. He hadn't meant to look, had tried like hell to keep his eyes up and meet her narrowed gaze. Those eyes framed by the thickest, blackest lashes he'd ever seen.

The swing of her long ponytail as she flicked it back over her shoulder was another distraction. Finn wanted to tug on it, twist it around his hand. Pull her mouth up to his. Kiss her until she was speechless. Shut her up long enough to stop all the put-downs she threw his way.

Yikes. If he continued thinking along those lines, he might as well volunteer to be her minion and let her stomp all over him. He had to remember that Cleopatra was also a destroyer of men. Whole empires. He needed to be on his guard.

Finn strode into the building and down the corridor toward his office. There, he locked himself in, wanting to get on top of the mountain of reading piled on his desk.

But the pages of text blurred before him since all he could think about were her eyes. Not quite blue, not quite gray. Some color that shouldn't be possible. Almost violet.

What the hell was he thinking?

Eden tapped her keyboard with trembling fingertips and reread his email. That's how he saw her? Cleopatra. The queen who destroyed Egypt, one of the greatest civilizations the world had known, because of love. Or, depending on your point of view, because of her ego and the way she used men to gain power. The churning in her belly set off her fiercest competitive instincts.

Okay, buddy, game on.

If Finn wanted to get cute, two could play at that game. If he wanted to test her, he'd find out she was no pushover. And if he wanted to compete, she'd win. She always won, having learned early on you don't let men push you around.

"I know that look. Who are you pissed at now?"

Felicity stood beside her desk, lips tilted up in a half-smile; her short blond hair, sky-blue eyes, and a lab coat about two sizes too big for her petite frame completing the picture of an impish pixie. A pixie with a brain the size of a small planet. Her research assistant was a force to be reckoned with, which was why Eden liked her so much.

Eden let out a slow breath. "Jeez Louise, I didn't even see you there. I had a little run-in with Finn Donohue." After casting a glance over her shoulder, as if she might find him looming again, Eden clicked on the cartoon attached to the email and pointed at her screen. "That's me, apparently."

Felicity snorted and shook with barely contained laughter, leaning on Eden's workbench until she regained her composure. "It's funny. He's got your number. Will you report him? Have him reprimanded like that jerk from IT who called you princess?"

A corner of Eden's mouth curled upward in a semi-smile. "Not yet. I was thinking... We've got our team's social event this Friday. The charity fundraiser potluck thing. I thought I'd invite Finn and his team. All friendly and collegial."

"Nice. Devious. Lull him into a false sense of security. You could bake cupcakes."

"Exactly. Maybe filled with marshmallow fluff and decorated with tiny butterflies."

"No man can resist your cupcakes and tiny butterflies." Felicity raised an eyebrow and grinned.

Not true, unfortunately. The last guy she'd dated had sampled her cupcakes but still hadn't been tempted to indulge in a relationship. And the three guys she'd dated before him weren't cupcake-worthy. Not even close.

Eden frowned and lowered her voice to a whisper "I'm not trying to seduce him. I only want him off his game. So when I submit the best proposal and win the special projects funding, he won't know what hit him."

Felicity grinned. "Of course, a little professional maneuvering and back-stabbery, nothing more. He is uber-hot, though. Objectively speaking."

"Objectively speaking, yes. But I won't go there, and neither will you."

Felicity tipped her head to one side and paused before replying. "No problem. Not even thinking about it."

"Good. Great. Get back to work."

Felicity snorted again. "You're a slave driver. Donohue may have a point."

Eden tore a sheet of paper off her notepad, balled it up, and threw it at Felicity's head. Real mature, not at all queenly.

She returned her attention to her computer and drafted a response to Finn's email. With tongue planted firmly in cheek, she swallowed her rage for easy retrieval at a later date.

Dear Mr. Donohue,

Your email and little cartoon were most amusing. I'm flattered, thank you. You compared me to one of the world's greatest and most beautiful queens while acknowledging my intellect, which was gratifying. I'm almost loath to tell you, but Cleopatra ruled many centuries after the pyramids were built, so the cartoon is historically inaccurate. But I suppose you didn't have a moment to check your facts on Wikipedia.

Anyway, no hard feelings. I hope you will accept my invitation to a cancer charity potluck event on Friday, 10.30 am, in the staff lounge in our wing of the building. Bring your team. Don't be late and remember your wallet. All for a good cause.

My cupcakes always go for top dollar and sell like hotcakes. Literally.

Regards,
Dr. Eden Robinson
Senior Project Manager and Lead Researcher
Magna Smart Pharmaceuticals

Sent.
The challenge had been issued. Now to see if he'd accept it.

Chapter Two

LittleMissPerfect: Where are you taking me on our date, big shot? Downtown?

Finn stared at his phone in the palm of one hand while rubbing the back of his neck with the other. LittleMissPerfect's opening gambit was a tease. Normally, he'd fire back, saying he'd love to take her downtown. Get down and dirty. But today? Another woman occupied his thoughts like an invading army.

Cupcakes? Doctor Eden bakes cupcakes?

Eden's email was perfectly reasonable, almost pleasant, aside from her Wikipedia dig. Probably fair enough. But it made his head spin. Because his mind went straight to an image of her swanning around her kitchen, wearing her white lab coat, a dusting of powdered sugar, and little else. Licking cake mixture off the back of a spoon...

Bloody hell. Seated at his desk, he adjusted his trousers, suddenly a fraction too tight.

Eden was inspiring some lurid fantasies during the middle of a workday, which was definitely a cause for concern. But the real reason he felt so uncomfortable, so *guilty*, was all the time he'd been thinking about her, he'd forgotten about someone who could really matter to him. LittleMissPerfect, his online dating partner. Date. Potential girlfriend. Whatever.

Time to focus and organize a top-notch date. Soon. Before he lost his damn mind. He was about to call his favorite Italian restaurant when a knock at the door startled him so badly that he banged his knee against the underside of his desk.

He cleared his throat. "Come in."

"Hey, Finn." Nate hovered in the doorway, awkwardly leaning on the frame. "Can I have a minute?"

"Sure. Pull up a seat."

Nate sat on the low couch by the wall, so Finn scooted closer on his swivel chair. Blowing his ratty hair out of his eyes, Nate gazed up at the ceiling and took a moment before speaking. Finn studied his ugly heavy metal T-shirt, torn jeans, and combat boots. The guy looked about sixteen instead of a twenty-four-year-old postgrad.

"I sent those web traffic stats to IT and was waiting for a reply, but something weird happened."

"Weird, how? Did they get back to you?"

"Nope. I had a visit from the big boss. Doctor McTavish stopped by my cubicle to 'say hello' and see how I was settling in."

Nate's raised eyebrows told the whole story. Finn's eyebrows shot up too. McTavish never stopped by to *say hello* to anyone who worked for him. He sometimes summoned people to his expansive office, but that was an entirely different ball game. Doctor Martin McTavish didn't really 'do' people.

Finn leaned back in his chair. "Huh. What else did McTavish say? Was he worried about you using IT resources? Checking if you had authority for the request?"

"Nope. He asked how I was settling in, and if you'd made me feel welcome in Marketing, that was it."

Finn had no words. The conversation was so out of character for McTavish that it was as if they were talking about a completely different person. Someone with an actual personality.

"Okay. Keep this to yourself, but let me know if McTavish pops by again or if he sends any other unusual communications. I reckon he might be fishing for information about problems in our team, asking the new guy. You know we're competing for that special projects funding." Finn breathed out, Zen style, finding his calm. At least trying not to let stress overwhelm him.

He stood and paced to the window. Watched the seagulls soaring high above the courtyard. "On a lighter note, we're all invited to a charity morning tea on Friday with the scientific research team. I'm told there will be cupcakes."

"Cupcakes? And plenty of hot, smart scientist women, I'm guessing?"

Finn turned and shot a frown at Nate. "Speaking in a totally politically correct and non-gender-biased way, I can confirm there will be both cupcakes and female scientists. But I won't comment on the temperature of either."

"Ha!" Nate's laugh was so loud that it made Finn jump. "I'll take my chances. Count me in."

Finn swallowed his chuckle as Nate loped out of his office. He was beginning to like the guy. There was more to him than first impressions suggested. Seemed there was a lot of that going around.

"The metabolic results are back," Eden announced, phone pressed to her ear.

She swiveled in her office chair, waiting to hear his voice. No, not waiting to hear his deep, resonant voice. Waiting to hear his response.

Finn wasn't going to like the story the results told. Why that made her so tense, she couldn't say. Eden stretched her neck from side to side, attempting to ease the crick in the muscles there. She'd sat in her private office far too long, poring over the bad news in the report, trying to find some positives in the information. Honestly, hiding out.

"Great. Can you finish your report today? I need to add my section and get it across to McTavish." Finn's tone was light, unconcerned.

"I'd better talk you through the results before I send it. It's not what we were expecting."

Finn groaned, and the sound vibrated through the phone, doing surprising things to her insides. Everything tightened and heated. If she didn't know better — if it hadn't been so long — she'd almost describe it as...sexual.

Oh no. Not Finn.

She couldn't be attracted to him. How inconvenient. Long months of not through choice celibacy, or longer, now she thought about it, since making out didn't count, were making her tense. It was closer to two years. And since there had been lackluster dating for much longer, her hormones were getting out of control. They had to fire up now. Because of him. Just perfect.

"I'll swing by your office in five," Finn said.

Brusque. Efficient. Nothing to get worked up about.

"Okay."

He'd already hung up.

Eden busied herself straightening the already perfectly aligned pens and notes on her white desk. Then she tried to focus on the report on her computer screen. Facts, not feelings. She needed to concentrate.

She crossed her legs. Uncrossed them. She didn't want to come across as all stuck-up and queenly. But then again, damn his annoying self. How dare he make her nervous!

Legs crossed.

He knocked once and strode into her office, but she still wasn't ready for him. No way was she ready for the look on his face—the clenched jaw, pinched forehead, and eyes that bored through her skin, heating her blood and making everything tingle down south.

Don't think about down south.

South of the border. Down Mexico way. Everything hotter and spicier. Sweatier. *Oh God.* Her hormones were officially going crazy. And she wanted tortillas.

She could be in serious trouble around Finn.

"So... *Doctor* Eden? What's the prognosis?"

"Not so good, but not terminal either. You'd better read the précis for yourself." Eden waved him in and slid a copy of the report across her desk.

He shoved it right back with one long finger. "No, you explain it to me. But give it to me straight. Plain English. Use small words." He rolled his eyes and jammed his hands into his pants pockets.

She couldn't help noticing how he'd pushed up his shirt sleeves, showing off his tanned forearms, sprinkled with a liberal cover of sandy blond hair, sparkling in the sunlight from her office window. Prominent tendons and muscles rolled and flexed when he moved. She'd always had a thing for men's forearms. And he had a fine pair. Strong. Manly.

"Eden? Are you alright?"

"Mmm? Yes." She took a breath and forced her gaze away from those yummy forearms. Checked her notes. Regained her composure. Crossed her legs tighter. "The trial examined the effectiveness of compound R22 on a group of subjects with congenital heart disease and some with acquired heart damage due to lifestyle factors or comorbidity with other conditions.

After the final analysis, the conclusions were inconsistent with previous trials, and no increased heart function was noted."

Finn's jaw clicked. "What? No improvement at all?"

She shook her head. "None of statistical significance. There was some anecdotal evidence of improved wellness. Participants reported feeling calmer and more rested."

"More rested? We didn't send these people to a summer camp. We provided them with next-generation heart medication, and it's supposed to improve their health. It's meant to be our new market leader."

Her jaw clenched before she spoke again. "I knew you'd be upset. Trust me, I'm not exactly doing a happy dance myself. I'll have to recommend a fourth round of clinical trials. We're not ready to go to market."

"Shit." Finn flopped onto the visitor's chair opposite her desk, his long legs manspreading all over her office. "Sorry, didn't mean to swear at you. What the hell am I meant to say to McTavish?"

"We have to give it to him straight. Facts, figures, risks associated with going for FDA approval on a drug that isn't yet fully tested." Eden winced, hating to even admit that the drug was not ready to market. Through no fault of her own—she'd pushed for funding for more extensive clinical trials and been denied. She still felt responsible.

"I know the drill. Send me the full report, and I'll get my part done tonight."

"Give me a call if you need me to explain any of the finer details." Eden smiled, hoping to get rid of him politely. Then she could fan her face and cool off in the privacy of her office.

Finn's eyebrows shot up perilously high. "Seriously? Thanks, but I should be right. I might not understand some of the big words, but I'm sure I can google them."

"I didn't mean... I was only trying to be helpful. There's some background material on the metabolic rate of various drug categories. It can be confusing for a layperson."

"Confusing for a mere marketing graduate, you mean. Bugger off, Doctor Eden. I don't need you to condescend to help me." He rose from his chair, shaking his head.

"Finn, listen—"

Slamming the door behind him, he was out of there before she could say another word. Before she could apologize.

Crap. She hadn't meant to talk down to him. Sometimes words popped out of her mouth before she could stop them. And she probably had on her resting bitch-face. According to Felicity, it made her look terrifying. This was why she was hopeless at dating... Which reminded her of her upcoming date with her online mystery man.

Why hadn't HotAussie007 responded to her last message? Was he having second thoughts? Was she? Perhaps she should message him and call the whole thing off. She could put herself to bed on Friday night and think happy thoughts of Chris Hemsworth as Thor and call it quits. That strategy had served her well over the past few months.

She'd relegate HotAussie007 to that spot in the back of her mind reserved for a couple of ex-boyfriends she still thought of fondly. It had been close to five years since she'd been in a proper relationship, but she didn't want to examine that too closely.

Anyway, if you didn't get too close to someone, they couldn't hurt you. Fantasy men came in handy from time to time, and they wouldn't make you cry, demand you quit your job, or scare you. Eden had come to a logical conclusion based on plenty of anecdotal evidence: real men were overrated.

HotAussie007: I want you by the beach. With pizza.

LittleMissPerfect: Kinky. You want to make a meal of me?

HotAussie007: Um... I lost my train of thought :)

LittleMissPerfect: You. Me. Pizza. When?

HotAussie007: Right. Friday night. 7pm. Allesandro's at Del Mar.

LittleMissPerfect: Great, see you there. My mouth's already watering!

HotAussie007: Reservation under MISTER BOND

LittleMissPerfect: haha!

Eden put her phone down on the kitchen counter in a ridiculously happy mood. And her mouth was literally watering. It wasn't just HotAussie007's flirty messages getting her juices flowing, although she was buzzing from head to toe with anticipation. She'd woman up and be brave. She'd finally meet him IRL. Tomorrow night.

It had also been a torturously long day, and she was ravenous. Of course, she should have whipped up a healthy salad or grilled some chicken for dinner. Instead, it was almost cupcake time.

From the stereo, Ella Fitzgerald crooned about having rhythm and music. Who could ask for anything more? Indeed. She had Ella, she had cupcakes, she almost had a date. Life was good.

Barefoot, Eden swayed across her open-plan kitchen/dining room, moving to the music, enjoying the swish of her 1950s-style skirt around her legs. When Ella came to the part about having got her man, Eden stopped dancing.

This time tomorrow, she could have her own man. Maybe. If she didn't jam her foot in her mouth. She'd scared off more than one date when the conversation turned to global warming or cloning. Some men didn't appreciate a woman who could counter their pig-headed opinions with scientific facts.

Stirring the decadent chocolatey-caramelly mixture in the ceramic bowl on her kitchen counter, she put all her weight behind it. Not that there was much weight to speak of, mostly on her chest and butt; hence, no good for power-stirring. She could have used her space-age electric mixer, but mixing the eggs, flour, and sugar with a wooden spoon added to the baking experience. It grounded her. There was much satisfaction to be derived from hand-beating eggs into submission.

The trill of her old-fashioned doorbell had her dancing her way to the front door of her bungalow. She peered through the peephole and grinned before throwing the door wide and pulling her little sister into a bear hug.

Faith's lips stretched into a broad smile, revealing perfect pearly whites. "Hey, Eden. What's cookin', Babycakes?"

Faith looked amazing as usual, dressed in her usual skinny jeans and leather combo, dark hair dyed extra black, and her own jewelry designs adorning her neck and wrists.

Eden squeezed Faith's shoulder before ushering her inside. "Cupcakes. In other words, you're just in time."

Her sister rubbed her hands together. "Yum. Lead the way."

Faith perched on a high bar stool at the counter in the open-plan kitchen. She swiveled from side to side, her knee jiggling up and down. It was just like when they were kids, back when their grandmother stood behind the counter, cooking them dinner. "So, what's the fashion emergency? I got here as fast as I could." Faith glanced up at Eden after hanging her jacket over a stool.

"A date tomorrow night. Actually, it's a blind date. Almost blind. We've only chatted online."

Faith drummed her fingertips on the countertop. "Go you! So, dish all the dirt. Who is he? Where did you find him?"

"Same anonymous dating site as last time, so I haven't even seen his face. But we've been chatting for weeks, casually, and I really like him so far. He seems smart, funny, and he likes old movies... I don't know. He could be nice."

"Great. The perfect man to get you out of your slump."

"Or he might turn out to be some perverted freak." She grabbed a metal whisk off the counter and smacked it hard against the wooden surface. "Perverted, I could deal with *if* it's the good kind." Eden winked and resumed her whisking. The eggs wouldn't beat themselves.

Her sister snorted. "Oh, you're such a badass. I'm impressed."

Eden glanced at Faith, her lips pursed. "But I won't settle for another man who tells me to shut up and stop thinking so much."

"Like hell you need to stop thinking. My big sister's a genius *and* a freakin' pinup babe, and if some dude can't appreciate you, he's obviously an asshole."

"Thanks for the vote of confidence."

Eden finished folding the flour into the wet mixture and spooned it into the waiting tray of paper liners. A dollop here, a glop there.

Faith shrugged. "My pleasure. Now, clothes. You need something knockout sexy with a touch of 'Whoa, Mama, you're too much woman for me.' Keep him on his toes. Then wow him with your smarts."

Smoothing out the last couple of cupcakes, Eden sighed. She popped the tray into the oven and set the timer. "Nice plan, sister mine. Only one problem—the menfolk don't seem to admire my smarts. Especially not the attractive ones."

For some reason, an image of Finn's muscular forearms popped into her head. What would they feel like wrapped around her waist? Probably all hard and powerful. *Inconvenient.* That was the word for it.

While wiping down the countertops, Eden contemplated how often Finn had invaded her thoughts in the past couple of days. The way her body sprang to life in his presence was most likely some strange side effect of all her sexy messaging with HotAussie007. Random aspects of her online life were bleeding into her everyday life. *Logical.* She was hot for HotAussie007, not Finn.

After a moment, Eden stilled and leaned on the countertop. "Sorry, but can we do the clothes thing later? I'm beat."

"Sure, hon. Anyway, I've got news. I got a commission from the gallery in Del Mar. They want a whole collection of necklaces and bracelets." Faith squealed and clapped her hands, her wrists jangling wildly.

Eden's mouth dropped open. "Oh my God. That's awesome! How did you not tell me straight away?"

"I'm not sure. I thought I'd burst with holding it in." Faith's knee jiggled again.

Eden grabbed two cans of diet soda from the refrigerator and settled into her favorite red velvet armchair in the living room, ready for a girly gossip session. Her sister plopped onto the floor at Eden's feet and leaned her back against the base of the chair.

Faith didn't disappoint on the gossip front. Aside from her golden opportunity to sell her jewelry in a gallery, she'd had her own flirtation. She told Eden all about the hot delivery guy who dropped off parcels at her day job in a boutique. Delivery Dude was apparently the object of rampant drooling amongst the store's female staff. They were all dying to receive his package, according to Faith.

Later, over steamy-hot cupcakes, Eden let her sister take control of her wardrobe. Faith talked her into choosing over-the-top clothes for her date. Eden had promised something strict, and the outfit certainly delivered.

Once Faith headed home, Eden wandered into the kitchen and bit into one more glorious buttery cupcake. It wasn't frosted yet, but she added a candy butterfly and groaned with pleasure.

"I've got cupcakes, who could ask for anything more?" she sang, channeling Ella Fitzgerald. But ever so slightly less tuneful. She imagined a crowd of adoring fans applauding her sugary confections and took a bow.

Then she headed to bed, where visions of candied butterflies and annoying men with dazzling green eyes danced in her head.

All. Night. Long.

Finn should have gone to bed hours ago, but instead, he banged his head on the desk in his living room for what must have been the twentieth time. He'd end up with a dent in his skull and his desk before long.

The words in the report swam in front of his eyes, even with the special font, and the text-to-speech software on his laptop hadn't helped him retain the information as it normally did. Too many charts and tables of results, not to mention all the jargon that made scientific language so impenetrable to a layperson, as Eden had pointed out earlier. Maybe she wasn't so condescending after all.

Then there was the Post-it Note she'd stuck to the index page. Eden had scrawled her cell number, along with the helpful note: *Don't let the science freak you out. It's basic once you get past the metabolic data.*

"Basic." He groaned, rubbing his eyes.

Yeah, thanks, Doc.

Finn slammed the lid of his laptop shut and stumbled off to bed. But before giving in to the tide of tiredness washing over his body, he reached for his phone and read over some of LittleMissPerfect's messages on the dating app.

At least there was one woman who seemed to like him. He had to focus on the positives. And when it came to work, he'd do what he was best at. Winning.

Chapter Three

LittleMissPerfect: Why do I have to work to-day? Can't we ditch and go to the movies?

HotAussie007: I wish. Sounds perfect.

LittleMissPerfect: Better go. Grindstone calling *sigh*

"Welcome. Come in, grab a coffee, and help yourself to a cupcake. Form an orderly line, please." Eden smoothed down the barbeque apron she wore over her work outfit.

She pasted a tight grin on her face, her cheeks stretching in a kind of premature rigor mortis. She'd die if this event didn't go well. At least, work death.

Be friendly. Nice as pie. She'd lull the enemy into a false sense of security. Sugar and spice and everything nice.

Eden smiled at the line of visitors entering the science wing's staff lounge. An odd assortment of geeks and lab rats, suits and admin staff in unfashionable, wrinkled clothes, most looking like they hadn't seen daylight in years. They lined up alongside a row of folding tables pushed together and covered in trays, a potluck banquet of deliciousness beckoned, including her own special butterfly cupcakes.

She nodded at a coworker holding his wallet. "Donations in the box. Thanks very much."

"Good morning, Doctor Eden," Finn said.

The voice coming from behind her had Eden frozen for a moment. God, even his 'Good morning' was laced with sarcasm or condescension. Some kind of undertone. But she refused to let him rile her up. He was on her turf now. She smoothed a hand over the ends of her ponytail and turned to face him.

"Hi, thanks for coming. Coffee's at the far end. Help yourself to a cupcake or sandwiches. All for five dollars. Donations in here, please." She rattled a cupcake-printed cardboard box at him, setting the coins jangling inside.

"What if I want to donate more than five dollars? Do I give you the check?"

Eden narrowed her eyes and cocked her head to one side, studying his expression. Open, guileless, deceptively charming. Those emerald eyes sparkled though, conveying all kinds of mischief. "Sure, if you want to be the big man on campus, show me the money! I'm guessing you're after your team's name on the donation leaderboard?"

She waved her hand over her shoulder, and his gaze followed. The colored poster featured a graphic of a thermometer filled with red liquid, sitting halfway to the top. At the very top, a figure of $1000 was highlighted. IT currently led the pack, their name written on a Post-it Note in silver ink surrounded by gold star stickers.

Finn leaned on the table in front of Eden. "I wasn't even aware there was a leaderboard. But now you mention it, I do love a challenge."

"I'll bet."

His left eyebrow shot up. "How much do you bet?"

She placed the donation box on the table, alongside a tray of pink-butterfly-topped cupcakes. They were gorgeous—if she did say so herself. "I'll take your money, Finn. Not everything's a competition."

"Clearly. Your team's sitting near the bottom of the chart, isn't it?"

Don't take the bait, don't take the bait...

Eden sucked in a breath before releasing a stream of words in a rush: "Alright. Two hundred bucks says your team can't eat as many cupcakes as mine."

She'd taken the bait. Hook. Line. And. Sinker.

Her heart pounded like she'd stormed through the outlet mall at sale time, looking for the last pair of size seven sneakers. She shouldn't have challenged him. She should have been sensible, but that ship had clearly sailed. Looking up, she found him staring at her, arms crossed over his broad chest and grinning like a maniac. His sparkly eyes met hers, and the higher-functioning parts of her brain forgot how to operate.

Oh crap.

Finn cleared his throat, loudly, and she had a bad feeling. A bad, sinkhole-ish, wobbly-legged feeling. She'd worked out a detailed plan for the proceedings this morning. Things were about to go off-plan in a major way, and somehow, she was powerless to stop it. She couldn't back down.

Finn strode to the center of the room before she could stop him.

"Ladies and gentlemen, colleagues, ring-ins from the tech company next door, I'd like to make an announcement," Finn said, drawing laughter from the gathered crowd. "This morning's event organizer, the *delightful* Doctor Eden, has just issued a challenge. She says my marketing team can't eat as many cupcakes as her research team. Two hundred dollars is on the line here. The game is on, people."

Eden stood there, dumbfounded, as a posse of Finn's staff appeared out of nowhere and surrounded him. They performed some kind of secret-handshake-slash-high-five thing like a coach does with their team at a basketball game. Joking and laughing, the men gazed up at Finn like he was their adored cult leader while the women blatantly fawned over him.

One blond woman in a short skirt touched his bare forearm in a proprietary way, her long, pink, salon-perfect nails dragging across his skin. Eden didn't like it at all. It was just... inappropriate. Her skin heated and her belly lurched before she looked away. She refused to examine the reason for her reaction.

Her own team was... nowhere to be seen. She turned and found Felicity cowering behind a cupcake-laden table, a pot of coffee in hand. Eden planted her hands on her hips and frowned at her research assistant, conveying her demands with the power of her glare. Felicity nodded silently, set down the coffee, and whistled. The kind of high-pitched, cut-through-the-air, silence-the-whole-room noise most commonly heard at dog shows.

"Science team, assemble!" Felicity ordered.

Amazingly, they responded en masse, like a band of geek superheroes coming to her rescue. They had her back now, positioned behind Eden in a semi-circle, resplendent in their lab coats or neat pants, button-down shirts, and sensible shoes. Felicity stood to her right, and Eden's confidence rose.

She nodded toward a table near the wall. "I suggest each team takes a table, two tray of cupcakes, and we set a time limit. Shall we say, five minutes?"

Finn nodded, still smiling. His teeth were blindingly white, and he had a dimple on one side. She'd never noticed before. It was *distracting*.

"You're on. But we need someone independent, an adjudicator. Any volunteers?"

A petite woman with a cropped curly hairdo stepped forward. Eden had spoken to her once or twice in the courtyard. Meredith from Finance. Some staff called her 'The Terminator' on account of her no-nonsense attitude and slash-and-burn cost cutting. Eden kind of liked her.

Meredith peered over the top of her black-rimmed glasses. She had a scary, stern look on her face that caused grown men, other accountants, to cower in her presence. After giving Finn a tight-lipped half-smile, she addressed the rapt crowd: "I'll adjudicate. Teams, take your positions."

One of Finn's team dragged an empty table across the floor until it sat directly opposite Eden's position. Two teams, opposing sides. Meredith distributed trays of cupcakes to each table and asked the teams to stand on their respective sides of the room, behind their fearless leaders. Only, Eden didn't feel all that fearless. Strange nerviness had her fingers trembling as she gripped the edge of her team's table.

"Each team can eat the cupcakes in any manner they see fit. But there will be no fighting, no bad language. Otherwise, anything goes. You have five minutes"—Meredith glanced up at the clock on the wall, and everyone's heads followed—"starting... now."

Eden gasped and looked around blindly. Where to begin? She stole a glance at the other table, where five young men were already face down, devouring cupcakes straight off the trays. Finn sat at one end, stuffing cake and pink frosting into his mouth by the fistful.

Felicity nudged Eden in the ribs and whispered loudly in her ear with a mouth already full of cake, "Eat. Now!"

Eden grabbed a couple of tiny cakes, one in each hand, and wished there could have been another way. She wanted to apologize to the delicate sugary butterflies for the sacrilege of eating them like a heathen.

But she bit down. She chomped, one handful, then the other. Her mouth filled with the cloying texture, creamy and sticky, coating her tongue and the roof of her mouth. It was gummy, like cement. Somehow, her creations lost all their delicate flavor this way.

Two cupcakes down, she chanced a glance at Finn. An empty tray sat in front of him, and his teammates were making short work of their share. She licked her fingers.

He looked up, hitting her with a gaze so hot, so intense that her internal temperature cranked up high enough to melt all the sugar into caramel. Set it on fire with a blowtorch. They locked eyes for the longest time, or so it seemed, while wanton cupcake desecration continued around them.

Once he'd finished mentally crème-brûléeing her, Finn twisted his head to the side and whispered something to Meredith, who stood in front of his table.

"Ladies and gentlemen, stop eating. Finn's asked for a time-out."

Finn and Meredith put their heads together again, conferring. *What the hell?* This stupid game had gone on long enough.

Eden was about to object to all the goofing around when Meredith spoke again. "Okay, everyone. At four minutes and thirty seconds, Finn has called it. It's a win for Marketing. I concur. Congratulations!"

"What did you say?" Eden shouted, much louder than she'd intended.

Silence rang out in the staff lounge as everyone fell unnaturally still. Eden turned and surveyed the scene. Marketing had indeed demolished entire trays of cupcakes, with nothing but smeared frosting and piles of crumbs remaining on the trays. The guys and women on Finn's side looked like they'd been on the wrong side of a childish birthday party food fight. Finn himself had frosting smeared all over his white shirt, up his arms, and across his jaw. A great glob of chocolate streaked his hair like a skunk stripe.

She looked around at her team members—Felicity, Candice, Bettina, and the other women. The lone man on her side, Dave, sank back in his chair with half a crumbling cupcake in his grasp, looking deflated and lost. True, there were at least ten cupcakes still intact on their table. Maybe more.

Eden exhaled slowly, then spoke in a clear, crisp voice. "Finn, can I speak to you, please?"

She stepped away from the table and paced toward the wall of windows at one end of the room, then through the door to the deserted corridor beyond. Finn's footsteps echoed behind her, sounding hesitant. When she turned to face him, his expression was guarded, but a muscle ticked in his jaw. He knew something was coming—he looked as wary as a defendant awaiting sentencing in a court of law.

A half-smile spread across his lips as he stuffed his hands in his pockets. "You summoned me, Doctor Eden?"

"What exactly was that little power play in aid of?"

He stepped closer, planting his feet within a few inches of her shoes. "Power play? The contest was over, so I called it. Fair and square."

Eden snorted. "Fair and square, my ass."

When his gaze dipped to skim over her hips, as if to catch a glimpse of said ass, Eden could have throttled him. So what if she was wearing pedal pushers instead of her usual skirt? So what if her ass looked great in them? There was no excuse for blatant ogling. Or perhaps he thought her ass was too big, and it offended him just by existing, all round and curvy in his presence. What a horrible idea.

"I didn't realize you'd be so sensitive about a little competition. I just wanted to blow off steam after working so late on the report for McTavish."

She huffed out a breath. "That's completely beside the point. You were trying to prove something about your team winning before the time limit was up. But now that you mention it, I was expecting my review copy of the report first thing this morning. I assume you're emailing it."

"Review copy? But you'd already completed your section. You've got no call reviewing my work. McTavish sent me a reminder email, so I forwarded him the report."

"Excuse me? You mean to tell me you've already sent the report to McTavish, sight unseen by me?"

"Eden, you saw it yesterday. Give me a little credit. I only added my update. I'd never touch any of your work."

She placed her hands on her hips. "Guess I should be thankful for small mercies. You're unbelievable. Do you have no concept of professional courtesy? Common respect? I'll have you know I received an important addendum from the lab I wanted to add to the report today. Now I'll look like the one who can't meet a deadline, all because I was waiting to hear from you." She stabbed a finger into the center of his chest, and Finn stumbled back a step, his mouth hanging open.

Eden snapped her hands back to her sides and breathed deep, a prickle of tears behind her eyes. No way was she going to cry in front of him. And her staff were in the next room, a dim memory in the back of her mind until now.

She breathed in and out while returning her hands to her hips. *Get a grip, Eden.*

Finn stepped closer again. He examined her face and raised a hand toward her cheek as if to touch her. His hand hovered mid-air, then dropped at the last nanosecond. "Sorry. Let's talk to McTavish, sort it out together. No harm done."

Eden kept her voice low as she answered, "Don't you dare try to manage me! I know your type, Finn Donohue, with your fluffy emotional intelligence and personality profiling." She crossed her arms over her chest, letting him know she was still in control. "Look at you, all covered in frosting. It's unprofessional and, frankly, ridiculous." Her hand shot forward of its own volition and poked him on the nose with her index finger, wiping off the daub of pink frosting there.

She was breathing too fast. Her chest rose and fell, rose and fell. She needed to move back, but something held her in place. Finn, apparently. His hand rested lightly on her hip.

Her fingertips traveled down the smooth plane of his face to his jaw; her thumb stroked across where his strong chin met his full lower lip, coated in chocolate cake crumbs. She felt rather than heard Finn's sharp inhalation, the way his lip trembled under her touch. *So soft.* How were his lips so soft?

Eden leaned in, and he mirrored her. His hand, suddenly heavy and warm on her left hip, pulled her closer. She glanced up at his darkening pupils, gold-tipped lashes fanning closed. Then her body swayed toward him, and her lips brushed his. Once. Twice.

She hummed into his mouth. He tasted delicious, like cupcakes with a hint of salty-sweet essence of... Finn. His lips parted, and he kissed her, gentle as a breath of air at first. Then deeper. His tongue slid against hers, teasing, dancing.

There was nothing gentle about what happened next. Eden tugged at the back of his shirt, pulling it from his pants, then slid her hand beneath the cool cotton and over his hot skin, up the indentations of his spine. Muscles bunched under her hand. Her leg had somehow wrapped itself around the back of his thick thigh until she rubbed against him, just so. Heat throbbed through her every nerve ending.

Finn nipped her lip with his teeth and nudged her back before breaking their kiss.

"Eden." He frowned, parallel lines furrowing his forehead.

She pulled away, panting. Up close, his eyes were enormous and gorgeously green.

"Eden, we shouldn't... We have to get back to work." He tilted his head toward the staff lounge.

She nodded. Too fast. "Of course. I never should have... I just... I'm sorry." Her chest constricted, and she closed her eyes. What on earth was she thinking? A lump formed in the pit of her stomach. She shouldn't have touched him, not at all.

Certainly not like her clothes were on fire, and she needed to get out of them ASAP.

When she reopened her eyes, Finn's gaze was on her, all over her. "You don't have to apologize for being attracted to me. I'm flattered." He grinned.

Damn him. Was he laughing at her?

A sinking sensation hit the pit of her stomach, dislodging some cupcakes. "This had nothing to do with attraction. Nothing. You hear me?"

Her voice had risen to a dangerous level. Any minute now, one of their staff would hear and come to check out what was going on. But what was going on, she had no idea. Her body was too hot, out of control, her brain clearly not in the driver's seat. Apparently, her vagina could drive now.

Eden lowered her voice to a whisper, "You and me? Never going to happen. You're not even close to my type."

He raised an impertinent brow. "Whatever you say. I take it I'm dismissed?"

Pain flared behind her eyes. "What do you mean?"

Finn sighed wearily. "You want me out of your sight. It's pretty obvious."

"Yes. I mean, get back to work."

"Your attitude could do with some adjustment there, Doctor Eden."

An inarticulate sound rose from her throat like a strangled scream. "What makes you think you can speak to me like that?"

"You really want to know?" His voice was low, with an edge of something dark and dangerous.

Eden nodded. "Yes, I want to know what makes you think you're better than me. I want to know in what possible universe you're so superior, Mr. The Customer Is Always Right, Mr. Marketing Double-Speak Blowhard."

It was his turn to cross his arms. "Right. So we're resorting to name-calling? Well, I think you're an arrogant, know-it-all control freak who wouldn't recognize good teamwork or a good time if it smacked her in the face."

She glared at him. His face was as red as Mexican five-alarm chili. Seemed she wasn't the only one fired up. Somehow, that didn't make her feel any better.

Finn turned away and ran his hands over his hair, then whipped his head back around. He wasn't finished. "And before you accuse me of being unfair or sexist, I'm only giving my honest opinion on your behavior. I've tried several times to work with you, to be friendly. When you simmer down, you can come and apologize. This time, you owe it to me."

He stormed off—it was the only way to describe it. She could practically sense the thunder and lightning follow in his wake, crackling along the fault line of the corridor.

Eden's stomach plummeted to her knees, the weight of his words making her legs tremble. It couldn't be true. Her attitude didn't need adjustment. She was a perfect model of workplace competency. He'd been the asshole. Hadn't he?

Except, as she watched him leave, his shirt untucked from where she'd almost ravished him in public, she knew two things: First, Finn was absolutely her type, from his emerald eyes and dimply smile to his soft lips and cheeky back talk. Not to mention those forearms. She'd denied her body's signals for too long. And second, she'd been a stone-cold bitch to the only man she'd felt compelled to kiss in nearly a year.

And what a kiss. Eden pressed her fingertips to her still damp lips. She'd loved every second of it. Until he pulled away. Then he'd said he was *flattered*. Not attracted to her, just flattered. He wasn't interested in her. Of course not, considering how she'd told him off and called him names. How she'd launched herself at him. Then he'd said all those things...

She trudged back into the staff lounge, her stomach lurching from too many cupcakes. Or something else. Everyone in the room turned to stare at her, open-mouthed, gawking like kids when a fight broke out in the schoolyard. Then they quickly looked away, pretending to clean up or chat with each other.

Eden waved a hand vaguely toward the folding tables covered in cake debris. "Sorry, everybody, party's over." Her voice came out squeaky.

Felicity hurried over to her side, and Eden mumbled another apology as she grasped her assistant's outstretched hand. Her colleague, her friend, led her back toward the door. Felicity had come to support her. Surely Eden couldn't be one hundred percent horrible if Felicity liked her?

As they passed by the table where some of her team still sat, Eden bumped it with her hip, dislodging a tray with a few lonely cupcakes that teetered on the edge. They fell, tumbling to the floor right in front of her. She could only stop and stare.

Smashed. Completely ruined. All her hard work for nothing.

Eden bit her lip and marched forward through the door. There would be no tears at work.

Chapter Four

LittleMissPerfect: Having the worst day. The movies was a much better idea.

HotAussie007: Tell me later...

Unbelievable.

She'd been called to a 'discussion of core values' meeting like some naughty schoolgirl summoned to the principal's office. Both she and Finn had. McTavish must be having conniptions.

Finn must have done something totally stupid this time—it was the only possible explanation. Her clinical trial report had been exemplary, as usual. If she did say so herself.

Staring down at her feet, Eden approached the meeting room, shuffling her sparkly purple Doc Martens on the polished concrete floor. Why hadn't she worn sensible grown-up shoes today? She dreaded the showdown with Doctor McTavish and Finn, obviously. The memory of their kiss still hummed through her body, but only if she thought about it. She pushed it ruthlessly from her mind.

Doctor McTavish had the power to make or break their entire project. He was the one who could recommend they receive a further twelve months' funding or make the whole thing go away with a snap of his fingers. He'd also make her go away if he was unhappy with her performance.

McTavish had never warmed to her, never joked around or been overly friendly. She wasn't sure if McTavish hated all female managers or if she was somehow special. He was a cold fish in general, so it was hard to tell.

Taking a deep breath, she straightened her cardigan and the folder full of paperwork in her sweaty grip and peered through the meeting room window. No one was inside yet. Her shoulders relaxed a teensy bit as her heartbeat slowed from a rapid be-bop to a more swinging jazz standard pace, letting her breathe.

She opened the door and stepped into the deathly quiet space, then chose her position. Like setting up a base camp ready for war, the seat you picked said plenty about your state of mind and strategy.

After eight years of working in labs, usually as the only woman in charge of significant projects, she knew the score. She had to radiate strength and power, even when feeling vulnerable and wobbly on the inside. Best to sit facing the door to get the jump on whoever arrived next.

As she arranged herself in one of the uncomfortable metal-framed chairs, the door lock clicked. Eden whipped her eyes upward, a small gasp escaping her lips. She cursed herself for reacting. Finn. Looking effortlessly hot, caramel hair flopping down over his forehead, framing those laughing green eyes. She noted the matching twitch of his lips.

With eyes narrowed and arms crossed under her breasts, she stared him down. She could tell the moment Finn realized how pissed she was, as his eyes widened a fraction, and he offered a terse nod. He strode in, chose a chair a couple down from hers, and sat with a loud huff. Was he worried about this meeting too? *Interesting.* He drummed his fingertips on the tabletop in an infuriating way.

She shot him a glance and found him already looking at her. At her breasts, specifically. *Bastard.* Her blood thudded thickly through her veins, but she wouldn't be turned on. She just wouldn't.

The door clicked open again, and Doctor McTavish entered, or rather his glasses and bushy beard entered, followed by his wishy-washy self. He was a gray man, from his tufty hair to his baggy suit. Baggy everywhere except for his middle, which had a touch of the Michelin Man going on. Eden snuck another look at Finn seated across from her. He was staring in the direction of the door, a scowl marring his otherwise smooth, tanned forehead.

"Good. You're both here." McTavish quasi-smiled as he shuffled in and took a seat. Their boss's expression reminded Eden of a snake: a poisonous snake poised to strike. "Let's begin. I understand there was an unfortunate incident in the staff lounge this morning. Some kind of disagreement that was heard all the way over in IT. Do I have any cause for concern?"

Eden raised her head and composed her features into a bland expression, blank as a sheet of printer paper, to hide her irritation. This was what he'd summoned them to discuss?

Finn leaned forward, resting his large hands on the table. He let out a slow breath. "I'd like to apologize for any disturbance we might have caused. It was a social event, and it got a little out of hand."

Eden sat back in the hard chair and smoothed her palms down her thighs. She was sweating, nervousness getting the better of her. Was she meant to say something? Why did their boss reduce her confidence to gawky-teenage-girl levels?

And Finn was studying her, his head tilted to the side in such a way that she could make out the slight trace of stubble across his jaw. It looked touchable, tactile. Something deep in her belly contracted. Hunger, perhaps. She'd skipped lunch again.

"Thank you, Finn, for taking the initiative here. Much appreciated. Eden, do you have anything to add about your behavior?" McTavish pressed his lips together as if tasting something disgusting.

Eden's cheeks heated. She hated the fact her anger was so completely transparent to both men. The way McTavish always spoke to her, well, it made her want to punch his lights out. A shame society frowned upon such behavior, at least when it came from women scientists.

"No, Doctor McTavish. I believe my colleague's covered it." The words leaked from her lips on a sigh.

She crossed her arms and waited it out. Sooner or later, they'd have to talk about something important. Finn watched her, his gaze tugging at her as if an invisible cord connected them both.

McTavish peered at her over his gold-framed glasses. "You're a scientist, Eden. You're supposed to be an intelligent, rational person. Are you not?"

She gritted her teeth before releasing the tension with a tight smile, then responded with as much magnanimity as she could muster. "Of course, sir. As you'd appreciate, I've been under some pressure working on the clinical trial, and I suppose"—she risked another glance at Finn, sitting immobile, one eyebrow raised—"I needed to let off some steam."

"Hmm." McTavish looked down at the pile of documents in front of him. "I was disappointed to read that the drug needs to go through a further round of trials. In your opinion, of course."

As Eden's skin prickled with an unpleasant combination of embarrassment and anger, she folded her hands on the table, fighting the urge to reach across and throttle her boss. It was a close call. He'd hired her to do exactly this job—to be the voice of reason when everyone was blinded by the dollar signs attached to market potential or the exciting phase of launching a new product.

With a shrug, she explained her position. "In this case, my opinion is crucial. We mustn't forget that many people's lives depend on the safety and effectiveness of the drugs Magna Smart manufactures. This drug simply isn't proving effective, not yet, and we've not yet fully examined some of the side effects reported in earlier trials."

Finn cleared his throat, causing Eden to spin around and face him. As their eyes met, his lips tipped upward in a hesitant smile. Then he completely ignored her and spoke directly to McTavish. "I agree with Eden. When I first read over the lab results, of course I was disappointed we couldn't go to market yet. But I now consider this potential time lag a bonus for marketing planning. We can use the extra time to gauge the market's readiness for the new concept we discussed."

He was on her side now? He supported her decision? Good. If they were allies, it would make her job so much easier. The warm, fuzzy goodness rising in her belly and squeezing her chest was a friendly feeling. Appreciation. He respected her more than she'd realized. But wait... What exactly was the 'new concept'? Eden needed to know what was going on, and hopefully, Finn wouldn't hold back any details.

"Is there something else I should know about this project? What's this new concept?"

A pinched line appeared between Finn's eyebrows. "Weren't you briefed on the PowerUp Portal proposal?"

McTavish butted in, barely letting Finn get his question out. "The board deemed it unnecessary for the proposal to be widely discussed."

"But Eden and her team need to be on board, or it's never going to work." Finn's voice shook slightly, and he'd straightened in his chair.

It appeared McTavish had hidden something from her, and maybe Finn too. Something big. Her gaze switched back and forth between the two men across the table from each other, the tension in the air almost palpable.

"Finn, we can discuss this later, privately." McTavish shut down Finn's concerns with a wave of his hand. "I have good reasons for establishing two distinct project teams, and you will each have an opportunity to submit your proposals in a month's time. The board may choose to inform each of you about our longer-term strategy then."

Her stomach dipped with a foreboding of bad news. The current board of directors, of which McTavish was a key member, was a secretive and conservative bunch, preferring to drip-feed information to staff and shareholders long after important decisions had been made. Theirs wasn't exactly a collaborative and open approach to doing business. Basically, she was a mushroom, being kept in the dark and fed manure.

One glance across at Finn's expression, and it was clear he shared her annoyance. When he spoke, his voice held a tone of cool steel edged with icicles. "When I accepted this position, I was assured the scientific research team was on board with marketing a new kind of product."

The sense of doom rose in Eden's chest again, her heart thudding. Surely an old-time movie villain would enter the scene at any moment, twirling his mustache before whisking her away to tie her to the railroad tracks. Somehow, she'd fallen into a trap. They were keeping something from her. Something important.

She straightened in her seat. "Tell me what you've planned. I can't, in good conscience, continue to research new drugs without knowing the strategy the company intends to follow. I need to ensure we're taking an ethical stance in our research operations," Eden blurted out. She'd said what she must, but had she been heard?

McTavish rose from the table, straightening his gray suit and adjusting his glasses on his nose before staring down at her.

Using his height to intimidate her. It wouldn't have surprised Eden if he'd sprouted horns during the last few minutes, but he remained remarkably bland.

Their boss turned away from her and spoke mostly to Finn. "You each have a month to put together an outstanding presentation to assist us in getting this drug to market in the fastest possible timeframe, making the best use of resources and providing evidence of how your proposal will positively impact the company's bottom line. Only one of you will be employed by next year. If the board isn't satisfied with your performance, you'll both be terminated, and your respective team members will also be given notice. Do I make myself understood?"

Eden's mouth dropped open. McTavish wasn't even bothering to veil his threats anymore. How could she continue working for the man?

"Good." McTavish nodded, agreeing with himself, as neither she nor Finn had said a word. "Now get to work on your projects. The clock's ticking." With that, he strolled from the room and closed the door behind him.

She turned to Finn, her arms wrapped tightly around her waist. Nausea threatened to take hold, but she pushed it down. She needed to get out of this meeting room without looking like a complete basket case. But first, she had to get his perspective on whatever had just happened.

"What have you done?" she asked flatly.

Finn leaned toward her until their faces were only inches apart. "Excuse me? I didn't do anything except for my job, and I don't need any more attitude from you."

Eden took a deep breath, inhaling a drift of his fresh cologne; it teased her senses, reminding her of the beach in mid-summer. His face was free of cake crumbs, and he wore a clean shirt. Maybe he'd showered at lunchtime...

She shook her head. His brand of distraction was absolutely not what she needed right now. "Sorry. I didn't mean to, um, accost you earlier. And I can't believe McTavish spoke to us like that. I knew he was an asshole, but —"

Finn chuckled, low and throaty, close to her ear. When had he moved closer? Her nipples beaded, rasping against the lace of her bra, and she shivered, silently cursing the air-conditioning duct blowing on the back of her neck and down the front of her neckline. Goosebumps racing across her exposed skin, she glanced down at her notepad on the table. When she looked up, Finn was staring at her. Still sitting too close.

"I'd call him a cock knuckle, actually." He flashed a crooked smile that was infectious. His dimple made an appearance.

"A what?" she asked with a snort-laugh.

"Cock knuckle. A useless appendage. Great Aussie slang term my brother claimed to have invented."

"Kudos to your brother. That's quite a descriptive phrase, and accurate in this case." Eden breathed out, releasing the stale air in her lungs.

Finn tipped his head forward and lowered his voice. "You don't have to like McTavish. You don't have to like me either. I know we're competing, but I reckon we have to work together for a while. This month, anyway. We should try to be friendly."

The mention of her possible dismissal set Eden's stomach churning again. She had so much riding on this job, more than she'd ever meant to gamble. Her late grandmother's house—her family legacy—mortgaged twice over, the money used to fund her own expensive postgraduate studies and the start-up costs for Faith's jewelry business.

If she failed in this project, if her carefully constructed house of cards collapsed, both she and her sister would be left with nothing. Less than nothing, with debts up the wazoo. And if she failed, she'd also dishonor her grandmother's memory in the process.

She tried for a smile. "Friendly. No problem."

But when Finn reached out to shake her hand, she hesitated. Touching him suddenly seemed like an extremely bad idea. He was a random element in this entire situation, and she had no idea what reaction his touch would elicit. Instead, she rose from her chair, flicking her ponytail over her shoulder. Leaving him hanging until he dropped his extended hand to the tabletop.

"Friendly's doable, but let's not go crazy. See you around, Donohue." Eden walked out the door with her head held high, putting an extra swing in her hips.

She couldn't see his face as she left, but she heard his chuckle, felt his gaze on her back. The weight of his scrutiny. Why did it feel like she'd risen in his estimation in the last few minutes? And why did she suddenly care?

"Absolutely, *Doctor* Eden."

She clenched her teeth but kept on walking.

It didn't take much to make Finn happy. Flowing curves, feminine beauty, sensual power. It was almost enough to make him burst with excitement. He ran his hands over her form possessively.

"Ahem, get your hands off my beauty." Sam's voice echoed off the concrete floors, shattering the intimate moment.

Finn removed his hands from his friend's property and slipped them into his jeans pockets instead. "Sorry, mate. But this chassis... She's a beauty for sure."

His friend nodded, then folded his arms. "She's my latest joy," he said with a lopsided smile. The proprietor of Grease Lightning Garage and Auto Repairs was a proud man. A genius when it came to restoring classic cars and previously in mechanical engineering. But this business was his real calling.

"She's a '65 Fairlane?" Finn squatted beside the rear tire and checked out the rims. He glanced up at Sam, who made a kind of coughing noise.

Sam ran his hands through his slicked-back, Elvis-inspired hair and pointed at the hood. "Yep. Got her direct from a dealer in New Jersey. Take a look if you want. She purrs like a kitten."

Finn strolled around to the classic car's front end. He flicked a latch and popped the hood. "She's gorgeous. How much do you want for her?"

"You serious?"

He nodded. "Dead set."

Sam's left eyebrow quirked, then relaxed. "I didn't think you'd be staying here that long. A car like this means a commitment. She needs looking after. I won't sell her to you if you're just gonna skip town and move back to Australia."

Finn shook his head and shoved his hands back into his pockets. Sam was his best friend here in the US, but his impending work visa crisis was a bone of contention between them. Sam kept telling Finn to leave his 'job full of stuffed shirts' and find something fun, even if it was in a completely different field. To get out before he lost his job at Magna Smart. Finn was sorely tempted, but no. He wasn't giving up. Not yet.

He shook off his gloom and doom with a shrug. "Promise I won't skip town. I'll give you plenty of warning if I have to leave."

Sam slung an oily rag over his shoulder. "Yeah, whatever you say. You want to tell me why you're really here?"

Finn leaned over the Fairlane's engine, checking out the authentic front fender before answering his friend. "I'm freaking out about a woman. You know that dating site I told you about? I'm about to meet the one I've been chatting with on the app."

"The One? Big call, buddy. You don't even know what she looks like."

"No, not 'The One' in capitals, but I can't get her out of my head. It might all go to hell, but I want to keep chatting with her. Maybe meet up. She could be a good reason to hang around in this city."

"And I'm not? Thanks for nothing, asshole." Sam punched him in the shoulder, not gently either.

Finn rubbed his shoulder, then closed the car's hood. "That's not what I meant, mate. It's just been hard to date here. I've been putting in the hours at work, learning all the science jargon, building my team. No time for anything else."

With a nod, Sam turned and headed toward his damn fine Italian espresso machine, taking prime position on a workbench next to the office at the back of the garage. "I get it. Then you find someone, and she's as busy as you are. I'm just as much of a sad sack as you."

Leaning his butt against the hood of the car, Finn crossed his arms over his chest. "Right, thanks. You've totally made me feel better."

His friend turned from where he was messing with the machine's group head, adding the ground coffee and heating cups. "That's why I'm here. Group hugs, fluffy bunnies, motivational speeches, and all that shit."

"Asshole."

Sam flashed a grin back over his shoulder. "Come on, man, you can do better. Hit me with one of your best Aussie put-downs."

Finn raised his eyes to the ceiling and came up with a new one: "Okay... you arse-backwards dingo's donger."

Sam snorted. "I like it." He hit the espresso button, and the bittersweet aroma of coffee suffused the air, like the promise of better days. "Seriously, Finn. If this woman doesn't like you, she's not worthy of your attention. You're a genuine guy who knows how to show a woman a good time. You're not butt-ugly. You're not into game-playing, and you're smart."

Finn snorted at this last point. He couldn't help it.

"You *are* smart. Like I keep telling you, dyslexia's only a challenge. We all have them. Some of us have anxiety"—Sam pointed at his own chest—"but it doesn't mean we're dumb or not good enough. We have to work harder on our own shit sometimes, but it's not the end of the world."

Finn's thoughts drifted to Eden as he nodded. She was smart. Successful. Beautiful too. But she was rude and arrogant, even when she probably didn't mean to be. She had a dragon's personality and breathed fire on him whenever she opened her mouth. Except when she kissed him.

It was confusing. And hot.

Maybe Sam had a point. Compared to Eden, Finn was an emotional genius. "Thanks. You've actually made me feel better. Wish me luck, I guess."

Sam raised his espresso cup in a toast. "Salute."

You never knew. LittleMissPerfect could be The One. He had to give it his best shot.

Chapter Five

HotAussie007: What's your favorite film?

LittleMissPerfect: To Catch a Thief

HotAussie007: Nice. Love Grace Kelly

LittleMissPerfect: Really? Old-school

HotAussie007: Yep but Vertigo is my fav Hitchcock

LittleMissPerfect: *sigh* You're my kinda guy...

HotAussie007: I hope so. Can't wait till tonight. ☺

Can't wait. Sure. His message from a few hours ago now taunted Eden like a bad omen as she placed her phone back on the table in front of her.

Her foot had gone to sleep under the table a few minutes ago, thanks to her crossing her legs so tightly while waiting for her mystery man on the terrace of the Italian restaurant. They were supposed to meet almost half an hour ago.

She let her gaze wander over the heads of the other diners. The view over the Pacific from the elevated restaurant was stunning, the crisp sea breeze refreshing after a hot day. But her patience was fast running out. She smoothed down her full skirt and massaged her right calf muscle. The shoes had killer heels, alright. And her internal monologue was getting depressing.

He's not coming.

Yes, he is. He's just running late.

Or he's dead.

Why hasn't he sent a message?

Eden checked her phone messages, but nothing new had popped up. Not in the last thirty seconds. Nothing from her date. Why did her stomach perform death-defying rolls whenever she thought of HotAussie007 as her date?

He'd probably changed his mind. Decided she was a bit of fun online but not worth pursuing. Perhaps he was married or a secret international cat-burglar like Cary Grant in her favorite movie.

Needing a lifeline before she drowned in an ocean of self-doubt, she tapped out a message to her sister.

Eden: Date may be a no-show *sob*

Faith: Shit. What do you always say? What would Grace Kelly do?

Eden: If Cary Grant stood her up? Haha. Never. Plus she wouldn't say *shit*

Faith: Sorry Babycakes. You're a babe and he's trash. Call me later xoxo

This would never happen to Grace. She'd just run off to Monaco and marry a real-life prince who'd drape her in jewels. Eden didn't need a prince or jewels. A nice, relatively sane man who wanted to kiss her would be a pleasant change. Handsome and smart, too, if possible.

She took a sip of her vodka gimlet, wondering if she looked like a desperate woman. Overdressed, sitting alone on the terrace of a crowded restaurant with an old-fashioned drink. But she liked it. It was in a pretty martini glass with a slice of lime. Plus, vodka. Calming for the nerves.

The dress truly made her look certifiable. Eden smoothed her hands over her skirt, watching how her own fingers trembled. An older woman from a nearby table glanced at her over her companion's shoulder, her eyes pitying. When the woman ran her gaze over Eden's dress and frowned, Eden realized she'd made a mistake.

She shouldn't have let Faith talk her into the sexy outfit. Should have known better than to agree to the blind date too. The SD Confidential dating site had seemed a good idea at the time. Like-minded professionals in the San Diego area, matched for their interests and goals, no photos or giveaway personal information. It should have made dating easier. Less confronting, less like a meat market. Also, less stalkerish.

Instead, she felt like a fraud. She wasn't sexy. Or confident. When you got right down to it, she wasn't even interesting. She was a scientist, and she loved her work, but she'd barely put any effort into the rest of her life. Her judgment was failing, and all because she was lonely. Eden gulped down a mouthful of gimlet and nearly choked on the slice of lime, making her splutter into her glass.

Excellent. Just perfect.

She was a sad, mad, old-lady-style, cocktail-drinking spinster with a PhD in stupid.

Allesandro's was always pumping on a Friday night. Finn strode through the restaurant's heavy wooden doors and scanned the room for his date. God, he was so late. Not intentionally. An unplanned phone interview had dragged on for so long, he nearly messaged his date to cancel. But it was better if he explained in person. Probably. He was exhausted and not thinking straight. His brain still buzzed with information, details he'd have to go over later. Anyway, he'd finally made it. The restaurant's host stopped him and asked if he had a reservation.

Finn nodded, scanning the nearby tables at the same time. "Yes, under Bond. I'm meeting a friend. Is it okay if I walk through the restaurant?"

The host waved him inside. "Si, molto bene. I have you out on the terrace."

Finn shot the host a smile and headed inside. It was difficult to get a clear view through the restaurant. A central bar dominated the front section of the building, opening out to a large bistro area and the outdoor terrace beyond. This place was one of his favorites in the area, with terracotta tiles on the floor, traditional wooden tables, and photos of Italian cityscapes adorning the white stucco walls. Great food, great atmosphere.

Straight ahead, rows of pre-dinner drinkers sat at the long wooden bench seats in the bar area, a mix of ages, some dressed up and others casually kitted out in jeans and T-shirts. A lot of after-work catch-ups, some couples, and families with young kids. A tiny boy seated in a high chair, slopping spaghetti all over his face and giggling, had him chuckling too.

Finn walked on, checking out the likely suspects. Where was she?

There were more than ten women in the bar area alone, sitting and gazing at their phones, sipping wine, applying makeup. A blond woman with impossibly long legs shot him a wide smile and tossed her hair in an obvious come-on. Not her. She couldn't be his date. He had zero interest. He'd be able to tell if it was her. Wouldn't he?

Why hadn't he found out what she looked like? He'd asked early on, but she'd always deflected. He guessed she was homely, perhaps a little overweight. That was the strange thing—he didn't care. She was LittleMissPerfect. He'd got to know her and liked her, was attracted to her already. The main reason he'd gone for an anonymous dating site was he wanted someone to talk to.

Since moving to California, dating had been trickier than he'd expected. In New York it had been easier, or maybe he hadn't been as jaded. It was all a game. All women cared about was what he did for a living, his looks, and what model car he drove. Then they wanted to know if he owned a home in swanky Del

Mar. He didn't. He rented a fully furnished condo and spent far too much time at work. Not prime dating material, according to many.

Seemed most of the guys were in on the game too. Creating an image of success, having the 'right' woman on your arm. The women he'd dated lately had been more interested in his salary package than *his* package, or his personality. *Whatever.* He hated it. Had it been the case back home in Australia? He could hardly remember.

These days, Finn wanted more. Not some shallow hook-up, not just sex. Although sex would be a definite bonus after such a long drought. He wanted, *needed*, a real connection with a woman he could trust. 'Chasing tail' as his American friends so charmingly put it, had lost its appeal a long time ago.

He should've asked her to wear a flower on her lapel or some other clichéd accessory. She'd messaged him earlier and said she'd dress in 'something strict.' But what the hell did that even mean?

"Excuse me." Finn weaved his way through the restaurant to the terrace, then hung back near the French doors as a large group pushed past to exit.

He scanned the outdoor area. There. Could it be? It was! His pulse thundered in his ears. It was definitely her. *Eden.*

She had her back to him, but he'd know her long hair any-where. Seated on a bench seat at the far edge of the terrace, against an iron balustrade, she gazed out over the ocean, the sunset fading from orange to soft pink like the backdrop in some exotic travel brochure. She'd flipped her loose dark hair over one bare shoulder, exposing the long line of her neck.

She was stunning. Her outfit was... wow. And he was the proverbial stunned mullet.

Christ, how had he never noticed her rocking those curves? She wore a strapless number in deep red, like wine, pulled tight around her tiny waist with some kind of black ribbon corset at the back. He wanted to unlace it. Immediately. With his teeth.

Then there were her legs, crossed to one side under a full skirt, pencil-thin lines running up the back of her stockings. Did they go all the way to the top? Finn's eyes meandered over her hips to her bare shoulders, then tracked back down again. Black gloves to her elbows. High heels with red soles. So elegant and yet *so strict*. Like his favorite classic Hollywood starlet fantasies come to life in glorious Technicolor.

Eden turned toward him slightly, and he backed up against the rough stucco wall, willing himself to be invisible. Her lips, painted blood-red, were full and wicked looking. *Tempting*. Then she sighed. Her shoulders drooped, her whole body deflating as if she'd given up. She worried at her lower lip.

Finn almost went to her. Almost called out 'Little Miss Perfect.' He could have let her know his secret identity, explained that he was her match. But she looked so damned sad.

He'd only make things worse. Eden had decided he was the enemy, and work was going to be hell with the two of them competing. How could he reveal his online identity? If she found out he was HotAussie007, she'd lose it, big-time. He'd already been on the receiving end of her wrath once—he wasn't sure he'd survive round number two.

On the other hand, she'd kissed him. Totally unexpected, and totally hot. Blood surged to his lower extremities, leaving him lightheaded. The way she'd touched him had made it near impossible to back away. One more kiss like that, and there'd be no more working together. He'd pin her up against the wall of her office and take her the way he wanted. It was what they both wanted, even if she wouldn't admit it yet.

The only problem was he knew what would happen next. He'd lose his job and his work visa along with it, unless he could find another employer to sponsor him. Highly unlikely. He'd be deported, his career in tatters. Nothing he'd done over the past few years would mean a damn thing.

"Bloody hell," he muttered as he stepped back inside.

Finn headed for the bar, plonked himself on a stool, and signaled the bartender. He needed a drink. Some fortification before either claiming Eden as his date, consequences be damned, or cutting and running like a coward. He needed to formulate a strategy.

His phone pinged, signaling a new message, and LittleMissPerfect's name flashed up on the screen. Finn stared at the glowing screen, torturing him from where it lay on the glossy wooden bar. It was crunch time.

Five more minutes. Eden could stand waiting another five minutes and still keep her dignity intact.

She sipped the dregs of her cocktail, drink number two. It slid down way too easily, leaving her brain a bit fuzzy around the edges. She needed to get home. No more drinking unless she planned to stay for dinner. And no way would she do a solo date. That was too depressing to contemplate when her expectations had been so high.

She tapped out a message. *Waited 40 mins. Where were you?*

It was her second such inquiry in the last few minutes. Her tone was no longer flirty but snarky and resigned. When she glanced at her phone's blank screen for the third time in a minute, she could no longer stand it. She drained the last of her drink, wincing at its bitter aftertaste.

"Okay, time to go," Eden whispered as she grabbed her clutch purse. She rose from the bench seat and steadied herself on her super-high heels before pushing back her shoulders and getting her stride on.

Wanting to avoid the embarrassment of walking through the restaurant, she moved around the outside tables until she spotted a server.

"Sorry, I can't stay." Eden pasted the semblance of a smile on her lips, noting the young woman's sympathetic half-smile in return. She gulped hard. Tears weren't far away.

She escaped, out the side gate leading through a garden to the parking lot.

Finn stepped out of the restaurant's main doors and stomped across the parking lot. It was cowardly, but he couldn't go through with it. He had to leave.

Eden was brilliant and beautiful, challenging for sure, but *so* not for him. Something churned in his gut, and he suspected it wasn't only the beer on an empty stomach. He ripped off his suit jacket and stashed it under his arm, the heat of the sticky summer night washing over him like a wave of nausea.

So he was attracted to her—he was honest enough to admit it to himself. *Big fucking deal.* That didn't mean he had to do anything about it. He didn't have to throw himself at her feet, so she could stomp all over him in her red-soled stilettos. They had to work together in a tense situation, and it made no sense to stir a whole lot of feelings into the mix.

The sight of his prized '67 Chevy pickup sitting at the edge of the lot by a line of trees cheered him up, as it always did. Her sleek lines and purring engine were as close as he'd get to anything sexy tonight.

Finn unlocked the door and climbed inside. Checking his rear-view mirror, he fired up the engine and threw the pickup in reverse. And gunned it. A grinding crunch of glass—*or gravel?*—beneath the wheels had him gritting his teeth and slamming on the brakes. Hard. He put his baby into neutral. Like hell did he need a puncture to top off his evening.

As he rounded the rear end of his Chevy, he scanned the ground behind his wheels and spotted the offending trash.

Some idiot had dropped a bunch of Skittles or some other hard candy, creating a slip hazard, but nothing dangerous like broken glass. After kicking the colorful spheres toward the trees, clearing the ground as best he could, he got back into the driver's seat.

He started the engine and reversed fast. The sound of impact hit him like a gunshot.

Crack! A thud. He'd struck something. Hard.

"Shit," he spat out, a hot roil of dread moving through his gut. He'd forgotten to check his mirror again before reversing. Too distracted by stupid candy on the ground and everything else.

Finn killed the engine and jumped out of his car again. He ran, pulse hammering, around the back of the vehicle to an awful scene. Sprawled on her side, a woman lay on top of an overturned motorbike, legs outstretched across the asphalt. One leg was scraped raw, grazed skin as red as her dress. A black helmet lay a few paces away The bike's engine was still running. As he crept forward and reached down to turn off the ignition, in the back of his mind, he registered it was a smaller scooter, a Vespa.

He swept the woman's black hair aside to see her face. Red lips and long, dark eyelashes fanned out over pale skin. Too pale.

His heart beat a dull rhythm in his chest as sweat trickled down his back.

Oh hell. Oh no. Eden.

"Eden, can you hear me?" He brushed his hand across her cheek, willing her to open her eyes. "Wake up. Are you alright? Talk to me."

Her eyes blinked open, but she stared through him, her gaze unfocused. He gritted his teeth and smoothed his thumb across her cheek again. So soft. So fragile.

"Eden, it's me. Finn. Can you talk? Should I call an ambulance?" He slid his hand under her head to cradle it. Holding her up. Another wave of guilt rolled through his body. "I'm so sorry. It's all my fault."

He'd make it up to her, somehow. If she let him.

She opened her eyes.

Chapter Six

Eden's ears rang, white noise rushing through her head. A pounding had started above her right ankle. She couldn't move her leg. Where was she? The restaurant. The parking lot...

Finn was there. She blinked again. Was he a mirage? No. He was really there.

Thank goodness.

Her lips parted, but at first, only a croak came out. "I - I'm okay, I think." She blinked slowly and exhaled, her body shaking. "Finn, what are you doing here?"

"I was meeting a friend... It's not important now." He shook his head and gazed into her eyes; his forehead creased with concern. "Do you want me to call an ambulance? We should probably have a doctor check out your leg."

She raised herself onto her elbows with Finn's arm wrapped around her back, providing some support. Luckily, she'd put her little bolero jacket on over her strapless dress, or her back would've been torn to shreds when she hit the ground. Her dress was probably ruined.

Focus, Eden. Priorities.

Glancing down at her leg, she gasped at the mess of rough skin, blood, and the way her ankle was twisted, already swollen. Once she made it home, she'd hit it with disinfectant to clean the raw scrape. It would hurt. But Finn had asked her a question.

She gazed up at him and shook her head. "I don't want an ambulance."

His forehead scrunched in concertina folds. "Are you sure? There's no way you can ride your scooter home."

The man was so *hot*, radiating body heat all over her. His arm wrapped around her, his thumb stroking her cheekbone. She shivered, enjoying Finn's touch. Or was she in shock? Probably shock. "Oh. You're right. I hate when you're right."

Finn chuckled, a deep, resonant sound that had thrilled her once It thrilled her more intimately up close. He eased her up gently until she sat to one side, her weight resting on her arms. "Better?"

When she nodded, he nodded.

He tipped his head to the side. "I've got a first aid kit in my car. Stay there—don't move."

As if she was going anywhere.

Eden closed her eyes and groaned as she shifted her leg slightly. A flash of red behind her eyelids told her how bad the pain was, even if she couldn't feel it fully. Yet. She blinked her eyes open and sat up straight. She studied her shaking hands, pale against her red silk skirt, looking like they belonged to someone else.

Finn jogged back to his car, while she sat there hobbled like a racehorse after the biggest race of its life. She should go to the emergency room right away, but the cost would be astronomical, and an ambulance was out of the question. Just the thought of it gave her chest pains. The last thing she needed was a heart attack.

She'd call Faith. Her sister would pick her up. Except it was Friday night, so she'd be working the late shift at the boutique. Eden turned her head to her poor, dented Vespa behind her, its storage compartment still shut. Her phone was in there.

Finn was back, crouched beside her, gravel crunching under his knees. He pressed a bottle of water to her lips, and she drank eagerly, water droplets spilling down her chin and onto her chest. She must look a complete mess. But it wasn't important right now. Her phone, she needed it.

"Can you pass me my phone? From the compartment?" She gestured over her shoulder, trying to ignore how he quickly lifted his gaze from her damp cleavage, his eyes now alive with mischief. Now wasn't the time to explore whatever physical spark was between them. She set her mouth in a hard line.

Without a word, Finn reached over and unlatched the small black box behind her scooter's seat, where she stored her purse, keys, phone, and other essential items, such as lipstick. He located her phone and handed it over. His face had gone blank, his shoulders tense, like he was waiting for her to yell at him.

Something about her cell phone had him watching her like a hawk. Was he worried she'd call the cops? Report him for reckless driving? If she were the cold-hearted bitch some people thought she was, perhaps she would. But the truth was, she enjoyed being in control. She liked being organized. Not being stood up on a blind date she never should have agreed to or being run down in a parking lot and sprawled all over a far too attractive man who shouldn't have been there.

It was his fault. Logically, she knew that. But she was partly responsible. She was upset and hadn't been paying attention. And she hadn't replaced her helmet with the loose clasp.

She didn't want Finn to see her like a damsel in distress. He shouldn't have to save her.

She messaged Faith, short and to the point.

> **Eden:** Little accident. Fell off Betsy. Not bad but hurt my leg. Pick me up?

Seconds later, her phone pinged with a response.

Faith: Shit. You OK Babycakes? Can't come now, big stocktake with the boss. Can u get a taxi home? I can be there by 10

Eden hissed through her teeth. She hated to ask Finn, but what other choice did she have? An expensive taxi, maybe. She glanced up to find him still watching her intently. Studying her, almost. As his gaze raked over her face and skimmed her body, her face heated like she'd been soaking in a steamy bubble bath for an hour.

She pressed her lips together, then took the plunge. "Could you give me a ride home? My sister's stuck at work. And Felicity lives too far away." She shifted, glancing down at her phone. "I can't think of anyone else to call." A lump formed in her throat. It was a sad state of affairs that she'd let other friendships wither.

Finn's eyes flashed. "No worries. I'd already decided I was taking you home, Doctor Eden." He uttered her name in a deep, throaty tone, matched with one of the cheekiest smiles she'd ever seen.

If it was even possible, her face flamed hotter. There was something about those words and the naughty intent behind them. A threat. Or a promise. Heat coursed through her body, chasing the earlier shivers away. *Phew.*

His expression turned serious as he mumbled, "Besides, this is all my fault. Taking you home is the least I can do."

Concentrating on controlling her trembling fingers, she messaged Faith again.

Eden: It's OK. Getting a ride home with Work Guy. See you at 10 for sister hugs x

When she put her phone down beside her, Finn picked up a small green box—a compact first aid kit with a white cross printed on the lid. He opened it and rummaged through it, the crinkling of plastic distracting her from any thoughts of him taking her home. But... he'd have to help her inside. He'd have to touch her hand, maybe wrap his arm around her again. He might even throw her over his big, strong shoulder and carry her inside like a fireman. The shivers returned, chasing across her chest and arms.

"I was a volunteer surf lifesaver back home, had a proper first aid certificate and everything." He touched the outer edge of the torn skin on her shin, which surprised another gasp out of her. "I'll clean the wound, see what we're dealing with. Is that okay?"

He seemed to know what he was doing, cradling her leg gently from underneath. What a relief. But when he pushed her skirt above her knee and began rolling her mostly destroyed stay-up stocking down her thigh, her heart rate skyrocketed into the stratosphere. Tingly tendrils of pleasure followed the trail of his warm fingers down her inner thigh and, thankfully, down past her knee.

Eden nodded, mute and compliant, letting him take control of the situation. Totally unlike her usual self. When he tore open a small paper package and swiped a cotton swab over her sore leg, she didn't complain. Until it registered that he must have soaked the swab in acid first.

She bit her lip to stop herself from howling. But a few choice words still escaped. "Ouch! Mother *firetruck*. You absolute *toolbelt*!"

Finn looked up, flicked his toffee-streaked hair out of his eyes, and flashed a movie-star grin. "That's the best you can do? Mother firetruck? *Toolbelt*." His shoulders shaking, he ducked his head and continued to work on her leg.

Eden gasped at the sudden stab of pain as his fingers skimmed the scraped and bruised area. "I don't like cursing, alright? It's undignified and unprofessional."

"We're not at work now. Anyway, I think your brand of cursing is adorable." He smiled, looking annoyingly smug. And then flustered.

Finn ducked his head again, but his fingers trembled, and his broad chest rose and fell rapidly under his thin cotton shirt. He continued doing something medical with antiseptic cream, rubbing it into her skin.

"Holy guacamole!" It stung like freshly squeezed lemon juice poured over a paper cut, maybe with some Tabasco sauce. *Like a mother firetruck.* A gasp escaped her lips. "You did not just call me *adorable.*" She squinted her eyes so narrowly he could have mistaken her for a half-blind mole person.

"No, never. I called your swearing adorable. Big difference." He nodded, his eyebrows knitting together.

Eden frowned. "Oh. Good."

She didn't want him thinking she was adorable. Such assumptions were problematic, especially when he'd seen her out of her work clothes. Well, not out of her clothes entirely, but in her sexy date clothes. It was weird when they had to work together. Still, it would have been nice if he'd agreed she was *a bit* adorable.

"All done." He applied a dressing over her wound, then rubbed his thumb across it to smooth it down.

Her heart hiccupped, interrupting her thoughts. Hearts weren't meant to hiccup. The way he touched her leg and took care of her, it was... kind. Something ached in her chest at the thought. A kind man. Kind and handsome.

"Thank you." Her words came out a little husky. Hopefully, he wouldn't notice.

Finn raised his head and smiled, softer this time. All melty and delicious looking. Were his lips always so full and inviting? They had been earlier when covered in cake crumbs. The kiss she'd tried so hard to block from her thoughts came flooding back with a wash of warmth across her skin, along with a thud of her heart. It was inconvenient.

"You're welcome. Looks like your ankle's sprained, not broken, and the abrasion's not too bad. Time to get you home." He stood and dusted his hands together before gathering up the contents of his first aid kit. With hands planted on his hips, he tipped his head toward her and tensed his jaw. "I'll have to carry you to the car. Can't have you putting any weight on your dodgy leg yet."

Without waiting for her response, Finn squatted next to her and somehow got his arms behind her back and under her knees. In one smooth movement, he lifted her into his arms.

Snuggled against his chest, she breathed in the fresh linen and citrus scent of his shirt, mixed with the sharp tang of clean male sweat. He was warm too. Toasty.

Eden had one arm wrapped around his neck, near the nape. Then she realized she was gripping his right forearm with her other hand, her nails digging into his skin. Releasing her death grip, she tried to relax into his hold as he strode toward his car's passenger door.

His skin was silky and surprisingly soft under her fingertips. *Oh no.* She was stroking his arm. Snapping her hand back, out of harm's way, she glanced away and got a clear view down the bodice of her dress. If she had a clear view, so did he. Pulling her jacket tightly closed over her chest, she closed her eyes and breathed deep. Her pulse was out of control. Everything was out of control.

Finn chuckled and patted her on the butt. "Nice save, Doctor Eden." He deposited her in the passenger seat.

Her internal thermometer spiked again. He'd noticed her reaction, enjoyed it even.

Then he was gone. Eden smoothed her hands down over her full skirt and stretched out her leg. There was quite a lot of space in the front of his truck, with the seats pushed right back. She craned her neck and caught sight of Finn rounding the back of the car through the rear window. He was messing around with something in the truck's tray, taking his time.

She checked out the Chevy's interior. Nice. Probably a late 1960s model. The seats looked like the original leather, in a pale blue pearl finish to match the paint job. No back seat. Her grandmother once warned her about hot boys who drove hot cars. They only wanted to get a girl into the back seat, she'd said.

Sometimes a girl should throw caution to the wind, or so she'd thought back in the day. But things were different now. She was a grown-up and had to think about annoying things, such as the consequences of her actions. *Son of a monkey!*

"I'm in love, in case you didn't know." Finn caught Eden's startled expression as he jumped into the driver's seat. Classic deer-caught-in-headlights look, complete with massive doe eyes. "My truck. She's my one true love."

Eden smiled, a special sparkly smile he'd never seen before. "She's beautiful. I feel the same way about my Betsy."

He blinked. "Betsy?" Did Eden have a daughter she hadn't mentioned?

An image of a giggling toddler with black ringlets popped into his head. Any child of hers was bound to be a stunner. Smart and independent. Eden would be a practical mother but loving too. She'd be great with kids. Finn shook his head to dislodge the random thoughts.

"Betsy the Vespa. Oh, what will I do about her?" Eden's hand flew to her mouth.

She'd named her scooter Betsy? Cute. She surprised him, not for the first time. He wouldn't have picked her for someone who'd be emotional about a scooter. But her Vespa was a beauty. "No worries. Betsy's safe in the back of my truck. But she's a bit banged up. I'll call my insurance company and pay for all the repairs."

Finn ran his hand through his hair with a sigh. He was an asshole for causing her so much trouble and ruining *Betsy*. It was the least he could do.

Eden nodded, staring straight ahead out the windshield. Her hands dropped to her lap, and his gaze followed; he couldn't help it. She'd folded her hands on top of her thighs like an old-fashioned lady.

Those smooth thighs he'd caught a glimpse of as he'd rolled one of her stockings down her injured leg. Those damned sexy stockings. He'd touched her skin, so warm and inviting, with the scent of vanilla and roses teasing him. As sweet as one of her cupcakes. The dress, her whole look: such a contrast to her usual uptight work persona.

Finn realized he wasn't driving or saying anything, only staring at her like some creeper. Totally going to improve his reputation with her. He blinked again. Did he want to improve his reputation? It was kind of fun to have her all snarky and on edge, with those pretty lips pouting at him. But what if she'd changed her mind about him? What if he could be more to her than an annoying coworker? Maybe he already was. *That kiss*. It'd come out of nowhere, but he couldn't forget it.

With a shake of his head, he pulled himself back to the here and now and turned to her. "You haven't told me your address."

Eden jumped as if startled from a dream. When she turned to face him, she opened her mouth as if to tell him where she lived, but nothing came out. After a moment, she said, "Right, of course. I live in Del Mar, near the fairground. I'll direct you."

"Cool."

Finn started the engine and focused his attention on the road, being sure to check carefully before reversing this time. Driving like a man in charge of his senses.

Chapter Seven

The drive to her house was silent and interminable. Although only a few minutes in real time, the tension in the air and an answering pressure inside Eden's chest made things move in slow motion. Finn's forearm as he wrenched the gearshift into second, the way his jaw clenched when he had to stop suddenly in merging traffic—everything about him spoke to her.

Things she'd never noticed now stood out in sharp relief—his strong profile, more angular than she'd thought. He swallowed, and her gaze followed the motion of his Adam's apple, shifting underneath his tanned skin.

"Turn right here, then take the first left." Her voice croaked on a dry mouth, and she twisted the fabric of her skirt between her fingers. He made her nervous.

As they turned into the familiar neighborhood, Eden's thoughts spiraled. What would he think? People often regarded her differently when they realized where she lived, and she didn't like it. She hardly ever invited anyone to her home. In many ways, life would be much easier if she met everyone's stereotypical ideas of who she should be, but she never had. Not even when she lived in a down-and-out neighborhood as a kid. Back then, she'd been the nerd who read books for fun and enjoyed learning about science in school.

Now that she lived close enough to touch Millionaire's Row, a couple of streets back from the beach, strangers evaluated her with other emotions besides pity. Cold and calculating, assessing her worth in purely monetary terms. She could practically see their brains ticking, wondering just what she'd done to amass such wealth as a young, single woman. Some people made assumptions and asked vague questions about who she knew, who she might have slept with or divorced.

They didn't realize her late grandmother left the house to her two granddaughters when she died after a long illness, and Eden wasn't exactly rolling in cash. Far from it, with a huge, refinanced mortgage to service. So people who judged her could go jump off the La Jolla clifftops. Judgy McJudgersons had no place in her life.

Finn slowed as he navigated the winding, narrow street, and she stared out the car window with fresh eyes. The wide, green lawns, palm trees, and monolithic mansions all screamed one thing—*money*, and plenty of it. Except it often wasn't true. Sure, some of her neighbors in the grand new houses were loaded. Others were in hock up the wazoo but lived here because it was a great location for work and the university. Then there were her grandmother's old friends who'd lived in the area for over forty years, since the time when inexpensive bungalows were the only style of home. They loved being near the beach and the old community feel. Although that was gradually fading away.

Eden pointed out the window, flicking her eyes across to Finn. "My house is at the end. The white bungalow."

He pulled up alongside the curb and turned to face her. "Nice." His raised eyebrows instantly communicated all kinds of emotions—surprise, interest, curiosity. But thankfully, he kept any assumptions or innuendo to himself.

"Thanks. I like it."

She reached out to grab the door handle, but Finn leaned across her, stopping her. He pressed his hand over hers, so she could feel the warm imprint of his fingertips on the back of her hand. His face was so close to hers, his scent surrounding her again. A dizzy rush of what she guessed were pheromones left her lightheaded.

He could have leaned in an inch or two more and kissed her. But he didn't. Still, she froze as ice invaded her veins, every muscle in her body tensing. The tiny hairs rose on her arms and the nape of her neck.

Fight or flight. There was no need to run, but her body reacted anyway.

With a frown, Finn shifted back to his seat. "It's okay, Eden. I just want to help you out of the car." He held up an index finger. "Wait one second."

As he disappeared out his door, she sank back into her seat. Inhaled. Exhaled. She rubbed her arms, and her body calmed. He'd seen her panic. What must he think of her? The next thing she knew, he'd opened her car door and was offering her his hand. She took it gladly. Finn wasn't a threat. She was just jumpy.

"Okay?" he asked gently while pulling her up and out of the car.

Eden nodded, leaning against him as he wrapped an arm around her waist. Tensing a little, she tried putting a little weight on her sore leg to see if she could walk on her own. She winced. No chance. She glanced down at her damaged ankle. It throbbed with internal fire, her foot feeling as big as an elephant's. She'd kicked off her shoes in the car and now held them in one hand. Her feet looked odd—one stockinged and one bare.

Finn guided her forward a step and slammed the car door behind them, then asked her again if she was okay. Every step of the way, he supported her, held her just tight enough and never too tight, helping her to skirt around a potted plant near her front door. She tripped over her own feet anyway, so clumsy it was embarrassing. His arm around her waist gripped her firmly, his hand on her hip squeezing a fraction tighter.

Something else throbbed now, deep inside. It felt so good, him holding her close, that she forgot herself for a moment. She almost asked him if he'd like to come in for a nightcap, which was ridiculous. They weren't on a date. Not even close. Her date had been a no-show, a disaster she'd blocked from her mind until now. But her emotions were yo-yoing all over the place.

They stood on her front doorstep, and he stared down at her in such a way—such a stunningly *caring* way—that everything clenched a little tighter. Her stomach, her chest, especially her thighs. Lifting her chin, Eden made herself meet his gaze.

"Could you help me inside? Just to the living room." She waited for Finn to crack a joke, to tease her for needing his help.

Instead, he smiled, flashing white teeth, and pressed a firm hand to the small of her back. "No worries. Lead the way."

She was barely capable of leading him anywhere, but she did her best. He waited while she unlocked her door, lending a hand to push it open while she balanced on her good leg. Only once she was inside did he follow, looking around her home, a small smile lifting the corners of his mouth.

Eden loved her house. It was modest in size but light and airy and decorated in a feminine retro style she adored. Hints of color popped from abstract paintings, old movie posters, and the scatter pillows on her vintage sofas, while a vase of bright pink and orange gerberas decorated the dining table. Happy flowers.

Then there was the sewing station, with her current work in progress. Her face heated. *Oh*. She should probably hide the curvaceous mannequin clad in scanty, half-sewn lingerie. No one needed to know what she sometimes wore under her conservative work outfits. She went to move toward the mannequin but tensed when Finn pulled her back with a hand on her upper arm.

"Wait," he murmured.

She was so unsteady on her feet that Finn expected her to crash to the floor at any moment.

"Lean on me." He supported her again, making sure she was stable before walking her toward the nearest sofa.

Finn waited until she settled, leaning against the end of the sofa with her legs extended along the seat cushions. He glanced at the mannequin. "Is she a friend of yours? Sexy ensemble."

Eden nodded and offered a half-smile. "Yes, we're kind of close. We share a couple of things, like our measurements."

He raised an eyebrow and turned to her plastic friend. "Really?" He cleared his throat.

Those were quite some measurements. The scraps of deep red transparent fabric stretched across the mannequin's ample breasts, barely held together by lace to form a teddy, were having an effect. He was sweating. He swiped a hand across his forehead. Imagining that lingerie on Eden's curvy form would keep him up at night. Literally.

"Do you sew a lot of your own clothes?"

"Only what I can't buy in stores. I love vintage styles, and they're getting harder to come by secondhand. And sewing relaxes me." She fussed with the pillow behind her back, trying to prop herself up. She looked uncomfortable, and he had to help her. Couldn't stop himself. He urged her to lean forward and rearranged a couple of pillows so she sat straighter.

Finn perched on the other end of the sofa, near her feet. He placed another small pillow under her injured ankle, then allowed his gaze to wander up her body. "Is this dress one of your creations? It's amazing." What an understatement. It had virtually disabled the speech center in his brain when he'd spotted her earlier at the restaurant.

She caught his eye and smiled, but it looked a little tight around the edges. "This dress was a remake from a 1950s pattern. I think it turned out nicely. Even if my evening didn't. I got stood up. And then run-down."

His stomach lurched, and he fixed his gaze on the hardwood floor. It was his fault. The botched date, Eden being stood up, her injury. All his fault. He was officially an A-grade asshole. Finn snapped his head up and faced her, determination rising to the surface of his mind, past all his murky intentions. He'd fix it. All of it. Somehow.

"Whoever the guy is, he'll regret standing you up. He doesn't realize what he's missing out on."

Eden snorted, shaking her head.

Right. She needed to hear something positive to take the sting out of the tail of a shitty night. "I'm serious, Eden. You're intelligent and beautiful, and you've got a killer sense of style. As the kids say, you've got it going on."

She laughed, clear and true, and the sound warmed something inside of him. At least he'd made her laugh. It was a start.

"You're *so* down with the kids. Look at you, Mr. Hip and Funky." She beamed up at him, and he returned the favor. She had gorgeous lips. It was all Finn could do to stop himself from kissing her.

Woah. Where had that thought come from?

Kissing her, trying to make a move on her when he'd ruined her night. It was not cool. Even if she had stopped smiling and appeared to be studying his mouth, with a similar thought flitting across her face.

Eden bit her full bottom lip, and the blood drained from his head, surging in completely the opposite direction. He shifted to the side and then stood with his back to her. She didn't need to see the physical evidence of his body's reaction to being close to her.

He needed a distraction. Why was he here again? Ah yes, he was meant to be helping her, making sure she was okay. "Right.

I should get you a glass of water, maybe some painkillers. Can I get an ice pack for your ankle?"

Eden murmured her agreement. Finn shoved his hands into his pockets and strode around the back of the sofa, headed toward her kitchen. He took a glass from a cabinet above the sink and filled it with water. Next, he opened her freezer at the top of her refrigerator. No ice pack, but she had frozen peas, so he occupied himself by wrapping the bag of peas in a clean cloth he found folded on the counter.

He studied the immaculate kitchen. It smelled of lemon, and everything gleamed. On the fridge, there was a photo of two dark-haired girls dressed in princess costumes, one taller than the other. The taller girl stared at the camera, her expression serious, while the other scrunched up her face in laughter. Eden and her sister, he guessed. Beside it, in an ornate silver frame, a photo of an older woman dressed in a fitted blue suit and elegant hat took pride of place.

Eden's voice rang out from the other room: "You don't have to stay. My sister will be here soon."

A heavy stone settled in his gut. She wanted to get rid of him. Fair enough, he'd most likely overstayed his hesitant welcome. He'd just make sure she was comfortable, then get going. "It's okay. I can stay until she gets here. Where's your bathroom? Do you have any ibuprofen?"

"Down the hall, on the right, top cabinet. But I'm fine, really." She sounded strange, like she resented having to talk to him.

Finn walked back to the sofa and handed her the glass of water. She drank but avoided meeting his eyes. He offered her the makeshift ice pack, but she shook her head. "You're not fine yet. You need to ice your ankle now to help reduce the swelling."

Seated back near her feet, he pressed the ice pack to her now purplish ankle. It would hurt like hell in the morning. Finn tried not to notice how her skirt had fanned out and risen above her knees, he concentrated on pressing the cool cloth against her skin. He tried not to notice but failed. Miserably.

Eden still wore one of those damned thigh-high stockings, and a ladder ran right up the inside of her leg. It wouldn't take much effort to tear the thing right off. Finn's grip on the ice pack tightened when his fingers brushed against her bare skin near the dressing he'd placed over her abrasion. She was so warm, her skin so silky smooth. Hot blood glugged through his veins like syrup.

She gasped and let out a shaky breath. "It feels so good." His gaze snapped up to meet hers. Her eyes widened. "The ice, I mean. The ice feels good."

Her pink tongue darted out to wet her lips, and he was a goner. Somehow, the next thing he knew, he was leaning over her, tracing a line up her arm, all the way to her shoulder. He took her chin in his hand, and she tilted her head to meet his gaze. They both stopped. She moved first; at least, he thought so. It happened too fast. Her mouth connected with his, so soft and inviting. The sweetest taste struck him as she opened to him. Strawberries and that vanilla scent again.

Finn tasted her, sliding his tongue against hers, wanting to be closer. Hands buried in her mane of hair, he tilted her head for better access. He groaned into her mouth as her arm wrapped around his back to pull him closer. His chest pressed against the curve of her breasts. *Hell yes*. Fine curves. How he'd never noticed until recently was a mystery.

And he wanted to get to the bottom of the mystery. Like those breathy little sounds that she made when he kissed her. How did they get him so worked up? He was so hard, he ached.

Finn worked his way down her throat, kissing her delicate skin, her pulse point behind her ear. Her breasts teased him, making him want to strip her bare and take her. Right there on her sofa. Her dress was in the way. All his clothes too.

He kissed her chest, the spot between her breasts where a little crease of cleavage began. A few freckles dusted her golden skin. His new favorite place in the whole world. Maybe he'd move in.

Ding-dong.

The doorbell?

Eden knew it meant something. But Finn was kissing her, deep and soft at the same time. His lips blazed a trail down her jawline to her throat, and she sucked in a breath. Her skin tingled. Everywhere. Her brain rattled.

Dingdongdingdongdingdoonnngg!

Kissing him was bliss—who knew he had such hidden talents? When he kissed the spot behind her ear, she shivered. He wasn't supposed to make her feel like this, but she was so turned on it would get embarrassing soon. She'd melt into a panting, begging puddle of goo.

She tried to squeeze her thighs together to relieve the building tension, but she couldn't. Finn was on top of her now, his body pressing down on hers, one of his thighs between her legs. The hot, hard length of him firm against her hip.

Eden's hips lifted, her body on autopilot. He felt so good. If he'd only move an inch or two, she'd have him exactly where she needed him most. And, God, she needed him. Needed this. To be close to a man, to feel sexy and desirable. Her hand wandered down to his tight butt, squeezing him through the thin fabric of his suit pants, pulling him closer.

Ding-dong.

Was her doorbell always so loud?

Mmm. Finn kissed the top of her cleavage, where the swell of her breasts spilled over the edge of her bodice. *Yes, yes, yes!* She wanted this. Her nipples were tight, her breasts straining against her strapless bra and dress, desperate to escape their confines. He'd push down her dress, kiss her breasts, tease her nipples until she was breathless. And then...

"Eden, are you in there? Shit, are you okay?" It was just Faith. Banging on the front door.

Faith!

Her sister had a spare key. She'd be inside any moment. Eden had to pull herself together. And get Finn off her.

"Finn," she stage-whispered, right in his ear, "my sister's here. We have to stop."

He pressed a kiss to the hollow of her throat before raising his head. "Bloody hell, she's got rotten timing."

So he didn't want to stop either. Good to know.

He smiled, and the flash of white teeth and dimples set her pulse throbbing. Everywhere. He rose and stood beside the sofa, none too subtly adjusting his pants. She shouldn't have looked. Of course not. It was awkward, especially seeing his prominent erection straining against the fabric right at eye level. But she couldn't help but notice he was a tall man, and everything appeared in perfect proportion.

Finn leaned forward and smoothed down her skirt, then brushed her hair back behind her shoulders. She had all the tingly feels when he kissed her lips again, light as a breath of ocean air. He kissed her like a gentleman. Then he bit her lower lip, just hard enough to sting. *So good.* Not so gentlemanly. She let out a long, slow breath and fought to calm her racing heart.

His voice low and gravelly, he said, "That's just a preview of coming attractions, *Doctor* Eden."

And didn't his words bring reality rushing back? *Doctor.* Couldn't he have called her sugar-pie or sweet cheeks or something equally inane? No, he had to remind her about work.

Thank goodness it was the weekend, and she wouldn't have to face him again until Monday. She'd have herself and her hormones firmly in check again by then. Probably.

The door lock snicked, and her sister rushed in, tripping through the door in her haste. She hauled herself up on the doorframe and stumbled into the living room.

Faith pulled up short and ran her gaze over Eden's leg. "Eden? Thank God you're here and in one piece. I came as soon as I..." She finally spied Finn lounging on the back of the sofa, leaning on those muscular forearms of his.

"Hi, I'm Finn." He stuck out his hand in Faith's direction. "I was helping Eden get settled."

Faith took his hand, her mouth hanging open as she shook it. "Oh, I'm Faith. Eden's little sister. Good to meet you, Finn."

Eden wasn't sure if she should say anything, explain who he was or why he was there. She couldn't explain exactly what they'd been doing.

Eden looked from Faith to Finn as they stared at each other while still shaking hands. Finn dropped her sister's hand. "I'll grab those painkillers and get going."

As he walked out of the room, Faith fell to a crouch beside the sofa. "He's your 'Work Guy'?" Faith's fingers made those annoying air quotes.

"Yes, he's a colleague. A friend, I suppose." What an odd thought. She didn't even like him. Not really. Weren't they supposed to be sworn rivals? But he'd been so kind to her and then so sexy... And that kiss. Kiss number two. She wouldn't forget it in a hurry. Even though she should.

"He's very handsome. Nice of him to give you a ride home." Faith's lips twisted into a kind of grin, as if she were trying to stop herself from laughing.

"He backed into me in the parking lot at the restaurant and knocked me off my scooter. It wasn't exactly nice. Helping me get home was the least he could do." And then he'd kissed her stupid.

"Oh. I didn't know he was the one who knocked you off your scooter. What a dick move! But then, he did help you." Faith examined Eden's ankle and replaced the makeshift ice pack, which had somehow slid off onto the sofa cushion.

"He said it's a sprained ankle with an abrasion on the shin. Nothing to worry about. He seems to know what he's talking about."

Faith nodded, running her fingers over the bruising. She looked up at Eden and grinned. "Your lipstick's all smudged, by the way," she whispered.

With a giggle, Faith got up and walked away down the hall, bracelets jangling. She shouted over her shoulder, "I'll go grab your pajamas and show Finn out."

Finn appeared in the doorway, and Eden craned her neck to see him better. He really was handsome. And tall. He looked like a friendly giant in her hall. A friendly giant who gave her heart palpitations and apparently wanted to see her naked.

The smile he shot her was pure sin, so shockingly sexy she had to look away before she hollered for him to take her to bed. When she looked back again, he'd turned and was speaking quietly to Faith. She lost sight of them as they walked toward the front door.

When Faith returned to her side, she sported the cheeky little girl smile that used to win her extra treats from their grandmother when they were kids. Would Finn be susceptible to Faith's charms? Her little sister was fun and easy to get along with, as opposed to smart but snarky and too demanding, like Eden. He wouldn't be the first guy to opt for the younger Robinson sister. Eden straightened her back.

Faith had her pj's tucked under her arm, the black silk ones with pink polka dots. Eden didn't know whether to be embarrassed Finn had seen them. He could be imagining her in bed right now in those pj's. Or out of them. She squirmed on the sofa, remembering how much he'd almost seen.

"Take these painkillers your *friend* found for you." Faith handed over a couple of capsules, and Eden downed them with a large gulp of water.

Faith studied Eden carefully. "I think you owe me a few more details. How about you tell me the whole story while we get you ready for bed, young lady?" She laughed.

"I can get myself ready for bed." Eden mumbled under her breath.

Faith shrugged, before awkwardly helping Eden out of her dress anyway.

Eden leaned on Faith's arm as she pulled on her pj pants. A random thought struck her: Earlier, she'd expected to kiss HotAussie007 tonight. But it was Finn she wished was here, helping to unlace her dress.

Funny how things turned out. Funny and super brain-scorchingly hot. She couldn't wait to go to bed and replay his kiss on the movie screen of her imagination.

Thor and her other fantasy lovers could take a well-earned vacation.

Chapter Eight

The next morning, Finn dragged Eden's scooter through the open garage door and into his friend Sam's workshop.

The guts and entrails of classic cars littered every available surface, but the place had a life, a vitality to it that made Finn want to breathe in deep, to fill his lungs with petroleum fumes. He gave in to the impulse, then coughed so hard he almost hacked up a lung. Not such a great idea after all.

Finn deposited the Vespa on the garage's concrete floor, stained with psychiatrist-style inkblots made of engine oil. The pattern nearest to his feet looked like an open umbrella with raindrops falling underneath it. What did that say about his state of mind?

The scooter looked sad and broken. *Betsy*. Eden had given it a cute name. Poor, mangled Betsy. He'd make sure she was all fixed up, good as new. Better than new. He smoothed his hand over the seat, causing the scooter to shift and clunk against the floor.

Sam slid out from under a gorgeous turquoise, semi-restored 1950s muscle car propped up on jacks. Dressed in his typical gear of ancient Levi's and black T-shirt, Sam had motor oil slicked across his face. When his friend glanced at the scooter and then up at Finn, he couldn't have looked happier. Like a pig in mud. Sam loved his work.

Sam's tanned face twisted into a wry smile. "What has the cat dragged in?" He pulled himself up to standing.

Finn tipped his chin at the metallic carcass at his feet. "Vespa scooter. I had a little run-in with her owner last night. Woman I work with. And I promised I'd get her ride fixed up."

"Ah, man. Hope the lady's alright. And your truck, of course."

Finn stuck his hands in his pockets and met Sam's eyes. "Sure, they're both fine. Me too, thanks for asking."

Sam laughed like the low rumble of a V8 engine before pacing over to the scooter and letting out a sigh. "This paint job's wrecked. I can respray it, but I'll need to order in the right shade of red mica. Might take a few days. Needs a bit of bodywork too."

Finn felt Sam's gaze on him as his own face stretched into a grin. An idea took hold that shouldn't have made him happy, but it did. Some might even say he was twisted. "Okay, no worries. I can drive her to work while her scooter's in the shop. We have a few things to discuss."

Eden's scooter would be out of action for days, and he already knew she didn't have a car. Finn could swoop in like a white knight to save her. She'd hate it. For some reason, the thought of getting her all riled up had him grinning even wider.

"Mate, you could have told me you're in love." Sam raised his eyebrows and waggled them so they looked like fuzzy black caterpillars wriggling around his forehead.

Finn crossed his arms. "I'm pretty sure if you're not an Aussie, you don't get to call me mate, *dude*." Then the rest of his friend's words filtered through, sending a blast of heat washing over his face. "What do you mean, *in love*?"

Sam wiped his hands on a cloth from his jeans pocket, transferring grease from one blackened hand to the other until he gave up and dropped the rag in the trash. He fixed his gaze on Finn, his expression serious. "Seems to me you're here bright and early on a Saturday morning, wanting to get this woman's Vespa fixed as priority number one. You've hardly mentioned a woman in months, only some faceless online hook-up and your Chevy. Sounds like lovesick-puppy territory to me." Sam scratched at the stubble on his jaw and crouched to inspect the damage to the scooter's paintwork.

That weird heat flared up again, and Finn swiped a hand across the back of his neck. It sure was humid in the workshop. "Yeah, right. Eden's someone I work with, and she's bloody annoying. But I need to keep things civil between us, or at least not declare outright war."

"Hmm, sounds like she's got you jumping through hoops. Just like when Gina and I first got together. I couldn't take her out for burgers, oh no. Had to be a fancy Italian restaurant where the waiters wore black, and she had her choice of fine desserts."

"But you're Italian, and you like fancy Italian food. And dessert."

"Sure do." Sam patted his stomach with a grin. "My wife was an excellent cook, and I love to eat. A match made in heaven, or in Italy at least. One of the many reasons I miss her."

"Yeah, I know. But my prospects of gaining a wonderful wife are slim to none. Eden can't even be civil to me." Except, even as he said it, Finn pictured her panting beneath him on her sofa, lips red and welcoming.

Sam tipped his head to look up at Finn, his expression now serious. "It's good. You need someone to give you hell and keep you coming back for more."

Finn sighed and ran a hand through his hair. "Let me know how much for the respray and bodywork. I'll leave the love stuff to you. I'm not cut out for it."

Sam straightened and glared at him. "That's not the go-get-'em attitude I'm used to hearing from you. What about the online dating chick?"

"I'm giving it a shot. But it's complicated." The whole situation with LittleMissPerfect-slash-Eden was complicated. And getting more so by the day.

"Sure, I get it. You're chatting to one woman, then along comes this work babe, and it's all you can do to think about anything else. Next minute, you're crashing into her Vespa so you can drive her to work..."

Finn's mouth popped open. "Shit, no. She wouldn't think so, would she? I swear it was an accident." He flopped down into the nearby visitor's chair against the wall separating the garage from the office.

Sam laughed again, shaking his head. "Well, my friend, yours is an expression I've seen all too often. You sure look like you've been sucker-punched by love." He walked past and patted Finn on the shoulder. "Come on. I'll make you an espresso, and you can tell me all about her."

HotAussie007: So sorry I missed our date. Helping sick friend. Forgive me?

HotAussie007: I won't blame you if you don't reply.

Eden stared at his messages over breakfast on Monday morning. She read them again, even though she'd read them about a million times over the weekend.

As a scientist, she preferred facts to fairytales and wasn't prone to exaggeration, but she really had read them numerous times. Then she'd scrolled back through their past messages and read them a few more times, index finger hovering over the reply she hadn't sent while trying to watch another Grace Kelly movie. Should she reply?

Her breakfast of organic peanut butter smeared on whole wheat toast followed by water and a small bowl of fruit salad topped with Greek yogurt left her feeling healthy and virtuous, so she washed it all down with a large mug of coffee and cream. She read a couple of work emails while she drank, but her messenger app called to her again. Should she message him back? The man who'd stood her up?

After telling Faith the story of her non-date and Finn's unexpected appearance on the scene, she'd listened to her sister's enthusiastic urging to jump Finn again at the first opportunity. Eden wasn't sure what to think or feel. Faith seemed convinced Finn was a good bet.

Finn was undoubtedly a great kisser. If she had to rate him on the one-to-five scale they used on surveys at work, she'd mark his kissing ability as 'Exceeds Expectations,' five out of five. Her lips and various parts down south tingled again from thinking about it. But there was the whole work situation to consider.

HotAussie007 had added a little love heart to the end of his last message, but Eden's heart wasn't exactly melting. She found the whole sick friend excuse a little hard to swallow. Was there some reason he couldn't have contacted her at the time? Even if he'd been in a hospital, he could have used his phone in the visitors' waiting room. And why had he messaged so late, after eleven o'clock on Friday night?

A message alert popped up on her screen, and her heart did a little flip-flop when she wondered if it might be Finn. *Finn,* not HotAussie007. Not good. Not good at all. Her primitive lizard brain and hormone-fueled body were leaping to all kinds of conclusions, colluding against her more rational self. Finn didn't even know her online handle. He only had her work cell number and email. He didn't have her private phone number.

She checked. It was only Faith, asking if she needed a ride to work. Eden didn't want to make her sister drive clear across town for no good reason.

Eden picked up her dirty dishes from the table with a sigh and popped them in the dishwasher, ensuring everything was clean and tidy. She hadn't decided what to do about a ride to work. Taxis, probably. It would be expensive. Betsy was out of action. Finn had left in a rush, and he'd probably forgotten about Betsy still in his car. But even if Betsy had been there and in full working order, Eden wasn't.

She'd visited her doctor on Saturday, and as Finn had suspected, she had a badly sprained and bruised ankle. As long as she took it easy, it should be healed in a couple of weeks. Her doctor had insisted on a few other routine health checks while she was there, but all in all, she seemed fine. *Fine.* She gritted her teeth as she hobbled across her kitchen.

She couldn't ride her scooter or drive a car, not that she owned one. Taxis were definitely out of her budget. All of which equaled one thing—public transport. Eden sighed again, letting the released air carry away some of her frustration. The idea of limping to the bus stop and the circuitous route to work, complete with noisy teenagers on board, wasn't something she relished. She'd like to take up Faith's offer of a ride on the one hand, but on the other hand, it was half an hour in the wrong direction for her sister. Eden hated being a burden almost as much as she hated things being out of her control.

She texted Faith back and let her know she'd get the bus. She'd be fine. Probably.

Just as she was slipping on her Converse and wondering whether to strap her ankle more firmly, the doorbell rang. That familiar *ding-dong* had become an omen of impending excitement around her place. She froze. Was Faith there already?

Eden hobbled to her front door, trying to keep the weight off her bad ankle. She'd left her new crutches in the kitchen. When she peered through the peephole, her heart stopped dead for a second. She backed up against the door and took two deep, calming breaths before looking again. Just to double-check.

Finn.

It was definitely Finn, definitely standing at her door. She wasn't ready to see him. Maybe after the long bus ride, when she got into work. Maybe sometime in the afternoon. But not straight up, after only one cup of coffee. But avoiding him was ridiculous. As if she was afraid or something.

Full of trepidation, she eased the door open, her heart *ka-booming* like she'd run a sprint. Not that she ran, unless something or someone was chasing her.

Was Finn chasing her? She bit the inside of her cheek, but not to keep herself from smiling. Nope.

His golden hair flopped to one side, luminous in the morning sunlight, and his shoulders looked impossibly broad in a plain green business shirt, the color of springtime, matching his eyes. She stared, waiting for him to say something. Finn's smile was infectious, like a disease. Obviously, she needed to be inoculated.

He leaned in her doorway, all large and sunny looking. "Good morning, Doctor Eden. Care for a ride?"

Oh. My. God.

"Oh. My. God." Eden stood there, tension holding her body perfectly still. She looked about ready to vomit.

Finn should've expected her reaction. Being pleased to see him was asking too much.

Eden stared him down, even though she wasn't exactly tall and had to tilt her head skyward to do so. Her right hand still clutched the doorknob, as if she might slam the door shut in his face any second. She was probably considering it.

"What are you doing here?" she asked, her tone frosty.

Finn had anticipated her question and, of course, had an answer ready to go, like a TV chef presenting a meal. *Here's one I prepared earlier*. He cleared his throat and stuffed his hands in his pants pockets. He had to do something to stop himself from grabbing her and kissing the hell out of her. Again.

He shrugged, acting calmer than he felt. "I figured you'd need a ride to work, and I wanted to tell you I delivered Betsy to the mechanic. You know we left your scooter in my car on Friday night." He waited for her to react. Instead, she continued to stare at him.

He carried on with his explanation, even though she didn't seem to want to listen: "I dropped her off to my friend Sam because he's kind of a genius with classic cars and bikes, so I called in a favor."

Finally, Eden moved, removing her hand from the doorknob and folding her arms under her breasts.

He wouldn't look, he wouldn't look... He looked. But only for a second. Then he took his time checking out the rest of her. She wore a white button-down shirt, fitted in all the right places, teamed with a slim gray skirt. Purple sneakers on her feet, ankle strapped in place. She'd tied her hair in a ponytail and small, black-framed glasses perched on the end of her nose. She looked adorable.

"I don't want you to give me a ride." She hesitated, closing her eyes.

Not entirely oblivious to his double entendre then. But she obviously wasn't about to mention kissing him, either.

She opened her eyes, black lashes fluttering, and stared at him. "I'll take the bus."

He shook his head. "Eden, you don't need to take the bus. I doubt you'd even make it to the bus stop, walking on that ankle. I'm here, so why not take advantage of me?" He tried but failed to contain his grin. Okay, he didn't really try.

Her mouth popped open slightly. She wasn't wearing any lipstick today, but her full, pink lips looked luscious anyway.

Then, out of the blue, she shoved him in the chest.

"Grr, stop it!" Eden growled as she attacked him like a cute grizzly bear.

Finn took a step back. "What's the matter?"

Her shoulders slumped, and she breathed out, then took another deep breath in, like his half-hearted attempts to meditate. "Stop it. Stop with your sexy one-liners and the turning up and rescuing me. I don't want you here. I don't need you."

Right. Of course.

How could he have forgotten her usual sunshine-and-lollipops attitude? But he wasn't taking any of her crap today. Not after he'd kissed her and held her in his arms, felt her melt against him. No, he *knew* her now. Knew the sexy, passionate side she attempted to hide. Whether she liked it or not.

Finn stood his ground and slowly shook his head. "You can pretend you don't like my 'sexy one-liners,' as you put it, but I know you enjoyed kissing me. I sure as hell enjoyed kissing you. And I'm going to do it again." He smiled, enjoying the look of stunned indignation furrowing her brow. "But I won't kiss you again until you want me to. Until you ask nicely."

She raised a haughty eyebrow. "Don't hold your breath. You'll be waiting a while."

"No worries, I'm a patient man. Good things come to those who wait." His mouth stretched into a wider smile. Teasing this woman was too much fun.

Eden growled again, softer this time, and he almost groaned at its effect on his body. It was like she was winding him up with a string, tightening his muscles, getting him ready for action. He laughed, unclenching his body. Time to get this show on the road.

Finn pulled his car keys from his pocket. "Okay, I'm giving you a ride today and every day until your ankle's healed. You might want to text your sister and let her know. She's the one who suggested I drive you to work this week." He paused, waiting for that to sink in.

Her mouth fell open, but she didn't say a word, only turned and hobbled into her living room. He followed her as far as the hallway. She picked up her purse and phone from the coffee table and retrieved a pair of crutches. A minute later, she was back by his side and locking her front door.

He could have offered his arm as they walked to the car. She was using the crutches but putting too much weight on her leg. But he didn't offer. Pride was important to Eden, both professionally and personally. He was getting to know her, and it was obvious she wanted to do things herself, to her own high standards, even if it was a struggle sometimes. He could respect that.

Huffing and puffing, she navigated the slight downward slope and approached his truck in the drive. He couldn't stop himself from opening the passenger door for her and watching to make sure she got in okay.

Eden puffed out another breath as she sat, blowing a couple of loose strands of hair out of her eyes. He resisted the urge to smooth his fingers through her hair. It wasn't easy. "You alright?"

She kept her eyes focused on her purse in her lap. "I'm not an invalid, you know." She glanced sideways at him. "Just drive."

"Yes, ma'am." Finn saluted and doffed his imaginary hat, acting the part of a proper chauffeur.

Then all was silent. No problem. He had more than enough conversation for the both of them.

After he settled in the driver's seat and revved the engine, he backed out of the drive and turned onto her quiet street. Then he began his life story—at least the parts he didn't mind sharing.

"I've never told you about my hometown of Melbourne. You know I'm Australian, right? Lived there all my life until I finished uni at the ripe old age of twenty-one. Then I worked in sports marketing for a while before I decided to try my luck at grad school in the States. Anyway, Melbourne's a great city. Really cool, lots of sporting events, and it's a cultural capital too. I'd love to show you around sometime if you ever visit. I lived right near the beach growing up —"

Eden shifted in her seat to face him, interrupting his flow of thoughts when her slim skirt rode up her bare thighs. He snapped his attention back to the road, just in time to get on the highway.

She kept her gaze on him the whole time — he could feel it, a palpable lick of flame against his skin. She narrowed her eyes when he glanced at her. "Why are you telling me all this stuff?"

Finn shrugged, keeping his eyes on the road ahead. "I thought you'd be interested, now that we're friends."

"Well, I'm not. And we aren't friends. Or anything close." Her voice was high-pitched and weird, as if her throat was constricted.

"We got pretty close on Friday night. I liked it. A lot."

Eden sighed but said nothing more. When he looked across, he found her staring at her phone, texting someone. He clenched his jaw, almost biting his own tongue.

Shit a brick. Was she messaging HotAussie007? With his phone sitting right there in the center console, next to the gearshift, if she sent a message now, his phone would ping like an alarm right in her ear.

But, of course, Eden wasn't messaging HotAussie007. She hadn't responded to his admittedly lame attempt at an apology on Friday night. He'd considered telling her the truth, mulling over the pros and cons all weekend.

Sam thought he should come clean, tell her he'd been attracted to her online long before he knew who she was in real life. But for some reason, Finn didn't want to drop his online persona. Not yet. Eden actually liked one version of him. Well, she had for a while.

He glanced across at her, staring glumly out at the beautiful sunshiny day. "Aren't you going to say anything about Friday night? About us?"

Eden huffed out a slow breath. "I don't want to talk about it. And there is no *us*."

"C'mon, Eden. I was there. You were into it, and I was *way* into it. There's definitely something between us, whether you call it physical attraction, chemistry, whatever."

She whipped her head around to glare at him. "I do know a thing or two about chemistry. Outside factors can influence the result of any experiment. For instance, if a certain element has an urge to merge, it will combine with another element, even if not ideal, to form a compound."

He chuckled. "Urge to merge?" Somehow, he suppressed another comment. Since when was science talk so sexy?

She crossed her arms. The frown on her face would've been cute if she hadn't looked so fierce. "You heard me. The resulting compound may be something useful, or it may be junk."

"Junk. Right." Finn nodded but couldn't help feeling discouraged. Feeling like shit, actually. Being compared to junk was never a good sign.

Eden continued her spiel, unaware of the way his guts were churning. She waved her hands around in the air, getting into her explanation. "Speaking for myself, I've been running a kind of experiment by dating new people. My date didn't exactly work out last Friday, hence the, um, random element and failed bond."

Great. Now she was describing him as some random element and their kiss as a failure. At least he knew where he stood with her. He didn't stand anywhere. She'd barely even noticed him, and she'd already kicked him to the curb.

Finn shifted gears and concentrated on the road ahead. "Far be it from me to adversely affect your grand experiment."

His words must have sounded colder than he'd intended because she swung around and stammered out a response. "Sorry, I guess I've done it again." She scrunched up her face.

He returned his eyes to the road as he spoke. "Done what, exactly? Kissed the hell out of some guy you obviously don't even like?"

"No, I don't do that. Not usually. I meant I tried to explain something of what I'm feeling, and it came out sounding bitchy."

"Yeah, you really should work on those people skills."

Eden huffed out another breath. "Let's just get to work."

"Fine."

By the time they reached Magna Smart's parking lot, the temperature within the confines of his car had gone from cool to scalding hot. And it wasn't just the summer sunshine warming up the early morning, glinting off his rearview mirror. No, Eden was fuming. He couldn't exactly say why, but he was too.

There was definitely some sort of chemical reaction going on between them, but he didn't dare risk Eden's wrath by disagreeing with her. Even though she was dead wrong.

The compound they formed when they were together wasn't junk. It was something new, something amazing. Something highly flammable.

Chapter Nine

Finn: I'll pick you up from your office at 5pm. No need to thank me.

Eden: Fine. But I wasn't planning on thanking you.

Finn: Oooh burn!

By the time five o'clock rolled around, the sun was streaming through Eden's office window, casting orange and gray stripes on the walls. She stretched her spine as if an invisible string pulled her upright from the top of her head. Her yoga teacher claimed it was invigorating. She rolled her neck in slow circles. She was done. Exhausted, hot, and itching to get home.

She'd spent quality time in the lab that morning, analyzing some results Felicity had ready to review. Later, she'd followed up on other work as part of managing her team. Completing paperwork for Human Resources, reviewing CVs sent in by postdoctoral students looking for a position, responding to emails, and catching up on reports requiring her signature. Boring stuff, in other words.

Her back ached, her ankle throbbed, and she'd long ago ditched her shoes. There were no more painkillers left in her purse. She'd have loved another drink of water. It was a hot day outside, and even with air-conditioning, it was unpleasantly sweaty in her office in the afternoon. Still, it was a long walk down the corridor to the staff kitchen on an injured leg. Tomorrow she'd bring in a huge water bottle to sit on her desk.

She flicked her eyes toward the open office door when she heard someone approaching her office, and a gigantic red takeout cup appeared in the doorway. A large, manly hand was attached to the cup, then Finn's top-quality forearm and the equally physically impressive rest of him came into view. He stood in her doorway like a mirage in the desert, something she'd conjured up in her imagination because she was dying of thirst.

Eden could have licked him. Or the drink. She could have licked the drink and only the drink. Because she was just thirsty. *For liquid.*

"Gimme," she all but shouted, gesturing for Finn to come all the way inside.

"A little politeness wouldn't go astray, you know." He raised his eyebrows, somehow making his eyes all sparkly.

"Gimme that cold drink now, *please*, Finn." She formed her lips into an approximation of a smile.

Finn laughed as he strode into her office and stopped on the other side of her desk. "You were almost polite. Here you go."

She snatched the icy cold cup from his outstretched hand. He'd taken mercy on her, thank goodness. After taking a quick sip through the straw, she winced at the biting cold and sharp lemonade flavor then sighed. Delicious.

"Oh, that's so good." She pressed the cup to her forehead, letting the chill seep through to her brow, then patted her cold fingers along her neck, along her collarbone, and down into her cleavage.

"Er, do you two need a moment alone together?" Finn pointed down at the cup, which she'd inserted into the neckline of her shirt to hold it in place.

The way it cooled her décolletage and caused her nipples to tighten was quite pleasant. But now she thought about it, probably not the most professional move.

"No, thank you. It's just so hot today, and it's too far to walk to the kitchen again." Eden caught herself before she started telling him how much her ankle hurt. It wouldn't do for him to think of her as weak and needy. "Can I help you with something?"

"I've come to pick you up. I'm giving you a ride home, remember?"

How could she forget when he was wearing out that turn of phrase? She was convinced he intentionally used the word 'ride' at every opportunity, so she'd picture herself straddling his lap, stark naked, rocking back and forth, drawing her fingernails across his fine, ripped abdominal muscles. It really wasn't necessary for him to use innuendo. She could imagine the scenario, *vividly*, all on her own.

God, it sure was hot in her shoebox of an office.

Eden took another deep suck of frozen sugar water and reluctantly put down the cup. "Sure, thanks. Just give me a minute to shut down my computer." She returned her attention to the screen, closed the confidential staff files, and logged off for the day.

When she looked up, Finn was taking a long sip of his own drink, studying her over the rim of his cup. Those sparkly eyes looked a lighter shade of aquamarine in the reflected sunlight.

What did he see when he watched her like that? She'd thought she had this attraction to him under control, locked down tight where he'd never notice, but no. It might take a few more days to forget their kiss.

Kiss*es*. Plural. *Oh boy*. There never should've been a second kiss. The first one had been a random error, but the second? The second could constitute a pattern.

Finn stepped closer. He crouched at her feet and helped put her shoes back on and, in doing so, touched the sensitive arch of her foot. As he laced up one sneaker, he paused near her injured ankle, gently making sure the shoe wasn't laced too tight.

He straightened and offered her a hand to get out of her chair, which she refused. It was bad enough he'd touched her bare foot. It was all tingly and prickly now, his fingers having left some kind of imprint. And her pulse throbbed heavily at every juncture of her body.

Eden struggled upright on her own: literally and metaphorically standing on her own two feet. "Let's go."

He nodded and held the door open for her. She let him do it. Strangely enough, she liked it when he played the gentleman.

She walked through her office door and locked it behind her, Finn by her side.

Finn walked toward the parking lot in silence, Eden close beside him on her crutches. He felt as sunbaked as the concrete courtyard between the two buildings where they walked. The sea breeze whipped through every few seconds, cooling the damp fabric at the back of his shirt and providing a brief respite from the heat. His fingertips tingled in that weird way they sometimes did after he'd been running for too long, working out too hard.

It had nothing to do with touching Eden's bare skin. It couldn't possibly.

He'd never been a foot man, but her skin was so soft, and her toenails painted a delicious shade of cherry red. An image of him kissing her toes, one by one, popped into his head. Like something from a 1970s porno.

Mad. She was driving him mad. A couple of kisses, and suddenly he was lusting after the woman's feet like a pervert. But maybe she had some sexy high-heeled sandals she could wear on their first date, whenever he finally managed to take her out.

Shit. Hold on, back up a second.

He came to a halt in the middle of the concrete forecourt. Eden stopped right behind him.

There wouldn't be a date. The date he'd been supposed to go on had been lined up between HotAussie007 and LittleMissPerfect. Him and Eden almost hooking up on Friday night was completely random in her book. The fact he knew better had been bugging him all weekend.

What was she thinking, arranging a date with HotAussie007 and then making out with *him*, Finn, when he dropped her home that night? Sure, she'd been stood up, and he felt bad about that. If he could go back in time and change how he'd behaved, he'd jump straight in his DeLorean and do it. It must have hurt her, not only physically.

He wanted a date with Eden. Whether it was with HotAussie007 or himself, it didn't really matter. But he needed a plan.

"What's up, Finn?" Eden's soft voice stirred him from his daydream state.

She was panting from the exertion of walking. She'd struggled to keep up with his pace despite him going slow.

"Did you hear from that guy who stood you up on Friday night?"

Her face crinkled in a frown. "Yes, he messaged me. Some excuse about helping a sick friend."

He flicked her a sideways glance, his heart beating too fast in his chest. "So, did you get back to him? Are you giving him another chance?"

"Where's this coming from? Who I choose or do not choose to date is none of your business."

"Come on, I think it might be a bit my business after the way you kissed me."

Her eyes widened. "Excuse me? You're the one who kissed me."

Nate, Finn's analytics guy, chose that exact moment to walk past. He must have overheard them because the guy's eyebrows shot sky-high. But he nodded once at Finn and kept walking.

Finn lowered his voice. "Let's not get caught up in the semantics. I'm pretty sure you were right there with me in the heat of the moment."

She stared at the ground. "Maybe, in the heat of the moment, as you say. But it has nothing to do with my dating situation."

"What is your 'dating situation'? Are you single, or are you seeing someone, Doctor Eden?"

She hesitated, and you could have cut the air between them with a knife. The warm air bulged and swayed with the thickness and humidity. "I'm thinking about seeing someone."

He clenched his jaw, trying not to get his hopes up, trying not to let it show all over his face exactly how disappointed he'd be if she chose the other guy. The 'other guy' being half of his own brain, but that was beside the point.

Eden shrugged, but her crinkled forehead betrayed her irritation. "I'm going to message him. Let him know I'm prepared to give it another try."

He cursed himself and his online alter-ego self. *Stupid*. She could have chosen him, Finn-him, but instead, she chose some faceless dude who'd stood her up. A faceless dude who was still him. But, hell, she didn't know that.

Finn could have been Eden's boyfriend for real by now if he hadn't been such a coward. He could have been going home with her and giving her a sexy foot rub, like a real man.

"You'll go out with him? After he stood you up? Far out, are you a glutton for punishment or what?"

No. He shouldn't have said anything. His stomach rolled over and played dead.

Eden's head whipped up, and she glared at him. Those violet eyes, almost shooting sparks, hurled bucketloads of hate at him with one look. It was probably dripping off him like mud.

She stormed toward his car, silently limping, then waited for him by the passenger door. At least she didn't try to walk to the bus stop. "Just take me home."

Finn nodded as he unlocked the car, not saying another bloody word.

Chapter Ten

Eden thought of sending a message to HotAussie007 over lunch. She'd deleted it. Maybe she'd message later, after work. Honestly, she didn't know what she was going to do.

The pipette slid from Eden's fingers before she could say, "What the hell are you doing in my lab?" She turned and said it anyway. The tiny glass dropper hit the hard floor and fractured. "Why do you always sneak up on me?" she shot over her shoulder at Finn.

There he was, taking up half the room again. It was a bad habit of his. Being all *big* and *there* when least expected. He'd popped in regularly, on the pretext of checking up on her side of the drug development project.

Wasn't it enough that she was with him each day, trapped in his car every morning and evening when he gave her a ride to and from work? No, he had to seek her out during the workday too. Was he checking up on her? Making sure she was coping with her injured ankle? It was infuriating.

She hated being incapacitated. Hated when her body didn't allow her to do all the things she needed to. From having to sit on a stool instead of standing at the lab bench to being unable to walk all the way to the cafeteria at the other end of the building, it was incredibly frustrating. She couldn't go to her yoga class or for walks along the beach. It was *boring*. She'd been thinking of setting up a date with HotAussie007, but not in her current condition.

In the office, it was like being held prisoner with no form of escape. But crutches were no longer an option. With Doctor McTavish also dropping in more than usual, it would be tantamount to wearing a flashing neon sign reading: *Female manager needs to lean on something.*

"Do I make you nervous, Doc?" Finn asked with a chuckle that she relished and loathed in equal measure.

It was a pleasant sound. Sensual, even. But it was inappropriate to make such a low, throaty noise at work. It made her belly clench and got her all hot and bothered, making her want to strip off her lab coat and a few other layers along with it.

Not going to happen.

"Why would you say that?" Her words sounded flat and sarcastic, even to her own ears.

Eden leaned forward and reached down to grab the broken pipette, but it was too late. He was there before her. She froze as he stepped closer and crouched on the floor. His face ended up rather too close to her knees, so she swiveled on her stool to get away from him.

Finn talked as he swept up the glass shards with a paper towel. "I don't know, do you always sacrifice so many innocent glass droppers in the name of science?"

With a sigh, she pointed out a dustpan near the back of the lab. He fetched it without having to be asked twice and swept up the remaining glass.

Eden tried not to stare at the backs of his hands or the length of his spine as he crouched at her feet. "Pipettes break. It happens. We move on. Can I help you with something? I need to finish this." She waved at the dishes on her bench, samples of heart valve tissue. She was trying a different approach to analyzing the drug's effectiveness.

He glanced up at her face, caught her eye, and smiled. A slightly crooked smile she now recognized as his thinking-naughty-thoughts smile. She got a proper look at him as he stood. He looked good. Tall and tanned and... Had he done something to his face? There was a red mark on his cheek, right under his left eye. He was talking. She hadn't even been listening.

"... McTavish asked me for it, but I thought I'd better check with you. It comes under your team's budget, after all."

"What happened to your face?" she blurted out. So much for tact.

Finn's hand automatically lifted to his cheekbone and smoothed over the reddened area. "Oh, it's nothing. Just a dodgy-looking spot I had lasered."

Her hand flew up to join his, testing the texture of his skin. "A what? A melanoma's not nothing. You should get a second opinion from Rupert Williamson. He's the best dermatologist in the city. I can email him if you like."

His smile was softer now, all the naughtiness gone. "Eden, it was nothing. Not even pre-cancerous. I got it zapped, so I don't have to worry about it. But it's nice to know you care."

Eden sucked in a shaky breath, and her hand fell to her side. "I... There's been a lot of cancer in my family. I believe in being vigilant." She looked down, concentrating on not crying. Why did talking about it still affect her so viscerally?

"I'm sorry. Did you lose someone close to you?"

She nodded, staring at her shoes. Her voice cracked when she spoke. "My mom when I was young. Then two years ago, my grandmother, who raised me." She said nothing more.

Finn reached out and touched her upper arm, a gentle pat. "God, I'm sorry. Let's get out of here for a few minutes. Come on, I'll buy you a coffee."

With another nod, she slid down from her stool and took a deep breath as she put her weight on her swollen ankle. Four days after the accident, it was dark purple with bruises. She winced and slowly followed Finn out of the lab, pausing only to let Felicity know she'd be back in five.

She didn't need to see Felicity's knowing smile. Her RA had on her match-making hat and wouldn't stop talking about Finn. It was like some kind of conspiracy cooked up between Felicity and Faith.

Her sister kept calling to ask if Eden had kissed any handsome coworkers lately. No, not lately. But she couldn't stop thinking about it. She'd quite simply never been the recipient of such a kiss before. It was worth studying as an exceptional physical experience.

Now she was intensely aware of her *kisser* holding the lab door open for her, waiting for his *kissee* to walk through it. Standing back, being polite, as he had been all week. Aside from when he'd challenged her about her dating status. It was as if he was waiting for her to do something. To say something, perhaps. But she didn't know what. She was a mess of indecision. And she'd nearly burst into tears in front of him and her team, thinking about her family's history of cancer.

Nice work, Eden. She was falling apart at the seams, and she couldn't even blame work stress this time. Well, not entirely.

Eden's job, her whole life, hung in the balance. Maybe her choices would be taken out of her hands soon, and she might not have this job or any income to rely on. McTavish seemed intent on firing her.

But she shouldn't focus solely on the negatives. She had a good brain, great taste in movies and cupcakes, elegant clothes, a loving sister, and an *almost* perfectly functioning body. Perhaps soon, she'd have a boyfriend.

She crossed her fingers. Scientist or not, she believed in luck.

Chapter Eleven

Eden: Heading home from work early. Come get me when you're ready to go.

Finn: No worries!

Finn knew Eden would tell him to get lost at some point. She'd stop accepting a ride home. She'd probably never message him ever again. And, bloody hell, he'd miss it. But today, she gave off vibes of being exhausted after a long day, and she didn't refuse him. She'd even texted him at quarter to five to remind him she was leaving early.

Now he got into the driver's seat after opening the car door for her and waited while she settled beside him. It seemed that her ankle was less painful.

"McTavish's got it in for me, you know. He wants me gone. I'm not sure why, but I know it's true." Eden stared straight ahead, out his windshield. "I met with him this afternoon, after we went for coffee. It was short and sweet. He threatened my team."

Seated in his car beside Eden, he was so close to her but unable to reach over and touch her because of their stupid stubbornness. It was driving him nuts. But he listened to what she had to say. She was stressed out, confused, and nearly at the end of her rope dealing with McTavish.

As he started the engine and headed out of the parking lot, she removed the elastic band from her hair and shook it out so it tumbled around her shoulders in shiny black waves. Finn watched out of the corner of his eye, without once reaching over to smooth her long silky hair back from her face. But he had to grip the steering wheel tight to keep from doing so.

He didn't squeeze her hand where it rested on her lap. Although it was so tempting. To touch her again, to see if the spark between them ignited again. However, despite the cost to his equilibrium, he didn't do it. He sucked in a deep breath instead.

Apparently oblivious to his frustration, Eden continued, "Why would McTavish ask me so many weird questions? Whether I always keep my staff pass 'on my person at all times,' and why I was having a coffee break with you."

Finn fully tuned into the conversation. "He asked you about us?"

Eden glanced at him, her eyes wide. "Yes. It was strange. He's never asked me about having coffee with Felicity or Juan from HR."

"It is weird." He scratched his chin, feeling the beginnings of a five o'clock shadow. "Hang on, you have coffee with Juan from HR? The big guy who looks like he could bench press my Chevy with one hand?"

Eden raised one perfectly curved eyebrow in his direction. "I like Juan — he's a nice guy. Anyway, not the point."

"Right." Finn tried to rein in the stray twist of jealousy in his gut. *Juan, huh.* He *was* a nice guy, which made it worse.

He could see Eden going for someone like him — someone who'd agree with everything she said. But, as she'd said, it wasn't the point. McTavish was their main concern now. Eden seemed interested in his opinion, using him as a sounding board. He liked it. "What do you reckon McTavish is playing at?"

"I have no idea." She sighed, and the sound was so world-weary it wasn't like her at all. Except, he had to admit that what he knew about her was still limited.

Eden seemed to present one face to the world while concealing a more private face, a different version of herself he'd like to coax out of hiding. The feminine, creative, sexy side. Yeah, he'd like to get to know the passionate side of Doctor Eden a whole lot better.

He caught her gaze and felt himself falling further under her spell. "If we put our heads together, we might be able to work out what he's doing."

Her eyes widened. "Are you offering to help me, Finn Donohue?"

"Why, yes, Doctor Eden, I believe I am. Is that a problem?"

They'd stopped at some traffic lights. He turned to face her, twisting around in the driver's seat so he could see her face, half in bright sunlight, half in shadow. Her expression was that of a kid whose birthday cake had just fallen on the kitchen floor.

She pursed her lips before replying: "I don't need your help. Men always want to help me. They think they can magically fix everything in my life. Let me make it clear — you can't."

He frowned and drummed his fingers on the steering wheel as he waited for the green light, then continued driving. What the hell was going on with her? It had to be more than McTavish and his sorely lacking management skills. But Finn wasn't sure he could handle it if Eden wanted to get closer or saw him as someone to confide in. Not with everything currently going on in his life. And he'd proven useless at being a boyfriend in the past.

His mother would say his heart was buried deep inside somewhere, and you just had to know where to dig. However, Finn had never met a woman interested in trying to find it under all the layers of mud and other crap that life had heaped on top of it. Now the weight of all those layers pressed down on his chest.

Finn's jaw tightened before he forced it to unlock. "What's up, Eden? I can just listen if that's what you want. I won't try to fix anything."

She nodded, tucking her face into her chest so her hair fell in dark curtains around her. Hiding from him. "My doctor called this morning. She received some blood test results back from the lab. It's probably nothing, but I need to get retested."

His heart thudded too loud in his chest. "It'll be alright."

Eden shrugged. "I hope so."

She went quiet, and it was hard for him to stay silent too. He could have told her she worked too hard, that she needed a rest, but it wouldn't earn him any points. She didn't want him trying to fix things. So he just drove.

Eden turned to him. "Remember I mentioned my family history of cancer? I have to get regular tests, to make sure there are no precancerous abnormalities."

It all sounded... scary. Finn kept his eyes on the road. "Sure. Good idea."

She sighed, turning towards him. "I don't want any surprises. But you can't control everything, I guess. My hemoglobin levels are unusual. It might be nothing, or it might be something."

There seemed no point in trying to make her feel better about potentially bad news. "That's truly shitty. I'm sorry."

To his amazement, she laughed. "Yes, it is *shitty*. I'll have to tell Faith at some point, but I don't want to scare her."

She was protecting her sister when she really needed someone to take care of her. Sounded about right. When they pulled up outside Eden's cute little house, he didn't want to leave. "I can stay for a while — if you need company."

Her answering smile was wide but strained. "Thanks, but not right now. I'm fried. Oh, and I'm taking the day off tomorrow, so you don't need to pick me up."

Finn nodded, and she got out of the car, waving away his offer of help. Soon, she wouldn't need his help at all. Could be time to call on his old mate HotAussie007 to make something happen.

"Faith, could you please bring me a soda? And a ham sandwich? Pretty please?" Eden called over her shoulder toward her kitchen.

Her sister's groan echoed around the kitchen, and she slammed the refrigerator door dramatically. Stomping sounds followed across the tiled floor.

"Yes, boss. You know, I do realize you're milking this injury for all it's worth. I'll get my revenge someday. Bwahaha!" Faith cackled like a cartoon villain.

Eden's lips curved upward, and she let out a giggle. She knew her sister was enjoying looking after her. Mostly. Faith had come over every night since Eden hurt her ankle, making sure she had food and was set up with something to watch or read. They'd watched a couple of movies together too.

Eden sat propped up on her sofa, scribbling in the little red leather-bound notebook she used to sketch her sewing projects. She was working on an idea for a fancy dress she had no need for and nowhere to wear it. But it would be fabulous. Elegant and feminine. She pictured the full skirt and a fitted bodice, an overlay of French lace with capped sleeves, like something Grace Kelly wore in the fifties. Emerald green, like Finn's eyes. She blinked and dropped her pencil.

Faith raised her voice to ask if she wanted mayo, so Eden asked nicely for mustard. Then Faith continued, "So, you've kept me in suspense long enough. What's going on with 'Work Guy'? Finn, isn't it?"

Squirming with the memory of his body pressing down on hers, their hips melding together, his lips tasting hers, she touched a fingertip to her lower lip. The way he'd kissed her... She'd replay that memory for a long time to come. But that's all it was. A memory. Another image popped into her head — his concerned expression that afternoon when she'd told him about her test results. It could be the start of a real friendship. Perhaps.

She'd been expecting Faith's question, surprised her sister had waited four whole days to ask for more information about the guy Eden had kissed right here on her sofa. She bit her lip. What to say? "You know very well his name is Finn. And nothing's happening. Absolutely, positively nothing, except colleague stuff."

Faith strolled into the living room, her arms laden with snacks. "You sound disappointed, Babycakes."

Did she? It was a relief to realize that she and Finn could never be anything more than colleagues. They struggled to hold a civil conversation for more than five minutes. How could they possibly pursue anything more when they didn't even like each other? Except, she liked some things about him.

When Finn wrapped his arm around her waist and helped her into the house after the accident, he was kind. True, he'd been the cause of her injury. But he'd been driving her to and from work, seemingly happy to chat and listen to her work woes. Even before any second kiss happened, he'd seemed genuinely concerned about her. He was friendly and funny too, most of the time. A nice guy. A nice and handsome guy. But not the guy for her.

Eden sighed, not even attempting to conceal her downbeat mood. "Not disappointed. Fed up, I guess. Where are all the decent men hiding?"

"Now *that's* a mystery for the ages." Faith placed the plate with a sandwich on Eden's lap and left a soda on the coffee table.

She shimmied down on the other end of the sofa, near Eden's feet, and shuffled back until her head flopped over the headrest.

Faith talked at the ceiling: "I thought Finn seemed sweet. He's driving you to and from work, isn't he?"

Darting a look out of the corner of her eye, Eden caught Faith's gleeful grin as she sat up straight again. Her sister's silver-blue eyes sparkled with barely suppressed laughter.

Eden's own lips twitched at the corners. "Yes, he's driving me — driving me crazy every day. Very sneaky of you, asking him to drive me. And sweet isn't a word I'd associate with Finn."

All the words she would use to describe him flashed through her mind. Stubborn. Obstinate. Annoying. Strong. Manly. Kind. Sexy. Friendly and funny and handsome. Now *nice*. Not to forget scrumptious. His lips were delicious.

A dastardly evil chuckle rose from Faith's chest, making her whole body shake. "You should see the look on your face right now, Babycakes. You're all steamed up. I'm guessing he's an okay kisser." Faith batted her eyelashes, all innocence again.

Innocent as sin.

Eden kept her expression neutral. "Yeah, he's okay." *Okay times infinity.* She squirmed again as tendrils of rampant hotness escaped her memory and lust heated every square inch of her skin. "You know, it had been a while."

"So why not go out with him? I don't get you sometimes."

Right then, Eden struggled to recall why she couldn't have more of Finn. More of his heat, his muscular arms around her waist, his lips like candy apples with a hint of spice. Then the way he'd pressed into her, letting her know exactly how turned on he was... *Phew.* A cold shower was on her horizon if she didn't block those steamy thoughts.

She smoothed down her skirt and let out a long, slow breath. "It can't happen. Not with this whole work situation. Our boss is determined to fire one of us if we don't deliver on this project. It's all tense and weird. And Finn's a real asshole most of the time."

Wasn't he? He had told her off more than once. But she'd told him off multiple times. And he'd also tended to her injury and helped her get home. It might have been guilt, but it felt like more. He seemed to want to get close to her. Friends, or maybe something else.

Faith placed a hand over her eyes with a sigh. "I thought I'd found a decent guy, but it's a no go. I told him where to stick it when he suggested we check out a weird bondage and discipline club 'for a laugh.' Once he started talking golden showers, I was out the door. No thanks, and *adios*." She waved in a bye-bye gesture.

Eden blinked. "No way. Simon? The accountant? But he seemed so..." *Boring*. The word was on the tip of her tongue, but she didn't want to upset Faith. Her sister had really liked him at first. She breathed out, then shook her head. "He seemed so normal."

Faith's new guy must have been hiding a kinky side all along. Perhaps he thought he wouldn't meet anyone if he let it show. It was a little sad.

Her sister lifted her head and clapped her hands in sudden glee. The complete change in mood made Eden's head spin. What was up?

Realizing she hadn't yet taken a bite of her sandwich, Eden chomped down on it now. Food for thought. She chewed, the salty goodness of ham and mustard invading her tastebuds.

"No more men talk — it's depressing me. We're meant to be having a girlie movie night." Faith hopped off the sofa and skimmed her fingers along the low bookshelf with the movie collection. "Ah, this is the one." She grabbed a DVD and flipped the cover around to show Eden.

"*High Society*. Yes, that's perfect." Eden sighed and took another bite of sandwich.

The movie would be a great pick-me-up. Grace Kelly swanning around looking elegant as always, Cole Porter songs, and a true love that withstands even divorce, temper tantrums, and silliness about money and class. Where could Eden find a modern Bing Crosby type to get her inadvisably drunk and dance with her in the moonlight? Someone who'd realize she wasn't an ice princess but a hot-blooded woman with feelings...

Eden leaned over to grab her soda from the coffee table and noticed her phone flashing. She'd put it on silent, needing a respite from work messages. But this was a different type of message, one she hadn't seen for days. *HotAussie007*. Her belly rolled, wanting to reject the ham sandwich.

How had she managed to forget about him? All this thinking about Finn was no good for her psyche. Or her digestion. She pressed a hand to her stomach and picked up her phone with trembling fingers.

Her virtual boyfriend had sent another message, this one demanding a response. It fired up all her senses, set her head aching, her heart ker-thumping, and nerve endings crazy with tingles. She loved it.

> **HotAussie007:** Enough games. I know I fucked up. Big time. We haven't met but I know. You. Are. Special. Talk to me...

Okay. Eden breathed in, deep. Relaxed her shoulders. Breathed out. Surprised to find her heart was pitter-pattering at double time, she stared at her phone screen.

Faith fiddled with the DVD, since the movie had started halfway through. Bing Crosby and Frank Sinatra sang from the TV speakers, swinging and grooving. Cool and smooth. As if nothing had happened.

Eden glanced back to her phone screen. She could do this. Message HotAussie007, get back in the game. But what should she say? Her fingers locked in neutral. As did her brain.

Firetruck! Damn and blast.

Faith's head whipped around, and she landed on her butt with a thud. "What the heck are you cursing about? Gran would have a fit if she heard such talk. Well, maybe not the firetruck part." A tinkling laugh matched the sound of her swinging bracelets as she tripped lightly back toward Eden and sat.

She'd said that stuff out loud? She must be losing the plot.

But perhaps Faith could help. Her sister had much more experience on the dating scene. She screwed her eyes shut for a second. When she blinked them open, her sister's gaze was silently interrogating her.

"Has something bad happened?" Faith pressed her lips together.

Oh no. She didn't want to freak her sister out. Eden squeezed the phone between her fingers. "No, nothing really. It's that guy from the app. The one who stood me up. He wants to chat again, and I can't think what to say." She stared down at her phone screen. No inspiration yet. "I'm drawing a total blank."

Faith crouched by the side of the sofa and then dropped to her knees. "You like this guy, more than I thought. You want to chat with him, don't you? Maybe meet up?"

Eden looked down at her lap, the phone in her hand like an undetonated landmine. What if she stepped on it, and it exploded in her face? What could she say? To him or to Faith? Why did it feel so important?

Faith prized the phone from Eden's grasp and read his message with one eyebrow raised. Super-fast fingers tap-tap-tapped away, and within a millisecond, her sister tossed the phone back in Eden's lap. It landed with a muffled plop but no explosion.

What the heck? Faith had sent him a message! Eden read it over quickly, trying not to let the words hurt her brain.

Her sister shrugged. "No harm, no foul. Don't overthink it." Was she always so casually annoying?

"Faith! What have you done?" Cold dread dripped off Eden's tongue with the question. Could you unsend an instant message? Apparently not. She stabbed at her phone with her index finger.

It pinged. She'd succeeded in turning the sound back on. It was another message, from him. Her belly flip-flopped like she'd been rolled over and sucked under in the surf.

> **HotAussie007:** And she's back. Sexy as hell and twice as deadly :)

She choked on a laugh. *Argh!* What had Faith's message said again? She scrolled back up and reread the words, registering their meaning this time.

> **LittleMissPerfect:** Cross me again and I'll poke you in the cajones with my stilettos. Missed you too.

She snapped her head up to meet Faith's eyes — her laughing eyes. And she'd bet her own expression was equally silly. Giggles bubbled up from Eden's belly and burst from her mouth. Her sister's instant laughter mingled with hers.

"There," Faith said, her voice soft now, "that's the happy Eden I want to see. Chat to him. I'll be in the kitchen, making popcorn." She strolled from the room, glancing over her shoulder with a grin.

Letting out another giggle-snort, Eden read his next message when it pinged through.

> **HotAussie007:** You there? *echo* Talking to imaginary hot babes now. I'm picturing you sitting in a bubble bath. Am I right?

LittleMissPerfect: Don't get ahead of yourself Hot Stuff. Babes? There's only one of me. My sis is here but no sharing.

Oh. She'd mentioned her sister. Eden bit her lip. She'd never revealed anything real about herself to him before. But perhaps it was time. They'd taken things super-slow on account of her nerves and his... She didn't know what. Work commitments? He always seemed so busy.

She reached for her drink on the coffee table. Maybe she should ask about his work? Something else personal?

HotAussie007: Pls tell me you and sis are having a lingerie PJ party. With pillow fights.

Taking a sip of her soda, she snorted and nearly choked on the effervescent fizz.

LittleMissPerfect: In your dreams. Movie and popcorn night.

Her fingers hovered over the glowing screen as a thought struck her like a truck veering onto the wrong side of the interstate. She could invite him over. Did he live close by? She had no idea. She only knew he lived in the greater San Diego area.

The throbbing in her temples arced up again. *Thump, thump.* Too much pressure. Now was not the time to meet him. Plus, she looked like a disaster. Swollen purple ankle propped up on a cushion, lank ponytail, T-shirt dress with tiny stars, more like a stretched-out nightshirt, and a lapful of sandwich crumbs. *Chicken.*

Yes, she was a complete chicken and wouldn't be the one to be brave first. The next move was his.

> **HotAussie007:** I want to take you out to a movie. Say yes.

Eden froze. Was he reading her mind? Okay, think fast. Did she want to go out with him? The answer came fast and absolute. Yes!

> **LittleMissPerfect:** Okay. But you have one chance. ONE. Better be a good movie.

There was a pause, a yawning, cavernous pause as wide as the Grand Canyon. Then her phone pinged again.

> **HotAussie007:** Thank you. I swear I'll make it up to you. How about an old James Bond movie?

> **LittleMissPerfect:** Sean Connery?

> **HotAussie007:** Of course.

> **LittleMissPerfect:** It's a date.

There. Done. But hopefully not 'done-ass' as in busted or over. According to Faith, all the cool kids were saying it these days.

If she was done with his ass before even seeing it naked, she'd be starting from scratch in the online dating pool. A damp, dark, and murky waterway infested with sharks and alligators she had no desire to swim in again.

No, this thing with Hot Aussie was on. All systems go.

Chapter Twelve

HotAussie007: I'll book movie tickets for us. Looking at Dr. No.

LittleMissPerfect: Perfect. But I'm at work. Chat soon x

Third time's the charm...

Eden bent over her microscope, adjusted the magnification, and blinked. For the third time, she examined the sample on the glass slide. It couldn't be accurate. Only, it was. The cluster of cells from the patient's blood sample wasn't normal. The white blood cell count was off, and the lab results attached to the patient's records confirmed what she saw.

She tried thinking rationally to determine the cause of these abnormal results. Something was different, and according to the records from the patient's physician, the only significant change in their treatment was the drug Magna Smart had supplied: an experimental drug, but it had previously proven effective.

"No way." Exhaling slowly, Eden stood as though carrying a load on her shoulders. A massive, heaving load of expectations, weighing her down.

Felicity moved to her side. "What is it?"

Eden waved a hand in front of her. "See for yourself."

While peering through the microscope, Felicity muttered, "Thickening of the blood. Not good, not good at all." She straightened and glanced around the lab, then spoke to Eden quietly. Confidentially. "Have you heard from the team at the hospital yet? Aren't they meant to alert you straight away about any unusual test results?"

As usual, her RA's mind had jumped to the crux of the problem. The hospital should've been on this. Immediately. "No, I haven't heard from them. But I think a visit to Doctor Zhang might be in order."

Felicity waved Eden away. "Let me know how you get on. I'll check out the rest of these samples while you're gone."

Eden nodded, her feet already moving. Back in her office, she hung up her lab coat and barely stopped to grab her purse before ordering a taxi to SD West General Hospital.

Then she called Doctor Zhang. No answer. He was most likely in surgery. She tried the cardiology department number and waited. No answer. She left a message, but as she thought, it would probably be quicker to go straight over there.

She doubled her pace as she made her way out to the courtyard.

Finn leaned back in one of the lounge chairs in the open-plan Marketing office, screwing up pages filled with website analytics stats. He had quite a collection of balled-up paper missiles sitting beside him on the black laminate desktop.

Glancing up, he grabbed one and raised his arm, aiming for the plastic basketball hoop stuck to the back of the office door with suction cups. He hurled the paper ball at the hoop, scoring a six-pointer.

He shoots, he scores.

Finn waved his hands in the air like he just didn't care.

His team were all out at lunch, but they were due back anytime. He'd eaten a Vegemite sandwich at his desk, the Australian staple food making him long for home. Although he was thousands of miles away, his mum sent him regular supplies via airmail care package. It made him feel both loved and hopelessly homesick at the same time.

The door opened inward, squashing the hoop behind it as Mimi rounded the corner and entered the office.

Damn. He really didn't want to be alone with her. The tall, slim, honey-blond woman with hazel eyes was pretty, in a superficial kind of way. Beneath the layers of makeup and a tight dress that barely passed as business appropriate, she was attractive enough, but not his type.

She was good at her job — managing ad bookings with an agency for the consumer side of the business. He had no complaints about her work. He'd just never warmed to her for some reason. It could've been the way she looked at him when nobody else was around. Now, for instance. A speculative gleam lurked behind that perennially perky smile.

"Hi, Finn. Great to see you taking some time out. You look a little tense." Mimi stalked toward him, tossing her hair. The action seemed a little contrived.

He generally had a good 'bullshit detector' as they called it back home. With Mimi, he sensed there was always some other motivation behind her words or the flirtatious way she sidled up to him. He didn't believe she actually liked him.

Finn had been careful not to encourage her, not taking her up on her invitations to go out for a 'casual drink' or to 'get to know each other better.' He hadn't gone to her Fourth of July barbeque, although a few of the other team members had.

Finn had the sense to steer clear, even if it made Mimi more determined than ever to get him alone.

He raised his eyebrows at her. "Yep. Tense. Which is why I'm heading out to the courtyard to meditate. Or at least give it a shot." He nodded once in her direction and was up and out of there like an Olympic sprinter at the sound of a starter's pistol.

Mimi called after him, "You can run, but you can't hide." She cackled, apparently finding herself hilarious.

As he made his way across the courtyard, heading for his favorite corner near the bonsai trees and granite plip-plop fountain, he spotted Eden. And he'd thought he was the one with a rocket up his butt.

She power-walked through the courtyard, limping slightly, heading toward the parking lot. Finn couldn't help himself. He had to find out where she was going.

Somewhere in the back of his mind, he realized following Eden wasn't a good idea. Still, there was something about her that shifted all rational thought sideways, making way for something else. A hot mess, probably. His distracted brain insisted that he get closer to the lovely doctor and find out exactly what made her tick.

"Hey, Doctor Eden. Care to split a cab?"

He needed a cab? That was news to his brain. His feet were moving in her direction, though and a taxi waited near the main building's front entrance.

She stopped and turned toward him slowly. "I don't think so." Her gaze flicked down over his body for a second. Two seconds.

Hold on. Was that a spark of interest from Doctor Eden? Possibly. He grinned. "Come on. I'm heading downtown. You goin' my way?" She brought out the tease in him.

Eden shook her head, staring blankly over his shoulder. "Sorry, headed to the hospital. It's urgent."

"Is something wrong?" Finn didn't want to ask if it was her own personal business. *Correction.* He badly wanted to ask, but he didn't think his inquiry would be welcome. He bit the inside of his cheek to keep the question in.

She hesitated, her lips parted as if about to speak. Then her gaze dipped to his lips. "Nothing serious. Just lab results I need to check on." She went to add something more, then apparently changed her mind. Instead, she raised her hand and waved. "Later, Finn."

His eyebrows raised as he watched her scurry away and clamber into the waiting cab. He found himself transfixed by the way her butt wiggled into the back seat, clad in a form-fitting black skirt.

Finn forced his eyes upward and met her violet gaze. He waved too, then smiled until his cheeks hurt as her cab drove away.

Damn. She'd hypnotized him or something. Again.

Work. Refocus. Get your act together.

Giving himself a bloody good talking-to, he turned around, only to see Mimi hurrying his way. Great. He'd made a fool of himself chasing after one woman, and here came another, chasing after him.

Later, Finn!

Eden shook her head as the taxi took off. She'd squeaked at Finn like a giggly high school girl flirting with the captain of the football team. Not something she'd ever done. The captain of the football team had once flirted with her, and that had ended in disaster.

Settled in the back of the taxi, she gave instructions to the driver and shut her eyes for a moment.

Pretty little nerd, he'd called her back in high school. Kyle: a typical jock, except when he was sweet and thoughtful. In private, of course, not where any of his goofball friends could see.

Eden had loved Kyle as only a sixteen-year-old girl could. She'd idolized him, all eighteen years and six-foot-four-inches of him, golden and broad, an oversized man-child with a smile like overly sweet chocolate syrup.

Then the confrontations began. His friends called him names. Stupid, immature, meaningless names like Nerd Lover and Geek Squad. But they came up with the worst one for her: *Spicka Chica*.

So what if her grandmother came from Mexico, her culture and traditions passed down? Eden hadn't understood why it was important or a bad thing. But they had. All of them, even Kyle.

Kyle had become a bully so quickly that the switch from sweet to scary had made her head spin. He'd cornered her by her locker after school one day, grabbed her by the throat, and slammed her hard against the wall. Afterward, her bruised body had ached, but not as much as her stupid, tender heart.

There were meetings with the school board, a restraining order, Kyle's parents calling her a little bitch for ruining his chances of a college football scholarship, like it was somehow all her fault. As if she'd instigated Kyle's hurting her simply by existing in his world, being who she was.

Her grandmother had been her champion, her defender, all through the next two excruciating years of high school. God, Eden missed Gran so much. It'd been two years since she passed from the breast cancer that had spread to her bones and ravaged her body. She hadn't deserved to go that way.

Eden's chest ached, tears prickling behind her closed eyelids. She stared out the window but barely paid attention. The traffic became a blur of gray and blue, a flash of red when they hit a traffic jam. She lost time, then pulled herself together, startled.

She had her work. It had always helped her through the tough times. The method, the structure, all the processes she followed as a scientist. She found them... comforting.

When Eden started university, she found her home among the science geeks and also a type of freedom. She dated smart, appropriate men on the PhD fast track, like herself, and never again entertained thoughts of hard muscles and slow smiles that simultaneously made her want to run away and orgasm on the spot.

Finally, her skin tingling and temperature spiking, she realized why Finn made her so uncomfortable. She shifted in her seat and watched city buildings pass by. Finn was like Kyle reincarnated — although Kyle wasn't dead, or not that she'd heard — plus years of experience and fifty pounds of muscle. The boy she loved could have become a man like Finn. If he hadn't turned out cruel.

Finn wasn't a man she could hate. Not anymore. Eden had tried not to think about him — his jokey flirtation, the way he kissed, those muscles. And she'd failed.

Failed, failed, failed.

Now all she could think about was the way he sometimes grinned at her — as if she were Little Red Riding Hood and he the Big Bad Wolf, waiting for his chance to eat her alive.

She shivered and jolted alert as the taxi slowed and bumped to a stop. They'd reached their destination. The hospital, the here and now. "Right here's perfect, thanks."

Eden stepped out into scorching sunshine and limped along the sidewalk beside the landmark concrete-and-glass façade at the entrance to the cardiology department. The department for people with damaged hearts, not so different from herself. Although theirs could often be fixed.

Doctor Zhang couldn't fix her wounded heart, but Eden could at least help his patients get the care they deserved. Even if she had to fight her own boss every step of the way.

The constant hair-flicking was beyond irritating. Finn tried not to stare. Should he tell her? No, Mimi would most likely take offense, then there'd be no working with her in peace.

Mimi shot him a smile, of sorts. "It's Doctor McTavish. He wants a preliminary proposal on the branding for PowerUp Portal, and he 'wants it yesterday.' Sorry to bug you when you're, um, meditating." He may have been wrong about her. Maybe she was on his side after all.

He nodded. "Right. Better get it over with."

Finn strode ahead of her into the building and down the corridor, his thoughts whirling like a tornado in the middle of Kansas. He didn't need this. McTavish seemed on the warpath at the moment. Finn would have to watch out. Something about Finn's work had piqued his boss's interest, and now Finn had to weather his increasing surveillance.

He stopped and turned to look at Mimi. "Where's McTavish? In his office?"

She flicked her hair again with gusto and raised one arched brow. "No. He's in yours."

Great. Why did the thought of his boss sitting in his office, lying in wait, make his gut clench? There was no solid reason for McTavish's behavior to cause concern, but... The man was creeping around. It was enough to put anyone on their guard.

Mimi caught up to him, high heels clacking on the polished concrete floor as she walked beside him. "So you're chasing the great Doctor Eden? She won't even give you the time of day."

He stopped dead in his tracks. "What do you mean?"

"Unless you've got a PhD or your own research institute, she'll keep running in the opposite direction. Her loss." She grinned, then flipped her hair and turned on her heel.

Finn called after Mimi as she walked away, "I'm not chasing her." He shook his head as she laughed. If only he could convince himself.

As he marched toward his office at the back of the marketing team area, he glimpsed McTavish through the window slit in the door of his office. Sitting at Finn's desk as if he owned the place. Which, of course, he kind of did.

Finn had recently discovered that McTavish had a personal stake in an investment company that sank millions into Magna Smart's research and development division. Finn wasn't sure where that money was coming from. But it was Eden's division in question. Did she know about their boss's investment in the business? Finn had no idea, but he reckoned she deserved to. He'd have to find a way to confide in her, sooner rather than later.

He pushed his office door open, bracing himself for a fight. It was a surprise when McTavish smiled and waved him inside.

"Finn, come in. I've been meaning to catch up with you, and I had an unexpected opening in my calendar. Sorry to ambush you like this." McTavish laughed, a dry, harsh sound like a shovel scraping across concrete.

Finn sat heavily in the visitor's chair in his own office, then leaned forward. "No worries. How can I help you?"

McTavish rocked back in Finn's leather office chair, his hands resting behind his head. His boss looked far too comfortable. "I've been thinking about the prospectus for investors. I'd like a high-quality publication I can send out ahead of the Chinese delegation's visit in a few weeks. Is that something you could manage?"

Finn tipped his chin at his boss, taking a second to process his request. McTavish was being unusually conciliatory and coy. But that wasn't the weirdest thing. He couldn't help but wonder what prospectus. No way were they ready to actively seek investors when PowerUp Portal was a vague concept, nothing more.

"Is this for PowerUp? I could have the team draft something based on the work in progress. Of course, it wouldn't be ready for serious investors to use as a guide. It would need to go through legal signoffs first."

McTavish nodded slowly, his expression turning stony. The crevice between the older man's eyebrows was so deep it looked painful. "I'm aware of the process, but at this point, we can't afford to have the project stall. We need to impress this delegation, Finn. Don't let me down."

Something sank deep into the pit of Finn's stomach. It was probably his guts trying to escape. He knew he should stand up to McTavish. At the same time, he didn't want to rock the boat, or not yet. "Okay. I'll have our designer mock up a draft prospectus and use my research to flesh out the content. Do you want me to ask Eden for some scientific data? It would add a bit of weight to the drug development information."

"No. Not at this stage. This is a PR exercise to drum up some interest, nothing more." McTavish rose and stared down at Finn, obviously enjoying their relative positions of power.

Finn couldn't forget he was a mere underling in McTavish's world. He had to tread carefully and continue doing his job. He needed it more than most people around the place, and his boss knew it.

McTavish had been the one to approve Finn's last work visa extension, which was contingent on him remaining with his current employer. No job at Magna Smart meant no more living in the States. He'd be packed off back home to Australia faster than you could say 'failure'. Which was pretty fast. Finn would be lucky to get out of there so easily, if things went to hell the way he suspected.

But for now, Finn's role was to smile and play happy camper. Even if he now realized taking a job working for an egomaniac such as McTavish had been a massive tactical blunder, he had to make the best of a bad situation. "I'll brief the team this afternoon and get back to you."

McTavish patted Finn on the shoulder as he headed toward the door. Patted him, like a compliant child or a pet.

Bugger that.

It might take time to work his way out from under McTavish, but he was bloody determined to do it. He had to kick his plans into gear. And now seemed as good a time as any.

Chapter Thirteen

HotAussie007: We're seeing Dr. No at the La Jolla cinema. Next Sat at 8pm. Sorry it's over a week away.

LittleMissPerfect: Perfect. Can't wait to see 007 in action...

HotAussie007: *grins* Should I pick you up or meet you there?

Eden read over his messages and sipped her second Mimosa of the morning. The orange juice and champagne combination was delicious, tickling her tongue with bubbles of sunshiny freshness. It was a little too easy to drink, though.

The sun was out, shining its summery golden rays on the crowd, half the population of Southern California having turned out for the festivities of Opening Day at Del Mar Racetrack. One of the biggest sporting events in San Diego, the first day of the summer horse racing season was a fashionista's and socialite's dream. Eden liked it for the fancy hats.

The day was already heating up, the sunshine warming the exposed skin on her arms and legs as she stood on a patch of lawn at the track. Thank goodness for her wide-brimmed hat casting some shade on her face and shoulders. Her ensemble of scarlet hat embellished with faux cherries teamed with her strapless red dress with white polka dots looked fabulous, fitting the bill of old-fashioned glamor perfectly—if she did say so herself. Anyway, she'd had fun designing and sewing the dress. Who knew, she might even have a chance at the Bing Crosby Grand Prize in the Opening Day Hats Contest.

She held her phone in one hand, rereading HotAussie007's last message. Her heart sped up at the thought of meeting him face to face. How far should she take this thing with him? Yes, she'd decided to give him another chance. But should she give out her real name and home address? Although they'd been chatting for a while, he was still basically a stranger. Inviting him to her home could be a step too far. Risky.

LittleMissPerfect: Meet you in the bar there at 7.30. Don't be late or I'll break out my assassin skills.

HotAussie007: Death by beautiful but deadly undercover Bond girl. Not a bad fate ;) I'll be there in tux jacket.

LittleMissPerfect: I'll be wearing an emerald-green dress. Looking glamorous.

HotAussie007: You'll be a knockout. Chat soon.

A thrill tingled through her body at the thought of meeting him, and on a whim, she sent him a kissy-face emoji as a sign-off.

She was already enjoying her Thursday off work, only reading the fun messages and ignoring the many and various emails pinging her cell phone. She popped the phone into her purse. It was an indulgence to take a day off work midweek, but one she relished.

Faith slinked toward her in a form-fitting turquoise sheath dress, decorated with all the silver and aquamarine jewelry her body could carry, a spiral-shaped black hat atop her shiny dark hair. Her sister had a broad smile on her face. "Looking good, Babycakes." She pulled Eden in for a hug.

"You too. Love the jewelry." She touched Faith's handmade necklace with an index finger. "Hope you've got your business cards on you. I'm sure you'll pick up some customers here."

Her sister grinned. "Great minds think alike. I'm meeting with an accessories buyer from Benedict's later. Sorry, I'll have to leave you on your own for a while."

"Wow, that's awesome news." Eden rubbed her sister's shoulder. She hoped her meeting with the department store buyer was a success. "Don't be sorry. I'll just hang by the track or in the bar."

Faith beamed and did a little happy dance in her strappy sandals. Eden couldn't wait for the event to get going. Forgetting all about work stress and men for an entire day would be bliss. She hadn't told her sister about her pending blood test results and didn't plan to. But she had told her about the recent semi-truce with Finn and the problems with the project at work. Faith had simply insisted Eden should go out with Finn. They agreed to disagree about that.

An announcement over the loudspeaker startled them both. The serious business of the hat contest was about to begin.

Eden drained her glass and set it aside before straightening the wide-brimmed creation sitting over her ponytail. She nodded at Faith and pointed toward the trackside area. "Let's do this."

Finn checked the time on his phone as the chair of the meeting droned on about the increasing competition from South America. He'd heard it all before. Only an hour to go, and then he could skip out of work early and head to the track.

It wasn't his usual form of entertainment, but the corporate box on Opening Day should be a sweet setup. Food and drinks laid on, and all he had to do was schmooze a few visiting doctors and head honchos from various hospitals. McTavish had insisted that Finn attend, which might have been odd, except Finn heard he'd invited most of the senior staff. Which meant Eden might be there.

Finn studied the PowerPoint slides projected on the screen, noting the high turnover products with the largest profit margins. Focusing on the international markets was key: more lucrative and less regulation. He'd provided most of the graphs, so it was nothing new but he'd have to remember to recycle some of the content for the annual report.

"Finn, what are your thoughts on selling directly online?" A voice floated into his brain, the accent taking a second to decipher.

He zoned back in, snapping his attention to George Petrov, vice-president of operations, visiting from the European office. Unannounced. Add in the unscheduled meeting he was now participating in, and it was all a bit odd.

Finn straightened in his seat. "Sorry, George, I was making mental notes for the annual report. Online sales have pros and cons, much like any retail operation. First, we'd need to consider the infrastructure investment. We wouldn't be looking at a pop-up e-commerce site. It would need to be state-of-the-art security-wise. Storing customer details, especially their medical details, raises a lot of privacy concerns." He drummed his fingertips on the heavy glass tabletop beside his phone.

George smiled, making his thick eyebrows dance and his dark eyes scrunch up at the corners. "Yes, so our IT team tells me. But what is your opinion from a customer-satisfaction perspective? Would it be a worthwhile investment?"

Finn paused to take a breath before plunging right in. "In my opinion, yes. Today's patients expect a customer-service experience from their health-care providers. Being made to wait in line at a pharmacy when they already have a doctor's prescription is a nineteenth-century concept. We all know that customers can buy some medications online and already purchase black-market drugs from international sellers."

Mumbled agreements rippled around the table. McTavish sat at the far end, grinning widely. It was a strange, self-satisfied expression, and it didn't sit right. Perhaps Finn was imagining things, but he didn't think so. McTavish was supremely confident that everything was going according to his plans.

Finn continued with his usual spiel, "Why not replace that market with a reputable source of genuine drugs, backed with professional advice? It's a win-win solution. We benefit from customer loyalty and repeat purchases, probably lifetime repeat business, while protecting patients from unscrupulous vendors at the same time."

He leaned back in his chair and scanned the faces in the room again. The two silent women who'd accompanied George from the European HQ office presented bland, pleasant expressions. The older woman, Marieke, broke into a broad smile. The younger, Isabel, was white as a sheet and didn't blink. Not once. She might have been a corporate vampire on retainer.

George laughed, a hearty *ha-ha-ha*, grabbing everyone's attention. "This, my friends, is why I suggested we visit our American colleagues. New ideas, new vision. Not set in the old ways. We should not be thinking simply in terms of cheaper manufacturing costs or reducing the size of packaging. Magna Smart must think big. For the future." He clapped his hands together once, loud as a slap across the face.

McTavish leaned forward and spoke for the first time in nearly an hour. "Excellent. I think we can all grasp the importance of the ideas discussed here today. Obviously, given the commercial-in-confidence nature of the strategy Finn outlined for us, it mustn't go beyond these four walls at this point in proceedings." His slimy smile was back, crawling across his face like a big fat slug.

Finn shifted in his already uncomfortable chair, trying to squirm his way out of the situation. Yes, he'd gone along with McTavish's plan so far, but not without serious reservations. He'd expressed his concerns many times, letting his boss know he wouldn't be a party to any marketing strategy that put patients at risk. Direct selling drugs online, particularly the way they were proposing, was potentially lucrative but also potentially deadly. All the checks and balances had to be put in place. Doctors and their own research and development scientists such as Eden also needed to be consulted.

A wash of dread crept over his skin. It was obvious Eden hadn't been consulted. She was the lead researcher on what was supposed to be the company's flagship heart medication, and yet she apparently had no clue about the PowerUp Portal approach. He knew McTavish intended to sell the drug direct to public, but Eden didn't.

The big question was, should he tell her? Should he directly and purposefully flout McTavish's instructions and let her in on the big plan? He was in two minds. Finn's gut told him that she should be informed, while something else nagged at him to protect her at all costs from getting involved in the debacle to come.

If his boss found out Finn had talked to Eden, he'd soon be out of a job. Leaving him without a work visa. He'd be winging his way back to Australia faster than you could say 'flying kangaroo'. And he'd be without any influence at all, unable to change plans that had been set in motion.

Even a couple of weeks ago, he wouldn't have been too sad about it. Disappointed, sure. Worried about finding another job back home? Definitely. Feeling disappointed he hadn't managed to achieve everything that his brother, Matt, might have if he'd lived and had the opportunity? Yes. Those thoughts were always at the back of his mind. But *sad*?

Now there was one big reason he'd regret leaving San Diego behind. One person. Eden.

"Doctor Robinson, is that you, looking so glamorous?"

Eden turned at the booming, distinctively English-accented voice coming from somewhere behind her. She'd been lined up at the bar, trying to get the bartender's attention. No luck so far.

The throng of horse racing fans and people partying after the hats contest was noisy and downright pushy. As she craned her neck under her wide hat to catch sight of the owner of the voice, a punter crashed into her hip, spilling their frozen drink down her arm.

"Hey, watch it." Eden shook her arm, and the sticky liquid dripped off her skin.

"Here, allow me." The voice was right beside her now, low and reassuring. That voice... She knew it.

Eden looked up. And up. Goodness, he was tall. The very definition of tall, dark, and handsome, with an extra serving of brilliant. Doctor David Zhang, cardiologist extraordinaire. One of the good guys—when he wasn't teasing her. He'd decided Eden was too serious, apparently. Or so he'd told her on numerous occasions. "Doctor Zhang, how are you? I didn't expect to see you here. And I've told you to call me Eden."

He chuckled, all six-foot-two of him. "Eden. You can call me David, of course. I didn't expect to see you either, but it's the highlight of my day. With a cherry on top. Nice." His hand brushed over the plastic cherries on top of her hat, making them shake. "Did you win a prize for your hat?"

She rolled her eyes at him but laughed. "No, only an honorable mention and a free mimosa. I'm happy with that. Who let you out of the hospital for the day?"

"I could ask you the same about your lab. But I was invited by your very own Doctor McTavish. A meet and greet with some of the staff from Magna Smart's European office, I understand. But you must know all about it."

Eden nodded, wondering if she'd missed a memo. Surely if McTavish were there with medical guests, people she'd personally cultivated a relationship with, he'd invite her to attend. "Really? I don't think there was an invitation for my team. I'm here with my sister today, but she has a meeting on the side."

David smiled at her, flashing blindingly white teeth. "I'd like to meet her. Anyway, when are you coming back to visit me?" He lowered his voice, his dark eyes glittering as he leaned closer. "I'll always have a place for you if you want to make a move. It would have to be a little less senior though. Get back to grassroots research."

Eden's lips stretched into half-smile. She'd always liked David, respected him, and it seemed the feeling was mutual. But she couldn't afford a less senior position. "Thanks, I'll keep that in mind. I was there yesterday, but I missed you. I spoke to your team and emailed you about some anomalous test results. You should review the results. But I'll stop by again soon. You can show me those new cardiac monitors you purchased."

"Sure. But right now, I'd like to buy you a drink." He stepped toward the long mahogany bar and whistled. Honestly, you'd have thought he was hailing a cab in downtown Manhattan.

With some space between them, she had a chance to study him. He looked handsome, as always. His tailored gray silk suit with a deep blue shirt suited him. In fact, he looked as suave as a Hong Kong movie star. Especially the way he wore his midnight hair, slicked back, uber cool.

A minute later, David was back, pushing a martini glass into her hand. A vodka gimlet. He'd remembered her favorite cocktail. It'd been a year since they'd met at a cardiology conference in San Francisco, where he'd commented on her drink of choice.

"Thank you. My favorite." She caught his eye, and he grinned, making his eyes scrunch up at the corners.

"I know. I have an excellent memory for the important things." David laughed again, the sound vibrating through her hand where he still touched her. *Interesting*. Was he flirting with her?

Just then, things got even more interesting. A large, warm, and slightly rough hand brushed her upper arm, and she shivered, even though it had to be close to one hundred degrees in the packed bar. A crisp citrus scent teased her senses. She didn't even need to turn her head to know who it was, but she looked anyway.

Eden nodded at him, keeping her expression neutral, resisting the urge to kiss his cheek. "Finn, hello."

Finn's face was stony. "Doctor Eden. Is this bloke bothering you?"

Laughter bubbled up, threatening to escape, until Eden pressed her left hand to her lips to hold it in. "No. Finn Donohue, meet Doctor David Zhang, a leading cardiologist at SD West General. He's a friend of mine. David, Finn's a colleague at Magna Smart. Our head of Marketing and Business Development."

David released her hand and extended his to Finn, who stared at it for longer than was polite. They shook hands, hard, as if competing to find out who had the toughest finger bones. They may as well have switched to arm wrestling on the bar.

She dipped her head for a second to hide her slight smile, then glanced up again to find the two men eyeing each other, sizing one another up.

David broke out his broadest smile. "Nice to meet you, Finn. You must be the marketing whiz kid McTavish mentioned."

Eden pressed her lips together. His use of the word 'kid' wasn't lost on her, or Finn, judging by his raised eyebrow. David was a few years older, maybe forty. But Finn was hardly a kid, and David wasn't senior enough to be throwing around such diminutives.

Finn straightened his tie, a stunning sea-green silk number he must have chosen to match his eyes. He looked across at her, and those eyes sparkled. "Just your average thirty-four-year-old whiz kid with a master's degree in marketing. Nothing as impressive as cardiology. You must have a steady stream of brokenhearted women throwing themselves at you, begging you to fix them."

Eden snort-laughed and nearly spilled her drink. She'd barely gotten herself under control when David kind of rumbled, then exploded into one of his trademark belly laughs.

"I think we'll get along just fine." David slapped Finn on the back, extra hard.

Eden swirled drink round her glass. "Okay, gentleman, now we've got the introductions out of the way, do you mind telling me what the deal is with this little party and why I wasn't invited?"

Their blank stares told her all she needed to know. They had no idea she hadn't been invited. They probably assumed she had.

Finn moved a fraction closer and spoke low in her ear. "McTavish has bigwigs here from Europe. Last minute visit, on the down-low." Then, in a more audible tone, he explained, "Eden's working on the research underpinning our new drug in development. But today's gathering is more of a marketing and networking event."

Except it wasn't. Otherwise, David wouldn't have been invited. She couldn't get around the facts—she was being sidelined.

Eden checked her phone, and sure enough, there was a text from Faith. She plastered on her happy face. "Anyway, my sister's looking for me, so I'll leave you both to it." She downed the rest of her drink.

When she looked up, David was studying her, a frown marring his brow. "I meant what I said earlier. Come and see me when you're ready to discuss my offer." He nodded in Finn's direction, then focused back on her. "See you soon."

David walked away, weaving his way through the crowd to who knew where.

"What was that about?" Finn gestured over his shoulder.

"David's offered me a job working for him, cardiac stem cell research with his team, attached to the hospital. It's not the first time he's mentioned it."

He raised his hyperactive eyebrow again. "Are you interested?"

What was Finn really asking? Whether she was interested in the job. Or the man? If she was completely honest, maybe a little of both, except he'd been married when they met. She'd heard he was separated now. David had offered her an interesting job, and perhaps he was looking for more. But overall, she'd say he was trustworthy. A known quantity.

Finn, on the other hand, was a random element. Then it dawned on her. Her hesitation in considering David's offer might well be tangled up with the other handsome man standing beside her, which wasn't ideal. Career decisions should never be influenced by a man, especially one who was most likely hiding something.

She shrugged, making her hat wobble. Her cherries trembled. "Working for him could be a smart move in some ways. In others, not so much." She lowered her voice to whisper, "The job wouldn't pay as well as my current position. And he's still a married man, even if he is separated from his wife. I suspect he has a little crush on me. It could make things awkward."

Finn nodded, a crease forming between his eyebrows. "He's definitely into you. Looked like he was trying to stake a claim when he saw me heading over. You're right to be cautious." He took a sip of his beer, then licked across his lower lip to catch the foam.

Eden's gaze dropped to his mouth before she could check herself. When she dragged her eyes back up to meet his, she found him studying her expression, and she forced herself to be affronted by him telling her who not to date. "By the way, why do you guys always go caveman when there's a woman around to impress?"

He tipped his head to one side. "Not always. It could have something to do with the woman and whether I think she's worth impressing."

Eden narrowed her eyes at him. Was he suggesting she wasn't?

Then someone pushed right into Eden's back. "*Ooof!*" All the air exited Eden's lungs in a great gust. She turned just in time to see it was Faith, who continued with barely a loss of momentum, pushing Eden into Finn's shoulder, sloshing his beer all over his shirt.

"Sorry, Babycakes." Faith patted Eden's arm. "Oh, Finn. Look, I've gone and ruined your shirt. Here, let me." She attempted to mop up the beer with a minuscule cocktail napkin.

Finn coughed and muttered, "It's okay." He smoothed down his shirt, making it stick to his body. He looked streamlined. Slick.

Eden stood hunched over, rubbing her back. Lucky she hadn't been in the full firing line. Sometimes her sister was a catastrophe waiting to happen. Other times, she didn't wait at all.

Faith took her arm "I'm soooo sorry. Babe, are you alright?"

"Uh-huh. Just battered and bruised." She rubbed the sore spot in the small of her back again. "You sure know how to make an entrance."

Faith giggled at that, raising herself to full height before hurling the soggy napkin onto the bar.

Finn tried to look dignified while wiping down his shirt front with his bare hands. Eventually, he gave up, straightening and grinning. "Guess I'll go find a new shirt somewhere. Excuse me, ladies." He tipped his chin at them before striding off toward the main doors of the reception room. Fleeing the scene.

Eden breathed out again, a little sore, a lot relieved that both Finn and David were gone, for now, but kind of pissed too. "Good work, Faith. I was trying to find out about this work party I'm not invited to, and now he's gone."

"Sorry." Faith rearranged her hair and adjusted her hat. "What work party?"

"The one the boss organized and forgot to invite me to. Feel like crashing?"

Faith nudged Eden in the ribs with her elbow and winked. "Like you have to ask. Let's go rock a party!"

Whether or not rocking the party was the best idea, Eden was going for it. She was over being circumspect. It was time to find out exactly what was going on.

Eden located the Magna Smart party in the corporate box and strolled in with Faith by her side, figuring she'd brazen it out.

The crowd mainly consisted of middle-aged men from Magna Smart and several she didn't recognize, milling around. A couple of younger women dressed in black mini dresses and little aprons were serving drinks. *Ugh*. It was one of *those* corporate events — male bonding based on inappropriate flirting with the servers.

An older man approached before they could get two steps inside the door. "Hello, my dear. Are you serving snacks? Hot dogs, maybe?" The gray-haired man snickered as he extended his arm, aiming for her waist.

She sidestepped right into Faith, who, as usual, was having none of it. "Dude, that's a top research scientist you're attempting to grope. Quit it!"

Eden sighed. "What precisely about my outfit suggests I'm a waitress?" She did look more like a trackside fashion model than a scientist today, but he could hardly have thought she was on the catering staff.

"My apologies." He raised his eyebrows, then turned away and joined a huddle of other older men in gray suits. McTavish was among them.

Eden wasn't sure what about that group set off alarm bells in her head. Perhaps it was that McTavish appeared larger, more aggressive, telling one of the other men off. Or it could have been the way one of the men, slightly younger, slightly nerdier, stared hard at McTavish without saying a word. With his nondescript short brown hair and horn-rimmed glasses, he looked familiar, though Eden couldn't immediately place him.

Faith nudged her in the side with a pointy elbow and whispered close to her ear, "Babe, isn't that the guy you matched with on that dating app? The one who loved cheese?"

Oh, it was him. Horn-Rimmed Glasses had been her date at a charity fundraiser event nearly a year ago, and he'd scoffed so much free cheese that Eden had seriously worried about the state of his digestive tract. There had been no second date. His name was something old-fashioned... Clint! That was it. He was a scientist too but focused more on data analysis. Why was he there?

Eden's lips twisted to one side as she whispered, "Yes, you're right. But I don't know if I should say hello. He's the one who called me 'uppity' for wanting to buy a glass of champagne instead of drinking the free beer." She scanned the room, getting her back bearings. The horse racing proceedings were playing on large flat-screen TVs on both solid walls, a bar stood to their right, and large windows to their left overlooked the grandstand and the racetrack.

Faith nudged her again and then shuffled her to the right. Finn had returned, looking casual but still sharp in a black Del Mar Racetrack T-shirt. He had another man with him now, possibly Italian, in a sharp 1960s-style suit. Totally channeling Dean Martin.

"Oh, hi, Eden. I didn't think you were... coming to this thing." Finn's eyes flicked toward McTavish's group.

"I changed my mind. Why not, right?"

Finn blinked and opened his mouth as if to say something, when the man by his side loudly cleared his throat. With a glance at him, Finn waved his hand around between them. "This is my friend Sam. Mechanical genius extraordinaire, lifesaver of random women's Vespas, and Elvis fan."

Sam coughed again, and Finn took the hint. "Sam, this is Eden, sometimes mad scientist, Vespa enthusiast, and creator of epic cupcakes."

Eden stuck out her hand and grinned as Sam shook it briefly. When she glanced at Faith, her sister mouthed, *"Wow."*

"Pleased to meet you, Sam. Also, not mad. Sometimes annoyed with marketing types, but you know how infuriating they can be. Thank you so much for agreeing to fix up my Betsy."

"You're welcome. I was glad to help. Especially because Finn here can't stop talking about you—"

Finn slapped his friend on the back so hard it made a walloping sound. "Don't mind Sam, he doesn't get out much. Um, Eden, can I talk to you for a sec?"

Eden nodded, her forehead pinching into a frown. "Oh, Sam, meet my sister. Faith is a jewelry designer." She stepped aside a few paces, following Finn's lead.

He cleared his throat. "I don't think you should be here. While I was in the gift shop, I overheard a few things. There's a guy here who I know is working on some research and development stats. It's... something they've kept quiet. I was going to stick my nose in, see what I can find out."

Eden glanced around Finn's shoulder, past Faith and Sam laughing together, to the huddle of serious-looking men clustered around McTavish. Their boss caught her eye for a split second, and his face contorted into a scowl.

She looked back at Finn and pressed her lips together. "Yeah, you might be right. I'll check in with you at work tomorrow. Let me know if you find out anything interesting."

He let out a loud breath, a lopsided smile crossing his face. "I will. Have fun with your sister. I'll find out how Sam's getting on with your scooter too."

Eden simply nodded and cast her eye in McTavish's direction again before asking Faith to go check out the horses. She didn't want to mess up this temporary truce she had with Finn. Or put their jobs in further jeopardy.

Chapter Fourteen

Finn: I want to drop off the Vespa to Eden. Get it ready for me okay?

Sam: Sure. I'm rooting for you!

Finn: Thanks mate. You know rooting means something else in Aussie right?

It was Saturday, two days since Finn had talked to Eden at the racetrack. Her sister had dropped her at work on Friday. Finn had been swamped with paperwork and had barely seen daylight, let alone Eden. Finn should have called first. It was probably a serious misdemeanor in Eden-land to rock up on her doorstep unannounced. But truth be told, he couldn't stop himself from going to see her.

"Alright, keep your shirt on," Eden yelled through her closed front door when he rang the bell and knocked for good measure. After a rustling and then banging noises, shuffling footsteps headed toward the door.

When she opened it, seeing her threw him. Heat prickled the skin across the back of his neck. He'd expected to be turned on—when he saw her at the racetrack, she almost took his breath away—but there was also this warm, happy-to-see-her vibe rushing through his stomach. It was a worry.

Finn was busy checking out her lush curves in her tight knee-length pants and little blouse, so he missed the exact moment she saw her Vespa on the drive. But he looked up when she squealed.

"You pimped my ride?"

Yeah, he'd pimped it for her. Nothing permanent, but she was now the proud owner of a scooter with silver floral decals that Sam had assured him were winners. All his Vespa customers apparently adored them.

Finn had been worried about it. Even now, he wasn't sure he should have done it without asking her permission first. His palms had been sweating on the way over to her place. He rubbed them down the side of his pants again.

"You did this?" She turned to him with one eyebrow raised. He caught the full force of those violet eyes, even brighter in the sunlight. Scrutinizing him.

"Me and Sam. He helped me do up the Chevy too. He's got some mad mechanical skills."

"I'll say." Eden cautiously approached her scooter, circling it as if it were a wild animal about to bolt. Then she crouched low and ran her fingertips along the outside of the Vespa's chassis. As her fingers skimmed its metallic surface, she sighed. "She looks gorgeous."

She sure did. Only Finn wasn't thinking about the scooter. He stopped short of imagining silver floral decals all over Eden's skin. But only just. There had to be some limit to his rampant reaction to her. Although, if there was, he hadn't found it yet. She moved to examine the re-chromed bumper, and there was something about her curvy butt in those tight little pants... It was hypnotic. What did they call them? Pedal pushers? Sounded about right for riding a scooter.

Still bent over, she looked back over her shoulder, flicking her ponytail. "Did you really get all the chrome refinished?"

"Uh-huh." Brilliant. Articulate. *Dickhead*.

"And added a new leather seat cover?"

"Yep." Finn crossed his arms over his chest. Surely he could manage to say something intelligent? "Sam fixed the suspension too."

Eden straightened and leaned one hand on the scooter's seat. Then she smiled with those pink lips, and it was like the sun breaking through the clouds in gloomy June, just before full summer hit. "She's beautiful. I'm almost glad you backed into me."

When she spoke that way, it was damn near impossible to stop himself from reaching for her. He wanted to kiss her again. Bad. Instead, he settled for grabbing the shopping bag that lay on the ground at his feet. His gift might have been overkill. Not usually one for extravagant gestures, he had no idea.

He pulled the gift from the bag and held it out to her, stepping closer. "I got you this too."

She took it from him, her fingertips brushing across the back of his hand. "A new helmet? A real Vespa one? From Italy?"

A laugh bubbled up, and he let her hear it. "Really, truly. I got the shiny black one because I thought it would suit you. You always look so... glamorous."

With her head tilted to one side, she examined him for a moment, as if he were a specimen under her microscope. "You shouldn't have."

"I wanted to."

"So I'll look glamorous?"

Finn sighed and shook his head. "So I'll rest easy, knowing you won't crack your skull if you and Betsy take another tumble."

She smiled, a shy expression on her face. "Thank you. It was very thoughtful of you."

Yes, the fact he'd been thinking about her nonstop had filtered through to the top of his brain. He lifted the helmet from her grasp and placed it on her head, and as he smoothed the long strands of her hair down her back, it felt like silk, warmed by the sunshine. Smelled of roses.

With her gaze fixed on him, she adjusted the strap under her chin. As much as he longed to touch her, he let his hands drop to his sides.

"Come on." Eden twisted away from him and swung her leg over the scooter. "I'll take you for a spin."

"For real?" Man, he sounded like a pimply-faced teenager being asked out by a girl. At least he hadn't turned her off by buying her an unexpected gift. He'd half-expected her to yell at him and say she could buy her own damn helmet.

Her lips tipped up at the corners. "Yes, for real. Climb aboard."

There were so many possible responses to her statement. And Finn had to clench his jaw to keep them from bursting out in a torrent of innuendo. Instead, he let the practical win out. "I don't have another helmet."

She hopped off the scooter and spoke over her shoulder. "I've got a spare in my garage. Faith wears it sometimes." Then she jogged across to her garage lifted the roller door and retrieved something from a hook on the wall.

She closed the garage and strolled back to him, holding the pinkest motorcycle helmet he'd ever seen. It looked like something a ten-year-old girl would wear. Her outstretched hand wobbled as she fought to contain her laughter.

Finn shook his head from side to side. "No. Just no."

"Oh yes. You're such a manly man. Surely a little pink can't hurt."

Manly man. That was a good sign. At least she didn't see him as a substitute little sister. He pulled himself up to full height, crossing his arms over his chest. He caught the way her eyelashes flicked down, her gaze skimming over his biceps. A *very* good sign.

"When you put it like that, okay. But I'm driving."

"You wish. My scooter, my rules." She swung her leg over the scooter, straddling it again.

As if he wouldn't join her. A chance to sit close behind her, his front pressed to her back, the curve of her butt, thighs against thighs... He'd be a prize idiot to turn down the opportunity. But he'd have to watch himself. Getting too worked up wouldn't do him any favors if she wasn't into it. If she wasn't into *him.*

Finn slapped the ridiculous helmet on his head and buckled the strap. Catching Eden's eye, he waggled his eyebrows, which made her giggle. Then he slid onto the scooter behind her and pushed himself forward until he sat flush against her. Placed his hands on her hips. Tried not to squeeze her.

He might have imagined it, but he'd have sworn that she shivered. It was damn hot in the full sun. Hardly shiver-inducing. But something had made her body react.

An excellent sign.

Eden stared straight ahead, tensing as Finn climbed on the scooter behind her. He'd helped wheel it down the drive and now they were ready to go. If she could only remember to breathe.

She never should have suggested he hop on the scooter behind her. So snug against her ass. So hot and hard, with all those muscles. The press of his thighs against hers made her shiver as she turned the key to unlock the steering. And when she took off from the curb, his hands tightened on her hips for a second. A thrilling, heart-stopping second. But it was wrong. His touch shouldn't thrill her. She should have hardened her heart and had her sensible brain tell her body to calm down by now. She was far from calm.

Eden zoomed down her street and out onto the main road, where she turned toward Torrey Pines State Natural Reserve. Finn held on tight as they took the corner, making her hold her breath. She forced her breathing to even out and listened to the wind rushing past as they rode.

On such a beautiful day, the view along the beach was spectacular. She soaked it in, the sunshine warming her bare arms. When riding, she was free. No work stress, no worries about mortgage payments, no concerns about a lack of personal life niggling in the back of her mind.

After a few minutes, they crossed the bridge that ran right along the coastline. When they reached the other side, Eden pulled off onto the shoulder near the clifftop. She took another deep breath, inhaling a lungful of clean, crisp ocean air, then tugged off her helmet and rested it on the handlebars. What to say to the man pressed up against her back?

Eden gazed out over the water. "I love this spot. Such a stunning view."

"Sure is."

She craned her neck to look at his face, only to find Finn staring at her. Somehow, she was trapped by his focus. He'd removed the glittery pink helmet that made him look like a rainbow unicorn. Now he was all sun-kissed, tousle-haired Aussie man. And as his gaze flicked from her eyes to her lips before sliding away to the view over the ocean, Eden's heart thudded loud in her ears.

This thing between them was ridiculous. It was purely physical. Empirically. But the purely physical thing with a man had been missing from her life for a long time. Far too long.

She hopped off the scooter and immediately missed the contact with Finn. But she forced herself to walk a few paces toward the cliff edge, away from him. Her legs wobbled.

"Eden." His voice was closer than it should have been. Right behind her. All deep and rough. "What's the matter?"

How could she explain? On the one hand, she wanted to jump into bed with him, consequences be damned. And on the other hand, she was scared of being hurt, of losing her job and her home, of trying for everything and ending up with nothing.

Most of all, she was terrified of him and all he might represent. Chances not taken; roads not traveled. All that jazz.

Eden shrugged. Without turning to face him, she tried to deflect his question. "I'm worried about Faith. She's starting up her own business and has no safety net apart from the mortgage on our gran's house. My house. That money's all tied up and basically gone. She could move in with me, but she's too stubborn and wants to keep her apartment with studio space. No compromise."

"But you admire her. I can hear it in your voice." Finn stepped forward until he stood at her side.

Shifting her weight, Eden glanced down at the water below, then back up at his face. "Yes, you're right. She's going after what she wants, even if it might end in disaster."

His eyes were on her now, the heat of his gaze burning through her. "You wish you could be more like her, but having a safety net is important to you." His assessment of her was too accurate. He saw something in her that she hadn't even realized she'd been trying to hide. "What do you want, Eden?"

Wasn't that the billion-dollar question? "Too many things. To keep my job, but to quit and do something more worthwhile. Proper, groundbreaking research. To keep my house, but not be afraid to travel the world. To protect my sister, but also to help her follow her dreams." She hesitated, closing her eyes. Her heart rate sped up at the thought of speaking the words threatening to spill from her lips. She wanted *him*. Her eyes popped open again. "I want to keep myself safe, but I want someone to love. And sometimes, I'm too cautious."

Finn nodded, his hair shifting in the breeze, shimmering, more golden than it looked indoors. "I knew you were smart, but now I reckon you're the most brilliant person I know. *Know thyself*, so the ancient Greeks said. You're way ahead of me. I struggle to decide whether to eat Cheerios or Cap'n Crunch for breakfast."

Laughter rose in her throat, and she let it burst out. "The wisdom of the ancients and breakfast cereal options all in one breath. You're a complex man too, Finn Donohue." He'd surprised her—in a good way.

He grinned at her. "Ah, you've discovered my secret. Complexity covered with a boyish grin and confident swagger. Come on, let's go. I'm in the mood for something sweet."

She blinked. "Something sweet?"

"Yeah. Banana split, or pancakes, or something. What do you recommend?"

Already nodding in agreement, Eden had to go with her favorite. "Churros. Mexican donuts with chocolate sauce. I know a great place."

"Now you're talking. Lead the way." Finn extended his arm and let her go ahead of him. The perfect gentleman.

He was being so polite. Sweet, even. Only, she kind of wished he'd drop the whole gentleman act and kiss her already. Again.

Eden eating sugar-frosted donuts dipped in chocolate sauce was a thing of beauty. A maddeningly hot thing of beauty.

If only Finn could stop the rush of heat that went straight to his groin every time she dipped her churros into the chocolate and licked it off. She couldn't just stuff the things in her mouth like he'd done. Oh no. The whole process had to be seductive, clearly designed to torment him.

She rolled her eyes to the heavens. "Oh. My. God. These are even better than I remembered. I haven't been here for a while." Eden proceeded to lick chocolate sauce from her fingers in such a way...

His body hardened immediately, so he stretched out his legs under the table, trying to get some blood circulation happening. Hoping the glass of cold lemonade on the table might provide some relief, he grabbed hold of it. Icy against his fingers and, thankfully, cool going down his throat. Finn downed half of it in one mouthful.

He swallowed, then cleared his throat. "Yeah, they're good. Best dessert I've had in a while."

Eden stopped eating, her hand resting on her belly. She rolled down the waistband of her pants. "I'm stuffed. But they were sooo good."

His eyes were drawn to her fingers, rubbing back and forth across the bare strip of tan skin between her shirt and waistband, exposing her cute little navel. Something inside him nearly boiled over at the sight, urging him to touch. To get his hands on her.

The slight curve and indentation beside her hip bone was interesting. There was a mark there, something colorful. A tattoo? She shifted in her seat, revealing the definite outline of butterfly wings, pink and purple. He hadn't picked her as a tattoo kind of woman. Unexpected. And completely, utterly hot.

Eden sighed, more of a groan, closing her eyes and rubbing her stomach.

His fingers shaking, Finn put down the glass and slapped his hands down on the edge of the table. Gripping much harder than was necessary, he dragged himself to his feet. "Let's get going."

She tilted her head but kept up the belly rub. "Right this second? I thought we'd hang out for a while." Her eyebrows pinched together.

Now she wanted to 'hang out' like they were friends or something. Of course. If he didn't watch his step, he'd end up permanently friend-zoned. Eden was a woman who liked things organized. Compartmentalized.

It was time to make sure he occupied the compartment labeled 'boyfriend.' Maybe. A rough outline of a plan formed in the back of his mind. Lots of things could go wrong, true. But if things went his way, he might dig himself out of the hole he'd found himself in at work, not only with McTavish, but with the other people demanding information from him. He could still win. What if he could win Eden too?

Doctor Eden got to her feet. Her lips tipped up on one side in a teasing way before an almost shy expression crossed her face. She batted her eyelashes, and for a moment he forgot his own name.

He shook his head. *Finn*. Finn Donohue. Man on a mission.

Chapter Fifteen

Eden: Hey, thanks for today. For my scooter and everything.

Finn: You're welcome. I'm dreaming of churros...

Movie night with Faith was usually the highlight of her week, sad as that sounded, and Eden had been looking forward to chilling out with her sister, eating some popcorn, and drinking frozen margaritas. Maybe she'd chat with Faith about what was going on with Finn.

But things weren't going quite to plan. One of her favorite DVDs was jumping and skipping all over the place. Looked like it might finally be time to sign up for a movie streaming service. She'd resisted so far, as she'd built up a rocking collection of vintage movies on DVD and didn't want to waste money on entertainment. Eden jabbed at the remote, trying to get the film to play.

A resounding thwack from the other room had her sitting bolt upright and staring, looking around for the source of the noise.

Faith hollered like a woman on fire, which, potentially, she was. *Yikes!* Smoke billowed from the open-plan kitchen, the rank stench clogging her nasal passages. She'd thought an earlier waft of smoke was a neighbor was barbequing outside.

"EEEEE-DEN!"

She jumped to her feet. And fell to the floor. Leaped up again. Her ankle throbbed, but she hobbled toward the scene of the catastrophe, trying to take it slow. Her sprain wasn't fully healed, and she didn't want to injure it again.

Shrieks bounced off the kitchen's laminate surfaces. Eden's heart skidded to a halt, along with her feet, and she snapped her mouth shut with a click of her teeth, because the shrieks were coming from her.

"What the *heebie-jeebies* happened here?"

While skirting around the body sprawled on the floor—a pint-sized person with blond hair, dressed in black, legs akimbo, and blood splashed across her face—Eden sucked in a breath of smoky air. The similarity to a TV crime show was all too real. She dropped to a crouch and touched a shaky hand to cold, clammy skin: a cheek, a forehead. Felicity appeared to be passed out on Eden's kitchen floor for some reason.

Heart hammering like a police officer trying to bang down a door, she raised her head to find Faith. A shaky, ashen version of her sister stood in front of the oven, waving a fire extinguisher around. Acidic fumes pervaded the space, mixed with a vile, smoky residue.

"I-I don't know what happened." Faith shook her head. "She just ran in the back door and fell. Boom!"

Eden's gaze returned to Felicity's face. Why exactly was her research assistant here? Let alone passed out on her kitchen floor. Eden's heart hammered in her chest. Something was very wrong, but she struggled to think clearly.

Finn's phone buzzed from where it was strapped to his arm. He slowed his pace to a jog, the reflected sunset blinding him for a second as he glanced out over the water from the clifftop running track. He palmed his phone and smiled. His mother. He hadn't heard from her in a while, as she'd been on a cruise. He stopped moving and took her call.

"Mum?" The gasping and sobbing on the other end of the phone set his heart racing, his mind jumping to conclusions at the speed of light. "Mum? What's wrong?"

"Sorry, Finn. It's just... you're so far away." She hesitated, her rough exhalation loud in his ear. "It's your dad."

Finn's heart shuddered, then stopped dead for a second. He pounded himself on the chest and leaned over the railing, sucking in air. "What about Dad?" His voice sounded strained, scratchy, even to his own ears.

"He's had a heart attack. He was out jogging. We're still not sure of the prognosis, but the surgeon wants to do a triple bypass as soon as possible."

A lead weight pressed down on Finn's chest, making it difficult to breathe. "Oh no. Is Dad awake? Can I speak to him?"

"Not right now. He's sleeping. But sweetheart... can you come home?"

The shakiness in his mum's voice threw him. It must be bad. She was usually so pragmatic that nothing stressed her out. "Of course. Of course! I'll get on the next flight I can find."

"Thanks, Finn. Let me know when you'll be home."

He closed his eyes, willing himself across the ocean. "As soon as I know, I'll send you the details."

"I'd better get going. The surgeon's coming back to speak to me."

"Okay. I'll get back to you soon. I love you, Mum."

"Love you too."

Finn stared at his phone, sitting like a bomb in the palm of his hand. If he had X-ray vision, it would have melted by now. He'd ended the call but seemed unable to move. Or think.

Minutes ago, he'd been happily texting Eden, flirting, if he was honest.

Now this.

He lifted his head and blinked a couple of times. The rising moon swayed unsteadily, like a mirage over the water. Finn leaned heavily on the wooden railing, high up on the clifftop above the beach. Sandy track beneath his running shoes, salty and a sharp ocean breeze in his lungs, cool against his skin. This had always been one of his favorite spots near Del Mar. He usually loved it there.

Now this.

Cooling now after running full-on for a couple of miles, his skin was icy where his damp tank top stuck to him, the breeze adding an extra chill factor.

He raked a hand through his hair while replaying the facts in his mind.

Dad was in the hospital. He'd had a heart attack. Mum was waiting in the hospital. Waiting for the surgeon to tell her the real deal. The *prognosis.*

Testing his breath, he shakily inhaled. Exhaled. Breathed.

His Dad wasn't dead. Gordon Donohue was alive, would probably be fine.

Except, what if he wasn't?

Here Finn was, Gordon's only living son, on the other side of the world. A son who hadn't seen his father for going on two years. Why? Because sometimes being home was too hard. He hadn't always been the only son. He'd been the younger son once. Twelve years ago. Or was it thirteen?

How could he not remember when Matt died? He wasn't great with dates, but it was important.

The wooden railing's edges dug into his palms as he leaned over, pressing down. His legs felt weak, and it wasn't only the lactic acid buildup in his quads. It was everything.

He'd put himself under a lot of pressure these past few years, trying to do a job he might not be capable of doing, at least not properly. Sometimes his typical M.O.—jump in headfirst, learn to swim later—wasn't such a great strategy.

With only a short time left to develop his project proposal, the countdown was on to win the special funding, and if he failed, it wasn't only the end of his job; it was the end of a dream.

Matt's dream.

When his older brother died from heart failure at only twenty-four, Finn knew what he had to do. Continue the work Matt, a brilliant young scientist, had trained for—trying to find a cure for the people like him with 'dodgy hearts.' Congenital heart disease.

His brother had died of a dysfunctional heart, and almost broke the hearts of his family too.

Finn had worked hard, much harder than most people thought he could. The guy who was good at any sport you threw at him, from football to swimming to running. The guy who'd been a natural sports marketing consultant if only he could get his head around statistics and other mathematical concepts. He'd stepped up and taken on a double load at university, studying business and marketing. He'd done it too. When the reading and analysis got to be too much, the pure weight of information he had to absorb weighing him down, he'd found new ways to learn.

He'd graduated with distinction, giving the one-fingered salute to dyslexia and every teacher who'd ever told him he wasn't smart enough. Matt was the only one who'd ever told Finn he could do whatever he set his mind to *if* he was willing to work for it.

But what now? What if Matt's dream was finally over? Finn had given it his best shot, but he had no idea if his work would pay off. And, the scarier thought, what if he had no dream of his own?

Before calling his mum back, he needed a plan. He'd fly home to Australia. Maybe he'd stay this time. He could find another job back home before things hit the fan at Magna Smart, and settle down near his parents. He'd never bought a house in the US, never committed to living there permanently.

Finn lifted his head and stared up at the darkening sky.

There was someone he needed to talk to before he could decide what to do next. Someone who'd help him find his way. Finn started jogging again, finding his stride, heading in the only direction that made sense. Her direction.

"Dammit, Faith, tell me again. What happened?" Eden flicked her gaze up to search her sister's face.

Faith remained silent, but her mouth hung open like the words were there; they'd just got lost on their way out. She stood, backed up against the oven, a heatproof mitt shaped like an alligator on one hand. A souvenir from a conference trip to Florida. Faith's hand idly opened and closed, making the little green monster's jaws *snap, snap*. Her sister's pale face contrasted sharply against her black hair and midnight-blue silk shirt.

Eden was afraid to touch Felicity again in case she accidentally killed her. Or worse. Although, when you thought about it, what could be worse than being killed? Her hands shaking, she reached for Felicity's pulse point on her neck.

She glanced around her white laminate kitchen, noting how the tiles sparkled under the downlights above the countertop. *At least the floor's clean.* She stopped, frozen in place. Being a neat freak was one thing, but being pleased about her friend's bloody body lying on her otherwise spotless floor was heading into seriously worrying territory.

"Faith." Eden stood, then reached over and grabbed the alligator's jaws. "Snap out of it. What happened?"

Faith shook her head, sending long strands of mirror-smooth hair flying every which way and back again. "She barged through your back door and said something about fish, then tripped and fell. She hit her head on the corner of the oven door. I was getting the muffins out. They're burnt, sorry. I think I spilled oil on the baking tray."

Eden shook her head. *Fish?* Okay. She'd get to the bottom of that later. Her biggest concern right now was Faith being charged with murder. Murder by muffin. This was not good. She was panicking, but couldn't seem to calm herself.

Eden sat on the floor and returned her attention to Felicity. She remembered her basic fire warden training. First priority, check the injured person for a pulse. Done. There was a definite thudding going on. "I've got her pulse. Thank goodness."

She brushed her hand across her friend's forehead. Short strands of hair got in the way. Under them was an angry-looking cut, leaking droplets of crimson.

Eden scooted over to the low cabinets under the sink and grabbed a clean dishcloth. Next, she pulled herself up to wet it under the faucet and wash the blood from her hands.

Seated back at Felicity's side, she pressed the cloth to the cut and cleaned it as best she could. It wasn't too deep. Should she dress it with something? Disinfect it? Probably.

Then came the fire safety awareness. Fragments of things she'd learned dribbled back into her brain. *Come on, Eden.* She should recall this stuff instantly.

"Faith, turn off the oven at the power."

Her sister rushed to the left and flipped the switch. Why couldn't she think clearly? Oh. The noise. The smoke detector's incessant beeping was mind-numbingly loud. How had she not registered it until now?

"Now the smoke detector, please."

While Faith dragged a chair across the floor to reach the smoke detector, Eden gazed down at Felicity. She was breathing but not responding to her name.

Then a familiar sound cut through all the other noise. Her phone in the living room, scatting with Ella Fitzgerald's voice: her ringtone. Who could be calling her?

A loud crash made her jump.

What the...?

The front door rattled on its hinges with the force of an enraged bull or something similar barging into it. Another almighty crash and the door struck the wall with a resounding thud. The bull charged down the hall and into the kitchen, only stopping when it fell on its ass. A mighty fine ass, she noticed as the man, not a bull, hauled himself upright.

Finn. In her kitchen.

Finn had knocked her door down. Because he worried she was in danger? Eden's heart thudded wildly at the thought of him caring about her.

He stood there, panting like he'd run a mile in seven seconds flat. Dressed like he had, in clinging running shorts and a tank top darkened with sweat across the front of his chest.

She'd never seen him so naked. Never seen his bare legs before. Extremely muscular, toned legs they were too. And none of this trendy metrosexual manscaping for Finn. He had proper golden-brown leg hair and tufts of chest hair sticking out of his top. Not too much, just right. She'd sure like to tug on it.

Finn stared down at her, his hand reaching forward. "I thought there was a fire. Are you alright?" he asked as he retracted his hand and ran it through his nicely tousled hair. "Is... she alright?" Finn nodded at Felicity, his biceps flexing and chunky shoulder muscles moving in all kinds of interesting ways.

Eden felt a lot better than she had a few seconds ago. Well, her lower belly was decidedly warm and tingly, along with her inner thighs. It was a teeny bit sexy, even considering the circumstances.

Wait, she looked a mess! Felicity was still unconscious, and Faith had a mangled, singed alligator hand. What was she meant to say to Finn in the current situation?

Hands shaking, she gesticulated wildly like a cop at the scene of an accident where all the traffic lights had blown, trying to find some way out of a bad situation while salvaging some dignity and avoiding a head-on collision.

She could still be polite amongst all the mayhem. "I'm fine, thank you." Eden nodded. "Would you like a muffin?"

Finn sucked in a breath. Acrid, smoke-tainted air greeted his lungs. He coughed, shaking his head. Eden was clearly out of her tree if she thought anything about this scene constituted *fine*.

And what the hell was he doing here in the thick of it? It was a good question, but one he didn't have time to examine just yet.

He leaned against the edge of a shiny countertop, catching his breath, then turned his head, following the stench of smoke, and spied the blackened muffin corpses on the stovetop. "No, Eden. I don't want a muffin. Do you want me to call an ambulance?"

Eden shook her head. "No ambulance. Felicity will be okay." She sounded more like she was trying to convince herself.

What the hell was going on tonight? Finn had been out for a run, feeling fine, when his world imploded as if struck by a planet-sized Death Star.

Before he'd even decided what he was doing, his feet had been in motion, carrying him directly to Eden's house. Whether he'd planned to talk to her, or yell at her to give him a reason to stay, or tackle her to the ground and kiss her into submission, he wasn't sure.

Probably a little from option A and a whole lot of option B. Option C would be cool. Although if she wanted to push him to the ground and straddle him, he'd be amenable.

Finn slumped back against the kitchen cabinets. He must be losing his mind. He should be thinking about his family. Eden had some sort of disaster going on, and all he could think about was sex. But who was he kidding? This thing with Doctor Eden was more than sex.

He watched her deflate at his feet, her shoulders slumping, air hissing out between her teeth. Silver stars dotted her over-sized gray T-shirt dress. They glinted under the kitchen lights, winking at him. The shirt had ridden up her smooth thighs and gaped low at the front.

Not looking, not looking.

Looking.

Hell, yes, looking.

His groin tightened as his gaze skimmed her shadowed neck-line and he caught a glimpse of black lace. Her nipples stood erect under the thin cotton fabric.

It was none of his business. He needed to get his eyes off her tempting curves. Stat.

His gaze darting left, he spied what would have been imme-diately obvious if he hadn't been so damned hung up on Eden and her outfit and what lay underneath.

The stove had been on fire, Eden's sister was standing there by the stove, and wore an alligator puppet on her hand. Felicity still lay on the ground. What the hell? Was this a fun girls' night in Eden's world?

He frowned down at Eden. "What did you do to Felicity?"

"Why do you assume it was me? Faith was the one who tried to murder her by muffin." She breathed out slowly, working to regain her usual calm. "Can't you help, Mr. I Know Everything About First Aid? She hit her head on the corner of the oven door."

He blinked at Eden. "*Okay.* Let's see how she's doing." He dropped to his knees beside Eden, and she scooted across to give him more room.

Checking Felicity's pulse at her wrist, he counted out steady beats. Good. She'd be okay, assuming that cut on her forehead wasn't too deep. He glanced at Eden. "Do you have some gloves?"

She nodded and left the room for a moment. When she returned, she held out a pair of disposable gloves and some alcohol wipes. Finn took them and offered Eden a tight smile.

He put on the gloves and examined the cut on Felicity's and saw Eden must have cleaned it up a little. He cleaned the area and noted Felicity's eyelids fluttering. Good. It didn't look major.

Finn looked across to Eden now sitting back on the floor, and noticed the way she stared at him. Eyes wide, lips parted, a tremble in her hands where they rested on her knees. She might be in shock. In no state for serious conversations.

He turned to Faith. Backed up against the kitchen counter, arms crossed across her chest, she stood silent and still. He caught her eye and tipped his chin. "Faith, could you go to the bathroom and check the medicine cabinet? I need some disinfectant and a dressing or bandage of some sort. And a clean washcloth."

Eden's sister shook herself slightly and headed toward the bathroom without saying a word.

Finn returned his attention to Felicity and smoothed back her hair. The cut on her forehead wasn't too serious on its own, but she'd struck her head. He couldn't rule out a concussion.

"How long has she been unconscious?"

Eden turned her head toward him, a confused frown crossing her face. "Not sure. A few minutes? I heard a crash and came from the living room as quick as I could. Faith said she ran in the back door, then tripped and smacked her head on the oven door."

Probably not enough to completely knock her out. Leaning close to Felicity's mouth to check her breathing, he almost choked on toxic fumes. The good news was she was breathing. The bad news was she was breathing out nearly pure alcohol. Felicity was smashed.

He nodded at Eden, who now sat on her butt, her long, bare, strokable legs stretched out in front of her. Cute pink socks with black bows on the edges covered her feet.

Focus.

"Does she usually drink much?"

"Felicity? No, only a beer or two after work. A glass of wine sometimes."

"Well, she stinks like a brewery right now."

Eden frowned, pursing her pink lips. She sniffed the air. "Oh."

"Let's patch her up and see how she goes."

Faith reappeared with the medical supplies, so he cleaned Felicity's forehead, then asked for some ice. Once he'd put together an ice pack, he applied it to the area too, hoping it would at least keep the bruising to a minimum.

Felicity's face contorted, then her lips parted, and she spat out, "S'cold."

Finn's mouth twitched at the corner. "She lives!"

He glanced over at Eden, who'd pressed a hand to her mouth, then she dropped it back into her lap and breathed out slowly.

Leaning over, he repositioned the ice pack. "Yes, it's cold. Talk to me, Felicity. How many drinks have you had tonight?"

Felicity gazed at the ceiling as if trying to remember something from a long time ago. "Um, beer, three maybe, couple of wines. Then Fish got tequila shots. Slammers."

Slammers. Causing her to slam her head into an immovable object. Sounded about right. "Who's Fish?"

"McTavish. Call him Fish for short. Suits him." She snorted and smacked her head lightly. "He got me drunk, but I got him drunker. Got him to spill some secrets." She tapped the side of her nose a few times, missing the first time.

Finn whipped his head around to look at Eden and noticed her eyebrows had shot up to somewhere around her hairline. He moved to sit behind Felicity and helped her sit up, supporting her shoulders. Eden took hold of Felicity's hands and hauled her friend upright.

Finn stared over Felicity's shoulder into Eden's eyes. "Okay, let's get you sobered up, and then you can tell us about these secrets." It was probably time more people knew what was going on with McTavish.

Eden turned to her sister, again hovering by the stove. "Faith, put the coffee maker on, please. We're going to need some caffeinating."

"Yes, boss." Humor had returned to Faith's voice.

It took them a while to get Felicity into a more sober state. Eden plied her with coffee and water, plus a couple of Advil. Now, seated at her small kitchen table, surrounded by smaller women, Finn felt like a giant in Fairyland as he sipped his coffee.

They listened in silence, and as Felicity's story unfolded, Eden's bright violet eyes grew ever wider, gleaming under the kitchen lights with a kind of righteous fury.

His own skin heated as his fists clenched and unclenched on the cool tabletop. But he kept his shit together and listened, letting the details tumble from Felicity's lips. It was worth the wait.

McTavish, the scumbag, had a lot of things coming to him, none of them good. And Finn would be only too happy to deliver them to the man's doorstep in a steaming pile. One look at Eden told him she felt the same.

He nodded at Eden, and a glimmer of a smile crossed her lips. Something passed between them, no words required. He wanted to be on the same side. For better or worse.

He had the feeling there was a hell of a lot of worse still to come. This workplace stuff, McTavish's transgressions, it could end up in court. He'd been forced to gather information already, but Finn couldn't say too much to the other people around the table or he could be on the wrong side of the law. But that wasn't all that was on his mind.

His father was sick, and he worried his mother wouldn't cope on her own. She'd fallen apart after her eldest son died. Matthew had been her pride and joy, her favorite, even though she denied it. If she lost the man she still called her sweetheart, she'd probably fall into a black pit of depression again. Who knew if she'd ever recover?

All things considered, Finn should quit his job and head home to Melbourne permanently. If he didn't get the special projects funding or if McTavish took his project over, there'd be no point staying on at Magna Smart anyway. If he could get out in time, he had options to consider.

There were other jobs, not as lucrative or potentially groundbreaking, but jobs he could do in Australia. He could buy a house back home.

But that wasn't all he was considering.

He glanced across the table at the woman with sparkling violet eyes. He had her to consider too.

Chapter Sixteen

Faith: Night, Babycakes. Don't let Work Guy keep you up!

Eden: Shut up

Faith: ☺

Two hours after Felicity's staggering revelations, Eden's head was spinning, but her friend was still basically a corpse on legs. Eden helped Felicity into her spare bedroom, where the bed was already made up.

Eden pulled the sheets up to her chin by lamplight. Felicity was petite, and with her hair all messed up, she could have easily passed for a teenager. Eden shouldn't worry about her brilliant research assistant, but somehow, as her manager, she struggled to switch off her concern.

Apparently, Felicity had arrived at Eden's on foot, having staggered down the hill from the bar attached to a Mexican restaurant in Del Mar. Eden was happier knowing she was tucked up here, safe and warm. With it being the weekend, she could stay and sleep off her hangover tomorrow morning if she wanted.

Eden flicked off the bedside lamp and softly shut the door, then took a deep calming breath before walking back toward the kitchen.

After cleaning up the aftermath of the muffin disaster, Faith had headed home. That left only Finn still awake and very much present in her quiet house. Just the two of them, alone together. Why had he stayed? She suspected it wasn't to chat about work.

Breathe, Eden. Don't forget to breathe.

Eden crept down the hall and into the living room. His presence affected her body even before her eyes registered his outline in the lamp-lit room. The skin prickled at her nape as goosebumps ran up her arms. But she wasn't frightened of him. Oh no. Tendrils of heat chased away the goosebumps not caused by fear.

Bent over her stereo on the low side table, he was flicking through the crates that housed her vinyl record collection. Finn was stupidly sexy in his black running gear, the soft light outlining the long lines of his muscular body. His perfect, taut ass was a fine display, along with calf and thigh muscles she'd like to lick. A completely inappropriate thought about a colleague. But he was more than that.

She liked the way he'd taken charge of the situation with Felicity. He'd been kind and attentive, as he'd been when tending her own injured ankle.

Finn had made polite conversation with Faith and Felicity. More than polite, he'd been... caring. Then he'd sat and listened to Felicity's story and gazed straight into Eden's eyes. What she'd seen there — concern, understanding, determination — had forced her to reassess her assumptions about Finn. He made her want to trust him, which was something she'd never have predicted.

She still didn't know why he'd shown up at her place tonight. Whatever he'd wanted had been forgotten in the earlier mayhem.

The song now drifting from her hi-fi speakers made her suck in a sharp breath: 'Dream a Little Dream of Me.' The song about whispered *I love yous* and craving someone's kiss.

Eden took a few more steps into the room and came to a halt on the edge of the wool rug. Its crimson red looked a deeper shade of wine in the half-light. Only a few feet of carpet lay between them.

Finn straightened, as if sensing her presence. Then he turned to face her and hit her with a devastating high-beam smile, followed by a smoldering full-body inspection that made her nipples peak, her kneecaps melt, and her heart pound.

Now she couldn't breathe.

Something in her expression must have given him pause because he dropped the smile and studied his feet. Lucky, or she might have been tempted to either smack him or rub up against him and purr like a cat.

Eden sucked in another fortifying breath and asked him straight up, "Why did you come over tonight, Finn?"

He tensed, then raised himself to full height, a slow smile crossing his face. "It was spur of the moment. I was running along the clifftop track and realized I was close to your place, so I thought I'd stop by and say hello."

Liar. She wasn't sure how she knew, but he was lying. Through his teeth. His tight smile didn't quite reach those stunning eyes, currently deep and stormy. An ocean at night.

Eden crossed her arms and tilted her head to one side. "I don't think so. Try again." Her gaze took in the front view of his fine form, the firm contours of his chest mercilessly outlined by his tight-fitting tank top. Not to mention the impressive bulge in his shorts. She flicked her eyes back up. "I believe the part about running. You look... fit." She swallowed on a dry throat.

His gaze roamed her face, then dropped to her breasts, where it lingered a while, a good long while, before running right down her body. It felt like a physical caress, the weight of his gaze tugging at muscles deep inside, turning her blood to a sticky syrup.

Finn stepped closer. Closer still. He cleared his throat and said, "I was worried about something. I wanted to talk it over with someone honest, and I thought of you."

He had? It was flattering, depending on what he meant by *honest*. Did he mean blunt? Rude? But since he'd been so helpful with Felicity, the least she could do was hear him out.

Besides, with what they'd learned about McTavish tonight, she needed him on her side. Eden waved him toward her sofa. Where, not so long ago, he'd leaned his long, hard body over her, pressed her down, and kissed her, sending her body into chaos.

She sat heavily and gestured for him to sit beside her. "Okay, take a seat."

Finn flopped down on the sofa and stretched out those long, muscular legs in front of him. One arm extended along the back of the headrest toward her. For a moment, she considered snuggling into his side, letting him wrap his arm around her.

But she didn't move toward him. She couldn't take the plunge. Instead, she scuttled to the opposite end of the sofa and sat with legs crossed, her stretchy T-shirt dress pulled down until it almost covered her knees. Nerves had her threading her fingers through her loose hair, pushing it behind her shoulders.

When she finally darted a glance at him, he was already watching her. His face was more serious now, his forehead crinkled into ridges like corrugated cardboard.

He started talking, his voice low and husky. "I had a call from Mum. Dad's sick. A heart attack. Sounds like he needs a bypass. I heard the news and just ran in this direction."

"Oh no. I'm so sorry." Eden's heart leaped up somewhere around her throat. She moved closer, reached for him without thinking. She touched his cheek, the rasp of stubble on his angular jaw.

Finn's hand was suddenly over hers, holding her fingertips against his face. His skin was hot, making her want to pull away. Making her want to press closer to him too.

He sighed. "Thanks. I mean, for caring. You seem like a caring person, Eden. The way you look out for your sister and friends like Felicity. I guess that's why I thought of you." His warm breath blew gently over her hand and arm. "I should fly home to Melbourne and help look after Dad, make sure Mum's alright. But I don't know if I can make the choice. I might be too selfish."

He turned and captured her with a glittering stare, at the same time rubbing his thumb across the back of her hand. Back and forth. She shivered, and not with cold. Although she was now acutely aware of how few clothes she wore — an oversized T-shirt dress with black lace underwear underneath. Her legs and arms were bare. Like she was ready for bed.

She whispered near Finn's ear, no need to shout when they were sitting so close, "You're caring too. Look how you helped me when I was injured, how you helped Felicity tonight." She took a sharp breath. Why was he telling her about his family? What else was he trying to say? "Why wouldn't you want to go home?"

Eden hadn't realized how much she wanted to know his answer until she asked the question. Would he miss her? It was crazy to think so. Presumptuous, anyway. But deep inside, she hoped so.

He shifted slightly, bringing her hand down along his jaw to his lips. He kissed her palm, a gentle brush of his lips. But the sensation radiated to every cell of her body, every inch of her skin.

Finn moved her hand back to rest on his cheek. "I wanted to ask if you think I should stay here. In San Diego."

He wanted her opinion? But why should it matter to him? Could it be what she'd hoped? He *would* miss her. But the way he said it made it sound like a bigger decision than she'd realized. Was he planning on moving back to Australia permanently?

At some point, she'd shuffled closer, and his hand now wrapped around her shoulders. He pulled her into his side.

Eden let out a shaky breath and stammered, "Would you be coming back?"

"That's the question." He shifted again, turning slightly, so they sat face to face.

Her hand traveled around to the nape of his neck. She was so close to him now that her forehead rested against his. How had that happened? He breathed out, invading her senses with his scent. Pure male. Clean sweat, salty like the sea. A hint of citrus and something else. Just him.

Finn's voice cracked on the words, "Give me something, Eden. Please."

Her heart flipped over and fluttered wildly at his honest entreaty. She wanted to be equally honest. "I can't ask you to stay." She hesitated, searching his eyes. Found a melting softness paired with a low smolder. She licked her lower lip. "But I'd like you to. More than I can explain."

Without warning, his lips crashed down on hers, and all she could do was cling to him, to save herself from drowning. He licked across her lower lip, tasting her until she opened to him.

Eden wanted to taste him too, to experience all he had to offer. Her tongue darted out to meet his, and they tangled together. Opening herself to him, she kissed him deeper, almost merging into him. She touched his face, threaded her fingers through his hair, and pulled him closer.

His hand moved from her shoulder, skimming her bare arm until his touch settled on her hip. The weight of his hand steadied her. Otherwise, she might have flown off the sofa, straight up into orbit.

Before she knew it, she'd shimmied onto his lap, never once breaking the kiss. With her legs straddling him, knees pressed into the sofa, she snuggled down, then gasped as his hardness pressed into her. The whole, long, manly length of him. Everything heated and throbbed.

It would take only the slightest of touches, exactly where she needed it, for her to go from zero to orgasmic in sixty seconds flat. But she wasn't at zero, no way. Her body was all revved up, like the engine of Finn's prized Chevy.

Finn's other hand came up to cup her breast, massaging her through the thin fabric of her dress. Eager for his attention, her nipples leaped up to greet him. It felt so good, so right that she forgot to freak out. For a moment.

She broke the kiss, pressed her lips to his neck, just below his ear, and subtly moved his hand from her breast to her other hip. He didn't seem to notice how she'd shifted his attention.

When he skimmed his hand down the outside of her hip, then back up her sensitive inner thigh, she was powerless. Eden couldn't stop him, didn't want to try. In fact, her legs fell open slightly.

He teased the hem of her dress higher, inch by tantalizing inch, rubbing small circles into her thigh. She glanced down to find her underwear exposed, his fingers skimming their lace edge. Looking up again, she found him staring down at her with darkened eyes, his pupils dilated. His full lips were parted, still damp from their kisses.

"Is this okay?" His words were rough and deep.

Eden nodded, and their gazes locked. "Yes. I want you to touch me." She hadn't realized it was what she wanted, but it was true.

With those words, some of the tension flowed from his body, and hers too. His fingers brushed across her underwear, leaving trails of tingles in their wake. He stroked her, slowly at first, then faster, teasing her, circling. When his fingers dipped beneath the delicate fabric and touched her hot flesh, the wetness between her thighs, she gasped. He found her tight bud, then stroked her until she moaned. Everything stilled, her vision dimming, everything within her poised on the brink.

Finn moved again, running his fingers through her folds, right into the center of her. His fingers slid in and out, finding a rhythm, driving her mad with desire. Finding the right spot deep inside. She gasped, gripping onto his strong shoulders.

Just. Like. That.

"Yes. Please, Finn." Her voice was breathy. Desperate. She needed this. Needed him.

A light flicked on down the hall. She could have sobbed. Felicity was up. Footsteps echoed, moving toward them.

Finn stilled his hand and withdrew it from her needy body. He kissed her lips lightly while straightening her dress. She sucked in a deep breath, then tried to stop from rocking her hips.

The kitchen lights flicked on now, only a few feet from where they sat entwined together, Eden on Finn's lap. It had to be obvious what was going on.

"Oh shit. Sorry, guys. Just getting a glass of water." Felicity's voice was high and squeaky. Eden watched her friend retreat toward the spare bedroom.

The hallway lights flicked off again, cloaking Eden and Finn in welcome semi-darkness.

Eden felt as if she'd ruined her younger friend's innocence. Although it wasn't really true. Felicity had a dirty mouth at times, telling stories that made Eden blush.

But Eden wasn't blushing now as she grabbed Finn's hand and placed it back on her upper thigh. Even in the dim light, she caught the way his eyes sparkled, more black than green.

His chest rose and fell heavily as he inched his fingers back to where he'd left off. She gripped his shoulders again, hanging on for dear life. She was so close that she could taste it.

"Oh, sweetheart. You feel so good." The hot words rushed from Finn's mouth to her ear, to everywhere else. "Show me how much you like it."

He'd pushed aside her underwear and thrust two fingers inside her, finding that perfect spot again. Golden stars twinkled on the edge of her vision. Suddenly, he pressed down on her clit with his thumb and sent her soaring.

A strangled cry escaped her throat, until he swallowed it in a deep, all-encompassing kiss. Their tongues tangled as wave after wave of pleasure crashed through her system. Finally, she stilled, raining soft kisses over his full lips and leaning her forehead against his.

This man. This man had given her so much pleasure, unselfishly. He'd surprised her, not for the first time. Eden breathed in his scent, waiting for her heartbeat to settle. She wanted to ask for more, for everything. Not only physical release, but the type of real connection she'd been searching for; so far, without any luck. Could he be the one to give it to her?

Maybe. He was a definite maybe.

He kissed her lips, her earlobe, her throat. Then his voice came out deep, with a tremor that made her heart beat faster: "Can we move this to the bedroom? I want to hear you moan some more." He kissed a path down her throat, warm, wet kisses sending bolts of electricity flying to all the best places. Almost zapping her good sense.

Her heart was still pounding. She'd love to say yes, but... "Not now, not tonight. Felicity's here. Anyway, it's a bit fast for me."

"Hate to break this to you, but I think Felicity worked out what we were up to."

Eden frowned, then clenched her fist and punched him lightly on the shoulder.

Finn chuckled. "Okay. Not tonight, but soon? Don't keep me waiting too long, Doc."

He trailed his knuckles over her right breast, across the hard tip of her nipple. Sparks shot from the tender flesh straight to her core. If she let him, he'd take her there again. Right to the precipice, then over the edge until she flew. And she could touch him too. All of him.

She nodded, lost in the gorgeous afterglow. He'd touched her, given her pleasure. But how would he feel about her once he knew all her body's secrets? She wasn't ready to find out. Not yet. But soon, like he said.

Finn gave one thrust of his hips, pressing himself against her, reminding her how much he wanted her. He groaned deep in his throat.

With a heavy sigh, Eden clambered off his lap, but when she tried to stand, she staggered. Finn was immediately there beside her, offering his strong hand. She took it just until she was steadier on her feet. Even standing inches apart, she felt his body's heat like a physical touch.

Every part of her body wanted him. Only her stubborn mind was stopping what she knew would be an amazing experience. But she wouldn't sleep with him just for the thrill — it had to be more. For her these days, it was a requirement. She was interested only in a permanent, ongoing position, nothing casual. Even so, she struggled to keep her eyes above his waist.

Finn placed his hands on his hips. "How's your ankle, by the way?"

"Good. Better every day." She flexed her ankle, showing him how it had loosened up.

"Glad to hear it. I wanted to say sorry again, for hurting you. I've felt so guilty about it and for pushing you into letting me drive you to work." He frowned, his eyebrows pinching together.

"It's okay." Eden was surprised but happy to find it was okay. "I might have secretly enjoyed it. A tiny bit. Not being injured, because that was maddening. But having you drive me around, spending time with you, that part was... nice."

Not at first. At first, she couldn't stand being in the same car with him, confined in close quarters. But after a couple of times, she'd enjoyed it. More than she cared to admit.

"Nice?" Finn sputtered out a laugh. "*Nice* is for little boys or old grandpas. Not someone like me."

"Someone like you?" She looked him up and down, starting with his eyes before running her gaze over his emphatically male form. Definitely not a little boy or an old grandpa; he was in his prime. So handsome, taut, and strong. Hard. But caring too. He'd even made her laugh. All the things she'd been fantasizing about lately.

He raised an eyebrow. "Someone you secretly hope will drag you into the back seat of his car and strip you bare, then touch you, and lick you, and ravage you until you can't think straight." His eyes sparkled, dancing with glints of reflected lamp light.

"Oh, right. Someone like that." She could no longer think straight, not when he'd reached for her hip and pulled her against his hard body, still clad only in tight-fitting running gear. She couldn't help tilting her hips to meet him until their bodies fit together. Perfectly.

"Someone who might do exactly that one day." His voice was low and rumbly, an ominous roll of thunder in the darkness.

His lips crashed down onto hers again. So unexpected that a yelp burst from her throat. But then he caressed her hip as he kissed her, taking his time.

Eden opened her mouth to him, welcoming him, tasting his lips. Every nerve ending in her body sprang back to life, although it had been only a few minutes since he'd debauched her. Desire rose inside again, heat pulsing insistently between her thighs, her heart pounding loud in her ears.

God, this man knows how to kiss.

He pulled away. As suddenly as the kiss had started, it was over, and she almost cried at the way the cool air swirled between them.

Finn ran a hand through his hair, his chest rising and falling. "I'll let you off the hook this time. Let you get to bed." His voice cracked on the word *bed*. He was on edge, so close to losing control. Over her. The thought shouldn't have made her belly flip over with excitement, but it did.

"Thanks for letting me know," he said.

"Letting you know?" she repeated like a mindless parrot.

"Thanks for letting me know there's a reason to stay."

Eden nodded, too worked up to say much of anything. At least anything coherent that required words or sentences. Her body was practically shouting, begging him to stay. Stay in the country, in her life, in her house, in her bed, right inside her.

Woah. Hang on, brain. Let's take a moment. If things were moving too fast before, her mind was racing ahead at turbo speed now.

Finn brushed shaking fingertips over her mouth. "Goodnight, Doctor Eden. I'll call you tomorrow." He turned and marched to the hallway and out her front door, closing it gently behind him.

Finn had thrown himself against that door earlier, but thankfully hadn't broken the lock. The door had probably had the shock of its life. Eden knew the feeling.

Alone now in her quiet house, she let her wobbly knees give way and sank onto the sofa with a loud *whoosh*. She ran her own fingertips over her lips, tracing where they tingled with the memory of his kiss. Not to mention the tingling from the other things he'd done to her.

Finn Donohue had touched her, made her gasp out loud with the force of a stunning climax. He'd made her want to shriek like a banshee, wake Felicity and the rest of the neighborhood.

She'd had a casual sex romp on her sofa, been carried away by the moment, and totally forgot to think for a while. Allowed herself to only feel. It had been far too long.

She'd freaking loved it.

Oh boy. What have I gotten myself into?

Come Monday, she had absolutely no clue what she'd say to the man.

Chapter Seventeen

LittleMissPerfect: I have to cancel our date. I'm sorry but I've met someone else...

Eden sat at her kitchen table the following morning with a steaming cup of coffee and a bowl of granola in front of her, staring at the message she'd tapped into her phone. Should she hit send? Then it would be done. HotAussie007 would remain a fantasy, someone who'd made her laugh, sure, but no more. She could say goodbye. *No harm, no foul.*

She crossed her satin robe more firmly around her waist and tightened the sash. She couldn't do it. Not yet.

Yes, something had happened with Finn. More than a kiss. *Oh yes*. She squeezed her thighs together. It had been much more than a kiss but less than a relationship. So where did that leave her this morning? She had absolutely no idea.

After deleting the draft message, she let out a long, shaky breath. There was still time to think about it — no need to rush her decision.

She looked up and caught Felicity's gaze. Her friend, who'd entered the kitchen in silence, stood on the opposite side of the table, dressed in Eden's old UCSD sweatshirt and pajama shorts.

Felicity stared at Eden before flicking her eyes sideways to the coffee maker. Eden took the opportunity to study her. She looked like a disheveled clown who'd been stomped on by a horse and rolled around in the hay and muck at the end of a hard circus night. Or something.

Eden tipped her chin at her friend. "You're looking better." No point telling her that she looked like she needed to be hosed down.

Felicity rubbed a hand over her fluffy mop of blond hair, making a clump stick out sideways. "Thanks. I feel like the proverbial something the cat dragged in. If it dragged in a dead rat, half chewed, maybe with its eyeballs hanging out."

Eden's mouth twitched, but she held in her laugh. At least Felicity had her mental faculties mostly intact.

Felicity placed her hands on her slim hips. "So, Finn, huh? Told you he was hot. But you were all, 'Oh no, I wouldn't touch him with a ten-foot pole.'"

Eden sipped her coffee, taking a moment to compose some kind of defense. But nothing sprang to mind. *Forget it.* Her research assistant knew her too well.

"I changed my mind." She placed her mug back on the table with a thunk and studied its design—a printed image of the periodic table with the slogan 'Scientists do it periodically.' It was true. But the period between the last time she 'did it' and now was quite long.

Of course, she and Finn hadn't 'done it.' Not quite.

"You changed your mind? I thought you hated him?" Felicity narrowed her eyes, apparently trying to read Eden's thoughts.

Eden shrugged. "We've spent a fair amount of time together, and we got talking. You know, the usual. I don't hate him. I *like* him." It was the first time she'd said that out loud.

She liked Finn. The idea needed some more considera-tion—later, when her friend wasn't staring at her. She took another sip of coffee, glancing at Felicity over the rim of the mug.

Felicity smiled, a crooked, knowing smile, and turned to shuf-fle over to the coffee maker on the counter. Slowly, carefully, she poured herself a mug and added three heaping teaspoons of sugar. No artificial sweeteners for Felicity. She wouldn't put on an ounce of fat either.

Felicity returned to the table, pulled out a chair, and gingerly lowered herself. She clutched her head between both hands and rested her elbows on the tabletop. "I've got a killer headache, so tell it to me straight. Are you in love with him?"

Eden's stomach rolled over, and something throbbed inside her chest. It couldn't be her heart; that would be too inconve-nient. She couldn't have fallen for Finn.

She worried at her lip and took her time before answering. "Of course not. It's just a sex thing. Obviously. I haven't had any action in who knows how long. Nothing that's got my heart racing, anyway."

Felicity tipped her head to one side. "But Finn did? He got your heart racing?"

Heavens, yes! Her heart, her mind. Also setting tingles racing to all the places he looked, let alone touched.

Felicity grinned, her blue eyes dancing. "No need to answer. I can tell what you're thinking by the look on your face. You might want to close your mouth, by the way. Anyway, I heard the noises you were making last night."

Oh. My. God.

Eden's face flamed, the heat spreading up from her chest, burning like an out-of-control wildfire. She clunked her head onto the table, sending her hair tumbling around her face. Per-haps she'd just live here in her hair cave until her embarrassment died down.

Felicity giggled, then spoke more seriously. "It's okay, you know, to fall in love."

Love? The word had nothing to do with anything. Eden peered at her friend through the curtain of her own hair.

"And it's okay to have sex occasionally, or whatever it was you two were doing," Felicity said with a grin. "Give yourself a break. Let yourself cut loose once in a while."

Eden lifted her head and nodded once. Firmly. "You're right. We didn't even sleep together, anyway." Not yet. Her body tightened, and every molecule screamed with frustration at the fact. "But he said he'd call me today, so it's all good. We need to talk. I can tell him that nothing should happen between us on a personal level. Right?"

Felicity sipped her coffee, her eyes filled with that annoying, knowing look Faith got sometimes. It said: *You're a naïve fool, but I like you anyway.*

A weird buzzing had Eden crinkling her nose. Her phone vibrated, still set to silent, and it danced across the table. Eden stared at it, unsure whether to freak out about her phone being psychic. Not that she believed in such things. She did, however, believe there was such a thing as an overeager *almost* lover calling at eight o'clock on a Sunday morning. The morning after the night before. Although she didn't recognize the number on the display.

She sighed and took the call. "Hello?"

"Eden?" There was a pause. Long enough for her to register that the deep male voice was Finn's, but it sounded weird. Thick and heavy, as if he were talking underwater. "Sorry to call so early, but I wanted to let you know I'm on a flight to Australia."

"Finn? You're where? What flight to Australia?" Babbling. She was babbling like a loon, but she thought they'd discussed this last night. As much as they'd discussed anything, in between all the kissing and touching...

"I'm calling you on the in-flight phone. Flew out of LAX a couple of hours ago. I wanted to tell you where I was so you didn't jump to conclusions. I haven't done a runner. After last night... you know."

She sure did. And the memory of it made all the blood rush to her cheeks and relevant pulse points around her body. She glanced up at Felicity and froze. Her friend was studying her expression, her no doubt strange, tense expression.

Eden closed her eyes for a moment. "I thought you'd decided. You told me you wanted to stay here in San Diego."

With me. You said I'd given you a reason to stay here.

The words perched there on the tip of her tongue, but she managed to hold them back. She didn't want him thinking she was the worst type of clingy woman, falling head over heels whenever shown the slightest affection.

Finn lowered his voice. "I do want to stay, like I said. But I called Mum again last night after leaving your place, and Dad's not too good. I need to see him ASAP, in case he takes a turn for the worse. I'll be back soon, though. Probably in a week."

Eden's hand covered her mouth. She spoke through her fingers. "Are you sure? Your poor mother, she must be out of her head with worry. Take your time. I can talk to McTavish if you like."

She could? Why she'd volunteered to talk to their boss about his personal issues was beyond her. Except, she had a tendency to take on other people's problems as her own, especially when it was someone she cared deeply about.

Eden rubbed her hand across her hot forehead and took a calming breath. How had her attitude to Finn changed so quickly? Just because he'd given her an orgasm? A mind-melting, spine-tingling orgasm, admittedly. But even so, she was an intelligent, self-sufficient woman who didn't want to feel like she couldn't breathe because the man she wanted to sleep with was flying to the other side of the planet.

Firetrucking feelings.

"No worries, I'll email McTavish. But it's sweet of you to offer." She heard his smile, the cheeky emphasis on the word *sweet*. As if she was sweet on him. "But you could wish me luck. And a safe journey. Or say you'll miss me, or you want to kiss me again. Or something more." He exhaled in her ear.

Eden wanted to breathe him in. Hug him close and kiss him goodbye, then ask him to come back soon. She wanted to tell him no one had ever kissed her like he had. Like he meant it.

"Of course. Good luck. Have a safe journey." *I'll miss you.* Pesky tip of the tongue. She tucked the words away for later. "Talk soon."

Finn chuckled. "I hope so, Doctor Eden."

With that, he ended the call, and Eden placed her phone on the laminate tabletop, staring at it for a few seconds.

Felicity cleared her throat, loudly. "That totally sounded like just a sex thing. No subtext hanging in the air or anything. Much."

Eden slid her eyes up to meet Felicity's and bit her lip before responding. "Am I really so transparent?"

Her friend nodded, her mouth tipping up in a smile. "As a pane of glass. But it's okay, it's different for you. It's kind of…"

"Sweet?" Eden winced. She was a lot of things, but sweet wasn't one of them. Not usually.

"Yeah, sweet. Like you're in *luuurve*." Felicity rolled her eyes and clutched her chest dramatically.

Not the 'L' word again. She'd been avoiding it in her own brain, ducking and weaving like she was back in high school playing dodgeball, trying not to get hit. Or if she did get hit, trying to minimize the damage. Minor bruising, she could deal with, as opposed to a smack in the face and a broken nose. She'd always sucked at dodgeball.

Eden threw her hands in the air. "What the hell am I doing? Finn's my colleague—we're competing against each other. I can't afford to be 'in like' with him, let alone the other thing. It's a crush. Nothing more. It has to be."

Felicity's expression turned serious. "Sure, if you say so. Tell me, does he have a nickname for you? Not your proper name, something else?"

"He calls me Doctor Eden. Sometimes Doc." Then, last night, he'd called her *sweetheart*. And she'd liked it.

"Then I'd say, in my totally unprofessional opinion but as somewhat of an expert in the Southern Californian dating scene, you're in trouble."

"I am, aren't I?"

"Yeah, *Doc*, you are."

Firetruck. Eden let her head bang straight down on the table.

Midwinter Melbourne was cold, way colder than he remembered. The moment he got out of the taxi he'd grabbed at the airport, a gasp of bitter wind whipped around Finn's face. Now he stood on a leafy suburban street in front of the place he'd once called home.

Everything looked the same, like he'd traveled back in time twenty years instead of sixteen hours by plane across the Pacific. His parents' house was still solid, immovable red double brick with white-painted windowsills. And the garden—with its oak tree, green lawn, clipped hedges, and rosebushes—was still perfectly maintained.

He tugged his coat collar up around his neck to protect himself from a fraction of the wind chill and walked around the back of the taxi to haul his case from the trunk. The *boot*. His Aussie dialect and speech patterns had drifted away over the past few years of living in the States. Unless he actively forced himself to remember. He tried now.

As Finn clunked his case up onto the concrete driveway, he spotted a familiar sight that made his chest tighten. *Mum*.

She leaned halfway out of the screen door, checking to make sure it was him. For some reason, she rarely stepped all the way outside when a visitor arrived—until she was certain it was someone she knew. He walked toward her, the tightness in his chest easing a little when she stepped another two paces out the door and reached for him.

With his arms wrapped around his mother's slight frame, towering over her by a good foot of height, he hugged her close. He inhaled the comforting scent of her floral perfume and the hairspray she'd used since he was a kid. They meant he was home.

She pulled back and smoothed her palms down his rumpled jacket sleeves. Her green eyes, so like his own, still sparkled. "Finn. So nice to have you home."

"I know, Mum." He kissed her cheek, noticing the thin texture of her skin. At close to sixty, she was aging faster than he cared to admit. As was his father. A sharp pain sliced through his gut. "How's Dad?"

Her long sigh said more than any words could. "Improving. Out of surgery but not out of the woods yet. The doctor told me to go home and get some sleep. Fat lot of good that advice did me. I can't sleep during the day at the best of times. Bloody doctor. Arrogant bossy boots, if you ask me."

He laughed. At least his mother still had her spunk and sense of humor intact.

She ushered him inside, down the hallway with its sideboard and hat stand, past the painting of a sailboat at the beach, then pushed him into his old bedroom and told him to settle in while she put the kettle on.

Finn stood there, taking a moment to check out the changes around him. His football trophies were no longer on display, no more posters of pop stars and muscle cars stuck on the walls, but more framed beach scenes instead. The decor was neutral, not the red and black of his teenage years, and there was a double bed with a dark blue quilt and white sheets. Nice, comfortable looking, but nowhere near as cool as the prized Ferrari quilt cover he'd saved up his pocket money to buy.

After dumping his suitcase by the bed and his jacket on the nearby chair, he strolled into the kitchen to find his mother making tea. White with one, just the way he liked it. These days, he was all about the coffee, but not if Mum was making tea the old-fashioned way. He hoisted himself onto the kitchen counter and nearly hit his head on the top cabinet with the china cups.

"So, when can we go and see Dad?" he forced himself to ask, despite wanting to delay going to the hospital for as long as humanly possible.

There was something disturbing about the idea of seeing his formerly strong, independent father lying in a hospital bed in the cardiac ward. It made his own heart squeeze tight in his chest.

Mum leaned back on the counter with a sigh and sipped her tea before answering. "Visiting hours start in about three hours, but they're pretty flexible for immediate family. We can go whenever you're ready."

"Right. Okay, I might grab a quick nap first—the flight was a killer. But after my tea. Don't suppose there are any Tim Tams to go with this cuppa?" He raised an eyebrow at her.

His question earned him a laugh from this mother, as he'd hoped it might, and she went searching in the pig-shaped ceramic biscuit barrel for the best chocolate cookies—*biscuits*—in the world.

"I don't think you should nap now, or it'll mess up your whole schedule," his mum advised as she found the biscuit she was looking for and passed it to him.

Although it had been a while since he'd had one, as he dunked the Tim Tam into his steaming mug of tea, it felt like no time at all. The chocolate coating immediately began to melt, then he lifted the biscuit to his lips and sucked the soft chocolate filling from between the crumbly layers.

Finn groaned. "Yum. This is so damned good. I'll have to take a packet back to San Diego for a friend of mine."

An image of Eden popped into his head, sitting on top of her desk, dunking a Tim Tam in her coffee before sucking out its gooey chocolate center. Slowly. Seductively. A woman who enjoyed cupcakes and churros as much as she did was bound to be impressed by the triple chocolate treat.

There must have been some note in his voice when he said friend or a weird look on his face because his mum narrowed her eyes at him. "Do you have a girlfriend over there in San Diego?"

Finn almost choked on his mouthful of Tim Tam as he tried to figure out what to say. Eden was probably a friend now, most definitely a girl, although she'd demand to be called a woman. Fair enough with those brains and curves.

He fixed his gaze on his tea, his face warming. "It's complicated."

"I worry about you, all alone over there in America." Her voice came out soft, her concern obvious. "Sometimes I wonder... Do you ever think about what your life would have been like if Matthew was still with us? Would you have done things differently?" She touched his arm.

He flinched. But then he let the tension drain from his body and sipped his tea. Finn nodded. Did he miss Matt? Every single day. If his older brother hadn't died, would he have stayed in Melbourne? Probably. Maybe he'd have found a senior marketing job in his home city with a football club, as he'd once dreamed.

In an alternate universe, Finn might have settled down, bought a house with a special woman, and had a couple of kids by now. Matt might have too. They could have been best mates for life. Finn might have been settled in a lot of ways. Happier. More content.

He caught his mother's eye. "Yeah, sometimes. But I've achieved something, and I'm still on my way up. This project

I'm working on now could mean big things for the way heart patients receive their treatment. It could make a difference."

And it could. Maybe. If the project continued, if they received ongoing funding, if the company saw the benefit in dollar terms. If he didn't stuff up the tricky, secretive side of his current work. It made him sick to his stomach with worry. There were so many *ifs*.

She sighed. "I know, darling. It's just when I talk to you, you never mention any personal life. No hot Californian babes burning up your sheets?"

"Mum, gross!" How old was he again? He put his mug down on the countertop with a clink. "Actually, there is someone, but it's early days. She's a scientist from work. Smart and, I don't know, beautiful like a movie star. There's something between us. It could turn into more. I hope so."

It was possible. The way Eden sounded on the phone during his flight, the softness, the slight edge to her voice he recognized as desire. It all spoke of possibilities.

"Good. That's all I need to hear. For now. It gives me hope."

"Hope of what, exactly?"

"Grandbabies. Gorgeous mini Donohues to bounce on my knee and cuddle and kiss. Before I'm too old, please."

Finn laughed. "Jeez, Mum. Put the pressure on, why don't you?"

He acted annoyed, but for the second time, he imagined a child of Eden's. This time, he pictured a child half hers and half his. A little girl with Eden's dark hair and his green eyes. It was a pretty picture.

His mum slapped a hand over her mouth and giggled, sounding about thirty years younger than her actual age. "I wouldn't have believed it. Finn, I do believe you're getting clucky."

Finn's mouth popped open, and he had to bite his tongue to stop himself from telling his own mother to stick her opinion where the sun don't shine. He wasn't really annoyed, but the choice of word was something. *Clucky*, like a broody hen. That label was slapped on single women in their thirties, not men. It was offensive either way.

He shook his head again and hopped down off the counter. He shoved his hands into his jeans pockets. "Yeah, right. Whatever." As his mother laughed, he glanced toward the hallway. "I have to make a call."

He excused himself and took his tea into his bedroom, unable to wait another second to phone her. Eden was on his mind, and while it might not have been the best idea given the thoughts Mum had put in his head, he had to call. He *needed* to hear her voice.

Having deposited his flowery mug of tea on the dark wooden bedside table, Finn flung himself onto his back and rested his head on a pillow. He pulled his phone from his back pocket and blinked at the screen.

There was a message notification from LittleMissPerfect. For a moment, he suffered a massive case of the guilts, his guts clenching with the unpleasant thought he was cheating on Eden with his online girl. Which was ridiculous on so many levels.

First up, he and Eden weren't exactly dating. Sure, they'd got hot and heavy, enough to get his motor running. But they hadn't even been on a proper date and things were left undecided. HotAussie007 and LittleMissPerfect couldn't seem to get it together either.

Second, Eden and LittleMissPerfect were one and the same. As were he and HotAussie007. Both with their online alter egos. It was all too confusing for his poor jet-lagged brain.

He read LittleMissPerfect's message and immediately wished he hadn't.

Chapter Eighteen

LittleMissPerfect: It's been a while. Talk dirty to me.

Had she completely lost her mind? Eden wasn't sure but was veering toward a big Y-E-S as the answer to that particular question. It was late, she was lonely and more than a little turned on by the events of the previous day. Her earlier conversation with Finn had done things to her heart. Uncomfortable things.

So she'd messaged HotAussie007, whom she'd barely given any thought to until she picked up her phone and scrolled through a few of their old messages. She wanted to indulge in some harmless flirtation.

She lay on her sofa, watching another old movie. Audrey Hepburn, this time—looking stylish as usual. Tucked under a soft blanket, she was dressed in her favorite black sleep shorts and camisole. A little sexier than what she normally lounged around in.

This sofa was starting to have sexy connotations too. *Starting to?* Who was she kidding? She'd had more sexy moments on this sofa in the past two weeks than she'd had in her actual bedroom for the past two years.

Hot restlessness pulsing through her belly and thighs, she checked her phone screen. Nothing. No response to her hastily typed message. Perhaps he'd fallen asleep. She pictured him in his bed, naked, black sheets barely covering him to the waist. Bare chest glistening with beads of sweat.

Eden sat bolt upright as she realized the previously faceless man she'd imagined as her online boyfriend suddenly had a face. A gorgeous, smiling face, with a sharp jawline and golden-brown stubble, and deep emerald-green eyes that sparkled like sunshine on the ocean, all framed by hair that was a combination of dark blond and brown: the exact shade of caramel fudge. Finn's face.

Wait a minute...

Finn was single. A professional. Australian. Funny. He lived in the San Diego area. Could he be HotAussie007?

No. No way was her annoying colleague the anonymous man she'd chatted to online for so many weeks. Except he wasn't really annoying at all. Only in the way he kept popping into her imagination and reminding her of all the times he'd been sweet and caring and downright sexy.

Eden's belly heated, a warm, fuzzy feeling spreading through her limbs, making them loose and languid. She shifted her legs up onto the sofa and tucked her feet under her butt.

It would be a major coincidence bumping into someone online who you knew in real life. Surely the chances must be minuscule. Or not.

The people on the SD Confidential dating site were from the greater San Diego area, and they advertised it as a meet-up site for single professionals such as herself. And Finn.

What if Finn was HotAussie007? It would mean... He was also the man who stood her up.

The liquidy heat of her insides bubbled over into boiling-hot lava. What kind of guy did such a thing? And why would Finn be on an anonymous dating site at all?

Finn was clearly far too handsome to live—what with those muscular forearms and thick bitable thighs, *which she'd scarcely noticed, of course*, plus his tanned skin that somehow smelled summery and lickable. Then he had to go and be so sweet on top of it all. Finn could have had practically any woman he wanted this side of the moon. So why didn't he? What was wrong with him?

Maybe he was like Eden, not wanting his work and dating personas to collide. It made sense. Perhaps he wished to remain anonymous online so as not to jeopardize his professional image. The mystery turned over and over in her mind, performing loop-the-loops as she flicked her gaze back to the television.

Audrey had escaped her everyday life as a princess, bound by protocol and rigid rules, and was riding through Rome on a Vespa scooter, much like Eden's. With the wind in her hair, she was smiling, so happy to be free, having escaped the confines of her strict royal lifestyle to live undercover in a big city, if only for a while.

The whole runaway-princess theme was far-fetched but fun. Classic escapism all wrapped up with a Hollywood happy ending and Gregory Peck as a suave and kissable bonus.

Eden closed her eyes for a second. Hadn't she joined the dating site to escape her normal, everyday self? To get away from the geeks and the nerds? The nice, intelligent, but deathly boring men she usually attracted? Those who weren't too terrified to talk to her.

What if Finn had tried online dating for the same reasons? She'd never thought of him as lonely, but he was living on the other side of the world from where he grew up, away from family and old friends. She knew very little about his past. For all she knew, he could have been married and divorced or had a string of unsuccessful relationships. Why didn't she know these things? She suddenly wanted, needed, to find out.

Ella Fitzgerald's voice rang out in her lap, making her gasp. Her phone's ringtone sounded so sassy when it sprang to life. She glanced down at the screen and blinked.

Finn.

Her fingers twitched, then she snatched up the phone and took the call, her breath coming out all shallow. *Get a grip.*

"Hey, Doc. What's happening?" His voice was low, rumbly. Rolled in butterscotch sauce with a dash of whiskey.

Eden cleared her throat. "Oh, just hanging out at home. Watching a movie."

"Really? What's on?"

"*Roman Holiday.* Audrey Hepburn riding a Vespa. You probably wouldn't enjoy it."

"Are you kidding? It's a great movie. I remember watching it with Mum as a kid. Audrey's stunning, plus I always wanted to be Gregory Peck. Either him or James Bond."

James Bond? 007? Oh God. What if Finn really is Ho-tAussie007?

Eden took a deep, calming breath and clutched the phone closer to her ear while smoothing her hair back from her face. Later, she'd think about all the implications, like whether or not Finn already knew about her secret persona. Maybe he didn't. To him, she might still be a colleague, now a friend. Something more, possibly.

"Eden? Are you there?"

She shook herself back into the present. "I'm here. Just a little distracted. How's your dad?"

"We haven't been to see him yet, but Mum says he's doing better. I've been on a plane for nearly a whole day, so I'm having a rest first, and I wanted to call you."

Her mouth popped open. "Why?" She winced and scrunched her eyes shut for a second. Now he'd think she was impossibly rude. "I mean, is there something you need to tell me? Like work stuff?" She shook her head, trying to get rid of the awkwardness. Couldn't she ever say anything nice to him?

Finn mumbled something she couldn't make out. "No, nothing work-related. I was thinking about you and wanted to hear your voice."

"Oh. Thanks? I mean, I was thinking about you too."

He chuckled, low in his throat, and she imagined his Adam's apple bobbing up and down. Running her fingertips over his skin to her jaw. "You were? Are you having a lend?"

"Teasing, do you mean? No. I was just wondering why you're still single." Whatever happened to tact? She smacked her hand across her forehead, letting herself curse properly. Inside her head.

Shit. Hello, Little Miss Hopeless.

"Er, don't beat about the bush, will you?" He laughed again, the sound sending sparks zipping across her skin. "It's a bit of a cliché to say I've never met the right woman. But it's true. There's been a few I've liked, one girlfriend from college who wanted... Never mind. Bad timing. When you're busy working hard and traveling, you hit thirty, and suddenly everyone's already paired up."

Eden nodded. Oh yeah. She understood exactly what he meant. "Same for me. I'd meet scientists at conferences or engineers, guys who look good on paper, but there's no real spark. And heaps of married men trying to pick me up." She spat out the words, making no attempt to hide her disgust for all the two-timers out there. "There have been a few guys who wanted to date me... indefinitely. But I'm tired of it. Now I want something more serious." She shut her eyes again and silently counted to three. Would Finn make his excuses and end the call?

Instead, he breathed out long and deep, vibrating the phone against her ear, even across the Pacific and half the planet. "How serious are we talking? Marriage, house, babies? That kind of serious?"

"Uh-huh." She waited for the *click*.

"Good."

"What?" Shock resonated in her chest like the kickback from a gunshot. At least she thought it was shock. As her heart thudded out of control, she grabbed her camisole in her fist, twisting the silk fabric.

"*Good* because I don't want to muck around either. I want you. Let's give it a shot. When I get back, I'll take you out for dinner. Let's see what happens."

Blood pounded in her ears. Could they really do this? She wanted to do it. And other things. "Jesus. You're turning me on right now."

"Really? How much? Tell me." The gruff order rang in her ears, making her skin heat under her tiny camisole and shorts.

Eden flung the blanket from her lap and leaned back against the stack of cushions. "Are we talking dirty now, Finn?"

Deep, delicious laughter resonated through the phone. "Hell, yes. What are you wearing? Don't spare the details."

Now her heart picked up pace, racing downhill like she was in second gear on her scooter. "Sleep shorts." *Come on, be brave.* "A silk camisole. Both black with little red dots. There's a tiny red ribbon rose in the middle of the cami. Right between my breasts." Her fingers stroked the smooth fabric, then circled the rose.

Finn groaned, making the phone vibrate against her skull again. "I want to see you like that. See your perfect breasts. Kiss you and touch you."

Lust surged through her system, pulsing between her legs, and her nipples tightened until it was almost painful. But she wouldn't touch herself. Not yet. She'd force herself to wait.

"Are you in bed? Tell me." His voice cracked on his order.

Eden sighed, letting her index finger stroke once across her right nipple. "No. I'm in the living room, on the sofa."

"The sofa where I made you come?"

A gasp of air rushed from her lips, pleasure spiking in her core. "Yes. Right here." She wasn't sure what she was saying but gripped the phone tight to her ear. Her other hand had inched down, fingertips stroking along her outer thigh.

"Are you touching yourself?"

Her hand stilled on the curve of her thigh above her knee. "No. Not yet."

"Why not?"

Tell him.

Eden wanted to tell him. To tease him so good. "I want to wait for you to touch me."

A windy noise blew down the line. He was breathing hard. Panting almost. "Fuck. Are you trying to torture me, Doctor Eden?"

She grinned. "Possibly. Some things are hard to do over the phone. Torturing. Touching. You'll have to come home and see what I have planned."

Finn laughed, such a dirty, male sound, sending goosebumps racing across her exposed skin. Her arms, her legs, probably even her toes. How did he do it? No one else had ever had such an effect on her with touch, let alone phoning it in.

A distant voice butted into their conversation. "*Finn?* Don't go to sleep now. We should get to the hospital."

He groaned, the sound so fierce she could feel his frustration, loud and clear. "That's my mum. I'd better get going. Call you soon."

"You'd better."

"Are you threatening me, Doc?"

Her mouth stretched upward in a smile. "Possibly." She pictured his eyes, sparkling with humor.

"Brutal. Lucky you're so sexy with it."

"You're sexy too. Bye, Finn!"

Eden cut the call before he could say anything more, but she knew he'd be laughing. Her own giggle sounded wild and crazy, bouncing off the walls of her quiet living room.

Flopping back onto the sofa, she squeezed her thighs together. It wasn't long before he'd be back. Only a week. Not long to wait.

Everything south of the border tightened in disagreement. But it had been so long; what harm was a few more days? Anticipation made everything sweeter. Or spicier, as the case may be.

Spice. Hot chocolate with chili: Mexican style. Eden had some cravings to save for later, but that one she'd satisfy right away. She hopped off the sofa and swayed toward the kitchen with a head rush.

Lightheaded. Unsteady on her feet. Over Finn Donohue. Who would've believed it?

Faith would. She needed to catch up with her sister, tomorrow, urgent girl talk required. Eden never had any dating gossip to contribute, but now she did. Faith would probably encourage Eden to have a fling with Finn but maybe not get serious.

It was a strange to want to plan a future before they'd even dated. Was she rushing ahead and sabotaging herself? Eden's belly lurched as if she were seasick. Why did her damn brain have to go and ruin her own good mood?

Intravenous chocolate. That's what she needed.

In the depressingly beige hospital room, Finn shuffled his uncomfortable chair closer to his father's bedside. His father, who lay there in a wafer-thin blue gown with his eyes shut and tubes running from his mouth and arm, didn't seem the same man who'd raised him. The strong, smart, loving man who'd seemed invincible. Once upon a time.

A shadow passed across his father's face as a cloud obscured the sun outside the window of the private room.

"What can I do?" Finn talked into his hands, his elbows resting on his knees. There must be something. Being right here, next to Dad's bedside but unable to help, made him feel helpless.

Useless as tits on a bull, as his father would've said. He'd always loved his Aussie slang.

Stretching his legs out in front of the hard, molded plastic chair, he took a deep breath of antiseptic-tinged air and sat up straighter. Looked his father over, from gray hair to pale, sunken cheeks all the way down to his toes, covered in anemic green hospital sheets. With a plastic tube attached to his wrist, and to a drip, his dad was still out of it, on some super-painkillers since surgery. Triple bypass. Even the thought of it freaked Finn out.

How would his mother cope? Sure, she had her sister and brother and a bunch of friends from their neighborhood: a support network of people to lean on. But she still must be scared. Finn's parents had been married for nearly forty years. No small feat.

Thoughts whirred around in his brain like the fan belt under the hood of his Chevy. He needed to talk, to break the eerie silence of the private room, which must be costing them a bomb.

Finn cleared his throat. "Dad, I've been thinking. I'm wondering whether I should change direction. You know, get a different type of job. See about getting a woman on board, like you suggested a while back. *No man's an island. Even a fine captain needs a first mate.*" He laughed, then rubbed his hands over his stubble. "You sure do use some crappy expressions, you know."

His old man didn't say a word. Not that Finn expected him to. But it was better to talk than sit in silence. "Is that what it's all about? Not just work and running around after money or trying to achieve your goals, but getting to know someone? Loving someone special?"

Finn leaned back in his chair again, working out some of the kinks in his spine and the problem occupying his mind. "I could see how you felt about Mum, even when Matt and I were kids.

You always made sure she was happy first—before you took care of anything else. Us too. You were always there for us."

Their father had always been there for Matt. His older brother was only a fraction taller than Finn growing up, despite their three-year age gap, and he could never run as far or as fast as Finn. Dad encouraged Matt to have a go, to be a good sportsman. But his heart wouldn't let him.

His heart condition meant it was harder for him than most kids, but he wanted to experience everything life had to offer. And he tried, until the ripe old age of twenty-four.

Ever since Matt's passing, Finn had felt honor bound to do everything his big brother never had the chance to do in life. Only, somewhere along the line, it seemed Finn might have forgotten himself. Who he used to be, or who he could be in the future.

When he was younger, Finn had held fast to his own dreams and ambitions, even thinking about whether he'd be as good a husband and father as his own dad. They were things he'd always wanted.

"I'm sorry, Dad, if I ever made you feel like you let me down, because you didn't. You were the best. Still are. And you need to get better. I mean it, no buggering off back to work as soon as you're released from hospital. Mum won't have a bar of it either."

Of course, his mother chose that exact moment to push open the door, bearing a plastic bag of dinner. Chinese food, Finn guessed, by the mouth-watering aroma of soy sauce and ginger.

She smiled over at him as she plonked the food on the table by the wall. "Now, what were you nattering about? Mum won't have what?"

"Dad's not to get out of here and go straight back to work. He needs a proper rest."

"Great minds think alike. I've been telling your father the exact same thing. Haven't I, honey?"

Finn tipped his chin upward in the direction of the bed. "Do you think he can hear us?"

"Absolutely. I'm counting on it."

His mum bustled around the hospital room, pushing a rolling tray table along the end of the bed until it was close to where Finn sat. She then grabbed an extra chair and took a seat beside him. From the bag of takeout, she pulled out cartons and plastic containers. Enough to feed a small army.

"I wasn't sure what you'd like, so I might've gone a bit overboard. Try the Singapore noodles, they're great."

"Sounds good. Thanks, Mum."

She leaned over and kissed him on the cheek before ruffling his hair like when he was a young boy. A lump formed in the back of his throat. This weird vigil was getting to him, waiting for his dad to wake up. But the doctors had said he'd be coming around anytime now, so all they could do was wait.

They ate in silence. Finn wasn't sure why he eventually broke it, but he had to say something. He surprised himself with what came out: "I can stay here, in Melbourne, if you want me to."

"I want you to do what's best for you. And your girl, of course." His mum smiled, a cheeky dimple on one side of her face. People often said his smile was identical to hers, but they were nuts. His mother was truly beautiful.

Finn shook his head. "Okay, Mum, whatever you say."

"Good boy." The words, croaky but unmistakable, came from his father's mouth.

Finn dropped his plastic cutlery and stood so quickly that his chair tipped over backward and crashed to the floor.

His mother also leaped to her feet and pushed the call button next to the bed, her hand pressed over her mouth. "Are you okay, love?" Then she was right at his side, holding Dad's hand.

Right by his side. Always.

Finn had never realized how much he wanted a real love story for himself or how his heart would hurt just watching his parents together when things got tough. How they leaned on each other to get through whatever obstacles they faced. How they were there for one another, no matter what.

He'd never realized a lot of things. Until now.

Chapter Nineteen

Eden: I miss you. I miss kissing you.

Finn: Aww, now I don't want to come back. You only miss kissing me when I'm on the other side of the world.

Eden: Not true. I miss you when you're not being insufferable.

Finn: I dreamed about you last night. It was a good dream. You were naked, baking me cupcakes. I helped you decorate things... with frosting.

Eden: That's a burn risk. BTW you haven't seen my cupcake tattoos yet.

Finn: ...

Finn: I'll see you at work tomorrow. Wear clothes or I'll be too distracted to think. ;0

Eden didn't know what had come over her. Well, she wouldn't lie to herself—she had some idea. Sex, probably. It drifted around her, an invisible, sensual cloud of light-headedness, teasing her senses like a waft of sultry perfume. She and Finn had texted all week while he was in Australia.

To cut a long story short, it was driving her crazy.

She sucked in a deep breath, pulled up her black stockings with shaking hands, and smoothed her skirt down over them. With her perfectly starched white business shirt tucked in straight and smooth, she stepped into high heels on the wrong side of practical, more on the sexy side of the equation.

Studying herself in the full-length mirror on her wardrobe door, she could see it. She looked different. Grown-up, almost intimidating.

Good. The right clothes could lend confidence and power to a woman, so Faith had taught her. And right now, Eden needed all the confidence she could muster. That was one way of viewing her choice of outfit.

There was another angle. Her subconscious whispered the real reason for her careful choice of sexy clothes. She was dressing up, which wasn't so unusual. But to admit the complete truth, she was dressing up for a man. At work. And Finn was the man in question, making it extraordinary behavior on her part.

Eden's hair hung loose around her shoulders, so she stood tall and pushed it back over her shoulders. She nodded to her reflection. "Give him hell, Eden. You can do it."

As pep talks went, it was kind of lame, but she'd have to work with it.

As Eden walked across the courtyard, an unseasonal wind whipped through the space. Specks of dust or sandy grit attached themselves to her eyelashes, and she blinked it away. The last thing she needed for the big presentation was smudged mascara like a sad raccoon.

Of course, the wind also gusted clean under the stack of papers balanced in her left hand, and while adjusting her grip, she tripped over a seam in the tiled courtyard. She pitched forward, reaching out to break her fall.

Her hands struck the pavement with a resounding thump. "Oh no!"

Everything went flying. Her hair, her shoe, her damned stack of research printed out but not bound... Eden scrambled to her feet and chased after the sheets of white paper, flapping like sails in the wind before taking off exactly like kites.

A sob rose in her constricted throat as she stood and jammed her shoe back on her foot, and watched her papers fly. All her hard work — literally gone with the wind. She could reprint most of it, but she'd made notes by hand, all of which would be lost. She spun around and snatched at random pieces of paper at eye level, knee level, along the ground.

Then... a deep voice echoed behind her: "Eden, do you need a hand?"

Every muscle in her body tightened. Of course he was here. She blinked and huffed out a breath, turning to face Finn. She couldn't look away. He was beautiful. Cool and calm, dressed in a sharp business suit, all long lines, emphasizing his height. He tore off his jacket and tossed it aside as he charged toward her, grabbing handfuls of paper on his way.

She'd expected to see him across the meeting room and been prepared for that. She'd planned to be poised and professional and, hopefully, a little sexy. Instead, she was chasing her own tail, unraveling like a spool of thread in her sewing box.

Eden straightened and brushed down her skirt. "Hello. And ouch." She'd grazed her right palm. She tucked in her shirt tails, now also flapping loose in the breeze.

When she looked up to meet his eyes, there was something unexpected in those green pools. Laughter, yes. But also something far sweeter. A strong dose of *like* lit up his springtime gaze. Not the other 'L' word, obviously.

She was staring so hard that she'd probably burn through his retinas and sear his brain.

Quit it, Eden. Pull yourself together.

"Here." Finn handed her a bunch of papers, haphazardly shuffled together. "Now let me see your hands."

Next thing she knew, he'd wrapped his fingers around her right hand while she stuffed the papers under her arm. His grip toasty-warm and gentle, he smoothed the pad of his thumb over her grazed skin. It smarted a little, but that wasn't why she gasped.

"She'll be right." He stroked his thumb across her palm, then down to the pulse point at the inside of her wrist. Trails of tingles followed his touch. "I missed you, Doc." He smiled, and everything twinkled.

Heat flared low in her belly, and her throat constricted, making it difficult to respond. Images of their night together flashed before her eyes as if these were the last moments of her life. She wasn't dying, of course, but she might have been having a heart attack.

How did he do that to her? She grunted something inarticulate, shook her hand free, and strode away from him.

Glee filling his voice, Finn shouted after her, "See you inside. We could get lunch after?"

Eden turned and stared at him, her mouth agape. Lunch. Such a normal-sounding suggestion. So why did it make her stomach feel like she'd just jumped off the nearby La Jolla clifftops without a parachute?

She nodded. "Okay." Her legs moved, propelling her away from him. It would be fair to say she fled the scene. She had to get away if she enjoyed breathing.

Eden knew now that whatever happened at the presentation this morning would impact her potential relationship with Finn. The presentation timeline had been moved up, neither of them were ready, and the pressure was on. Finn had only just flown in from Australia the night before, for goodness sake. The work situation could implode, and the personal thing between them could be over before they'd even begun. Whatever she might want personally—and God, she *wanted*—a relationship with Finn was a risk. It had 'PROFESSIONAL MISTAKE' written all over it in huge, red capital red warning letters. The kind they put on hazardous substances in the lab.

The two of them mixing it up could well be a disaster waiting to happen — one that could completely derail her career if she wasn't careful. And her project proposal was lacking detail about key elements she hadn't had time to include.

Her stupid high heels clickety-clacked across the pavement as she walked, her heart thumpity-thumping in time inside her chest.

Eden sucked in one last breath of fresh air before crashing through the doors to the air-conditioned but stuffy science wing. Her first priority was to find a quiet place to steal a few minutes alone before facing Finn and McTavish across the boardroom table.

Before putting both her professional reputation and personal life on the line.

Eden stood behind the desk in her office, trying not to cry. She'd attempted to salvage her research papers, so carefully arranged and tagged with Post-it Notes the night before. But everything was hopelessly out of order now. She'd have to speak from memory and a few hastily scrawled notes. The drug trials they had been working on were just the beginning. She'd envisaged a reduced time-to-market with expedited trials, for a new class of heart medications. Without her notes, she was hopelessly underprepared. She would have to go with the flow.

Oh, how she hated going with the flow.

Unlike, say, Finn, who grinned at her as he strolled into her office. His look said *I know you've been up to no good.*

God, how her body responded to him. Heat suffused her cheeks and throat as her heart pounded against the confines of her blouse, and her legs acquired a sudden jelly-like consistency. Letting them wobble her downward, she sat with a huff, dumping her pile of papers before her.

"Good morning, Doctor Eden," Finn announced cheerily. As if the morning was bursting with rainbows and unicorns, free cupcakes raining down from the sky.

She shrugged, trying to avoid falling into his distracting eyes in case she sank and drowned in their tropical, ocean-like depths. "I've had better."

Those eyes sparkled and danced, warning her of impending cheekiness. "Hey, it's going to be okay. I've had a tremendous morning, thanks for asking. I got to see you again, for one thing. But there seems to be a certain song that's stuck in my head..."

He hummed, infuriatingly in tune, and she immediately recognized it: 'Dream a Little Dream of Me.'

It'd been stuck in her head too. The instant replay in her memory was a dangerous thing, as it came packaged with intense, hot, sticky sensations that thundered through her body with an energy that left her breathless. Not to mention a firetruck-load of feelings.

Lucky she was already seated.

With a grin, Finn reached down to straighten her pile of papers, brushing his fingertips along her forearm as he did so. Eden watched as all the tiny little hairs stood to attention, goosebumps pebbling in the wake of his touch. She rubbed her hands up and down her arms, although she wasn't cold. Not by a long shot.

She gasped and whispered, "You can't just, not here..."

He laughed, damn him. "It's okay, Doc. Relax. See you in the boardroom." He sauntered to the door, looking totally relaxed. And limber. There was something about his long-legged stride that made her want to tackle him to the ground.

Finn glanced back over his shoulder at her. And his smile nearly melted her jelly legs into a puddle of Kool-Aid.

Eden picked up a sheet of paper and flapped it in front of her face. If she were online, she knew exactly what she'd type: *fans self*. Then, head down, she read over her first page of research.

A few minutes later, Eden sat in the boardroom, waiting for the meeting to start. Gazing over the heads of several silver-haired and besuited board members, plus a chatting contingent of guests she didn't recognize, she spotted him.

Finn now sat at the opposite end of the long plank of a boardroom table. He raised an eyebrow and then glanced down at his assortment of papers, laptop, and black stainless steel coffee mug.

Coffee. She'd been so knocked off-center that she'd forgotten her own caffeine fix. But no time now. Eden straightened her spine and faced the chair of the meeting, who stood beside a flat-screen monitor attached to the wall.

McTavish stood front and center, looking less disheveled than usual. In fact, with his oddly slicked-back hair and well-pressed navy suit, he appeared almost sheveled for a change.

When McTavish addressed the guests, naming them individually and nodding at each of them before speaking to the room. "Welcome, everyone. Before we get underway, some introductions are in order. I've taken the opportunity today to invite a group of guests from Magna Smart's new partner in Europe. Please join me in welcoming the international partnerships team from DCM Pharma."

Eden blinked at Finn, who looked utterly confused. What on earth was happening?

Finn tore his gaze from Eden and looked around the boardroom. He had no clue what was going on. Around the table, his colleagues fidgeted, looking everywhere but at McTavish and his guests. Finn was no wheeling and dealing stock market guru, but he followed the market reports in their industry. And this wasn't right.

DCM Pharma wasn't exactly who he'd imagined when McTavish mentioned potential investors. Anyone with a basic understanding of math knew the company's plummeting share price on the back of some dodgy investments in eastern Europe start-ups equaled a bad bet.

Finn took a long gulp of coffee, eyeing Eden over the rim of his mug. She looked shell-shocked, glancing between the guests and McTavish, then finally meeting his own eyes again. When she inclined her head slightly, asking him a silent question, he shook his head equally subtly. *No.* He'd had no idea about this development.

McTavish turned to Finn, clapping his hands together once. "There'll be time to talk informally later, but we should get started. Finn Donohue, our manager of Marketing and Business Development, has an exciting presentation prepared. He's been developing a new concept in direct patient management and will now offer an insight into Magna Smart's future. Over to you, Finn."

Eden inclined her head at almost a right angle this time. Curious, he guessed. And, judging by the frown on her forehead, worried too.

Finn would've liked to discuss his presentation with Eden beforehand—to mull over the implications. He wished he could've asked her advice about whether to continue playing along with McTavish. But he hadn't had a choice. He was compelled to report to an outside agency now, and they'd made their expectations clear. Continue doing as McTavish says, until such time as they have enough evidence to shut him down.

He rose from his seat and brought up his presentation on his laptop. A few clicks later and his opening slide appeared on the screen on the wall.

"Good morning, everyone. As Doctor McTavish has asked me to give a presentation on our new direction, I'd better introduce you to Kelly. Kelly is fictional, but also our ideal customer in an online, self-service healthcare model." He gestured to the screen.

A smiling image of blond, picture-perfect Kelly surrounded by a spotless kitchen and two point five children filled the screen. She rested a hand on her baby bump while well-dressed preschoolers sat at a kiddie table with a bunch of crayons. The image was cheesy, but he'd understood this was what McTavish was looking for. Family-orientated, wholesome. As opposed to corporate greed personified...

He clicked through to a video his TV producer friend had put together for him at the last minute. The words 'Patient 360' filled the screen as the music started.

Finn looked up and caught Eden's expression across the table. The room was darker now, but he couldn't miss the narrowed eyes and crossed arms, her *no way, Jose* body language. He glanced across to McTavish, whose grin was smug. Their boss appeared in his element.

Returning his attention to the screen, Finn continued with his memorized script: "Our Power Up concept is nothing short of revolutionary. In the US, millions of dollars are wasted on doctor and hospital visits each year. These visits could be replaced by a simple online drug dispensary. The difference with other online drug sites being, we will utilize an artificial intelligence 'doctor' to lead patients through diagnosis to treatment with appropriate prescriptions. AI will learn from patient input in real time and analyze trends to improve over time, and help us develop new and better drugs before our competitors."

On-screen, the animated version of Kelly, now looking as happy as a kid on Christmas morning, logged in to Magna Smart's patient portal to view her medical records with a toddler on one knee. She sent a two factor authorization code to the smartphone in her hand. Words like 'Convenient, Easy, Online' flashed across the screen.

"For patients such as Kelly, time is in limited supply. By using Magna Smart's new patient portal, she avoids wasting this precious time in waiting rooms. She reorders her birth control pills online, and the AI doctor approves the transaction. Done."

"Kelly's pregnant." Eden's voice rang out over the top of the video soundtrack. "She's quite clearly sporting a baby bump, so she's not currently ovulating. Why would she need birth control pills?"

Shit. He'd hoped to avoid the whole twenty questions routine, but Eden obviously intended to call him out on the holes in his presentation. He took a breath and answered as he'd practiced: "She's ordering ahead, for after the baby comes. Three kids is more than enough for Kelly."

A light titter of laughter followed this statement. Eden, however, was not amused. "I see. And her robot doctor will just approve it? Without even knowing if she'll experience complications at birth, blood loss, or hemorrhage. What about post-natal depression? And is Kelly planning to breastfeed? Because, as I'm sure you're aware, the mini pill is the only recommended oral contraceptive pill for breastfeeding women."

Finn sighed and drew himself up to full height. "I didn't know, but the possible risks and side effects will be outlined clearly online. The doctor wouldn't approve it if there were any potential problems."

Eden slowly shook her head from side to side. "I see where you're going with this proposal, and I think it's extraordinary that this is being pitched to prospective investors when the concept is so obviously flawed. Not to mention potentially dangerous for patients."

A muttering from one or two of the guests had Eden turning to them, then pointing at the screen. "Let's say Kelly has her baby in a couple of months. She has her ready supply of birth control pills, which she begins taking immediately after the birth. All of this is unknown to her admitting doctor in the delivery ward. She's had a C-section, lost a significant amount of blood. She's at major risk of clotting and stroke. The medication would undoubtedly affect her ability to breastfeed, or her hormones, transferred via her breast milk, would adversely affect her baby. This is unacceptable."

A chair leg scraped across the floor, and Finn turned his attention to McTavish, who now stood at the other end of the room. "You've said quite enough, Eden."

Eden stood too. She leaned on the table, as if her legs couldn't support her. "I'll say my piece, Doctor McTavish. And I'll thank you to address me as Doctor Robinson, as a matter of professional courtesy."

"Of course, Doctor Robinson," McTavish forced through gritted teeth. He sounded as benevolent as King Henry VIII addressing one of his wives. Right before their public beheading. "Please, take your seat, and you'll have your chance to speak in a few minutes."

Finn stared at Eden, willing her to be sensible.

Careful, Eden. Don't do anything stupid.

Finn held himself perfectly still, hoping Eden would back down. But he couldn't stop this, whatever the hell it was, playing out in front of him.

She pointed an index finger at McTavish. "Just out of interest, what are your thoughts on this proposal, Doctor McTavish? I assume you're the barely scientifically literate, incompetent, decision-making-by-threat, over-the-hill fool who dreamed it up."

Shit, Eden. Don't hold back. Tell it like it is...

"That's quite enough. Eden, who I will not be addressing as Doctor after such an appalling outburst. Please clear out your desk and report to HR. Immediately. Your services are no longer required."

Aaaannnd, chop. Off with her head.

Eden gasped and sank back into her seat as if she were a balloon that had suddenly deflated. Finn guessed it was how she felt. All the wind taken from her sails, the petrol from her engine, whatever metaphor he could think of, she was done. Kaput.

His own stomach felt filled with lead.

As he watched, Eden rose slowly, carefully, reaching for her pile of papers.

"Leave them," McTavish ordered.

Struck mute, Eden nodded, grabbed her purse from under the table and phone from in front of her, and quietly walked toward the door. When she reached it, she stopped and turned toward Finn.

The look she shot him was filled with icy scorn, then her face froze completely. Blank. She opened the door and left without uttering another word. It was like being ghosted in real life.

Unable to stop himself, Finn called out, "Eden, wait."

He stepped forward, about to chase after her. He needed to talk to her. Needed her to know he didn't support any of this stuff but was biding his time, waiting for the ideal moment to let it all fall in a heap at McTavish's feet.

McTavish had walked across the room, and stuck out a hand and touched Finn's arm, stopping him in his tracks. "Finn, she's of no concern to us now. Please, continue your presentation."

Finn stepped back and closed his eyes for a second. He couldn't risk getting fired too. Not with the situation he was in, stuck playing the role of loyal lapdog to McTavish, all the while gathering evidence to take the bastard down.

He couldn't risk anything. Not with how things were going with Eden. How they *had* been going, anyway. His work visa would be nonexistent; he'd be sent packing back to Australia immediately. Any burgeoning relationship, any feelings he might have for her, would be as kaput as Eden's job.

Finn had no doubt McTavish would fire him if provoked, especially if the boss got wind of the growing connection between himself and Eden. He stalked back to his laptop and hit a key to restart the video.

Words he'd written filled the screen. He no longer gave a shit. Eden must have assumed he'd kept her in the dark on purpose. Normally, nothing could have made him drag her into this mess, but he'd been trying to protect her. To make sure her professional reputation wasn't dragged into the mud as his would be.

Marketing professionals often managed to swim in murky waters without getting pulled under. He could only hope he managed to pull this off. Sink or swim. Goddammit, he needed a life jacket and sea rescue.

Finn sank into his chair and let the video do the talking. His mind whirled in a vortex, thinking ahead to everything else he had to do.

Eden packed her personal effects from her office into a storage box, hands trembling the entire time. A small painted ceramic vase held an imitation rose, a souvenir from a trip across the border to Mexico. The photo of herself and Faith dressed up at the track for last year's Hat Parade on Opening Day.

She crouched and deposited all the items neatly into the storage box at her feet, then straightened and scanned her desk.

Her coffee mug with the cartoon Little Miss Perfect... It had been sitting right next to her computer monitor all along. Had Finn ever noticed? She shook her head. What did it matter now? She was on her way out of the building, never to return. McTavish had made it crystal clear. Then, for good measure, he'd called Security.

Finn had called after her in the boardroom, but so what? One word from McTavish, and he'd toed the line.

Deano from Security stood right outside her open office door, arms crossed, watching her. His saddened expression warmed her a little. He'd always been nice to her. Deano was a good guy, unlike some she could name.

McTavish could go to hell. And Finn could join him since he'd obviously decided where his loyalties lay. Her heart squeezed in her chest. No. She refused to cry.

Chapter Twenty

Finn wanted to shout blue murder, to run after Eden and make his feelings known until no bloody uncertainty remained. Kiss her like there was no tomorrow. Because, apparently, there would be no tomorrow for the two of them.

She was gone. She wouldn't be back. But he was still in the thick of it, standing at the front of the boardroom.

Back to business. Finn needed to keep his eye on the ball. Get back in the game. All the usual sporting analogies had helped him to claw his way up over the years and to keep going. His presentation was a piece of crap with a bow on it, but he'd known that all along.

If Eden had given him just a few minutes more, she would have understood his game plan. He'd counted on her trusting him, giving him the benefit of the doubt, but obviously, they weren't there yet. Which cut deep when he thought about it too hard.

He glanced at McTavish, who glared at him from the back of the room.

"Mr. Donohue, continue." McTavish's voice was icy cold.

"Excuse me for interrupting, but I think we should discuss the doctor's comments." A woman from the European team spoke softly and calmly but with a steely undertone that demanded attention. "It would appear Doctor Robinson has significant reservations about the company's new direction. Perhaps she is right."

Finn breathed out slowly without making a sound. *This.* This was what he'd been trying to stir up. Questions, dissent, bringing out all the stuff McTavish was attempting to cover up. This had only been the start.

McTavish fumed but responded reasonably: "Of course. We're happy to discuss any issues or queries regarding the project. As I explained earlier, this is simply a proposal."

Like hell it was. In McTavish's mind, the deal was no doubt already signed. But if Finn played his cards right, it wouldn't make it past the proposal stage.

Finn: Eden, can we talk? Please? I can explain everything.

Finn: I miss you. More than you know.

A few hours later, Finn entered the lab, looking around for Eden's offsider, Felicity. She was a smart woman, and Eden respected her, so Finn did too, by default. He needed to talk to someone who knew Eden to get some advice on where to start in smoothing things over with her. And if he managed to win over Felicity with his plans, it would be an added bonus.

As he strode across the gleaming white space, he spotted Felicity in a corner alcove, standing behind a partition. She was deep in conversation with someone. Meredith?

What was The Terminator doing here in the lab? Why was Meredith talking to Felicity? They had no reason to be working together.

Finn hung back, not wanting to interrupt what appeared to be an intense discussion. Felicity, who wore a frown, was waving her hands around until Meredith reached out, took hold of them, and smoothed them down by her sides. Meredith released the younger woman's hands, then touched Felicity's cheek with her thumb, gently. With affection—or love? Felicity's expression softened, and she sighed.

Oh. Generally, he was good at reading people, but he'd always had a hopeless female gaydar. However, now that he saw them together, it was plain as the nose on his face. Another romance between coworkers had been going on right in front of him.

Now he knew where Felicity had gotten hold of her information about McTavish's financial dealings. From Meredith, not just McTavish. That night at Eden's house, when Felicity had been drunk, she'd spilled some of the beans. McTavish had a gambling problem. He owned a stake in an investment firm that was doing badly, and his racehorses hadn't come through like he'd hoped. Felicity had also hinted at him having offshore accounts with money coming from somewhere else. Finn hadn't realized Meredith had been the source of the details about those accounts.

Finn strolled toward the two women, giving them a chance to notice him before butting in. They'd stopped touching but stood close together. Felicity still appeared upset, with a tell-tale redness around her eyes.

There was no point in pulling any punches. "Excuse me, but I was wondering if I could have a word — with both of you. It's about what happened at the presentation this morning. About Eden."

Felicity crossed her arms and narrowed her eyes. "You've got some nerve talking about Eden when you're the one who got her fired."

Shit. This was going to be hard work. He turned and checked out the other lab staff. A few had tuned into their conversation already. "Can we discuss this in private? You'll both want to hear what I have to say."

Felicity nodded, and Meredith's eyes flicked from Finn to Felicity again. She nodded too.

Finn led the two women out of the lab, at least twenty pairs of eyes trained on his back. He half expected someone to throw a dagger at any moment.

Felicity and Meredith gaped at Finn, who sat back in the leather seat at the diner a few minutes' drive from Magna Smart's office. They could have been in a spy movie, with the secret meeting in a neutral, public venue. All he needed was a roll of microfilm hidden in his pancakes for the perfect setup.

"I knew you were investigating what McTavish was doing. But... You're a corporate spy." Meredith crossed her arms and stared him down. "And you have evidence that he's trying to pin his financial fraud on Eden?"

"Yes."

Felicity blinked, then said quietly, "Let's say I believe you. You understand what you're trying to do will most likely end your career in big pharma?"

Finn nodded as he stirred an extra spoonful of sugar into his coffee. "Yes, but that's not a major concern for me. I don't particularly want to work in this field anymore. I can get a marketing job in another healthcare field or high tech, probably back in Australia. This whole experience has left a bad taste in my mouth."

With her head tilted to one side, Felicity studied him. "What about Eden? You said you wanted to protect her. She liked you. Trusted you. I don't want to see you hurt her."

Hurt her any more than he already had, she meant. The mention of trust stung somewhere inside his chest. He'd been double-dealing with her from the start. But she'd done the same—with the online dating thing. Maybe she'd understand. Maybe he could still fix it.

Finn clenched his jaw, then released it. "I can help her, but I need to talk to her. I've tried calling and emailing, sent loads of messages, and she won't respond." He leaned forward and dropped his spoon with a clatter. "I care about Eden, and hurting her is the last thing I want to do. I just need a chance to explain."

He let out a long breath and took a sip of coffee, watching as the two women turned to each other. A moment of silent communication took place between them.

Meredith bit her lower lip. She'd sat quietly until now, listening to what he'd said, but finally, she spoke up. "I can give you more details about Doctor McTavish's financial investments, shell companies, offshore investments, that kind of thing. If it would help."

Finn nodded, relief flooding his body. "Yes, that would be great. I've already got a stack of research papers and reports on the clinical trials Eden sent to me, stuff about the new drug and how it's not performing as well as McTavish makes out. And there's something about a patent, but it's not clear what it means. I could use some help with interpreting the science-speak." Finn glanced at Felicity, his eyebrow raised.

Her lips quirked up on one side. "Can do. Science-speak happens to be my specialty."

Meredith leaned over and took Felicity's hand where it rested on the table. "We make an awesome team."

Finn couldn't help smiling in return. They did look happy together. "So I see. Thank you, I'll be in touch." He stood and placed enough cash on the table to cover their meals and the tip.

As he was about to walk away, Felicity called out to him, "Finn, wait." She tilted her head to one side, her blue eyes wide. "I'll talk to Eden and tell her you'll be in touch. I'll give her a heads-up on what you've told us. It might help you get your foot back in the door."

"Thanks. I appreciate it." He gave them a nod, then headed for the exit. For his plan to work, he needed information from people in several different areas of the company who'd support his version of events. Or corroborate his evidence if it came to a trial down the line.

But most of all, he needed Eden on his side.

Chapter Twenty-One

Felicity: Just give him five minutes. I think you'll want to hear what he has to say.

Eden: But I hate him!

Felicity: Really? I think he's in love with you.

Eden: Am I an asshole magnet?

Felicity: No, just unlucky in love... so far. Talk to him!

Eden's head ached, and she could hardly move from her spot on the sofa. Her ankle had healed, and the bruises faded. But this morning, it throbbed, along with her head. And her heart.

Finn's performance in the boardroom yesterday and the aftermath had made her physically ill. She'd vomited twice, then spent a restless night, unable to sleep for replaying how her life had detonated in one afternoon.

She had no job, no reputation, no references, and no scientific papers published in the past two years. Maybe she was being dramatic. She could take a lower-paid job working for David, but the sums didn't add up. Soon, she'd have no money. Not to mention, no Finn.

Finn had obviously known what McTavish was up to for some time. He'd been involved in the planning stages of a massive change to the company's direction, with dubious moral underpinnings and a lack of interest in patient care, yet he hadn't said a word.

Eden's phone buzzed from where she'd left it, set on silent on the kitchen counter. She dragged herself up and across the living room and picked up the phone just as it stopped ringing. Felicity. Again. Should she call her back? She'd already texted her, but she didn't want to hear any more about Finn. The phone rang again in her hand. With a groan, she answered the call.

"Eden, how are you doing?" Felicity shot out her words rapid-fire.

Eden shrugged and pulled her robe tighter around her waist. "Okay, I guess. Didn't get much sleep, though."

Felicity sighed. "Listen, I had a chat with Finn yesterday, and — "

"Let me stop you right there." Eden closed her eyes. "I don't even want to hear his name right now."

"This is important. He's got a plan to take McTavish down. There's more to this whole situation than you know. They brought Finn into some planning meetings months ago, and he's got hold of a bunch of research McTavish had about the AI for the new patient portal and something about an international patent. McTavish was looking at your heart drug research as something to sell, and more. Finn's investigated more of McTavish's personal investments, offshore accounts and stuff. Meredith told me she'd given him some financial data too."

Eden straightened, pressing the phone hard to her ear. "Meredith from Finance?" This situation was getting stranger by the second. "What's she got to do with anything?"

"Oh, I meant to tell you, we're dating. We have been for a while. I trust her. And she uncovered some murky crap in McTavish's declaration of personal investments."

Eden blinked, trying to figure out what was most surprising in this conversation. "You and Meredith? I'm aware that you bat for both teams, but I didn't think you went for older women?"

"That was before I met Merry."

Merry? The woman seemed about as merry as a funeral to Eden. But if she made Felicity happy... Felicity and Merry. They sounded like a perfect match based on their names alone. "Wow. I'm happy for you. But what's this got to do with Finn's presentation yesterday?"

"Everything. Finn's been playing along with McTavish, acting like his golden marketing boy. But he's actually been investigating the project and where the funding's coming from, and what he's planning to do next. What McTavish is up to, it's sneaky. Criminal even. If Finn calls you, please hear him out. It's about much more than you and him."

Eden had to think. But it was impossible with the image of Finn in yesterday's meeting still so clear in her mind. His emerald eyes sparkling, the way he'd looked so shaken when she'd been asked to leave. He'd called out, asking her to wait, but she'd stormed out of the boardroom.

But why hadn't Finn tried to talk to her before now, to explain exactly what was going on? She'd thought they had a connection.

At the very least, he could have hinted about the company's reputation being at stake. If he cared, he should have made sure she understood exactly what was happening. Or told her to get out quick. She could have begun looking for another job.

Eden ran her hands through her hair with a heavy sigh. "I'll think about it."

"Good. I'll miss you at work. Let's catch up soon, okay?"

"Of course. I'll call you."

Eden ended the call and stared at her phone for a moment, scrolling through her messages. Finn had texted, left several voicemails, and even emailed her work account, before it was disabled. She set the phone back on the counter and went about the mundane task of making coffee.

It was strange, hanging about in her kitchen in a bathrobe on a workday. Nothing to do, nowhere to go. Not even the beginning of a plan so far.

She'd have to tell Faith sooner or later. Eden sucked in a sharp breath. *Later.* She couldn't face that call just yet. Her sister had drawn money against Eden's mortgage to establish her jewelry business. Eden didn't want to ask Faith to pay it all back, but she may have no choice. With no job and probably no income for a while, she may have to arrange a payment plan... or worse.

While homelessness was not an appealing option, nor was selling her grandmother's house in the current market. She'd never afford to buy in the same area. Eden could always rent out the house and move somewhere cheaper. Maybe a tiny apartment over a laundromat or something.

The coffee maker bubbled away, a slow stream of black liquid filling the mug she'd placed underneath. The bitter but appetizing aroma teased her nostrils, perking her up, even if only temporarily. Eden picked up the cup and brought it to her lips. Black today, no question of sweeteners or cream to soften the harshness.

Sunshine burst through the kitchen window overlooking her back lawn. Summer carried on relentlessly — cheerful and bright — regardless of her mood.

The doorbell, followed by a clunking knock at her front door made her twitch and spill a few drops of coffee on the counter. She wiped it up with a cloth, her mind ticking over. Could it be Finn? He wouldn't just show up at her door uninvited and unwanted, would he? Although, if she was honest, he wasn't really unwanted. She wanted him — so much she ached. But she wanted pre-presentation Finn, the one who seemed to care for her, who hadn't let her down.

The knocking came again: loud and insistent.

She tugged her robe tighter across her chest and walked to the door with hesitant steps. It might be Finn. He'd turned up unexpectedly a couple of times now, each time bringing a cataclysm of events along with him. Eden stood tall, sucked in a deep breath, and pulled open her front door.

The sight before her was blinding. Golden sunshine silhouetted a tall, broad-shouldered man, his face in shadow. The sunlight glinted off his caramel hair, lightening its shade to the palest of yellows. He was stunning, of course. Always had been. Her lower belly tightened in recognition and longing.

Why she had to fall for him now was a mystery that only her hormones were in on. Her brain was clueless and stumped for words.

"Finn." Her voice sounded cold and deadly even to her own ears.

He shifted, a beam of sunshine illuminating his hesitant smile. "Before you shut the door in my face, I came to say I'm sorry, first and foremost. I shouldn't have kept things from you, Eden. Not the work-related stuff, and definitely not the online-dating stuff." He shrugged, a playful gleam in his eye.

"You're my perfect match, my Little Miss Perfect, and I don't want to lose you."

The air whooshed from her lungs, and her knees threatened to give way, so she grabbed hold of the doorframe for support. With all the work drama, she'd forgotten about her interrupted online dating life. She'd forgotten how she'd connected with HotAussie007 and found him so attractive, even before they'd met. She'd forgotten what a disaster it would be if someone at work found out about it and her two worlds collided.

Who'd take a research scientist seriously when, after hours, she was LittleMissPerfect, online flirt? Eden shook her head. It didn't matter now, when her reputation was already in shreds. And they no longer worked together...

She closed her eyes for a moment, trying to figure out a way to keep her humiliation to a minimum. "Are you telling me we've met online?"

"Come on, Eden. You must have guessed it was me. The guy who wants you so bad, the one who likes old movies and flirting by instant message, the one who stood you up. Which I'm not proud of, by the way. I've wanted to apologize to you for a long time."

She huffed out a breath and stood tall again, crossing her arms under her breasts. "You were suddenly there in the restaurant parking lot. When you hit my scooter."

Finn nodded. "Yes."

"You were there to meet me."

"Yes."

"You're the only man I've been messaging for weeks."

"Well, I hope so. I'm HotAussie007, and you're Little-MissPerfect. We belong together."

She stared at him, this man who'd lied about everything and ruined her life. "Was your father even sick? Did you lie about that too? What about when you had to fly back to Australia? Were you really cheating on me?"

Finn stared at her, his mouth hanging open, his whole body frozen. He took far too long to respond. Like a liar!

"Eden, all of it was true. My dad's okay now, but he had a triple bypass, and it was touch and go for a while. I had to go to him. I'd never lie about something so important."

She tilted her head, sizing him up. "And cheating? Seems like that's second nature to you. I'll bet you have a whole string of women lined up on the app."

"What? No. I dated a few women, but it was a while ago."

"How long?"

Finn shook his head. "Months ago. These past few weeks, I only ever wanted to hook up with you."

Eden couldn't breathe. *Hook up?* Was that how he saw her? Just a cheap fling for something to do? For a second, everything stilled. Her mouth fell open, and she couldn't say a word. If there was a worst possible reaction to his admission, her body found it.

She clutched her stomach as the too-bitter black coffee surged up, burning her throat. With a heavy lurch, she leaned forward and vomited all over HotAussie007's shoes.

Finn winced and looked down, checking out the damage. Tan loafers plus pissed-off scientist/potential girlfriend vomit was not a winning combination, but he yanked off both shoes and flung them aside. Then he grabbed Eden by the upper arms and pulled her close, wrapping an arm around her back. The way she gasped and smooshed up against him, breasts crushed against his chest, would have had him backing her straight into the bedroom at any other time.

But today, he lifted her and carried her over to their favorite sofa. He deposited her on it and took a step back. After grabbing a glass of water from the kitchen, he stood over her, making sure she drank some.

"Sorry." Eden mumbled.

She made an unmistakable sobbing noise, then swiped the back of her hand across her mouth and struggled to pull her silky black robe together in front.

"This sofa rendezvous thing's becoming a habit, Doc. But the vomiting's new."

Her head whipped up, her violet eyes flashing. "Don't you dare tease me, Finn Donohue, Hot Aussie, whoever you are! You've destroyed my life single-handedly."

He sank to his knees and sat heavily on the floor beside her. Pain slashed through his gut at the distraught look on her face. "Oh bugger. This is worse than I thought, isn't it? What have I done? Come on, tell me. I can take it."

She blinked at him. "You don't even know? For starters, no one's going to want to hire a research scientist who's published no papers in the past two years. This clinical trial meant everything to me professionally after my... setback. Two and a half years ago, I had to quit my last job when my gran was sick. This project was my way back into the field, but now it's all been for nothing. Putting up with McTavish, developing a drug that's probably no good to anyone, it was all a complete waste of time."

Finn let out a slow whistle. "Right. Not good. Tell me more."

She shook her head, strands of black hair tumbling around her shoulders. "I have a massive mortgage. Huge. This was my grandmother's house, and she left it to Faith and me when she passed away. But she'd mortgaged it to pay for my education. It was important to her that I kept her home. I had to refinance it to help set up Faith's business. I can't lose the house, but I can't pay the mortgage with no damned job."

"Shit, yeah, that's awful too. Your grandmother's house. Makes sense. It's a really great house." He shot her a half-smile.

She sniffed, wiping her nose on her sleeve. "It *is* a great house and a great neighborhood. I'll never be able to afford to live around here if I lose this place. It was my childhood home after our mother died when I was eleven."

"Oh, Eden. I'm so sorry. I know what it's like to lose someone close to you. It's not something you recover from. Ever."

This time, she stared at him, eyes wide and watery. "You lost someone too?"

Finn's chest constricted. He didn't want to talk about it. He never did. But he owed it to Eden. From now on, he'd be nothing but completely honest with her. If he wanted a chance with her, she needed to know the full story. Why he'd pushed himself too hard to work in a scientific field when it made him feel like an elephant balancing on a tightrope.

He shrugged, attempting to unburden his shoulders. "My older brother. He was only twenty-four when he died, and I was twenty-one. But he'd been sick all his life. We were close all through our childhood. Best mates. He couldn't run and play football like me, but we stayed in and watched old movies with Mum. And he was so smart, like you, Doc. He wanted a career as a scientist, but he never had a chance to get his PhD. Guess I reconsidered everything when he died. I'd been so selfish. I hadn't spent enough time with him in the last year or so. And then, suddenly, he was gone."

Eden's sob surprised him; it sounded as if it'd been wrenched from the depths of her soul. And when she spoke, her words came out choked. "God, that's awful. What happened? How did he die?"

"Heart failure. He had congenital heart disease."

A touch on his cheek, soft and warm, made his own heart stutter. Eden smoothed her fingertips across both sides of his face. His wet cheeks.

She let her hands drop back to her lap and hit him with a quizzical look, one eyebrow lifting. "Is that why you wanted to work for Magna Smart? To develop a heart drug to help people like your brother?"

Finn nodded. "It's always been about Matt. He was the smart one with the science brain. I'd been studying marketing and got an internship in the sports industry. When he passed away, I knew I owed it to him to pursue his line of work somehow. I couldn't do the research side, but I could help make sure new drugs made it to market. Try to make a difference to another family."

Eden stared at him, sitting up straighter. She breathed out long and slow, her next words coming out on a sigh: "You're making it difficult to stay angry at you, even though I am. What you said about your brother, it makes total sense to me. I was good at math and science in school, but the only reason I pursued scientific research was to try to put a stop to cancer. Breast cancer took my mother and grandmother. I'm scared for myself and my sister too."

Finn rose from the floor and scooted onto the sofa beside Eden. She glanced at him and shifted to one side, making room for him. This was progress, at least. He sat facing forward, his hands resting on his knees. He wanted to reach out and touch her, but it was too soon. "I'm sorry about your family, and for all the trouble I've caused you. I'm sorry I lied. But I hope you can forgive me. You're important to me, Eden. I genuinely care about you."

She shrank back a little, watching him. "I want to believe you. I think you've been trying to do the right thing. But that doesn't mean we can just pick up where we left off. I need a man I can rely on. Someone who won't stand me up or turn his back on me when things get difficult. Or see me as a casual hookup."

Finn sighed, rolling his shoulders. He was a selfish dick. Of course he wanted it all. The job, a successful project, and Eden. But he probably had to face facts and admit it wasn't going to happen. "I understand. If you want nothing more to do with me, I'll back off. I'll leave you alone to get on with the rest of your life."

Shit. Why had he said that when leaving Eden alone was the last thing he wanted to do?

She'd become the first person he thought about each morning and the last one he thought about each night, when he imagined her lying beside him in bed. And she popped into his head at least fifty times a day in between. The way she told him off, the way her hips swayed as she walked, how brilliant she was, how she'd told him she wanted someone to love. How beautiful she was, and how his whole body ignited with a touch of her lips. How amusing she was, even if she didn't realize it.

He was in deep. Way too deep. Cutting himself off from Eden even for a while would hurt like a gaping wound. Cutting himself off from her forever would be bloody murder.

She shook her head, then did something totally unexpected. She took his hand. Her fingers entwined with his, and the softness of her skin, the tenderness of her touch, had him wanting to pick up exactly where they'd left off before he went to Australia.

Eden's lips parted with a sigh. "Let's back up a bit. Why don't you explain all this cloak-and-dagger business? Felicity told me you're investigating McTavish. Is it true?"

Everything churned inside him, mixed signals and warring emotions turning his insides to rubbery goo. Eden was being kind to him. Why, he wasn't sure. But he'd take it. If she was throwing him a bone, he'd jump up and catch it, then say *bow-wow.*

She'd asked about McTavish, so now he had to put his thoughts in order and answer her. "Felicity's right. I've been tracking the boss for months now, on the down-low. Ever since I learned of some strange financial details to do with the patient portal concept and the product development budget. I'm not as stupid as you think, Doc. I immediately knew the concept was flawed, a potential disaster. But what interested me was why."

Eden let out a grunt of frustration. "First of all, I don't think you're stupid. I've always thought you were bright and great at your job. Just annoying at times. And why what? Why did he pursue the idea?"

Finn's lips twitched. Nice to know she didn't consider him a dumbass. "Exactly. Why float the concept when it's likely to be shut down by the head honchos in Europe or the FDA? Why try to push it through in such a short timeframe? Alarm bells rang. But I played along with McTavish and waited."

Eden sat forward, her eyes locked with his. "Waited for what?"

He raised an eyebrow at her. "Waited for more information to fall in my lap. I played the 'yes man,' did whatever McTavish asked, and pretended to be enthusiastic. And information did turn up. Reports, memos, research from competitors, and financial papers. Some of them Meredith forwarded because she knew I was involved in the project. I'm not sure yet whether she knew exactly what they contained. Possibly she did. It wasn't conclusive, but a pattern soon emerged."

"Don't keep me in suspense. What kind of pattern?"

"Funds disappearing from the research and development budget. Also from business development, but mostly from R&D. Separate accounts for new projects that never came to fruition. There were significant funds assigned to them. Sometimes the funds would be drained, then later, money would reappear. Less than before."

Eden held up a hand like a stop sign and twirled her index finger in a circle. "Hang on, rewind. Funds disappeared from the R&D budget? But that's my area. At least, I manage some of it."

Finn sighed. "I know. That's why I've had to keep some things close to my chest. All signs pointed to McTavish embezzling company money, probably significant amounts. But I didn't think he could be doing it alone. Sure, he's the boss, but he can't approve funds transfers on his own. Meredith, other senior staff, or the manager responsible for each department has to cosign *if* things are being managed above board."

Eden moved as far away from him as possible while still staying seated on the sofa. She stared at him, her mouth hanging open like he'd slapped her. "You thought I had something to do with it. Stealing from the company."

With a shake of his head, Finn looked down at his hands. Ran his hands over his face and through his hair. "Months ago, I didn't even know you. Before McTavish announced the special projects funding, you were just a name to me, someone on an email distribution list. I was digging for information, poking around where I didn't belong. I had to be sure of everyone I worked with, including you."

He turned to face her, and those beautiful eyes of hers looked gray now but sparkled with emotion. Hurt, probably. "Then I got to know you a little. You were fiery and passionate about your work, a pain in the butt sometimes, but so dedicated. Your team clearly respected you and wanted to help you win the funding. I knew you didn't have a dishonest bone in your body. And when we got closer, I still couldn't tell you what was happening. I wanted to, but I needed to protect you."

Eden's forehead crinkled in a frown. "Protect me? By leaving me in the dark? God, Finn. You should have trusted me." She rose from the sofa and strode toward the hall. Then she turned and stormed straight back to him again. "I've done nothing wrong. Not one single thing. Except yell at McTavish, which I admit was a mistake. But am I in trouble? Real trouble, I mean. Will the cops come knocking on my door?"

Finn got to his feet and took a step toward her. Eden shivered as if cold, and he placed his hands on her upper arms. "As far as I can tell, you're okay. McTavish might have planned to use you as a cover, but he made mistakes. Remember that day he asked you about us having coffee together? I had my suspicions... Nate from my team found something. Someone accessed the financial database from your terminal while you were out of your office, but I don't think they made any transactions. Then there was how he kept you out of the loop on the patient portal project. No one's going to believe you were kept out of the way for any reason other than having too much integrity."

Eden bit her lip. "I can't believe it. Oh, I can believe McTavish is a sack of turds, but not the rest. He tried to set me up?"

Finn nodded, gazing down into her eyes. "You're not the only one. I think he tried it on me by taking funds allocated to business development. Meredith's worried. It's her reputation on the line here too. Which is why she asked external auditors to analyze the accounts about three months ago. Before we even discussed it, we'd both realized something wasn't right."

Eden sighed and took a step back.

Finn's arms dropped to his sides. He realized he'd been rubbing his hands up and down her arms. Soothing, yes. But he was also touching her as if he had a right to. She didn't need him demanding things of her. As much as he wanted to wrap her up in his arms, she wouldn't welcome it right now.

She pressed her lips together, then breathed out slowly. "I need to think about what you've told me. I'm going to call Felicity too, just so you know." She turned and walked toward the front door, clearly expecting him to follow.

"I have to get to work anyway. The show must go on. But I appreciate you giving me a chance to explain."

Eden opened the door and held it for him. "Goodbye, Finn."

He only hoped she wasn't saying goodbye forever.

Chapter Twenty-Two

Finn: Hey Mum, miss you. Having a rough week. Work sucks right now.

Mum: Give them all hell! Call me later. Dad sends his love too xxx

Finn walked into the open-plan Marketing office around nine o'clock, hoping no one would hassle him. He scoped out who was in and who was missing. Mimi appeared to be MIA, but she had a client appointment downtown, or so she'd said.

A few guys were drinking coffee and playing some complicated world-building video game when they should have been working. Finn glared at them but walked past without saying anything. For now.

Nate sat at his desk, tapping away on his keyboard, looking diligent, and raised a hand in greeting. "Hey, boss man. How's it hanging?"

Heat rose from Finn's chest and crawled up his neck. Nate's comment wasn't so offensive, but for some reason, that morning, it was annoying enough to tip him over the edge.

He strode across to the website team's corner and hovered in front of Nate like an angry storm cloud about to hail down on him. "Will you quit it with the frat-boy nicknames? And how is *what* hanging, exactly? Are you asking about the state of my private parts? Because, frankly, I should haul you into HR and give you an official warning for that comment." Finn turned to walk away, then called out, "And the rest of you, do some actual work."

Nate's mouth hung open, but Finn didn't stick around long enough to watch him catch flies. He stormed into his office and slammed the door behind him. His conversation with Eden had left him fuming, and he wasn't even sure why. She'd listened to him, given him a chance to explain, even let him touch her for a moment.

That was it. She'd pulled away from him, then said goodbye. It all seemed too final. And the more he rolled it around in his mind, the worse it sounded. Who could blame her? He'd lied to her almost from the second they met. Sure, he'd been trying to do the right thing, but what did it matter when the actual result was him ruining Eden's life? He was angry at himself. That was the plain, unvarnished truth.

Finn slumped into his office chair behind his desk and toyed with the rubber stress ball shaped like a cartoonish hot dog someone had given him last Christmas.

Maybe he should talk to his team. Explain he might be called away suddenly on urgent business... He struggled to think of a good enough excuse. If he had to leave on short notice, to give evidence or to go back to Australia, what could he tell them?

Finn was sick of all the subterfuge. He wasn't 007, not for real, wasn't cut out to be a double agent, pretending to go about his work while actually investigating the people around him. He squeezed the rubber hot dog tight in his fist. Its eyes bugged out. Why did a hot dog have eyes anyway?

He needed to do something, anything, to make himself feel he was getting somewhere. He sifted through the pile of papers on his desk, searching for... There it was. The blue folder with copies of the financials for the patient portal project, innocuously labeled 'Ad Spend.' Eden needed to look at the file, to see what he'd seen.

Finn was no math genius, not by any means. But he'd studied accountancy as part of his marketing degree and then managed some major marketing dollars. Budget figures and comparisons with actual spend were something he understood. At least, he understood the legitimate way it should be done. And he was good at recognizing patterns.

A light rap on his office door had him tensing and stuffing the papers back in the folder. Nate opened the door and stuck his head around the doorframe.

"Finn, I want to apologize." Nate's gaze tracked to Finn's hands as he stuffed the blue folder under a stack of plain beige manila folders. His filing system sucked. But now wasn't the time for paper-shuffling.

Finn sighed. "Apology accepted. I'm sorry I snapped at you. I've been in a mood since yesterday."

"Because Eden's not around anymore?"

Finn tried not to react but felt his eyebrows lift to somewhere around his hairline. "I'm concerned for Doctor Robinson, but I meant because the presentation didn't go to plan. Now I have to smooth things over with McTavish."

Nate dropped his head, dark hair curtaining his face. "Oh, right. Do you need me to help? I'm happy to download whatever stats you need, like that stuff McTavish wanted last week."

Finn rested his elbows on his desk and leaned forward, taking a moment before asking the inevitable question: "What stats did he request last week?"

"The usual. Traffic on the email servers between here and Europe, web search activity within the company, employee internet usage."

With a shake of his head, Finn rose and rolled his shoulders. "None of those things are *usual*. McTavish shouldn't be asking you for any of it. He should not be monitoring individual employees' internet searches, not unless he's formally investigating someone. You report to me, not him. Okay, here's what we'll do. Let's head over to HR and talk to someone, confidentially, about what you've just told me. We'll inform them of McTavish's requests and let them decide what to do."

Nate started walking backward, fast. "Nah, man. I can't."

Finn stood and strode across his office. He grabbed the door and called out to Nate, who'd already reached the far side of the larger team area, "Wait, what's the problem?"

The younger man shook his head. "I can't lose this job. I'm sorry, but if you think what I just told you is weird, you don't want to know what else the boss asked for."

Finn stepped outside his office door. "What? Nate, you can tell me. If you're honest with me, I can help. You won't lose your job." Finn blew out a breath, watching Nate, hoping rather than believing what he'd said was true. He was damn worried about his own job, his own life plans, the consequences of what he already knew. How could he protect Nate?

Nate stood frozen to the spot. Except for his head, which moved from side to side like that carnival game where you pop a ball in a clown's mouth to win a prize. He was obviously checking out the other guys from the team, who sat there staring, trying to figure out what was going on.

"Promise? If I tell you something in confidence, it has to stay anonymous. You didn't hear it from me," Nate stammered, his words tripping over each other.

With another sigh, Finn weighed his options. While he could promise not to reveal Nate's name, chances were, he'd have to at some point. "I can promise I won't reveal your name unless I have to, by law."

Nate nodded, suddenly serious. He caught Finn's eye and held his gaze. "I can live with that."

Finn extended his arm toward his office, waving Nate through. The younger man loped inside, and Finn followed, making sure to lock the door behind them.

Cupcakes. The world needed more happiness, but for now, cupcakes would have to suffice. Everyone knew they were the next best thing. Anyway, Eden needed something to do to keep her mind off all the worries circling in her brain.

Eden held onto her sifter: a metal cylinder with a handle she turned with a grinding noise. She sifted the flour into the mixing bowl, making sure all the lumpy bits stayed behind.

Her phone rang, buzzing on the countertop. When she saw it was her doctor's office, she wiped her hands on a kitchen towel and took the call. "Hello? Eden Robinson speaking."

"Hello, Eden. This is Catherine from Doctor Fernandez's office. She has your blood test results, and she'd like to discuss them with you."

The receptionist wouldn't give her the results over the phone but said the doctor had asked her to come in as soon as possible.

Eden agreed, in a voice that held a kind of dead calm. Faith called it Eden's Meltdown Phase One voice. Her sister always got well out of the way before Eden got really pissed and entered Phase Two.

The next available appointment was later that afternoon, so Eden took it and got off the phone as fast as possible.

A roil of nausea tipped her belly upside down, nearly landing her flat on her ass on the kitchen floor. Eden hadn't been feeling great lately. Low energy, lightheaded at times. And she'd vomited on Finn's shoes... She'd put it down to skipping a few meals, wonky blood sugar levels, and stress. But she shouldn't ignore it. It might be something, as it had been for the other women in her family before her.

Don't jump to conclusions. You need evidence. Facts.

Eden's eyes landed on the photo stuck to her refrigerator door. Her grandmother, all dressed up to go to Opening Day. A bit over three years ago now. She'd been so glamorous, so beautiful, always smiling. It was before she'd found out the breast cancer.

Her mother. Her grandmother... Would she be next in her family to suffer the scourge? Eden refused to say the 'C' word. Refused to even think it.

Her legs no longer wanted to hold her up, and she crumpled like a soufflé pulled out of the oven too soon. As she sank to the floor, the dam wall broke, releasing her tears to flow freely.

"So you're saying we're up shit creek without a paddle?" Finn sat at his desk, trying to absorb the salient facts in Nate's story. He squeezed the hot dog stress ball in his right hand until its guts nearly exploded.

His head resting in his hands, Nate looked up. "Not sure I even know what that means, but yeah."

"It's Aussie for *we're fucked.*"

Nate shrugged. "Oh yeah. We're totally fucked with a paddle."

That about summed it up. The situation was worse than Finn had thought, even worse than he'd suspected it might be when busy imagining worst-case scenarios. He'd be lucky if he didn't get fired. But he could also be deported and still have to testify against McTavish in a US court. There would be no escaping the situation he found himself tangled in.

Nate wouldn't escape either, poor guy. Finn didn't believe for a second that Nate had any idea of the bigger picture when he took the job or when completing the tasks McTavish assigned. He was a talented website data analyst, but he was young, straight out of college, and clueless about the corporate world.

How would he know a corporation could be like a bog, with all sorts of things sucked down and hidden underneath layers of mud? Nate was the perfect combination of technical skills and naïve trust. A gift dangled like bait in front of the predator's jaws.

Finn stopped recording their conversation on his cell phone. "Off the record, so to speak, I believe you did the right thing. There's no way you could've stopped working for McTavish without him noticing or inventing some offense to get you fired."

Nate nodded. "Exactly. Man, I've been worried. I'm putting my kid sister through school, and without this job, I can't afford it."

With a sigh, Finn leaned back in his chair. "I understand. You're doing a good thing for your sister."

Finn should have taken more of an interest in Nate since he came on board. He hadn't known much about the guy's background. Now he'd discovered Nate was trying to get his little sister back on the straight and narrow after a wild few years in high school. Their single mother was unemployed most of the time and unreliable at best. Nate had stepped up. He was more mature than Finn had given him credit for.

"Okay. Let's go over this again. I'll talk to Eden tonight and make sure she's got all the facts. Afterward, we'll prepare our paperwork for the meeting I'm setting up with the FDA and state investigators. We need to keep our heads down at work. We'll still do what's required and try not to draw any attention."

"Got it." Nate rose from his chair and headed for the door again. "But first, coffee."

"Got to agree. Coffee's a sound plan."

Finn waved Nate out of his office, then checked the time. Only nine-thirty. Hours until he finished work and could see Eden again. That was assuming she agreed to see him. And given that he'd pretty much ruined her life, it was a big ask.

He bent forward and clunked his forehead on his desk. He had to try.

Chapter Twenty-Three

Finn: Can I please talk to you later? In person?

Eden: Don't harass me

Eden was pissed with the world, and the ringing doorbell didn't help. Maybe she should yank the little button out of the wall so she wouldn't hear anyone who came by. It was the magical age of text messages and email. What was wrong with a little faceless, impersonal communication? Why couldn't people just send an emoji and leave her alone with her bad mood?

She hauled herself off the sofa, pushing her damp hair back over her shoulders, and shuffled toward the front door in her ankle socks.

After the doctor's appointment, she'd needed a shower. The warm water had been soothing against her body, chasing the deadness away. Her skin was still numb, from anesthetic and the mental fatigue was numbing her too. It might be something, her doctor had agreed. Eden was in a high-risk category, so they shouldn't take any chances. The biopsy had stung, but the implications stung worse.

It could be cancer. The C-word played on a loop in her head, like an ominous incantation.

Cancer, cancer, cancer.

Wrapping her silk robe tighter around her body, she almost stopped to pull on her pedal pushers. But, no, whoever it was annoying her at the door could deal with her half-dressed. Or they could take a walk.

She turned the key in the lock and opened up to a sight that made her stomach tighten. But she didn't think she'd vomit again.

Finn, looking slightly rumpled, overheated, and close to divine. His white business shirt was partially unbuttoned, sleeves rolled up to reveal his tanned forearms. His hair was tousled, and she could picture him running his hands through it. The way she wanted to. And his aviator sunglasses had slipped down his nose, so his green eyes sparkled over the top. And over the top was the only way to describe him.

Eden was in a foul mood, the worst, but in no way did that allay her horniness. Finn had no idea what he was getting himself into.

She smiled, resting her hands lightly on her hips. Her breaths came out shallow and reedy, too fast. "Well, if it isn't HotAussie007 gracing my doorstep again."

"Look, Eden, I've already apologized for the online dating stuff. That's not why I came to see you."

"No? Then I guess it's to do with work. Because coming to see me for some other reason would be extremely presumptuous." She raised her eyebrows and flipped her hair back imperiously.

Eden wanted him to presume. Wanted him to presume all over her body. Wanted him to kiss her, touch her, make her scream with pleasure. She shook her head since she was over-heating, and her ears were ringing.

She could do this. Seduce Finn. It was what she needed after the horrible day yesterday and her even worse doctor's visit today. She deserved some pleasure, and chances were good that this man could deliver.

Eden had decided. She wanted Finn, and he'd have to get with the program.

Finn whipped off his sunglasses and hung them in the V of his open shirt collar. His full lips tipped up in a smile. "Doctor Eden, anyone would think you're flirting with me."

"Flirting, having a conversation, call it what you will. Come in, either way." She opened her front door wider.

"Okaaay." Finn took a second to stare at her, his eyes roving from her damp hair down over her body, lingering on all the parts she longed for him to touch. Her nipples peaked under her robe, and she was sure he noticed. His eyes snapped back up to hers.

Then he strode forward and turned sideways to shuffle right by her, much closer than necessary. Certain parts of their bodies almost collided, like her breasts and his chest. She turned in his wake, and other parts came even closer, like her hand and his ass. She might have imagined it, but she'd have sworn he cursed under his breath.

Eden swayed forward, holding on to the wall for balance now. She took a moment to close her eyes and breathe before following him. Finn wasn't wasting any time—he'd gone straight to her kitchen and started up her coffee maker.

Okay then.

She stomped across the kitchen as best she could in her socks. Looked like he was going to make this hard for her, so to speak. Just when she wanted him hard and ready, he was playing coy. She wasn't having it.

Eden leaned on the kitchen counter in such a way he couldn't fail to notice her cupcakes. She'd baked a large batch that morning and was happy to share. But in case he didn't realize what was on offer, she'd make it obvious. "Did you see my cupcakes?"

Finn stiffened, his whole spine straightening like the mast on a sailboat. As he turned toward her, his back to the coffee maker, Finn sighed. "You made cupcakes?"

"Uh-huh."

His gaze flicked from the tray of cupcakes on the counter to her nicely framed cleavage above them. He swallowed. "Any particular occasion?"

"I was feeling down, and cupcakes always cheer me up."

"Me too." He gestured to the tray of dainty rose-colored cakes lined up like tiny ballerinas. "May I?"

She nodded. If he wouldn't taste her, it was the next best thing.

Finn stepped over to the counter and came to a halt on the opposite side of the island from her. He reached out and took a cupcake, raised it to his lips, then bit into it. It was one of the most devouring attacks on a cupcake she'd ever witnessed. The pink frosting covered his fingers, and his eyelids fluttered closed. He groaned, the noise reverberating through her like the engine rumbling between her thighs when she rode her Vespa.

"This is a bloody delicious cupcake, Doctor Eden. You know, they say the way to a man's heart is through his stomach."

"I'm glad you're enjoying it." She studied his mouth as his tongue darted out to retrieve a stray bit of frosting. "But 'they' say a lot of things, and I haven't found it to be true."

"No?" He chewed thoughtfully. When he swallowed, Eden watched the muscles in his jaw and throat work. "This cupcake makes me want to write you sonnets and name stars after you. 'An Ode to Doctor Eden's Pink Cupcakes,' or Alpha Eden Cupcake Nova."

Giggles rose from her belly, so unexpected she spluttered. "Finn, you're sweet." Her cheeks stretched out in a grin. Also unexpected. She was feeling better, happier, since Finn arrived.

"Come and sit down." She gestured toward the living room, waving her hand vaguely like a game show host.

Finn smiled, the expression flitting across his face like a cool breeze at the beach in summer. He messed around with the coffee maker for a moment before grabbing one of her favorite cups from the overhead cabinet like he owned the place.

Eden blinked. He'd been in her kitchen a few times lately, like a friend. Or boyfriend. He was starting to know his way around her house, except for her bedroom. He hadn't been in there. Yet.

She turned on her heel and hurried into the living room, making a beeline for her sofa. The Sofa of Sexy Times. Perhaps it was the wrong choice, but it called to her for reasons she didn't care to examine. She shuffled her butt down to one end and smoothed her robe over her thighs. The robe was suddenly too thin, too flimsy, and altogether too sensual for conversation with a colleague.

No, not a colleague. She no longer worked at Magna Smart, no longer worked with Finn, or competed against him. The zing of excitement at that thought was responsible for the heat surging through her limbs, nothing more. Certainly not Finn sauntering into the room carrying two coffees and bending down in front of her, just so. He was merely placing cups of coffee on the low table, not displaying his fine, rounded butt in his perfectly fitted suit pants for her benefit.

Finn straightened, tipping his chin at the cups. "Strong and sweet, just how you like it," he announced with a grin bookended by dimples.

Oh boy, did she ever like it! After the day she'd had—actually, the whole week—he was a super-cute mirage in the desert. Eden wanted to reach for him, but what if he rejected her? She untwined the ribbon belt of her robe, somehow twisted around her fingers.

Finn settled beside her on the sofa, leaving a vast empty expanse on his other side. He almost snuggled into her. He bent forward and picked up his coffee, then settled back again while taking a sip from his cup.

The spice-accented aroma and steamy warmth wrapped around her nostrils and tickled her tastebuds, even though she hadn't tasted it herself. He smelled delicious drinking her coffee. Like a cinnamon roll brunch treat. Her mouth watered.

Eden needed to get this visit back under control. "So, how were things at work today?" She pressed her lips together. Stupid question. It sounded too domestic, too '*How was your day, dear?*' Like she was his wife or sitcom love interest. It was too obvious an attempt at small talk to cover her nervousness. She snatched up the other cup from the table and glugged down a mouthful of coffee.

"Ah, now we get to the point. I've enjoyed this pleasant visit charade, but I guess it's time for me to ask you to help me with the McTavish situation or for you to tell me off. Then I'll ride into the sunset and leave you alone."

Eden sighed. "There's no need for you to ride off into the sunset."

"There isn't?"

"No. Everybody makes mistakes. Me as much as anyone. I never intended to get tangled up with someone I work with. But here we are, tangled."

Oh, what a tangled web we weave when first we practice to deceive.

The line, often misattributed to Shakespeare, floated into her head uninvited. Her quote of the day app was teaching her things, and the snippet seemed apt, whoever wrote it.

Eden's life had become complicated over the past few months. Things always got complicated when people started lying. Finn had been lying for months, of course. But so had she. She'd lied to others and, worst of all, to herself.

She'd pretended to be someone else to find love.

She'd continued working for McTavish, a man she hated.

She'd ground herself down, trying to pay off a huge mortgage rather than sell their grandmother's house, and she'd lied about it being easy.

She'd tried to look after Faith, put everyone else ahead of herself, and lied whenever she said she was fine.

All of those things, all those lies, stopped now. It was time to make some changes.

Eden knew the lies we tell ourselves could be the most destructive to our happiness. She was about to start being truthful. The results couldn't be any worse than what had already happened. Since she'd started lying, she'd nearly lost everything important.

Perhaps the truth would set her free.

"I want you, Finn."

Finn's head spun, and he suspected the double hit of sugar and caffeine wasn't responsible. The cup trembled in his unsteady grasp, threatening to spill its contents, so he leaned forward and deposited it safely back on the table.

Eden's words swam upstream into his conscious mind. "But here we are, tangled." Then, before he caught his breath: "I want you, Finn." Her voice was husky.

She shifted, her thigh pressing against his where she sat beside him. The heat of her skin through her thin robe was tempting. No longer the straitlaced scientist, she was all sexy, glamorous woman. His gaze caught on the sliver of skin revealed by the silky fabric loosening where it crossed over her chest. The hint of the upper slope of her breasts.

As Eden flipped her hair back over her shoulder, he focused on her face, her mouth. She hesitated before speaking so low it was almost a whisper: "I don't want you out of my life. It's not what I want at all."

Finn froze. His gaze snapped up to hers and snagged there. The tension between them was sharp, an invisible fishing line pulled taut, ready to snap.

He clenched his jaw, waiting to find some words. When his voice returned, it was low and uneven. "What do you want? Because I'll work as hard as I can to give it to you."

Eden's mouth softened, then stretched into that enigmatic Cleopatra smile, making him hold his breath. He waited for her command. "I was hoping you'd say that. I want us to try dating exclusively. We can see how things go without the pressure of work. I... like you, Finn. Surprising, but true."

What the hell had gotten into her? Doctor Eden had turned all *sexy*. Well, she'd been sexy before. But now, she was transmitting some hot infrared waves, and he was one hundred percent tuned in to her frequency.

She'd shifted closer, physically and mentally. Her smile and the way she stroked her thigh with her fingertip. And her scent: like heaven just crashed into a gourmet bakery. The vanilla and roses with a hint of musk did dangerous things to his self-control when he breathed her in.

He'd forgotten to respond to whatever it was she'd said. Something about dating? Being exclusive? Sounded good to him. Especially if it involved untying that damned ribbon around the waist of her red robe. She looked like a Christmas present in that thing, and he was dying to unwrap her.

Finn shook himself, shifting in his seat to hide his reaction to her words. His firm, upright, and definitely male reaction. "A good surprise or a bad surprise?"

"A good one." Eden leaned in and kissed him, once, on the corner of his mouth. Now *that* was surprising.

He stared into her eyes, the heat emanating from them making him suck in a sharp breath. The way his blood surged through his veins in response, no surprises there. How he reached for the lengths of her hair and ran his fingers through it, making her sigh was unexpected. Then, when he tugged at the bow at her waist with his trembling fingers, the way she didn't resist but leaned forward and kissed his throat... That was the biggest surprise of all.

The best surprise. Like the special item at the top of his Christmas list.

Eden shivered down to her toes as Finn tugged on the ribbon at her waist. The red satin fabric loosened and parted to reveal a slash of skin straight from her neck, between her heavy breasts, to her navel, the curve of her belly, and lower. He exposed the matching red lace underwear she wore for no other reason than a need to feel attractive. Desirable.

Now Finn's eyes were on her skin, his breath warm and close to her cheek. His desire filled the air, surrounding her. The very atmosphere was thick and syrupy. He sat close, his leg pressing against hers. Then he leaned forward and eased the robe from her shoulders so the fabric drifted down her arms and pooled in red ripples behind her.

The day was warm, but her nipples tightened beneath Finn's scrutiny as he sat back and stared at her. His ragged breathing quickened, she resisted the urge to cover herself. It had been a long time, and he was about to discover she wasn't perfect. Nobody was, she knew it, but she was flawed. Her eyes fluttered closed for a second.

What if he rejected her now? She'd probably wilt and die on the spot like a week-old rose in a vase.

"Oh, Eden. So beautiful." Finn had been stroking her shoulders, but now his hands feathered along her collarbone, moving downward.

She opened her eyes and watched as his fingertips stroked in gentle circles. Finally, he cupped her breasts in his large, warm hands. She gasped. His groan of appreciation sang through her body, making her tremble, making her want to grab and kiss the hell out of him before he changed his mind.

But she waited for the inevitable questions.

His hands stilled. Then he asked, "What's this? A cupcake?"

His index finger made contact with the outer edge of her right breast and traced the scar there, now covered by a tattoo of a cupcake. She wanted to whimper. Instead, she simply nodded and bit her lip. She held in the explanations, the apologies for being less than model perfect. All the reasons why men usually fled like rats from a sinking ship the moment she took off her clothes.

"So. Fucking. Hot." He bent and pressed his lips to her skin, right there, kissing once, twice, three times. "Pardon my French, but you have a cupcake tattoo on your breast. I think I nearly came."

Eden giggled, the noise rising from her throat so unexpected that she slapped a hand over her mouth. She spoke through her fingers. "I have another one on my butt."

What had made her share that interesting little tidbit?

However, she didn't have time to regret her words, as he basically fell on her, humming against her flesh, licking the outline of the cupcake's delicately rendered frosting and the cherry on top until she trembled. Then he shifted across and took her taut nipple in his mouth.

This time, she cried out as every nerve ending in her body tried to explode. His hand made its way to her left breast, squeezing and rolling the flesh until she had to stop him. It was too tender. She placed her hand over his. He moved back and searched her face.

"Sorry, it's a little tender today. I had to... have a test." She sucked in a deep breath, willing herself to stay calm. "A biopsy."

Finn sat back beside her, watching as she raised her arm slightly to reveal the dressing over the spot near her armpit. The doctor had assured her she'd be fine for normal activities, but this probably wasn't what she'd had in mind. Her stomach rolled over as Finn's mouth fell open, but no words came out.

He was going to run. Just like that loser she'd dated months ago. *'Too complicated,'* he'd said. *'What a load of horseshit, you coward,'* she'd responded. She'd shown him the door, and he'd never bothered to call her again.

Finn slowly shook his head. "Eden, I'm sorry."

His brow crinkled. He looked so concerned, so *kind*, that she wanted to shake him out of it. That wasn't what she needed right now. She needed to feel like a woman, wanted pleasure with a man who desired her, something she'd lacked for a long time.

With a sigh, Eden gathered up her robe to cover herself. "If you want to leave, I understand." Most men didn't have the gene for sympathy or acceptance. Not exactly a scientific conclusion, but in her personal experience, the evidence supported the hypothesis.

He lifted his hand and stroked her cheek. "I don't want to leave. I want you so much that, frankly, it's getting uncomfortable. In fact, I suspect I'm about to do myself an injury any minute. Unless you're asking me to go?"

She closed her eyes again, gathering her courage. When her eyelids fluttered open, he was watching her, and she was gratified to see his gaze flick down to her breasts again. "I want you to stay. But not because you feel sorry for me."

Finn stroked his finger over her jawline and down her neck. "As if I'd feel sorry for you, Doctor Eden. You're the most amazing woman I've ever met. You're magnificent."

Her heart thudded in her chest as her lips stretched into a smile. "In that case, guess I should finish showing you my house. You haven't seen my boudoir yet."

His left eyebrow quirked upward, his half-smile highlighting that boyish dimple. "Your *boudoir*? No, I, um, haven't had the pleasure."

Eden rose from the sofa, letting her robe fall to the floor. "And you haven't seen all my tattoos."

Finn's gaze roamed her body, almost a touch as it skimmed her skin. Or the promise of many touches to come. His attention settled on her skimpy red underwear. "Ah, the other cupcake tattoo. On your ass. No, I haven't seen it. But examining it is definitely on my to-do list. If we could, er, pick up where we left off?"

"I think we should." She pivoted in her silly little socks, then strolled toward her bedroom, putting an extra sway in her hips. "Before I die from the anticipation."

Finn's groan reverberated off the walls. They probably heard it all the way downtown.

Eden wanted to shriek with joy and punch the sky or do something stupid. But she settled for hurrying up. Her bedroom suddenly seemed too far away.

He followed her down the hall, his footsteps a staccato beat on her hardwood floor. "Your wish is my command."

Finn was panting by the time he crossed the threshold of Eden's *boudoir*. The enormous bed with its black satin sheets and thick ivory quilt was a surprise, but along with the Art Deco lamps and black-and-white photos of old Hollywood movie stars on the walls, it suited her. The room was elegant without being fussy.

Eden stood at the foot of the bed, removing her tiny white ankle socks. Why such a thing turned him on when she was almost completely naked, he couldn't explain. Then her red-polished toenails appeared with a wiggle, and he remembered. He'd had a thing about her feet ever since the first time he saw her with no shoes. His cock hardened to the point of pain, pressing against the zipper of his pants, trying to escape.

Finn cleared his throat. "Bend over." The words came out of nowhere.

She glanced at him and blinked, then bit her lower lip. It was slick and pink, calling him to kiss her properly. "Ask me nicely, and I'll consider it."

Fuck. His dick had started calling the shots. He had to remember his manners. She was entrusting him with personal secrets and her body, and he wouldn't disappoint her. "Please, Eden. Let me see your cupcake."

She burst out laughing, and, damn, the sound was music to his ears. "Alright." Eden bent over the edge of the bed, lying on her stomach and leaning on her forearms. She looked back over her shoulder at him, and he nearly lost it.

Her gorgeous peach of an ass was rounded and ripe, clad only in the delicate lace panties. Panties as red as the blood rushing through his veins, like a red flag to a bull. He wanted to charge in, lay claim to her, take her. But he had to slow down and think through the lust haze clouding his brain.

He dropped to his knees behind her and, slow as he could manage, inched her underwear down. His fingers skimmed the outline of her curves, the stunning softness of her skin making him sigh. And there it was. As the lace settled below the curve of her right ass cheek, a pretty pink cupcake was revealed. The swirl of frosting looked edible. He traced its outline with his fingertip, making her shiver.

"You didn't mention the butterflies." A group of tiny butterflies looked like they were about to take off and fly right out of the tattoo design. Just like the sugar-candy butterflies on the real cupcakes she'd brought into work that day... when he'd devoured them like a heathen. The day she'd kissed him senseless.

"Do you like them?"

Finn leaned forward and kissed her, right on the frosting. "Dammit, Eden, I want to eat you for dessert." He nuzzled his cheek against hers, then kissed his way across to the valley between her legs.

Eden made a sound in the back of her throat, as if drowning in need. He could relate. His whole body was heavy and aching. She widened her legs without him asking, and he slid her underwear down until they puddled around her ankles, then lifted one sexy foot so she stepped out of them. Grasping her hips between his two hands, he pressed his lips to the slickness between her thighs.

Tasting her was a treat. Sweet, with a hint of musk. Finn kissed her with an open mouth as he would her lips. Licking deeper, he found her entrance and dipped his tongue inside. She squealed, the sound coinciding with the start of her trembling thighs. He pictured his cock tracing the same path as his tongue and nearly had an embolism.

Finn licked a path farther up and found her hard bud. He teased her there, laying soft kisses on either side of where she wanted him. Then circling, circling, closer and closer until the tension spread through her limbs.

She leaned forward on the bed. "Now, Finn. Oh fuck. I need to come."

He spluttered against her, her swearing and frank sex talk unexpected. But he took heed. While pressing the flat of his tongue hard against her clit, he plunged two fingers deep inside her, triggering her climax.

She shuddered and cried out, "Finn!"

She said his name, and it was the most beautiful sound he'd ever heard. Finn kissed his way down between her thighs while easing his fingers from her body. She was relaxed, soft against him, but he was still coiled tight, ready to snap. Breathing hard, he sat back on his haunches.

Eden shuffled onto the bed and lay on her side, one arm flung over her forehead. "Phew. Thank you, Mr. Hot Aussie. I needed that. But I think you wore me out."

He slowly straightened to standing, then sat on the edge of the bed and stroked his hand down her leg. Smooth and more muscular than he would've guessed. How he'd love to have those long legs wrapped around his waist. "If you're too tired..."

She propped herself up on one elbow, her breasts jiggling so languidly that he couldn't help but stare. "Don't you dare go anywhere! Do you know I still haven't seen you naked? You might have all kinds of tattoos I haven't seen."

"So you want to see me naked? You only have to ask."

Eden's smile melted his insides. "Yes, I want to see you naked. Pretty please."

Finn was on his feet and out of his clothes fast, faster than Superman in a phone booth. And more naked. He'd toed off his shoes, yanked down his pants and boxers, and was halfway through unbuttoning his shirt when he registered the dead silence from Eden.

She sat fully upright now, staring at him with her mouth hanging open. "You could have warned me you were"—she ran her gaze down his body — "prodigious."

"Oh, you mean..." He followed her line of sight to the guy currently calling the shots.

His heart pounded, matching the throbbing in a certain other area, but he continued unbuttoning his shirt as if he had all the time in the world. As if she hadn't just complimented his cock for being on the large side. At least, he hoped it was a compliment. He discarded his shirt and stroked himself. Only once, no more, or it would be game, set, match. Advantage, Doctor Eden.

She raised one arched eyebrow. "You're a beautiful man. It's been a while since I've been with anyone... for lots of reasons. Oh God, you must think I'm such a prude."

With a shake of his head, Finn sat on the bed and bent to kiss her gorgeous mouth. She kissed him back, pressing those lush curves into him. He leaned against the headboard beside her, just resting there, not wanting to push his luck. "It's the last thing I'm thinking. You're looking for something special, and I'm honored that you're considering me. I think I'm a lucky bastard."

She sighed and pressed herself against him, linking her fingers through his. "I'm doing much more than considering. I want your cock inside me."

He shuddered, the intense surge of heat passing through him making him want to throw her down and take her. Hard. Closing his eyes, he breathed deep, ending up with a lungful of her scent, designed to drive him crazy. When he reopened his eyes, the look on her face shocked him. Her forehead creased, she was worrying at her lower lip with her teeth.

Eden slapped her hand over her mouth, then whispered so he had to strain to hear her, "Don't you like me talking dirty? An ex once told me I was crude. Apparently, I look innocent and seem like a nice girl, then I say these things... I don't know what gets into me."

Finn pulled her closer and kissed her. "I do. Passion gets into you. You're a fiery, passionate woman, and I can't get enough. I want to fuck you now. And I want you to say all the dirty things on your mind. Because I fucking love it."

"Oh." Eden shuffled over to the other side of the bed, and for a moment, he thought he'd lost her. She was backing away. But she opened the drawer of her bedside table and grabbed a small box, which she tossed to him.

He caught it and grinned. An unopened box of condoms.

"I've not had much use for them lately." Eden shrugged. "You'd better check the expiry date."

With a laugh, Finn read out the date and declared, "We're good to go." He placed the box on the pillow beside him.

As he pulled Eden closer and wrapped his arms around her, he knew this was a make-or-break moment. Finn rolled on top of her and kissed her, relishing the moment she softened beneath him with a moan. Tugging on her lower lip with his teeth got a reaction. She made that noise again. The hungry, carnal sound had him shifting his weight and pressing himself against her, at the same time tasting her, exploring her delicious mouth.

The taste of her was like nothing else—a feminine warmth and sweetness wrapped in a deeper floral scent. Heat surged through his whole system with such urgency that it had him pulling away from their kiss to catch his breath.

Finn reached for the condoms and tore the box open with no finesse, but Eden laughed lightly. Within seconds, he'd sheathed himself, protecting them both. He rolled on top of her and propped himself up on his forearms, which she began to stroke with her fingertips.

"Have I told you how much your arms turn me on?"

"Really? My arms?"

Eden nodded against his chest. "Then there's your gorgeous green eyes and your chest and all the handsomeness, but I can't look at your arms too long, or else I want to bite them."

He laughed, but it came out sounding choked. All this time, he'd assumed the attraction was one-sided. He'd been ogling Eden for so long now, wishing she'd want him too, but he hadn't registered that she'd been checking him out. She grabbed his bicep and squeezed.

Damn, at this rate, she'd make him lose control before he'd even sunk inside her. It was time. No more waiting. "Eden, I need you now. Bite me if you want."

She pressed her face against his arm and laughed, which turned into a gasp when he aligned himself with her body. He nudged at her entrance, and she took him in hand, guiding him with a sure touch. He glided halfway in at least, and she gripped him, the rush of sensitivity making his head spin.

"Fuck, Eden. You feel too good. Give me a sec." He closed his eyes and sucked in a calming breath of air. Where were his meditation skills when he needed them?

"That's what you're meant to be doing. Fucking Eden, it's your priority number one right now."

"Shut up and bite my arm."

Giggling, she did as instructed. Bit him, nipped at him, really, but the slight edge of pain had him groaning with pure lust.

Finn thrust into her tight heat, so they both sighed. His heartbeat sped up like he'd revved the engine, shifting into overdrive. Again and again, he thrust deeper, finding a steady rhythm.

Eden's lips opened on a silent gasp as she arched her back, pushing her breasts into his chest, her softness driving him wild. He kissed a path down her throat and across the slope of her shoulder, making his way to the peak of her right nipple. The light cocoa-colored bud called to him, and he licked a circle around it until she responded in the best way. She pushed her breasts upward, wanting more.

He closed his lips around her nipple and suckled her, the sweet taste and the way she responded, the peak hardening further under his tongue, making him dizzy. She was intoxicating. But he broke off for a moment. "Is this okay? I don't want to hurt you."

She let out a shaky sigh. "Okay. More than okay. Keep going." Her hips kicked up to meet him, then she wrapped her legs tight around his back. She clung to him as her inner muscles clenched around him.

He moved in and out of her, slow and steady, while sucking at her breast. He leaned back and met her eyes. "Eden." He repeated her name like a mantra. Or a promise.

She thrashed against the pillow, her dark hair fanning out around her beautiful face. "Yes. Finn, I love it. I love your cock deep inside me. I need it. Harder."

God, she'd be the death of him with her spicy talk. He nuzzled her throat. "Take it. Come for me." He thrust into her with everything he had, leaning on his forearms and letting her thrust back at him, hips rising to meet him.

"Yes, I'm coming..."

She screamed, her release arrowing through his own body like a bolt of electricity from where they were connected. Eden shuddered beneath him, her legs tightening around his back.

Finn couldn't hold on for another second. Didn't want to try. Heat radiated from the base of his spine, spreading to every part of him. His vision darkening, he surged into her with one final thrust, and his climax rolled over him like the surf at the tail end of a storm. Then he was washed away, rolling out with the tide.

When his eyes flickered open, he found himself on his back, and Eden shifted to lie on top of him. Still joined. She kissed his chest, and he lifted his head, apparently full of bricks, to kiss her forehead. His head flopped back until he lay prone. Spent.

Eden sighed and rested her cheek on his chest, snuggling against him. "Well now, seems you do love my dirty talk."

His heart seemed to beat just for her. "God, Eden. I love everything about you. I just love you."

Her head popped up, and she stared at him, her eyes wide and more violet than ever. Full of disbelief or anger, he couldn't say. She rolled off him and stood too quickly before stumbling away from the bed, her feet tangled in the sheets.

She righted herself and walked from the room, her naked ass swaying and cupcake taunting him. Leaving him lying in her bed, alone.

Chapter Twenty-Four

Eden leaned back against the closed bathroom door, shivering. The coldness seeped under her skin now that she wasn't pressed against Finn, so warm and hard. Now he wasn't inside her, making her body come to life, loving her.

I just love you.

He'd said he loved her. But did he really mean it? She'd waited so long to find someone like him. Strong and caring, funny and smart, willing to listen to her secrets and touch her — body and soul. He'd wanted to touch her, even though she was imperfect, scarred.

Now here she was, hiding out. Naked. Cold. Alone.

She'd run, as sure as she'd run from him before. After their first kiss, he'd strode away, but she had to get out of there just as badly. After the first time he'd made her orgasm on her sofa, she couldn't wait to get away from him. But why?

With a shake of her head, Eden forced herself upright and took a few steps toward her shower. She pulled back the curtain to turn on the water and waited for it to warm up.

A loud knock on the bathroom door reminded her she wasn't alone. Finn was still in her house, although apparently not in her bed. What must he think of her? She was fully aware she was behaving like a weirdo or, at the very least, a woman who couldn't handle the slightest affection from a man she'd just slept with. Not that they'd slept.

He knocked again. "Eden, are you alright?" His words were hesitant, muted by the running water. "Did I do something wrong?"

Oh no. Finn had done nothing wrong. By any measure, he'd done everything right. All the kissing and touching. Making her cry out with pleasure so intense that her brain had ceased to question everything for a few wonderful minutes. It had been so very right.

So why had she run out on him? Because she was scared. She knew half the problem with her love life wasn't the men she dated; it was her impossibly high standards, her wanting a man who'd adore her while she offered barely a hint of feelings in return. She'd protected herself at any cost.

Eden flicked off the shower and grabbed a large fluffy white towel to wrap herself in. "I'm okay. I needed a moment." She reached for the door handle and eased it open.

Finn stood framed in the doorway, dressed only in his navy-blue boxers, looking like a dream. His hair was all ruffled, and the sight of his bare chest with its light covering of downy hair made her want to lick him. Which would be entirely inappropriate. His expression was taut, lines creasing his forehead and his sharp jaw clenched. She had to fix this.

"You shocked me before with what you said. About *love*."

"It was too soon. I knew it, but I couldn't help it." Finn crossed his arms in front of his chest. "But I'm not sorry. Because it's true." He caught her with his gaze and wouldn't let go.

Eden was falling, and it was too late to stop her descent. "God, Finn, I want... I want more than anything to say it back to you and mean it. But I'm not ready." She shook her head, and he leaned over and brushed her hair back behind her ears.

"I get it."

"No, I don't think you do. I've never said it before — to any man. It's so hard for me to talk about my feelings. Facts I'm okay with. But this?"

"This?"

She grabbed hold of his arm. To steady herself. It felt good to touch him. She squeezed his amazing bicep. "It's like my heart's going through a meat grinder, and I don't know if I'll survive or be turned into hamburger. At the same time, my belly's turning over so much I might be sick, like I'm on a carnival ride and can't get off. But I don't want to get off either because it's exhilarating."

Finn's lips quirked up on one side. "I see."

"You do? Because that's not the worst part. I'm worried I might hurt you so badly that you'll leave and never come back. And I don't want you to leave. I can still feel you inside me."

He stepped toward her and ran his hand down her exposed arm. "How does it feel, Eden? Explain it to me."

"Like everything. The end of the world and the start of something amazing. I've never had an orgasm like it. So intense, so perfect. I feel so connected to you, as if you're my favorite person in the whole world. I don't want it to end."

He stroked her skin, his fingertips traveling up to her chin, and he took her face in his strong hands. "It doesn't have to end. And, by the way, I'd say you're doing just fine talking about your feelings."

Finn leaned down and kissed her, light and tender. Something must have misfired in her brain because her face overheated, and her whole body was aflame. Eden burned for his touch, more of that incredible connection. This kissing in the doorway wasn't enough.

With a sigh, she melted against him as he kissed his way down her throat. She had to let him know what she wanted. What she needed. "Come back to bed with me. I need you again."

He chuckled against her skin, making her shiver. "See? You're doing great. Come on."

Finn led her back to her bedroom, smiling over his shoulder when she lost her towel along the way. She didn't even mind being naked in front of him. Not when he looked at her in such a way. He couldn't be faking the hunger burning in his emerald eyes, making them glint and sparkle in the low light.

Finn held her hand and pulled her closer to the bed, and she tripped into his arms. His strong arms wrapped tight around her, and he kissed her again, but differently this time. Coaxing and teasing, exploring her, making her moan into his mouth. His hands tangled in her hair, and she stroked his warm skin, down the muscular planes of his back to his exceptional butt. They made out like teenagers until they fell together onto her unmade bed.

They lay face to face, Finn letting her set a slow, sensual pace. She kissed her way down his chest as he watched her. And when she licked lightly over his nipple, the little chest hairs tickling her nose, he tensed and swore under his breath. Eden felt him harden, his length pressing up against her belly, and she wanted him in her mouth immediately. She wanted to give him pleasure.

She shuffled down the mattress and took his erection in her grasp. He was so hot and hard but smooth and sensual at once. He groaned, and when she stroked him, he swelled in her grasp. Then she dipped her head and kissed the tip, savoring his musky scent. Eden opened her mouth, taking him inside, tasting him. She ran her tongue down the underside, then moved until she felt him tense.

The feel of him was insistent, making her hyper aware of him. With her other hand pressed to his chest, she kept going, taking him deeper.

Finn's whole body shuddered. He gripped her hair in his fist and held her still. "No more. Not this time. I want to be with you again."

She released him and moved back, stunned to see his clenched fists and hardened jaw. Almost as if he was having trouble holding on to his control... because of her. She kissed his lips, the lightest of touches, to let him know she cared. Because she did care, more than she could admit in words.

Finn pressed against her where they lay, beside each other once more. "Have I told you how gorgeous you are? How much your body drives me crazy? Your legs, your mouth, these breasts." He lifted her right breast with one hand, stroking her nipple with his thumb, and it instantly stiffened in response.

Eden watched as he ducked his head and kissed each of her breasts, so gently that it made her heart ache. Slowly, he worked his tongue over her right areola, around the point of her nipple, until finally, he took the peak into his mouth. Eden's breathing grew shallow and rough. He worked her sensitive flesh until she was hot and trembling, sparks of sensation shooting to the most unlikely places — her scalp, the soles of her feet. She curled her toes and rubbed her legs against his.

Low in her belly, muscles tightened, the spot between her legs swollen and aching. Her body was ready, anticipating what came next. Her heart, on the other hand, wasn't so sure. It thumped beneath her breasts, warning her to run away.

Not this time. She wouldn't run, wouldn't hide from his gaze or how he held her now. The way he caressed her. His hand grasped her hip, then he leaned over and slid his hand under her top leg and lifted it so it wrapped around his waist. In this position, she was open to him. Vulnerable.

Finn raised his head and kissed her lips, then fumbled for something near the headboard. Another condom. He smiled at her, the cheekiest grin she'd ever seen from him. And that was saying something.

He tore open the little foil packet in no time, and she watched in awe as he stroked himself. Her heart squeezed when he took her hand, guiding her with his palm until she'd rolled the condom down his length. Hands trembling, she tried to focus. He was beautiful. Every inch of him. So thick too. And, judging by the way that he held her hand still, also very sensitive.

Finn kissed her again, his tongue stroking hers as he grabbed her hip and pulled her close. She was still holding the base of his erection, so she guided him to her core, and he groaned as she used the head to stroke exactly where she needed him. Her clit pulsed, and she gasped with the exquisite pleasure pouring through her system. Slick with wanting him, she moved her hips as he entered her, this time in one long, perfect stroke until he filled her completely.

The deep, rumbling noise emanating from his throat was such a turn-on that she struggled to think. So she didn't. Her conscious brain slid away somewhere, and she didn't mind one bit. Letting her body take over, she rocked her hips while he followed her lead. With him so deep, he touched the spot inside that had her tensing and twisting, working herself against him feverishly. She panted, couldn't get enough air, couldn't get enough of him.

Finn gripped her knee and stroked into her long and smooth, each time taking her higher. He kissed her throat and whispered low in her ear, "Tell me. Tell me how much you want it."

Her eyelids fluttered closed. "I want it. I want you so much."

"Like you mean it."

Eden nodded. "Yes, fuck me like you mean it."

He half-laughed, half-groaned. "Not what I meant, but okay." Stepping up the pace, he thrust into her harder.

She clung to him as she cried out, "Finn! Now, now, now." She clenched her inner muscles. "Come inside me."

Finn tensed, and as he moved inside her one last time, his cock throbbed, and he came with a harsh cry, setting off her own release.

Showers of sparks tumbled down on her as waves of glorious energy left her floating somewhere in space. Then shivering, shaking, lying sprawled half beneath Finn, her head on his shoulder.

Finn breathed heavily, stroking his hand up and down the base of her spine. Tingles followed in his fingertips' wake, wonderful little bursts of light behind her closed eyelids. Her body loose and languid, muscles unresponsive to any kind of orders, she flopped there, exhausted. But at the same time, dazzlingly alive.

After a couple of minutes, he shifted, gently kissing her forehead before gently rolling away from her. He strolled through to her tiny en suite to dispose of the condom, his fine ass and thigh muscles bunching and flexing.

What a sight. What a night. Great, now she was rhyming like Dr. Seuss. Maybe her brain was scrambled permanently. Eden stretched her arms above her head and then snuggled down under her quilt, pulling it up to her chest. She couldn't remember ever feeling so warm and fuzzy, so generally well-loved.

There was that word again. This time, in her own head.

Hips swinging, Finn strolled back into the room with a lazy smile on his face, and her eyes couldn't help but land between his legs. He was still semi-erect. She caught her lower lip between her teeth.

"Don't get too excited. I need a rest."

"Oh, I wasn't... Okay, I totally was checking out your *condition*."

"Eden, you're insatiable."

She let out a slow breath. "Only with you."

He grinned, this time in a blush-inducing, panty-melting way that had her dropping the sheet so he could see her body. And he definitely looked.

Finn's gaze brushed over her skin as he spoke. "I'm so glad you said so. I've never experienced anything like what just happened between us." He climbed back into bed behind her and wrapped one arm around her waist. Kissed her neck.

Eden sighed with contentment. All was right with the world. "It was amazing."

He pulled the quilt up over them both and held her until she could no longer remember anything except it was nighttime. It was quiet.

She was safe in Finn's arms.

Finn had nearly lost his mind. Seriously, he wasn't sure where he'd put it. Lying there next to Eden, a naked Eden, napping in her comfortable bed, it would be so easy to drift off to sleep for the night and forget all about the outside world. But he had to get up.

He was hungry. His stomach growled like an angry lion at San Diego's open range zoo just before feeding time. The last time he'd visited the zoo, he'd kept away from the animals until they'd eaten. He didn't want to hunt Eden, though, unless it was a more passionate attack. He'd be up for it again soon. But first, he needed sustenance.

Finn rolled out of bed, flicked on a lamp and grabbed his boxers from where they'd landed on the floor. He pulled on his shorts, then he found his phone on the bedside table. He flicked a glance at Eden, snoozing quietly with her hair wild around her flushed cheeks, her face framed by the black satin pillowcase. The ivory quilt only just covered her full, tempting breasts. A sexy woman in sexy sheets. No better sight in the world. Except if she was in *their* bed. Now that was a goal worth shooting for.

He stepped through to the en suite for a pit stop, then crept from the bedroom to avoid disturbing Eden. Standing in her kitchen, he gazed out the window over her small backyard while calling his favorite local pizza joint that delivered. He wasn't sure what toppings Eden preferred, so he ordered half pepperoni, half barbeque chicken. As he ended the call, he opened her fridge and leaned in, searching for something to drink.

A patter of footsteps told him Eden was up and about. The warmth at his back as she placed a hand on his butt was confirmation. "Hey, why did you get up?"

"I ordered us a pizza. Should be here in twenty minutes."

"My hero."

He grabbed a bottle of white wine from the fridge and turned to face her. Probably with a goofy grin on his face. She'd slipped into her tempting red robe again, but now she looked tumbled in the best possible way. Her lips were a little swollen and deep pink, her eyes heavy-lidded.

"Wine?" he asked.

Eden nodded, wrapping her robe tighter around her body. "Yes, please." She stretched, reaching up to the high cabinets above the stove for two wine glasses.

Finn kept a close eye on the hem of her robe. It skirted her curvy bottom, and her legs looked long and strong, thigh and calf muscles tensing. The burn in his abdomen and tightening below told him he wasn't done with the beautiful Doctor. Not by a long shot.

As she placed the glasses on the countertop, Eden caught him staring, his gaze tracking back up her body. Her lips tilted at the corners. "Thirsty?"

He groaned. "Abso-bloody-lutely." He poured two generous glasses of wine and handed one to her.

Eden sipped hers, licking her lips after she swallowed. Suddenly, he was stiff as a plank of wood again. He didn't miss the way her gaze tracked down his body now or how her nipples hardened to definite points underneath the thin fabric of her robe. He took a large gulp of his own drink and watched as she placed hers on the counter.

She leaned into him and grabbed his biceps, then raised herself onto her tiptoes. And as she kissed him and licked along his lower lip, something tightened in his chest.

Finn raised an eyebrow and pulled back from her lips long enough to ask, "Is twenty minutes long enough to make you scream again?"

"I'll set an alarm." She raced off toward the bedroom, giggling as she went.

With a laugh, Finn took off running after her. His legs pumped fast in a piston motion, and he caught up to her before she reached the bed. He rolled onto it with her.

Chapter Twenty-Five

DOCTOR'S OFFICE: Dr. Eden Robinson, your test results are available. Pls call Dr. Fernandez to discuss at your earliest convenience.

Eden pulled up outside Faith's work and cut her scooter's engine. She flicked the kickstand into place and sat, delving in her jacket pocket for her phone. She stared down at the screen, the message notification seeming to blink at her, daring her to make the call. But Eden didn't dare. Not yet.

It could be good news, a huge relief if her test results were all clear. Or it could be bad news. Meaning more tests, treatment, and in the worst-case scenarios, hospital stays and surgery. Perhaps another lumpectomy, another scar. Or it could be worse. Chemotherapy worse.

She needed a few more minutes of the happy, sparkly feeling still pulsing through her body and lighting up all the dark places, all from spending the night with Finn. She sat in the summer sunshine, her hair loose and legs bare, breathing the fresh air deep into her lungs.

Eden spluttered, diesel fumes assaulting her nostrils as a semi-trailer pulled into the lot. Okay, so not everything was fresh air and sunshine.

The parking lot outside her sister's workplace was half full. The boutique where Faith worked sold cute but overpriced outfits to women with too much money and an overabundance of time on their hands. Eden spotted Faith through the floor-to-ceiling glass windows and waved.

Her sister, busy with a woman holding an armload of clothes in front of the counter, waved back and held up an index finger, letting her know she'd be a minute. She should be out soon on her lunch break, and they'd walk down the street to grab something to eat.

Eden closed her eyes for a moment, letting the sun warm her face. She should call her doctor's office for the test results, but she needed fortification first. She needed to hear Finn's voice. He'd make her happy. The thought sent her heart skittering with an unsteady beat.

He could make me happy.

Before she could overthink it, she scrolled through her contacts and found Finn. She'd renamed him Hot Aussie in her main contacts list. She pressed her phone to her ear.

"Finn, hey."

"Hey yourself, Doctor Eden. How are you on this fine California day?" Finn's voice was deep and soothing, yet delicious sounding, like it was drizzled with melted butter.

Her lips stretched in the smile he'd put on her face. "I'm great. You sound pleased with yourself — anyone would think you got lucky last night."

"Anyone? Really? Or someone in the know? Someone sexy and sensual and sophisticated and stunning. All the 'S' words."

She laughed, a little off-balance on her scooter. "Saucy? Stimulating? Um, Sugar Mama? No, scrap that last one."

He laughed. "Okay, but I like saucy and stimulating."

Eden sighed as she slid off her scooter to lean against it. "Can't wait to see you tonight." She hadn't planned to say so. But now that it was out there, she didn't mind. Except there was a pause at Finn's end of the phone.

He groaned softly, which was delicious. "Me too. I can't wait to kiss you. Touch you." Finn cleared his throat. "Bring your toothbrush if you want. Pj's too. Or not. I'm flexible."

Eden giggled, waving at Faith again as she walked out the boutique's front door. "*Very* flexible. But you haven't experienced my full repertoire of yoga skills yet. You'll be panting before my Downward Dog."

The spluttering at the other end of the call had her laughing too. "Eden, you just ruined a two-hundred-dollar shirt. I spat my coffee all over it."

She spoke through a no-doubt goofy grin as "Sorry. I'll, um, pack my overnight bag and make it up to you later."

"My day's looking up. And Eden? Good luck with those test results."

She breathed out slowly, letting the exhalation calm her. She'd told him early that morning that she was waiting for results. "Thanks. I'd better go. Faith's buying me lunch."

Faith walked across the parking lot towards her, messenger bag slung over her shoulder, and wearing a cute dress and cardigan.

Eden ended the call just as her sister joined her and stuffed the phone back into her pocket. As soon as she got home, she'd call him back, once she had the results. She hadn't told Faith about her latest health scare. She'd told no one except Finn.

Faith leaned over and kissed her on the cheek. "Hey, Babycakes. You're looking hot."

Funnily enough, she knew she looked hot, unlike most days. A black skirt showed off her legs, while a floral shirt cinched at her waist, a short leather jacket, and her hair tied up in a swishy ponytail had her feeling like a 1950s bad girl. But it wasn't the outfit that made her look different today. It was the post-orgasmic glow emanating from her pores, doing amazing things for her skin, not to mention her confidence. Her hormones were screaming, *I'm a goddess!* And who was she to argue with her own hormones?

She straightened, tilting her head to look up at Faith, towering a few inches above her in her all-black outfit and killer red heels. "Hi, sister mine. You're looking gorgeous yourself. Let's do lunch."

"Mm-hmm. And then you can tell me what or *who* you're doing."

Eden's mouth popped open, a denial poised to burst forth. But she didn't deny it so much as blush with a furious power, radiating from her chest and rolling up her neck and face like a wildfire licking at a line of trees. Ready to combust.

"I was talking to Finn, that's all." Eden fiddled with her jacket before stripping it off. It was hot standing there in the glaring sunlight.

"That's all, sure." Faith leaned in to whisper in Eden's ear, "I want details. All the hot, filthy, dirty, delicious details."

With a laugh, Eden wrapped an arm around her sister's waist. "That pretty much sums it up."

Faith gasped. "Good for you, Babycakes." She started walking toward the nearby taco place, all but dragging Eden along the sidewalk with her. "I was hoping you'd find someone like Finn. Totally hot and a nice guy underneath all the muscles."

Eden's heart squeezed, constricting her breathing for a moment. She concentrated on her footsteps on the sidewalk. One foot in front of another, the shuffle of her purple shoes literally grounding her. She shouldn't get too excited about this thing with Finn. But her sister's opinion was interesting — and important. Faith was the only family Eden had left, and Eden had always put her little sister's well-being first. Probably always would. Eden needed her to approve of whoever she was dating.

Eden shrugged with a nonchalance of the fake variety. "Do you think he's genuine? I mean, he comes across as nice, but it's hard to judge someone's true nature in such a short time."

Faith shrugged right back. "I get that you're cautious with men. Unlike me." She laughed, but it sounded hollow.

Eden hadn't enjoyed being a bystander during some of her sister's breakups, filled with fireworks and passion. But in some ways, she secretly envied Faith's ability to throw her heart into the ring.

Faith smiled at her. "You probably don't want my advice, but you tend to let your head rule everything in your life. But life's not an experiment you can control in a lab. It's more volatile, more exciting. And if you let things happen naturally, every once in a while, you might find something incredible."

Eden took a deep breath. Her sister smelled of gardenias, an expensive perfume, of course, but it reminded Eden of the laundry spray their mother used a long time ago. It was comforting, that hint of home. She nodded, letting her sister's words soak into her mind and surge into the blood pumping through her veins to her heart.

They arrived at the restaurant, and Eden fell into step behind Faith, who pushed open the heavy wooden door, then turned and let loose with a dazzling smile. Wait staff rushed to help Faith, whose friendly demeanor and easy way with people quickly won hearts. Like Finn, now Eden thought about it.

Her sister picked out a great table by the front windows, overlooking the busy street. Eden sat, watching shoppers walk past, some solo, some in pairs, chatting and laughing, then the workers rushing by, talking or texting on their cell phones, scarcely noticing their surroundings. But she could feel her sister's eyes on her.

Faith reached over and took her hand. "Margaritas. And spice. We need to spice up your life, Babycakes."

She nodded, checking out the specials menu on the wall. "Good. Let's do it."

Faith flicked her long hair back over her shoulders and grinned. Silver flecks shimmered on her eyelids while mischief sparkled in her eyes. "So, how did Finn like your *cupcakes*?" She gestured with her hand, waving in the direction of her boobs and butt.

Eden clapped a hand over her mouth to stifle her laughter. Then she let her hand fall, and a throaty laugh escaped. "He loved them."

Faith grinned before turning her attention to the laminated menu on the table.

Eden would see him tonight. After calling her doctor to get her test results. Her belly flip-flopped like she was being tossed around in the surf.

Faith then chattered away, explained about her upcoming gallery commission and all the materials she needed to purchase in advance. It was exciting but also scary. Eden knew the feeling. Faith threw herself into her work with the same determination Eden usually applied to a challenging scientific project.

Eden poured herself a glass of water from the jug on the table. She should tell Faith what was going on with her health. But she couldn't, not yet. She didn't want to worry her sister, who had enough on her plate with her head full of designs for her big commission and not enough money. The last thing Faith needed was to worry about looking after Eden if the diagnosis was something serious.

Think positive. Eden gulped down half of her water in one swallow.

She'd told Finn about her tests, although she still couldn't believe how much of herself she'd laid bare to him. Hopefully, she'd have good news to share with him later, something to celebrate. But if not, maybe he'd be the supportive friend she needed.

Eden wasn't one hundred percent sure she could trust his words last night, but she was hopeful.

Hope. It was something she hadn't allowed herself to feel for a long time.

It felt like freedom.

Finn planned to crash-tackle the next person who walked through his office door. No joke. His mood was murderous, and it was in his team's best interests to stay the hell away. The Finance and HR departments had been on at him with email after email about cutting the marketing budget and reviewing staffing levels, and all the while, he was acutely aware his own job was on the line.

Then there was his earlier meeting with Meredith. She'd found evidence of someone in his own team making copies of his emails and creating backups on the Finance server. And now that he knew who the culprit was, his blood heated to volcanic levels. Not Nate, the poor guy had just been trying to keep his job. Not one of the other website team members.

No, the person who deserved his anger had been right under his nose the entire time, and he'd failed to notice because she was an attractive woman. Because she seemed to like him. Because he'd seen only the surface and not what was going on underneath. Despite being conscious of disliking her.

The only positive in this whole situation, as Meredith had reminded him, was that there was no doubt of Eden's innocence. He'd known it already, without any actual proof. Instinct told him he could trust Eden even before they'd slept together. Before he'd fallen stupidly in love.

In love. Now, there was a thought and a half. But no way did he have enough time to psychoanalyze himself about it now.

The footsteps in the open-plan area beyond his office door could go walk straight off the pier. He hoped it wasn't the boss. He'd heard McTavish was on the rampage after a meeting with the board, so Finn was keeping his head down.

Finn raked his hands through his hair and swiped his phone's screen. Four more hours until he saw Eden again. He loved how she'd called him at lunchtime, apparently just to check-in. His own hand had hovered over her name in his contacts list all morning, as it did again now.

But instead of calling, he laid his phone on his desk and hit the text-to-speech app on his laptop. He needed to catch up on some reading — of the dense and scientific variety. The monotonous drone of a voiceover read him a journal article explaining the reactions some patients were having to a subcategory of heart drugs overprescribed by physicians in the US. He closed his eyes, but it didn't help him absorb the information. It all seemed pointless when he suspected he'd be out of a job any day now and probably out of the pharmaceutical industry for good.

He didn't register the knock on his door immediately, but when it opened a crack and Mimi stuck her head in, he stopped the text-to-speech app and hit the voice recording function on his phone instead.

"Hey, Finn. I missed you yesterday, but I wanted to share the good news. I landed us a deal with Crane Corp to advertise in their business magazines."

He drummed his fingertips on the desk in front of him. "Mimi, come in. And close the door behind you."

Her bright smile wobbled, but she walked in, putting a little extra swing in her hips. It didn't go unnoticed, but he wasn't interested. By this point in time, she should know that.

Mimi perched on the edge of his visitor's seat and crossed her legs. "What's up?"

Finn folded his arms over his chest and leaned back in his chair. He wouldn't give her the chance to escape today, but he'd be fair. "I'm giving you an opportunity to explain your actions of the last several weeks before I lodge a formal report with HR." He watched her and waited for a reaction to his bald statement.

Mimi shrank down, wrapping her hands around her knees. "I won't pretend I don't know what you mean, but I'm surprised. I didn't think you'd noticed my meetings."

With his head tilted to one side, he considered the brazen, ambitious woman before him. If she thought he wasn't paying any attention to what was going on around the company, she was a fool. "I've been keeping careful notes of all my team's activities for the past few months. You managed to fly under the radar for a while, I'll admit. Trying to flirt with me to suck me in. Not that it worked."

She shook her head, her bright pink lips twisting into a wry smile. "No. I told McTavish I thought you were gay, but I guess not if the rumors about you and a certain female scientist are true."

Finn clenched his jaw, taking a couple of breaths before responding. "My personal life is none of your business. Let's get back to what McTavish asked you to do. Were you supposed to steal confidential correspondence from my office, or did you do that on your own initiative?"

Mimi batted her eyelashes. "A girl's gotta have some secrets. I'd like to call my lawyer now." She pulled her cell phone from her jacket pocket.

He raised an eyebrow and watched as she tapped her phone's screen. "Sure, go ahead. I'll ring HR." Finn reached for the office phone, but noticed his cell phone on the desk showed a new message notification as he did so. He opened it and rolled his shoulders while letting the words wash over him.

Eden: Test results are good. We're celebrating
tonight xxx

Three kisses. He could think of a few places he'd kiss her
tonight. And thank God her test results were okay. Warmth
flooded his body, but he bit the inside of his cheek to suppress
his smile.

Mimi was talking into her phone, leaving some vague message
for her lawyer. Once she ended her call, they stared at each
other across his desk. He'd put in a brief call to HR, requesting
assistance with an employee issue. It wouldn't be long now.

One way or another, shit was about to get real.

Eden tugged at her sparkly buttoned cardigan, fitting snugly
across her breasts. Matched with the 1950s-style sundress, she
looked pretty. But would Finn think so? Nerves crawled around
her insides like the swarms of ants that congregated that time
she'd left the honey and toast crumbs on the counter after
breakfast. It was ridiculous, being so nervous to see him again
after last night. But nervous she was.

The wooden door loomed in front of her, blank and forbid-
ding, but she raised her hand and rapped her knuckles against
it. Once, twice. Three times for luck.

Glancing over her shoulder, Eden spotted a young, tanned,
and implausibly large-breasted woman flouncing past in a green
bikini top and sarong. Finn's apartment complex was the kind
so many professionals in the area lived in — rows of cookie-cut-
ter condos with a central courtyard and swimming pool.

Did they all have affairs with each other in these places, or was
that only fiction? Ms. Tanning Bed strolled past, hips swinging.

Was that Finn's view out his window each morning? How could Eden ever compete?

The door clicked behind her, and she turned her head to face the now-open door. Finn stood there, his worn blue jeans slung low on his hips, snake-like, in the best possible way. His chest was broad and contoured like a mountain range in a tight athletic shirt. *Oh boy*. She had to remember to breathe, then to swallow the saliva pooling in her mouth. And she had to remember to look up at his face, not keep staring at his muscles, her gaze filled with reckless intent.

She caught his eye, and something melted in his expression, making her want to weep. He really was too handsome to be hers.

Finn's eyes glinted aqua in the early evening light. "Eden, it's great to see you, but…"

But what? Had he changed his mind? She glanced down at her pointlessly pretty clothes and red stilettos. And the overnight bag slung over her shoulder. "I'm overdressed, right? I should have worn jeans because I knew we were just hanging out, but I wanted to look nice, and I like dresses, and anyway, here I am." She was rambling.

Huffing out a breath, she pushed her loose hair back behind her ears and gazed up at Finn. She had to breathe deep, filling her lungs with oxygen to get them working again.

He was staring. And the *way* he stared, eyes heating with what she now knew was desire, stole her breath again. Eden let her gaze drop and stared at his large, bare feet. Why was she checking out his feet anyway? She was completely distracted until she heard the door click shut. Her head snapped up.

Finn jerked toward her in two forceful strides. She watched open-mouthed as he closed the distance between them. Then he enfolded her in his arms and murmured in her ear, "You're gorgeous. Even if I don't deserve you, I'm a lucky bloke."

After that startling comment, his lips crashed down on hers, inundating her with handsome man. His herbal-lemony scent enveloped her as his tongue slid against hers. Her knees wobbled until she braced herself against him. He explored her mouth, all the while holding her in his arms, keeping her wrapped up tight against his body. He was warm and hard, where her breasts pressed up against his chest.

She tilted her head to the side and kissed him back. Took from him and tasted him, nipping at his lips with her teeth as he tangled his right hand in the back of her hair. This made her groan, the sound overly loud in the tiled courtyard. If he kept up the kissing, she'd melt right through his arms and slide into the swimming pool.

God, he was delicious. Like summer and melt-in-your-mouth cotton candy. Lemonade and sunshine and everything good.

Finn broke their kiss. "I'm so pleased to see you, but I don't think you should stay. It's a long story." He dragged his hands through his hair.

Eden stared up at him again, trying to unravel the loose threads of their conversation. Something didn't make sense here. He'd just kissed the hell out of her on his doorstep but was asking her to leave?

"Finn, do you mind if we grab a beer?" Felicity came into view leaning through the now open door behind Finn, sticking her head outside. "Oh hey, Eden. What are you doing here?" Her eyes widened.

Eden stepped back a pace and twitched, staring past Finn as he held her close with one hand. "I came for dinner. With Finn." She gulped on a now-dry throat. Felicity was at Finn's. Why? They hardly knew each other. What was going on?

Her research assistant's head bounced up and down in an exaggerated puppet-like nod. "Um, good, right. We should go. Merry, grab your bag, babe."

Finn turned to speak to Felicity without letting go of Eden's shoulder. His grip was too tight. "Don't go. We need to plan what we're going to say to the investigators." Felicity puppet-nodded again before disappearing from view.

Investigators? This was all wrong. Eden placed her hand over Finn's and squeezed, demanding his attention. "Finn, what about our dinner-and-extras date?"

Finn let go of her shoulder and stroked the pad of his thumb across her cheekbone. "I'm sorry. This isn't how I wanted things to go down." He dropped his hand and stepped back, allowing a gust of wind to whip between their bodies. "You should go. McTavish set the cops on a wild-goose chase. He told them you've been stealing chemicals from the storeroom to sell on the black market." He took a long breath and hit her with a precision-laser, green-eyed gaze. "There's a warrant out for your arrest."

So this was what it was like being a bad girl. Not all it was cracked up to be. So far, jail sucked. Eden had waited forty minutes in the gray, fluoro-lit corridor in the local sheriff's office, which wasn't exactly prison, but also wasn't much fun.

She glanced across at the front desk clerk, then craned her neck, trying to see through to the back office, where a couple of sheriff's officers shuffled paperwork. They'd interviewed her about McTavish's allegations, but due to a complete lack of evidence of any wrongdoing, no charges had been laid. They were letting her go. Apparently, McTavish himself was being interviewed about something else. 'An unrelated matter,' according to the sheriff. *Interesting*.

It was all a big letdown, considering what she'd expected to be doing with her evening. Finn could get the hell out of her mind and stop making her blush. The way he'd kissed her... But no. The big, muscled, sexy man, who she'd started to think of as sweet, had nearly landed her innocent ass in jail.

Eden should have listened to him the previous night when he tried to discuss what was going on at Magna Smart. But instead, she'd tripped over her own hormones and lost her head.

She sighed and made her phone call. Faith answered right away, thank goodness. "Faith, I need your help." She paused, and waited for her sister's annoyance. The tone that sounded exactly like their grandmother's.

"Of course, Babycakes. Finn's already called me. Are you at the sheriff's office?"

Finn called her. Okay, maybe he was trying to make amends. Well, he could keep on trying.

"Yeah, cooling my heels in the corridor here. What did he tell you?"

"Just that your ex-boss accused you of stealing, and it was all bullshit."

Eden sighed. At least Finn didn't believe she'd done anything wrong. But she wasn't sure what Finn had been up to. Her eyes prickled with the beginnings of tears. "Right. Well, I'm allowed to go home. I'll see you soon."

She ended the call and squirmed on the hard plastic chair, her head in her hands. When exactly had her life become one big, failed experiment? Was it when she took the job at Magna Smart? When she decided to work in big pharma rather than academia? Or was it when she let her body and heart rule her head, and she gave Finn a chance?

Fifteen minutes later, her sister pushed through the double doors of the waiting area and rushed toward Eden with the power of a whirlwind. She enveloped Eden in a hug, almost squeezing the life out of her.

Faith took a step back and met her eyes with a hard-assed stare. "What exactly is going on with you?"

Eden's gaze dropped to the vomit-brown linoleum floor. "You know I lost my job."

"Yes, so I've heard, but you should have told me sooner."

"I know, and I'm sorry. The boss wanted me out. I knew it. Finn knew it. We butted heads at the big presentation, and I blew it. I had to speak up — they were going to introduce a seriously flawed concept that would have put lives at risk. I knew I was right, but I lost my cool and handled it all wrong."

"So you quit."

"Not quite. McTavish fired me, in front of everyone. I think Finn might have stood up for me, but I didn't hang around to find out. Anyway, we kind of made up later. I'm still not sure how it happened."

Faith's half-smile was full of mischief. "This part, I know. But what's your boss thinking, making false allegations against you?"

Eden shook her head. She didn't know enough to explain properly. "McTavish has been up to something for months. Shifting money around, embezzling, I think. He wasn't just trying to get me fired, it's more complicated. It seems like Finn and someone from Finance have been investigating McTavish. He tried to tell me what was going on, but he didn't share all the details. He kept me in the dark."

"Sounds like Finn wanted protect you."

Eden considered it. Yes, he probably had been trying to protect her, was probably still trying. But that didn't give him the right to make all the decisions. "Maybe, but that's not all. Finn's been busy as some kind of corporate spy, and now he's dragged me into his mess."

Faith remained silent for a moment. "It's some loco stuff alright. But do you think Finn meant to get you involved? He sounded unhappy when I spoke to him. He asked if I thought you'd forgive him."

Eden leaned her head back against the wall and lowered her voice. "What did you tell him?"

"I said I figured you would, seeing as you're halfway to madly in love with him already."

"Oh, Faith, you didn't?" Eden clunked her head against the wall. "He's caused me a hell of a lot of trouble lately. I was arrested, I'm out of a job, and who knows how long I'll be able to keep making the mortgage payments —"

Oh, firetruck. She hadn't meant to mention her money worries to Faith.

Her sister frowned, the overhead fluoro lights casting gloomy shadows under her eyes. "We're family. If something's wrong, I want to help. You have to stop shutting me out. I'm twenty-eight years old, and I can handle a little stress. I'm not a little girl anymore. You don't need to keep trying to shield me from all the bad things in the world."

Six-year-old Faith swam in front of Eden's eyes, a tiny girl with long, dark pigtails who still played with dolls. A girl whose mother had just died from an aggressive form of breast cancer, leaving a gaping hole in the heart of their little family. They'd moved straight in with their grandmother, who was kind and brave, a great role model, if a little strict and old-fashioned.

Eleven-year-old Eden had tried to be perfect. Wanting to be as little trouble to their grandmother as possible, she'd appointed herself as Faith's guardian, thinking she was grown-up enough to handle it. She'd made dinner and washed clothes and still managed to do all her own homework. Faith was allowed to play and be a kid, while Eden became serious and determined. She'd stepped up to the role of mother and hadn't stepped down since.

Faith's fingertips brushed Eden's cheeks, and she whipped her head up to meet her sister's gaze. "You're crying," she said, shock coloring her voice.

Eden wiped her eyes. She had to be honest, even if it was hard. "I'm scared. I don't know what's going to happen."

"None of us do, Babycakes. None of us do."

The car horn blaring in the street outside his condo was getting on Finn's already-frayed nerves. He closed his eyes and shuffled the papers into a neat stack on the floor beside him. Sometimes people got locked out by the security gate in front of the complex's parking lot, but there was no need to blast the eardrums of the entire neighborhood.

Felicity rose from the leather armchair she was sprawled in, but Finn motioned for her to sit. He got up and stretched out his spine. "I'll go see what all the noise is all about."

Meredith whispered something to Felicity as he headed for his front door, but he didn't catch it. They'd been a big help tonight, sorting through the piles of emails and financial statements that bamboozled him. He was having trouble concentrating, worrying about Eden. He hadn't realized McTavish would be vindictive enough to try to get to him through the woman he loved.

When he opened the door, he spotted an old Mustang he didn't recognize, but with the streetlamps casting light on its passengers, it was easy to recognize the two women with long dark hair, one dressed in black leather, the other in a pale sweater. Faith sat in the driver's seat with Eden beside her.

His heart hammered in his chest, threatening to knock down the last of the internal walls he'd built in an effort to keep from falling for her. But it was too late. He was already her slave.

Leaving his front door open, he jogged down the sloping lawn and across the small parking lot to the gate, his footsteps echoing his thumping heartbeat. He stopped beside the car and crossed his arms as Eden got out of the passenger door.

She rose to stand and smoothed down the fabric of her dress. Eden glanced up at him, her lips pressed together. It was clear she was angry as hell. Not that he blamed her. "I left my scooter in your parking lot. I need to get it, and then I'll leave."

Finn took a couple of steps closer, jamming his hands in his jeans pockets to stop from reaching for her. "Eden, please, just wait a sec. I'm so sorry for what went down with the cops. McTavish was trying to get at me, but I didn't expect you to get caught in the cross fire."

"You're blaming this all on McTavish? At least own up to your part in this mess. I don't need your excuses."

"Right. It was my fault he went after you. I've been tracking his moves for a while, but I didn't realize he was also tracking mine. And yours. He worked out we're seeing each other and tried to use it to his advantage. To get me to back off."

"We *were* seeing each other. Not anymore. Now, I need my scooter." She placed her hands on her hips and stared him down.

Finn glanced at Faith through the car windshield, but she just shook her head and shrugged. Although Eden's sister seemed to like him, she was obviously fresh out of ideas. Looked like he'd have to wing it and see if he could get Eden back onside. When he flicked his gaze back to Eden, she was focused on his chest for some reason. At least the heat between them hadn't dissipated since yesterday.

He tipped his head to one side and met her eyes as she looked up. "Please, give me a chance. Come inside, and we'll talk. Felicity and Meredith are still here. No pressure." He watched the indecision drift across her face like clouds, her expression shifting and changing direction. "Please, Eden."

She huffed out a long breath while clasping her hands in front of her. "Fine. But only for a few minutes." She raised her hand and waved to her sister, who grinned in reply. Finn chuckled when Faith winked at him before driving off.

Finn punched his ID into the entry gate and extended an arm, indicating that Eden should walk ahead of him. He was being a gentleman. And if he happened to get a top-notch view of her hips and ass swaying in that dress, it was a bonus.

He followed her past her scooter to his front door and let her waltz inside first. Or maybe it was a flounce. Either way, Eden's walk was bursting with attitude. His lips stretched into a smile. He couldn't pretend he didn't admire her spunk, even if it meant he had a lot of work to do to get back in her good books. And her bed.

When he rounded the corner to his compact living room, Felicity and Meredith were packing a bunch of papers into folders.

Felicity smiled over-brightly, her eyes wide and sparkly as they zig-zagged between himself and Eden. "Sorry, we can't stay. We've got to go. Work tomorrow, early start, you know how it is." She slung her shoulder bag over her head, crossing it over her chest. "Okay. I'll call you tomorrow, Eden. We'll catch up — on everything — soon."

Meredith turned to Felicity. She looked like she was swallowing a laugh. "Yes, better run. I've got a breakfast meeting with Doctor McTavish. Wish me luck." Meredith waved over her shoulder as she hurried out behind Felicity. The front door shut with a click a moment later. Leaving Finn and Eden behind in stunned silence.

Finn took a step toward Eden, now standing with her hands fisted at her sides. She bit her lip, and damn, he couldn't help staring at her mouth. Those lips, so ripe and ready to be kissed...

"What did you want to talk about, Finn?"

Right. Talk. He cleared his throat and stuffed his hands back in his pockets. "Why don't you take a seat?"

Eden didn't say a word but backed up to one of his armchairs and perched on the edge, keeping her eyes trained on him the whole time. As if afraid he'd pounce on her or something. Maybe she was right to be wary. She looked gorgeous.

Her deep-red dress fanned out over the seat, and she'd crossed her long legs at the ankles, drawing his attention to those heels. A siren went off in his head as his eyes tracked back up her body.

The little librarian-style cardigan she wore made him desperate to tear it off. And her dark hair fell in glossy waves around her shoulders, loose and curling at the ends. Then there was her mouth, set in an angry pout, daring him to kiss her.

But no. The previous night, he'd let the physical take over and hadn't been able to talk to her. Tonight, he had to. Kissing would have to wait, assuming he ever got the chance to touch her again. With a huff, he sank into the chair opposite Eden's, separated by about six feet of blue rug and his low coffee table covered in papers.

"I want to tell you what's been going on these past few months. The whole story. I apologize in advance for not telling you the complete truth months or even a week ago. But at the time, I didn't feel like I had a whole lot of options."

Finn leaned forward, his forearms resting on his knees as he studied Eden's face. The shutters were down, hiding her true emotions. He'd seen the expression often enough at work. Finn used to think it meant she didn't care or was self-involved. But now he knew it signaled careful thought and self-protection.

"McTavish has been working at Magna Smart for close to ten years. But it's only relatively recently he was given sole authority to approve spending on research and development and new product marketing. Our respective areas of responsibility." He glanced down at the stack of financial papers in a blue folder. When he looked back up, Eden's gaze was focused on him, her eyebrows pinched together.

"This pile of paperwork came my way via Meredith. It's taken me a while to make sense of it, but I noticed a few odd purchase orders had been approved, supposedly for a new marketing project. But it was one I'd never heard of."

Eden's forehead scrunched into a frown. "McTavish was redirecting funds? Where to?"

"I wasn't sure until I also started reading the background material on the new heart drug under development by your team.

The marketing funds were being directed to R&D, supposedly for drug research trials."

Eden shook her head. "But our request for further funding was declined."

"Exactly. Then I noticed the timelines for my own project. Everything McTavish was trying to push through was happening in a truncated time frame. It appeared he wanted everything done and dusted by the end of the financial year. I had to ask why when it didn't relate to the actual project goals."

"Because of the government funding through the university?"

"I think so. McTavish was asking for a huge cash injection, but first, he had to prove he'd spent most of the existing project funds. However, that wasn't what concerned me the most. My biggest concern as the project manager was the lack of transparency. Funds weren't available to develop a prototype website, but I knew they'd been itemized in the budget. Later, this money had apparently disappeared. And then there was the push for early FDA approval."

Eden nodded. "Yes, I'm sure you know I was concerned about pushing through drugs when they weren't fully tested."

"I do. I shared your concerns, and I made discreet calls to the FDA. It turned out they already knew exactly who I was. Then I received a call from the Office of Criminal Investigations. Actually, it was the night I was supposed to meet you for dinner, I mean, LittleMissPerfect. They were already looking into some of McTavish's activities and they interviewed me, asking for lots of details. That's why I was running late."

Eden stared at him. "The OCI? That's serious stuff. Criminal offenses, charges referred to the FBI..."

Finn nodded. "Exactly. They were looking for evidence of systemic fraud and possible rerouting of controlled drugs into eastern Europe. And they wanted my help."

Eden let out a low whistle. "Are you saying they roped you into spying on McTavish?"

"Spying or documenting his activities and copying files. Whatever you want to call it."

She pressed her lips together tight, then ran her tongue across her lower lip before speaking. Finn tried not to notice how wet her lips were... but failed miserably.

Eden tilted her head to one side. "You tried to protect me."

It wasn't a question. Finally, she understood, at least partly. It would take her a while to come to grips with the full scope of the fraud McTavish had planned.

Finn sighed, the air coming out stale, his mouth dry. He picked up the glass of water he'd left on the table earlier and took a gulp, then looked over at Eden as he clunked it back down. "Sorry, I should have offered you a drink. Or food. I had dinner ready to go but..."

"Felicity and Meredith came over, and I was arrested. I was kind of pissed about that. Still am, to be honest."

He ran his hands through his hair. "Fair enough."

Eden stretched out her neck and tucked her hair behind her ears. "I'll take a soda. Diet, if you have it."

"Diet? *Blech*. That stuff's rubbish." His face contorted, and she laughed as he stood and moved toward his kitchenette.

Eden remained seated, her hands clasped tightly in her lap. "The doctor said I need to reduce my sugar intake."

Finn's eyes snapped to hers. "Oh man, I'm an asshole. I should have asked about your test results already."

She shrugged, but her posture was stiff. "It's okay, I'm fine. The lump under my arm was benign, just a cyst, thank goodness. But my blood glucose levels are too high. If I don't watch it, I could end up with type two diabetes."

"Bloody hell. I'm glad you're okay, but stick to soda water in that case."

Eden nodded, staring up at him with huge eyes. She blinked, her eyelashes fluttering. "I'll have to focus on my diet and exercise and do less baking."

"Too many cupcakes?"

A small smile curved her lips. "Not looking after myself properly. Maybe too many cupcakes."

"I happen to like your cupcakes." He couldn't help the way his gaze lowered and skimmed over her breasts to the curve of her hip. A pity he didn't have X-ray vision and the ability to see around corners.

"Yes, I remember." She huffed out a long, slow breath, making the hairs on the back of his neck and arms prickle with awareness.

Finn tried to keep his reaction to her under control as he asked the burning question on his mind, "What about us, Doc?"

"I'm not sure there is an *us* anymore."

"What if I said I want there to be an *us*? In a permanent-type situation."

"There are two people in an *us*, you know."

"That's why I'm asking."

Eden nodded, keeping her eyes on him. But he couldn't help noticing she wasn't leaping into his arms and kissing him or asking to see his etchings or his Netflix watch list. So he obviously needed to lay his cards on the table and go for broke.

Finn clenched his jaw, then breathed out. He had no desire to wait and wonder. He had to know how she felt today. "I want you, and I think you want me too. We haven't had a chance to give it a proper go, and I know it's too soon, but I reckon we could be great together. The real deal. Love, marriage, kids, great sex, the complete package. Not necessarily in that order. *If* you can trust me."

Trust. That was the tricky part. Eden shifted in her seat, avoiding Finn's eyes.

Kissing him, touching him, jumping into bed with him, those had been surprisingly easy. But for her to trust him? He must realize it was asking a lot. For someone like her — trained to question and analyze everything, to prioritize head over heart — it was almost impossible.

She had to weigh up the facts. A pros-and-cons list materialized in her head, a balance sheet of her association with Finn to date. It might not be romantic, but times like these called for the full force of her analytical skills. Finn had lied to her, deceived her, and kept information from her for months.

On the pro side: He had tried to protect her from McTavish's vindictive behavior and possible involvement in criminal activities. And Finn probably had no choice but to keep matters close to his chest once the OCI became involved. He was trying to assist with a lawful investigation.

He'd also been the first man to kiss her properly in close to two years, and he reduced her body to a trembling mess of hormones. Finn was the embodiment of the expression *sex on legs*. That had to slot into the pro column.

As for the cons: She wasn't sure, even now, whether Finn's interest in her was based on mutual attraction or on what he could gain. Did he need her onside to help his case? To help protect his professional reputation?

The con side was too horrible to contemplate. The idea he might have been playing her for a fool, even while in her bed... Eden shuddered, despite the warm evening, tingles of ice pricking at her spine.

All those things Finn had said about a future — sex, marriage, kids, the whole lot — it was so tempting. But could she trust it? She had no need for a man who considered her a convenient bed warmer when it suited him and a 'desperate, aging geek' when she was ready to get serious. She hadn't realized that the loser she used to date still had the power to affect her, but even now, his words stung. She'd rather be on her own than settle for a man who'd proven himself unreliable at best, vindictive at worst.

Eden's face heated as blood rushed to the surface of her skin. She'd almost forgotten Finn was there, and she was still sitting in his living room. She needed to leave. Too bad if he thought her rude. Or scared. She couldn't think clearly. She couldn't deal with these hormonal fluctuations or whatever they were.

She lifted herself from the armchair and stood on shaky legs, smoothing down her dress. When she raised her chin and looked at Finn, he opened his mouth to speak, but she held up her hand in a stop-sign motion. "Sorry, I've got to go. I can't... talk about this right now. I need some time."

As she scurried from the living room, she felt him close behind, the rush of warm air as his scent hit her, then a deep, visceral pull toward him. Somehow, he'd gotten under her skin, and she couldn't think straight with him so close. Only a foot from the door, from freedom, she spotted her overnight bag leaning against the wall. She picked it up, and as she slung it over her shoulder, she turned to see Finn running his hands over his stubbly jaw, the bristly, prickly sound giving her flashbacks of kisses, touches.

"Goodnight, Finn."

"Wait, take this. Read it. I need you to understand what I was trying to do." He thrust a folder full of papers at her, and she took it before she could think. His fingertips brushed against the back of her hand, and she quickly retracted it.

Eden tucked the folder under her arm and fled before he could touch her again, her heart thudding in her chest, deep and syncopated, like the backbeat in an old swing record. They couldn't keep dancing around each other this way.

She might have said goodnight, but she meant goodbye. Her heart could take only so much.

Chapter Twenty-Six

Finn: Eden, I miss you. I wish you'd reconsider.

Finn: I'll message you after the meeting today.

Finn's head ached, and his Achilles tendons screamed for him to stop, but he kept on running. The steady beat thudded through his body, from his feet pounding the dirt track up through his straining calves and quads through his temples, right into his blood. Pumping all the way to his heart.

He ran along the beach track, up the steep hill to the clifftop, and when he reached the highest point overlooking the beach, he stopped. Hands resting on his knees, he sucked in the air blowing fresh off the Pacific.

Today was the day. The sun had risen, but it was still early, and the sky was a hazy gray over the ocean. Later, the heat would be on.

He'd go into work, clear out his desk, and email McTavish his official resignation right before driving over to the OCI headquarters to give them a full interview as requested. All of this could go two ways — he could get out of it relatively unscathed, perhaps clutching a plane ticket back home to Australia. Or he could be called to testify before a jury, whether local or federal, he didn't know. He hoped for the best. The best being his own exoneration from any wrongdoing and McTavish's arrest.

In the second scenario, he could be left hanging in California or asked to fly over to Washington for a trial that could drag on for months. Without a job, possibly without any hopes of getting another. It sucked, to put it mildly.

Floating.

As he stared out over the water, a hang glider drifted past, riding a current of air like a surfer on a wave. He'd lived here for years and always wanted to try it. But he hadn't.

Finn hauled himself upright and stretched out his neck, then all the other aching, complaining muscles. He grabbed his phone from his pocket and searched for the details. Hang gliding. This weekend. No excuses. Soon, he might have to leave, and this was one thing he could tick off his bucket list. Other loose ends might prove more difficult to tie up.

On impulse, he snapped a photo of the hang glider and texted it to Eden along with a message.

Finn: I want to try this while I live here. One day.

As he started a slow jog along the clifftop again, heading back toward his condo, an image of Eden's face popped into his head. Her sweet taste the first time she kissed him, lips covered in sugar frosting.

Eden.

Her name pounded through his skull. A paradise lost.

No, bugger that.

Finn powered along the track with renewed energy. He had to give it one last shot with Eden, even if he ended up being the laughingstock of San Diego.

Eden propped herself up higher where she sat on her bed, flipping through page upon page of notes and reports. This wasn't merely a little research Finn had put together — it was a truly damning dossier of evidence against Doctor McTavish and possibly others on Magna Smart Pharmaceuticals' current board of directors.

Finn had done a great job of documenting everything of concern. Names, dates, meetings, excerpts from financial statements, it was all there in black and white.

Eden knew she should call him, talk it through with him, and, most importantly, find out what he planned to do next. Her chest tightened painfully. She wasn't ready to face him yet. The more she thought about it, the more she wanted to take back her behavior from last night.

Before she realized she'd done it, she grabbed her phone and hit the call button next to Felicity's name. Her friend answered after only a second. "Felicity, hey. I'm reading through Finn's files. Did you know about all this? This is big."

"Huge. I knew about McTavish gambling and maybe misappropriating funds, but it's worse than that. I only started helping Finn recently, when he needed someone to decode scientific results. Anyway, are you okay?"

Something surged in her blood, and her heart sped up. "Yes, why shouldn't I be?"

"Oh, I just assumed... You've read the section about how McTavish tried to set you up, right?"

"What?" Eden jammed the phone in place with her shoulder, freeing her hands to flip through the pages of reports on her lap. A bunch of papers held together with a metal bulldog clip came loose and fluttered to the floor. "Damn, I — which document?" She opened up a blue folder on the bed beside her. Her own name, highlighted numerous times in fluoro yellow, jumped out at her. "I think I found it."

As she read, her eyes misted over. Maybe it was her stupid reading glasses, or maybe not. She whipped them off and polished the lenses on her T-shirt. When she put them back on and flipped through to the next page, she sucked in a sudden gasp. It stuck in her throat and made her cough.

"Make sure you read to the end. Finn really stuck up for you."

Eden nodded, even though Felicity couldn't see her. "Thanks. I'll call you back later."

Finn had stuck up for her. She saw at once how he'd taken note of the careful work she'd undertaken, how she'd pushed for another round of clinical trials while noting the problems with their existing data. He had copies of her memos to McTavish and the board stating her case, then the full report they'd compiled together weeks ago.

She'd never seen Finn's section of the report, and what she read made her nauseous. McTavish had already applied for a patent for the R-22 compound. Under his own name. As if he'd discovered it, not Eden, not the team or the company, and he would therefore be the one to profit from its commercialization. McTavish intended to market it as the flagship product on the new marketing portal Finn had researched.

But that wasn't what made Eden gasp. Another name stuck out on the page like a red flashing sign. Meredith suspected McTavish had been redirecting funds to an offshore account, a shell company set up jointly with a man Eden never wanted to see or hear from again.

Kyle, her high school boyfriend, had turned out to be an untrustworthy bully. But his father, Peter Quade, was a nightmare. Over fifteen years ago, he'd tried to block her scholarship applications to multiple colleges and spread rumors about her ruining his son's life. Then, once she was a student, he almost got her excluded from the university's honors society. The dean had given her copies of the letters Peter submitted — luckily, the dean had understood Kyle's father had a personal vendetta against Eden.

According to the dossier in the back of Finn's folder, Peter was also one of McTavish's oldest friends and business associates. A recent photo of Peter made her gasp a second time and break into a cold sweat because, although he'd changed a lot since she first met him, she knew this man's face. She'd been on a blind date with him about a year ago — after she'd started working for McTavish. She'd known him as Travis Townsend, an engineer, but it was the same face.

Eden slammed the folder down on her bedside table. How many ways had McTavish and his friend tried to take her down? How long had they been tracking her? How many times had Peter attempted to ruin her life? And what on earth was she going to do about it?

Chapter Twenty-Seven

Faith: Hey Babycakes! Can you help me move some stuff in my studio tomorrow AM?

Eden: I guess, but I'm not made of muscle. Should I bring coffee?

Faith: Yes! Thanks x

Eden gazed around the large space where she stood. The sunlight through the narrow row of windows along the rafters slid into Faith's warehouse-style workspace like a fugitive on the run. You couldn't quite catch it, but it was there, lurking.

As she picked up a heavy box, she noted the dust motes dancing in the diffuse light. Piles of paperwork sat on a desk in the corner beside an old PC, while metalworking hand tools, offcuts of silver, and tubes full of beads and gemstones covered all other available surfaces. The lamps over the main workspace were switched off, but when they were on, the contents of the tubes sparkled and shimmered. It looked like a fairy's workshop.

"A little to the left. There, back toward the workbench." Faith directed Eden with a raised eyebrow and a tip of her chin.

Her sister held one end of the box and walked forward, while Eden, who'd drawn the short straw, held the other end, walking backward. She couldn't really see where she was going.

"Okay..." Eden shuffled back across the polished floorboards, the heavy box of materials and small tools shifting in her grasp.

Eden was hardly the best person for the job, but she suspected Faith wanted to talk to her, not just put her to work hauling jewelry-making supplies around her workroom.

Now Eden's butt bumped into the wooden bench, and Faith helped her turn and deposit the box there. Her sister grinned and leaned back against the edge of the bench while Eden dusted off her hands.

"Here, I want to give you something before I forget." Faith rummaged through the box and pulled out a small black velvet drawstring pouch. She dangled it in front of Eden's face. "For you, Babycakes. A new design I'm working on. They made me think of you."

Eden took the pouch in both hands and carefully opened it to find a delicate pair of earrings nestled inside. She tipped them into her cupped hand and turned them over with her index finger. Hand-worked silver highlighted the purple stones set inside, their square shape unusual and interesting. A tiny round stone dangled from each earring, hanging from the larger square stones.

She looked up at Faith. "They're gorgeous, thank you. I love the color. What's the stone?"

Faith smiled, her eyes lighting up as she tucked her hair behind her ear. "Amethyst. The lavender color reminded me of your eyes. And I thought you could use some calming energy."

Eden's eyebrow muscle twitched, but she managed to suppress the frown itching to spread over her face. Although she didn't believe in Faith's crystal-healing theories, she wanted to hear what her sister had to say. Faith sometimes gave people gifts of jewelry she'd made instead of having long-winded conversations about feelings. Her sister called it her 'love language.'

Eden undid the clasps on the earrings and slid the posts through her pierced ears one at a time. "Calming energy? Like, relaxation?"

"No, more to help you disconnect your overactive brain. So you take a breath and shift your energy and focus back to your heart."

Oh right. 'The Talk,' about love and stuff. Faith had hinted at it when they'd met for lunch, and now Eden suspected a more serious chat might be on the cards.

She nodded, turning to admire her reflection in the antique hand mirror Faith held up for her. The earrings suited her and made her eyes look brighter; it was true. But as for the love stuff... She wasn't sure it suited her at all.

Eden sighed. "They're beautiful, really. But I don't think they'll help with my love life."

"You never know. You shouldn't dismiss intention and the power of positive thinking. Have you heard from Finn lately?"

Eden pressed her lips together and glanced down at her sneakers. No, she hadn't heard from him. But it was all her fault. She'd ignored his texts.

She looked up and met her sister's gaze. "I think I've ruined things with him. He said he loved me, but I pushed him away. I wasn't sure if he meant it, and I didn't want to make a complete fool of myself by falling for a smooth line."

Faith crossed her arms over her middle, causing her tight black T-shirt to ride up. "What makes you think it's a line? From everything I've seen, the guy's crazy about you."

"I don't know." She ran her hands down the front of her pedal pushers again, her palms inexplicably damp. "Why would he want me when I'm too stuck in my head? I'm the kind of woman men see as difficult. I'm not sexy or beautiful. Really, I'm just a nerd in lipstick."

Faith threw her hands up to the sky, setting her bracelets jangling. "Bull crap. That's such a pile of manure I don't even know where to start. You, Babycakes, don't see yourself very clearly. You're smart, successful, and caring, and you're absolutely sexy. Tell me again what Finn thought of your cupcakes?"

As Eden's lips stretched in a smile, her phone vibrated in her back pocket. She pulled it out and saw Felicity's name on the screen. "Sorry, I'd better take this." She hit the button to accept the call and pressed the phone to her ear. "Hey, what's up?"

"Eden, I'm the bearer of bad news. Finn's going hang gliding this morning."

"Um, so? I can't think of anything worse than jumping off a cliff, but if it's what he wants to do, what's the problem?"

"You don't understand. I spoke to him just now, and he told me it's the final thing he wants to do before leaving the States. As in, permanently. He's booked a flight back home to Australia tonight. Did you know he loses his work visa if he quits his job at Magna Smart? But I guess he decided to quit before the board fired him."

Eden shouted, "Holy shitballs!"

Silence descended like a heavy blanket. On the other end of the phone, Felicity was obviously stunned, while Faith was staring at her, mouth hanging open. Her sister roused herself first, heading over to the corner sink to grab Eden a glass of water.

"Are you okay?" Felicity asked the question carefully, as if fearful Eden may shatter into a million pieces at any moment. She feared it, too, since her heart appeared to be fractured.

Eden nodded. "Yep. Fine and dandy. I've got to talk to him, that's all. Do you know when he'll be at the hang gliding place?"

"He said he was heading there as soon as he finished breakfast. Eden, he sounded sad. Not like his usual self."

Sad? Flying home to Australia? *Oh, firetruck.* This was serious, and probably all her fault, somehow. She pulled herself up to full height as she ended the call. Her sister placed a glass of water beside her, then commenced rubbing Eden's arm in a soothing motion.

Eden spoke to Faith, her words coming out flat. "Remember how Gran used to say that sometimes you have to take a leap of faith? I guess today, I've got to jump."

The wind in her hair, the highway buzzing along beneath her scooter, the vibration of the engine. Normally, she enjoyed the freedom of riding her Vespa, but today, it wasn't fast enough. Eden knew the way to the Gliderport at La Jolla, as it wasn't far from Magna Smart's office, but this morning, the traffic was a snarling nightmare.

It was Saturday morning, for heaven's sake. Where were all these people going?

She came to a stop at the end of a snaking lane of cars held up behind the turnoff. What if Finn had jumped off a cliff already and was halfway to the airport by now? She didn't even know if he'd want to see her, but she had to find out.

Eden veered off to the right, bumping over the curb and onto the grass strip separating highway from beach. Riding overland, she broke a couple of traffic laws and sped past the stationary traffic jamming up the road.

If she made it past the gridlock, she could be at the Gliderport in around twenty minutes. With any luck.

The wind was sharp and cool against his bare arms and legs thanks to the outfit of shorts and T-shirt he'd worn, ready for the heat predicted later in the day. Finn hadn't realized it would be so much cooler up on the cliffs overlooking the beach at La Jolla. He'd arrived at the Gliderport early, hoping to beat the weekend crowds. He still had to wait for an instructor. He grabbed his phone out of his pocket and sat at an outdoor table at the café, typing then retyping his message into his phone's email app.

What he'd planned was probably a dumb idea. He'd called in a favor from a friend who worked in advertising. High-impact outdoor advertising, as they called it. He was aiming for impact, so maybe it would work.

Oh hell. What to write?

What message could possibly convince Eden that he loved her, wanted her, would do almost anything for her—barring murder but including buggering off to Australia and staying out of her life—if it would make her happy?

He needed something short and snappy to convey everything left unsaid between them. Too bad the words weren't flowing. Or they were flowing, but slowly, thickly, like rapidly hardening cement.

Finally, Finn had a message. He wasn't sure it was a winner, but he'd give it a shot. He sent the email to his friend and waited for confirmation.

After ordering a coffee, he kept his eyes on the view over the ocean. Soon, he'd be out there. With any luck and Felicity's help, Eden was on her way too.

Eden ditched her scooter in the parking lot and hurried to the Gliderport on the clifftops, sure she was too late. Felicity had said Finn would be there straight after breakfast.

A swathe of baby-blue sky with a matching sweep of deep-teal ocean made up most of the panoramic view. It was stunning, and if she'd had time to admire it, she would have snapped a photo or two on her phone.

Shading her eyes with one hand across her forehead, she turned left and right, searching the grassy slopes for a tall, caramelly, delicious-looking man. There were plenty of people on the grassy area, with parachute contraptions spread out and some hang gliders ready to go.

Intrepid-looking folk in skintight Lycra or weekend-warrior combat gear organized equipment while jovially calling out to each other. As if they weren't about to risk their necks. But there was no sign of Finn. Not there, not anywhere. And further afield, the sand below showed no signs of life.

That sinking feeling in her stomach was probably due to her lack of breakfast. Fruit-free granola with skim milk simply didn't count.

Who was she kidding? She couldn't stand the thought that she might have missed her chance with Finn.

Eden hung back from the café and ticket office, watching a terrifying event about to occur right before her eyes. Was there anything worse than jumping off a cliff? Perhaps dying from cancer. Her anger and, yes, fear burned bright and fierce inside her once more.

As a rational person, she couldn't abide taking risks for no reason. The decision-making process behind this activity was all wrong. Then she turned her head, her heart leaped. Over there, someone was strapping themselves into a bright red hang glider harness. None other than Mr. Hot Aussie himself. Looking cool, calm, and collected as he prepared to do the unthinkable.

Eden stood rooted to the spot, her entire body frozen as she stared, wanting to tell him to stop. Her mouth opened, and a gush of air escaped, but no words. From her position about twenty feet away, she observed Finn as if he were a lab rat—a fascinating specimen but surely doomed.

An instructor helped him tighten the straps while something that looked like a combination of a sleeping bag and a cocoon hung behind his legs. The thing was obviously supposed to support his weight as he dangled midair above the ocean. What if it didn't? He'd plummet from the sky and land hundreds of feet below... Could you even survive such a fall?

A small sound escaped Eden's throat, like a mouse squeaking in the presence of a cat. She slapped a hand over her mouth to stop herself from calling out to him. But maybe she should say something.

Stop him! her brain screamed at her. She had to try.

"Finn." Her voice was wispy, carried off in the wrong direction by the wind. She cleared her throat, suddenly clogged by a sob. She had to get his attention. Charging forward on shaky legs, she shouted, "Finn, stop!"

This time, Finn turned toward her and hit her with a flashing grin, then he looked straight ahead, over the cliff. The instructor was strapped in now too — it was a kind of dual-harness glider. Before she could reach them or even think, the instructor and Finn both jogged along the ground, down the slope toward the drop-off. Running now, heading for the point of no return.

Then up, up, and away...

The glider swooshed off the edge of the cliff and the two men swung their legs into the sleeping bag things. They swooped upward slightly, veering off to the right. They must have caught an updraft. Finn's triumphant "Woo-Hoo!" carried back to her on the same gust of wind.

Good. Not dying then. But before he jumped, he'd smiled at her in such a way... As if he wanted Eden to watch him. As if he wanted her, period.

A flare of hope ignited, burning bright inside, warming her from within. But the wind whipped around her body, and she was wearing only a lightweight shirt and pants. She crossed her arms and rubbed her goose-pimpled skin. In the distance, the blue-and-red striped glider shimmered as it caught a glint of sunlight. They tacked downward, gliding along the beach.

If he could be brave, why couldn't she? Fear was no excuse. She'd forced herself to do plenty of things she didn't want to in her life. At least this time, there was a chance she might get something she wanted in return. Something she'd been too afraid to even hope for. *Someone.*

After years on the dating scene, she'd all but given up on finding love and a partner, and this year, she'd turned thirty-three. The whole online dating palaver had been a last-ditch attempt at finding someone to love.

Now she'd found a man, a good man, one who made her laugh and sigh with pleasure. He thought she was beautiful. *Magnificent,* he'd called her. He loved her. He'd said so—more than once. She should give him the benefit of the doubt and tell him the truth.

Eden loved him too. So much her chest ached with the emotion ballooning from her heart, inflating with the enormity of it.

It was time for that leap of faith.

She couldn't let him get away. Even if she had to chase him while he plunged to his imminent death like an idiot. Okay, she could be overdramatizing the situation, which went to show her state of mind. She'd heard hang gliding was safe, probably more so than riding her Vespa on the highway. But it didn't help to steady the thud of her heart as she walked over to the Gliderport flight school area.

As she approached the ticket office and information desk, Eden pictured herself gliding like a bird or a kite. She could do this. Taking a deep breath, she caught the eye of the smiling woman behind the counter.

Eden shook her head. No, she really couldn't do it. Jumping off a cliff was a step too far. But she could still go and find him.

"Hello." Eden cleared her throat, sticky with the unfamiliar emotions welling up. "The man I love just leaped off the cliff. I need to know where to meet him when he lands."

Air rushed by Finn's face, dragging the skin of his cheeks back in a flappy way. His pulse raced as his stomach dropped to somewhere below sea level, and it wasn't only the rush of endorphins or gliding above one of the most beautiful coastlines in the world. Gold and blue streaked beneath him as he clung to the grip of the A-frame glider, wearing the special gloves provided by the instructor.

He grinned, ecstatic from the jump and the rush of emotions when he'd spotted Eden at the top of the cliff. She'd come looking for him, exactly as he'd hoped.

Not long now, and, hopefully, she'd be back in his arms, where she belonged.

Eden had been ready to jump on her scooter for a daring ride down the winding road to the beach, but it turned out the gliders landed back up on the clifftops. So she waiting in the viewing area and cooled her heels. A few gliders were circling high above before slowly descending. She could see Finn's glider now, heading for earth.

Once back on solid ground, Finn was unstrapped from his glider, grabbed a backpack he'd left in the launch area, and eventually sauntered toward her as if he didn't have a care in the world. Maybe he didn't. She might have gotten it all wrong. Maybe he didn't care about her at all, not anymore. No! She needed to stop overthinking.

She walked towards him and rearranged the loose strands of hair that had escaped her ponytail. She most likely looked a mess. Wild hair, cheeks flushed by the wind, even her shirt and pants were crushed to her body.

In contrast, he looked amazing. Finn smiled at her and it certainly had an effect on her body. It was impossible to concentrate when the rush of hormones was making it difficult to function. There seemed to be red-hot liquid spreading beneath her skin—syrupy and thick. It might have been her blood, but obviously, something was wrong with it. Perhaps she should get it checked out by her doctor next time.

Suddenly, Finn was all up in her face, taking up the whole view. He was so gorgeous—tousled and sun-drenched. His skin seemed more tanned in his white T-shirt, and his khaki shorts were amazing in their own special butt-and-thigh-enhancing way. Eden was staring at his legs. She had to stop. Reluctantly, she dragged her gaze up his body and met his eyes.

His full lips hitched up at the corners. "Eden, what are you doing here?"

She shrugged. "Thought I'd try something adventurous. Start a new hobby."

He raised an eyebrow, daring her to tell the truth.

Eden sucked in a deep, cleansing breath. "Okay, fine. I was looking for you."

Finn stuffed his hands in his pockets and then met her gaze. "I didn't think you wanted to see me again."

"I didn't. Until this morning."

"This morning?"

"I was in bed..." The tail end of her dream drifted back into her head, flooding her body with happy chemicals. The dream was all about the man standing in front of her now. Except he'd been wearing fewer clothes, and she'd been biting his arm. When she woke, she was biting her pillow. And now she was sweating.

Finn raised one sexy eyebrow, as if able to read her X-rated thoughts.

Eden shook her head. *Focus.* "I reread your folder of notes with the evidence about what McTavish had been planning. How he planned to frame me. He was going to leave false information, the money trail, all leading to me."

"Ah, I didn't think you'd grasped the full extent of what the boss was up to. But now you do."

"Now I do."

Finn took a step closer, until he was close enough to breathe him in. "I hope you don't think too badly of me."

Eden tilted her head to one side and examined his expression—serious, eyebrows knitted together and tension in his sharp jaw. "No, I don't. I'm smart enough to admit when I've made a mistake, and it seems I was wrong about you, Finn. You weren't lying to hurt me. In fact, I suspect you saved me."

"I'm pretty sure you didn't need me to save you."

She sighed. "Maybe not, but you helped, and I plan to dig myself out from under the rest of my problems, don't you worry. This morning when I heard from Felicity that you were going hang gliding, then maybe leaving forever, it upset me. I needed to see you."

Finn grabbed a water bottle from the backpack by his feet and tipped it over his head. Droplets of liquid trickled down his face, making her want to lick them off. He set the bottle down on the ground.

She shook her head again, trying to shake loose some good sense. "So, you jumped off a cliff?"

"Yeah, I guess I did, but just for fun."

Her eyes widened until they probably bugged out of her head. "You sure have a twisted sense of fun, Finn Donohue."

He grinned, those gorgeous green eyes of his sparkling. "True fact. I'd also like to swim with sharks one day."

Eden goggled up at him. "Sharks? Not dolphins or perfectly nice blue whales?"

Finn's smile tilted up on one side like he had a secret. "Nope. Where's the fun in that? I prefer a challenge." He ran a thumb across her cheekbone and cupped her face in his hands. "Why did you come looking for me, Doctor Eden?"

She trembled beneath his sun-warmed fingertips. "I needed to talk to you."

"About?"

"Leaving. Don't leave. Felicity said you're going back to Australia and just... don't."

He gazed down at her, his green eyes glittering in the sunlight. "Why not? I've got no job, no visa, no house, no family here. Nothing to keep me here. Tell me I'm wrong, Eden."

Eden stomped her foot. "You're wrong. You're so, so wrong, you infuriating man. I want to help you nail McTavish. And then you can nail me. I mean, we can be together."

His laugh was throaty, dirty. "Eden, you crack me up. The only time I've known you to act out-of-control is when we're together. When you want me." Finn smiled down at her, smoothing his thumb along her jawline.

"I knew I had to find you. I had to tell you that you were the one for me."

"*Were*? Don't tell me you've changed your mind again?"

"No, never." She grabbed two fistfuls of the front of his shirt, the stretchy fabric warm and soft to the touch. And he smelled so good, like citrus and sea air. "You're mine now, Hot Aussie. And I'm never letting you go."

"Glad to hear it. Little. Miss. Perfect." He tapped her on the nose.

Eden snorted, quite possibly ruining their moment. "I'm far from perfect. Are you sure you want an uptight control freak like me?"

"As it happens, Doc, you're perfect for me. Anyway, I've seen you lose control. I like it."

"Really?"

"Uh-huh. In fact, I love it."

Heat surged across Eden's cheeks, chasing away the chill breeze, and her heart refused to keep quiet. It boomed and pounded in her chest until he could probably hear its bass beat. But, just in case, she needed to make her feelings absolutely clear. "I-I love you. For real."

Finn's smile stretched across his tanned face, making his eyes scrunch up at the corners and her belly flip and roll like she was swooping through the sky.

He stared up at the heavens, then back into her eyes. "Finally!"

Finn twined his hands through the back of her hair, pulling her closer, and when his mouth landed on hers, their teeth clacked together. It was awkward and cute all at once. He tasted like maple syrup. If it wasn't magical and meant to be, she didn't know what was.

A giggle rose in her throat, but he captured her lips before it escaped. Then he pulled her against his long, hard body, and her laughter became a muffled groan. Finn kissed her deeper, knocking her off-balance until she fell fully into his embrace. His hands wandered down her body to cup and squeeze her ass.

For her part, Eden clung to his biceps, feeling them up shamelessly. To anyone who happened to be watching, they must have looked totally inappropriate. But she'd never been so inappropriately happy in her life.

As a low rumble came from the sky above, a vibration down her spine made her break their kiss. Finn stared at her for a moment, his eyes dark and melting with passion. Then he lifted his head.

Eden looked up too and spotted a vintage bi-plane zooming in their direction. A flash of white unfurled beneath the plane — a banner. It rippled and spread out like a great white bed sheet to reveal a message. Her own name jumped out at her.

Eden stared up at the banner, then flicked her gaze back to Finn. He appeared to be chewing his lower lip, and it looked delicious. She wanto bite him — more than ever.

"That's *your* banner? You want my heart forever?"

"Yes. And your cupcakes."

"Your spelling's atrocious."

"You knew that already. And there was a character limit." He grinned at her.

Eden nodded. "Right. Do you mean it? The forever part?"

"Absolutely. And the cupcakes part."

"I took that as a given."

"Good."

"Good."

A moment's more staring into those glittering eyes, then Eden's gaze dropped to his mouth. Finn must have had the same thought because his lips crushed hers again.

After a few minutes of hot, unbelievably delicious making out, Eden spoke. "Take me home, Finn."

He nodded against her cheek. "You got it, Doc."

Chapter Twenty-Eight

Six Months Later

Finn: Meet me for lunch? I feel like something spicy...

Eden: Sounds good. Can you pick me up from the hospital?

Finn: Yep, see you about 1. Love you xxx

Eden: Love you too :)

"I need the new equipment for the lab. Don't make me come over there." Eden injected some extra menace into her voice as she tried not to laugh at Doctor Zhang. She pressed her cell phone to her ear and smiled. Seemed she was always smiling these days.

As she spoke, she strolled across the hospital's inner courtyard, right outside the cancer research institute where she worked, the sun warming her bare legs under her lab coat. It was a beautiful day. There was a breeze, but it felt refreshing. Cool, but there was never much bite to winter in San Diego.

The man chuckled darkly in her ear. "Who exactly is the boss around here?" David asked on the other end of the line, muffled laughter in his voice. "I know, I know, I'm not really your boss. I just work for the university. You're one hundred percent in charge of your research, and you've got approval for the new equipment. Anything you need, Eden."

She smiled, though he couldn't see it. He'd managed to find the funds for a more senior role for her, and she wouldn't forget about his support. "Thanks, David. You're the best. But I have to go. I've got a hot lunch date."

"Okay. Enjoy your lunch. Say hi to Finn for me."

"Thanks, I'll give him your best. I think he's going to invite you to that charity fun run he's organizing. Oh, and I won't be back in the lab this afternoon because we have that silly TV thing this afternoon."

David snorted through the phone. "Right, I forgot. I can't wait to see your interview when it airs. I might even hold a watch party and invite the whole team."

"You wouldn't dare!" Eden laughed, knowing David was only teasing.

It was good to hear him laugh after the awful time he'd been having with his divorce. It turned out the rumors about David

were untrue, and his wife had been the cheater in their relationship.

"See you tomorrow," he said.

Eden ended the call and watched as her hot date approached
from the direction of the hospital parking lot. Finn worked only
a few blocks away at the We Heart Kids charity headquarters.

Her handsome fiancé had transformed the charity's events
over the past few months, creating a sports partnership program
between professional athletes and kids with congenital heart
disease and heart failure. The athletes arranged VIP tickets to
sporting events around the country for the children and their
families. Eden was so proud of him and everything he'd already
achieved.

Her heart thudded with the knowledge that her hot date was
about to get a whole lot hotter. Even if he didn't know it yet. She
fiddled with the stunning antique princess-cut diamond ring on
her left hand. She loved it, but not as much as she loved the man
who'd given it to her.

"Hey, Doctor Eden," he called out from a few feet away. Finn
walked with a certain swagger, a loping, long-legged stride. It
meant only one thing: he wanted her. Luckily, they had that in
common.

Eden wanted him so much that it took her breath away. Especially when he smiled, eyes crinkling at the corners, flashing
white teeth. Everything about him was perfect. His now almost
too long caramel hair that she loved to run her hands through in
bed, was her new favorite thing. He'd grown it out a little, just
for her.

She twisted the ends of her ponytail around her fingers. Finn's
eyes followed the movement. She knew him now, knew his
reactions. He loved her 'librarian' look and ponytail, especially
when she added her reading glasses. Not to mention the tight
pencil skirt and heels she wore with her white lab coat.

Finn's eyes flared with heat, and he quickened his pace. He
marched straight up to her, grabbed her around the waist, and

pulled her close to whisper in her ear, "You know what your outfit does to me. Are you trying to make me swallow my tongue?"

Eden tried not to laugh. Speaking for his ears only, she whispered back, "No, but a reminder popped up on my calendar app. It's that time of the month. We shouldn't let the opportunity pass us by."

Finn shifted to meet her gaze. His delicious lips were within kissing distance if she launched herself at him. His focus moved to her mouth. They were on the same page. "Oh, but we can't just... I mean, we have the TV thing."

"I know. But later..."

"What's the plan, Doctor Eden?"

"Felicity's holding the fort in the lab. I can take the rest of the afternoon off."

"Okaaaay."

"I figured we could go parking. Get a head start on our baby-making plans."

He raised his eyebrows, then kissed her so thoroughly that she nearly fell off her high heels. Later, indeed.

The TV studio lights were hot on Eden's skin and almost blinding. She crossed her legs and glanced at Finn, seated beside her on the leather sofa in his sharp gray suit, white shirt, and green silk tie that matched his eyes. When he smiled, a slow, sexy smile, his handsomeness nearly blinded her too. He reached out and took her hand.

In the green room, they'd eaten the most delicious buffet lunch, including mini tacos and sugar-free cupcakes, then practiced their responses to the list of questions they'd received in advance. Eden should be ready. But nerves tickled her insides, making her jump when the host strolled onto the stage and sat next to her in the familiar blue armchair.

Dorothea Hart was one of the biggest names in talk shows, in TV generally, and from what Eden had seen, a genuinely lovely person. *Hart Talk* was a huge show, and Eden still couldn't believe she and Finn were about to be featured guests.

Dorothea clapped her hands together. "Okay, Eden, Finn, we're going to take our time with the interview today to make sure we get the full story. We'll edit it later in postproduction. We've got some footage of Doctor McTavish's arrest and background on Peter Quade's business affairs from the news team for our intro."

When Dorothea motioned across the stage to the floor manager, video footage played on big screens on either side of where they sat. Dramatic music accompanied the headlines flashing across the screens: 'High profile fraud in big pharma,' 'Heart drug saga in San Diego,' 'Magna Smart share prices tumble,' and finally, 'McTavish jailed for fraud and tax evasion.' The footage of McTavish hiding his face, doing the walk of shame out of the Magna Smart offices escorted by the FBI, never failed to warm Eden's heart.

Eden sighed as the music changed, and Roxy Music's 'Love Is the Drug' blared from the studio speakers. The screens cut to some different quotes: 'Love match at the heart of drug scandal,' 'Dating app meet-cute of the century!', 'When Hot Aussie 007 met Little Miss Perfect,' and 'Love Is the Drug,' just like the song.

When Dorothea signaled for them to turn on their lapel mikes, Eden tensed. Although she was confident this was the right thing to do, her hands still shook.

Dorothea smiled at them both and whispered, "Relax, you'll do great!"

Eden watched the monitors as Dorothea turned to the camera with a beaming smile, like the seasoned pro and Emmy Award winner she was, and launched straight into the intro.

"Welcome to this evening's edition of *Hart Talk*. My guests tonight are Doctor Eden Robinson and Mr. Finn Donohue, who were recently at the heart of the Magna Smart Pharmaceuticals scandal. Tonight, we'll hear how this dynamic duo not only uncovered one of the biggest corporate scandals in recent history but also fell in love in the process."

Dorothea turned to Eden, her smile reassuring. "Eden, can you tell me a little about how you met Finn? I hear it's an amusing story."

Eden cleared her throat and met Finn's sparkling eyes for a second before turning back to Dorothea. "Well, funnily enough, I knew Finn quite well before I ever got to know him at work. You see, we were dating online, anonymously, for a while. This guy—HotAussie007—seemed to get me. He loved old movies and wanted someone he could talk to, not just jump into bed with. That came later..."

Finn's laughter woke her from a kind of trance. She bit her lip. "Um, can we edit that last bit out?"

Dorothea smiled again and patted Eden's arm. "I'd leave it. You two are so cute. If I could bottle your energy, I could power a rocket to Mars and back. Trust me, the audience will love it."

Oh right. The audience. Eden had temporarily forgotten people would be watching this interview on TV soon. She simply nodded, her face practically on fire. They were really doing this. She smoothed her hands down her skirt.

Dorothea turned to Finn and cut to the chase: "Now, Finn, can you tell us about your investigation into Doctor McTavish that led to the eventual court case against him and the Magna Smart Board of Directors?"

Finn nodded. "Absolutely. It all started with a random note left on my desk by a colleague in Finance, which said, 'See me about this line item for new website.' You see, there was no new website, and even if there had been, there was no way we'd have spent eighteen-point-seven million dollars on it."

Dorothea gasped. "That's a whole lotta moola!"

"Sure is. I had a gut feeling something weird happened in accounting, so I dug a little deeper with the help of my colleague. One set of accounts appeared totally aboveboard, while a deleted file from another department's server had a completely different set of figures. Turns out my website analytics guy used to be a hacker, and he has some mad skills."

Finn explained more about the false trail McTavish left, the anonymous bank accounts Meredith uncovered in the Bahamas, and even his connection with Peter Quade, his so-called 'fiscal advisor.' When Finn got to the part about the man who'd attempted to ruin Eden's life, he took her hand and held it.

"McTavish had hidden yet another set of financial papers and sent emails supposedly from Eden's work account when other people knew she was out of the office. They'd set up remote access to Eden's computer. They were covering their own gambling debts and funneling money offshore. But they made it look like Eden had tried to get away with close to twenty million dollars. I couldn't let anyone frame her. Even if Eden hated me in real life, I liked her. Actually, I'd been in love with her since the beginning, online."

"And, Eden, did you realize what was going on with Finn and his investigation?" Dorothea asked.

Eden shook her head vehemently. "Absolutely not! He kept everything under wraps for so long... I'm mad at him in retrospect. The authorities asked him to work undercover, to continue his investigation and funnel information back to them. But I just thought he was annoying, hovering around my desk and being demanding. Not to mention, I had a huge crush on HotAussie007, which clouded my judgment."

Dorothea chuckled, shaking her head. "But Hot Aussie was Finn all along, right?"

Eden smiled. "Yes! But I didn't know it. Then he stood me up *and* crashed into me on my Vespa, so the date we'd planned was a disaster."

With a grin, Dorothea turned and spoke direct to the camera. "The course of true love never does run smooth."

At this point, Finn cut in: "I had a lot on my plate, but I couldn't get Eden out of my head. I had to decide if I could trust her because I'd discovered something strange with the funding and planning of her research project. Especially the patent application for a heart drug still in the testing phase."

Then Finn shared the real kicker—when he found out McTavish was a scammer. "McTavish saw the potential to earn millions, possibly billions, from marketing a potential heart drug for a secondary purpose—as a treatment for depression. He'd setup an unauthorized, secondary research team in eastern Europe and attempted to bypass Eden's team and US law. He forgot that patents could be challenged, or his name would be publicly searchable online. Let alone the website traffic and data saved on Magna Smart servers. Being greedy was the number one thing he did wrong, apart from messing with Eden. I'd do anything to protect her."

Eden ducked her head, fighting back the tears. Finn was fine with expressing his feelings, even in public. Sometimes it embarrassed her, but now, she almost had to pinch herself to check it wasn't a dream. She couldn't have asked for a more wonderful man if he'd been made to order.

As if noticing her quietness, Dorothea directed her next question to Eden. "Doctor Robinson, when did you realize Finn was *The One*?"

Eden grinned. "When he jumped off a cliff to get my attention, I knew he was a keeper."

"I was hang gliding!" Finn shouted.

Dorothea laughed long and hard, wiping her eyes with a Kleenex. She turned to Finn. "You two are the real deal, aren't you?"

Finn's eyes lit with emerald fire as he answered, "Yes, we sure are. This is my Little Miss Perfect, right here."

Eden climbed into Finn's lap, flung her arms around his neck, and kissed him like she meant it. For a moment, she even forgot they were being filmed.

Three weeks later, Finn emailed Eden while she was dealing with paperwork in her office, which wasn't so unusual. What was unusual was the invitation he sent her.

My dearest Doctor Eden,

> *Love of my life, creator of epic cupcakes, woman of my dreams, certified genius, my regular hot date... You are cordially invited to a roast in your honor (and mine). Dr. David Zhang is making good on his threat to hold a watch party. 7pm for 7.30pm screening time in the hospital staff lounge. Bring your sense of humor and leave any weapons at home, just in case.*

Love, kisses, etc. (use your imagination),
Finn.

Director of Marketing and Corporate Social Responsibility
We Heart Kids

Eden sighed and emailed back a meme of a woman calmly drinking tea, surrounded by monkeys. She'd have a word with David about his need to laugh at her, but somehow, she didn't think it would help.

Her colleague and her fiancé were now the best of friends, and sometimes they ganged up on Eden. All in fun, of course.

She'd talk to Felicity about pranking the men for April Fool's Day. They'd come up with something diabolical.

When Eden walked into the staff lounge on Finn's arm at seven o'clock, whoops of joy and laughter greeted them. Eden waved to the crowd like the Queen of England, then blew kisses to all her friends and colleagues. There was Felicity, seated right next to Meredith — the two of them looking cute as two buttons in matching tailored suits. Outside of work, they were inseparable, now living together in a fancy beachside condo. Meredith had scored a job as Senior Financial Advisor to a big pension fund for the healthcare industry and was doing great. Eden had heard all about it over lunch at their place.

Faith sat on Felicity's left, beaming at Eden as she mouthed, *'Good luck, Babycakes.'* Then she not so subtly pointed over at Nate, Finn's website guru/hacker friend, and fanned her face. Eden had to agree: Nate did look hot in his all-black suit, especially now he'd cut his hair and grown a hipster beard — channeling a young Keanu Reeves. *Interesting.* Perhaps Eden could set the two of them up.

Finn took off, and Eden watched as he stopped to chat with his friend Sam, the mechanic, seated near the back of the room with his new special friend, Constance. Eden had a good feeling about those two. Constance loved to bake macarons and cupcakes, so logically, she must be an awesome person.

When they took their seats, Finn leaned over and kissed her on the cheek, then whispered, "Remember, I love you. And your cupcakes. Can't wait to taste them later."

Heat crept up from Eden's chest to her cheeks, so she kissed him full on the mouth. The whooping and whistling in the room increased exponentially.

As they settled in to watch the program on the huge portable screen David had found in the medical students' lecture theater, everyone went quiet, except for the background noise of crunching popcorn.

Finn looked great on camera; no denying it. Eden squeezed his knee, so he leaned over and nibbled her ear. She nearly expired as a wave of desire rolled through her belly.

The episode was airing on national TV, and as soon as it started, a meme of their on-screen kiss began trending on Twitter under #LoveIsTheDrug, and she had to slap Finn's hands to stop him from constantly retweeting people's comments on his phone.

They also happened to appear in a commercial for the SD Confidential dating app—which totally paid off Eden's mortgage—through pure luck. Finn's friend at an ad agency had proposed the idea, and the app developers were totally into it. The ad was fun and made everyone laugh. Eden was pleased the app's creators had also made a sizable donation to the charities Eden and Finn nominated.

Once the screening finished, Finn grabbed Eden's hand and tugged her toward the door. She happily went with him. They made their excuses before escaping with everyone's congratulations.

Finn had organized an actual date to celebrate—with dinner and everything. But Eden kept her head and ordered a club soda with lime instead of the champagne she would have liked.

Eden knew life with Finn was about to get a whole lot more exciting, all because of a little blue positive sign on a stick. She dug the test out of her purse and slid it across the restaurant table toward Finn's plate. He glanced down at it, then looked up with a slow smile, his eyes wide and suspiciously damp.

Eden pressed her lips together, attempting to contain her joy. But happiness radiated from every cell in her body. "Congrats, Hot Aussie. Or should I call you Daddy?"

As he licked his lower lip, her heart kicked into high gear. Her man's voice was deeper than usual when he murmured, "Only in the bedroom, Doc. Come on, I'm taking you home."

Finn escorted her out of the restaurant double time and helped her into his recently purchased vintage Ford Fairlane. As he strapped her into her seat belt and placed a gentle hand on her belly, he whispered, "I love you, so much." His kiss left no doubt he was telling the absolute truth.

Eden knew things were about to get wild in the bedroom. Even wilder than usual. But in a few months, they'd have a new little person to share their lives with and too much love to measure. In other words, everything was perfect.

Acknowledgments

All writers probably have a project that's sat in their bottom drawer or on their laptop for a long time, waiting for the right moment for the problems to unwind themselves, and for it to be completed and published. This book is mine – a story idea I had in 2015, that became a short, category length romance that eventually morphed into a full-length, single title novel. Through several iterations, multiple hero names (Brandon, Dylan, and now Finn!) and a lot of rewrites, I finally managed to get this baby into ebook and print!

The first person I'd like to thank is my sister, Doctor Deb. She inspired me to write about a brilliant scientist heroine, because she is one in real life! While I have a degree in Communicating and Publicity Stuff and Phaffing About With Words, she has a PhD in Science Stuff and has been working to improve treatments for several diseases for years. She also inspired the location in this book (though I was oblivious at the time) when I visited her in Del Mar near San Diego, California in 2005. Deb, I hope you're not too harsh in your critique of the sciencey talk in this book. It's fiction, and a romance novel after all. Establishing a believable Happy Ever After was the most important objective of this experiment.

I'd like to acknowledge a fabulous team of professionals who helped me bring this book to life including:

Cover designer - Kylie Sek from Cover Culture, whose custom illustrated cover and character designs are just amazing!

Copyeditor - Liz Dempsey, The Error Eliminator, who absolutely eliminated so many errors, I'm a little embarrassed I thought my draft was finished . . . I've never met a story timeline I couldn't break. Thanks for not letting me destroy the space-time continuum.

Beta reader - Kelsey from AJ Collins Editing. I won this beta reading service in an auction to raise money for charities after the 2020 bushfires in Australia. Kelsey offered some wonderful, constructive comments on the draft of the longer novel.

Special thanks to my writer friends in the Melbourne Romance Writers Guild who helped with brainstorming ideas for this book years ago, including Michelle Somers, PJ Vye, Andra Ashe, Savannah Blaize, Lauren Harbor, Katerina Simms and probably more. My memory of a long ago writing retreat is hazy due to excess consumption of Cosmos, but I know you all gave me some great feedback.

My gratitude also goes to the online writers group I was a member of when I started writing this draft, back in about 2015. The brilliant international writers in that group gave me so much encouragement and advice, so thank you. We all met on the old Harlequin romance writing discussion boards, had some fun, and in short, you all rock.

I'd also like to thank the anonymous judges from the Lone Star Awards, Northwest Houston Romance Writers of America, for the finalist placing I received in that contest in 2015. The shorter version of this manuscript was something you enjoyed reading, and the longer version I drafted was better because of your feedback.

A huge thank you to Creative Victoria and Regional Arts Victoria, who chose me to receive an arts grant at the end of 2021. This money has helped me get this work (almost) over the finish line, and hire the wonderful professionals listed above. Covid-19 and other illnesses delayed it a little more than I had planned, but now it's published and I'm so happy I could demolish a cupcake or ten.

I may not have published this book the way I thought I would, or when I thought I would, but who knows what can happen when you dream a little dream?

Song and movie list

Songs and movies were hugely inspirational to me when writing this book. I thought my readers may be interested in the background soundtrack of my brain, which can be a crowded place full of movie quotes and lyrics. Here's a curated list of my playlists if you want to check them out!

Song list

"I Got Rhythm," Ella Fitzgerald

"They Can't Take That Away From Me," Ella Fitzgerald and Louis Armstrong

"Well Did You Evah?/What a Swell Party" (from *High Society*), ft. Bing Crosby and Frank Sinatra

"You're Sensational" (from *High Society*), ft. Bing Crosby

"California Dreamin'," The Mamas & The Papas

"I've Got You Under My Skin," Neneh Cherry

"California," Lana Del Ray

"Faking It," Calvin Harris ft. Kehlani

"Let It Happen," Tame Impala

"Everything I Wanted," Billie Eilish

"Dream a Little Dream of Me," Ella Fitzgerald

"From Eden," Hozier

"The Time is Now," Moloko

"Love is the Drug," Roxy Music

Movie list

"You've Got Mail" (1998), starring Tom Hanks and Meg Ryan

"Cleopatra" (1963), starring Elizabeth Taylor and Richard Burton

"High Society" (1956), starring Grace Kelly, Bing Crosby and Frank Sinatra

"Vertigo" (1958), dir. by Alfred Hitchcock, starring Kim Novak and James Stewart

"To Catch a Thief" (1955), starring Grace Kelly and Cary Grant

"Dr. No" (1962), starring Sean Connory and Ursula Andress

"Thor" (2011), starring Chris Hemsworth and Natalie Portman

"The Avengers" (2012), starring Chris Hemsworth, Chris Evans, etc.

"Roman Holiday" (1953), starring Audrey Hepburn and Gregory Peck

"Charade" (1963), starring Audrey Hepburn and Cary Grant

"When Harry Met Sally" (1989), starring Meg Ryan and Billy Crystal

Read next . . .

Girl on a Plane

**WINNER OF THE GLOBAL WE HEART NEW TAL-
ENT CONTEST!**
**Perfect for fans of *The Unhoneymooners* by Christina
Lauren and *The Layover* by Laci Waldon, *Girl on a
Plane* is an entertaining summer read for grumpy-sun-
shine romcom lovers.**
Sparks fly in mid-air when Sinead, a fun and feisty Irish flight
attendant, meets Gabriel, a gorgeous but grumpy Aussie CEO
in First Class.
When a storm hits during their flight from Melbourne to Lon-
don, they are unexpectedly grounded in Singapore. No-one
could predict Sinead and Gabriel would be locked-in together
in the same hotel suite...with only one bed! One steamy night
could lead to more as they chase each other across the world.
Sinead doesn't know if she can follow her heart after her disas-
trous relationship with her stalker ex-boyfriend. He shook her
so much, shattered her confidence in men, and made it hard to

trust. Her connection with Gabriel is powerful, a call to throw caution to the wind. Maybe it's time to find love, a man to call her own. To heal her broken heart.

But Gabriel isn't exactly an open book. He wants Sinead with an intensity that scares him but he can't afford to let a woman in, to pursue anything besides a hook-up. What if Sinead doesn't understand the limits he has to place on relationships? What if she cracks him wide open and disturbs the careful balance of his life? He may never recover.

Follow Sinead and Gabriel as they navigate a new relationship while dealing with the excess baggage of their pasts. Will love take flight?

Out now in ebook, paperback and hardcover!
Buy now – cassandraolearyauthor.com/books

Hot in the City: A Romcom Story Collection

Hot In The City is a collection of romantic comedy short stories and novellas from award-winning author, Cassandra O'Leary. Perfect for reading on your lunch break, on the go or anytime really!

Never before published in one book, this collection includes:
- *Chocolate Truffle Kiss: A Romantic Comedy Novelette* - An older woman meets a younger man in a story full of pining. A lonely writer, a hot rockstar barista, a cafe setting with stolen moments, poetry and chocolate . . .and a steamy happy ending.
- *Tree Love: A Romantic Short Story* - A short story with a sweet second chance romance, an urban lumberjack and emails to trees!
- *Girl Under The Christmas Tree: A Steamy Holiday Romance Novella* - A prequel to the novel *Girl on a Plane*, featuring Yuki, a hotel staffer looking for adventure, and Declan, an

Irish IT CEO with a broken heart, and too many Santas. They come together right before Christmas for just one night . . .

- Friday I'm In Love: A Short and Sweet Story - A brand new story set in a pyjama company in the middle of the city. Featuring a Japanese-Australian beefcake, a wacky computer nerd, workplace romance, spying and wardrobe malfunctions.

. . . and a new novelette. . . *Girl On A Babymoon*! Sinead and Gabriel from *Girl on a Plane* return, five years later. It's their anniversary, and Sinead has a big surprise for Gabriel. A romantic getaway and steamy role-playing feature in this laugh-out-loud story of a marriage in trouble, or maybe, a marriage that will be stronger than ever!

Each story is set in the author's home city of Melbourne, Australia, with a cameo or two from other fabulous destinations around the world. These stories will introduce you to a world of steamy kisses, swoony couples and funny love stories each with their own a happy ever after (or happy for now) ending.

Out now in ebook or paperback!
Buy now – cassandraolearyauthor.com/books

About Cassandra O'Leary

Cassandra O'Leary is an Australian author of steamy rom-coms, swoony romance and women's fiction books with all the feels.

Living in Melbourne, Australia, Cassandra has also travelled the world. If you want to send her on any research trips, Ireland, Italy and Spain are at the top of her list. Cassandra is a mother to two mini ninjas and married to a superhero husband. You'll find Cassandra reading, drinking coffee and buying shoes online...oh yes, and writing.

In 2015, Cassandra won the global We Heart New Talent contest and her debut novel, *Girl on a Plane*, was published by HarperCollins UK in 2016. Since then, she has independently published several novels and novellas, including a romcom story collection, *Hot in the City*.

Cassandra's favourite romance and romantic comedy authors include Beth O'Leary (no relation), Christina Lauren, Sally

Thorne, Amy Andrews, Kylie Scott, Alexis Hall, Talia Hibbert, Lucy Parker, Mhairi McFarlane, Penny Reid and Emily Henry.

Cassandra O'Leary is a proud member of Romance Writers of Australia, the Australian Society of Authors, and the Melbourne Romance Writers Guild.

Read more at **cassandraolearyauthor.com**